Praise for *The Long Con*

"*The Long Con* is for all of us who are still mad that *Ocean's 8* wasn't sapphic. The heartwarming found-family dynamics had me rooting for our con artist antiheroes from page 1, and the chemistry between Chloe and Harper is as scorching as the Miami sun. Jenna Voris has written the ultimate 'be gay, do crime' thriller!"

—Layne Fargo, bestselling author of *The Favorites*

"With sizzling tension, laugh-out-loud humor, and a cast of crime-loving characters to root for, *The Long Con* is the romantic heist thriller we all need—a whip-smart, high-stakes thrill ride!"

—Olivia Worley, author of *So Happy Together*

"A glittering, dynamic, captivating story full of characters that dazzle and sky-high stakes . . . Voris expertly hooks the reader from the start and deftly navigates every thrilling and unexpected twist."

—Christina Li, author of *The Manor of Dreams*

"Jenna Voris has written the rival-thieves romp I didn't know I needed in my life. *The Long Con* is slick and sexy, with a delightful cast of characters and the eat-the-rich vibes we're all craving. . . . The most fun I've had in a long time!"

—Alison Cochrun, author of *Every Step She Takes*

ALSO BY JENNA VORIS

Made of Stars

Every Time You Hear That Song

Say a Little Prayer

The LONG CON

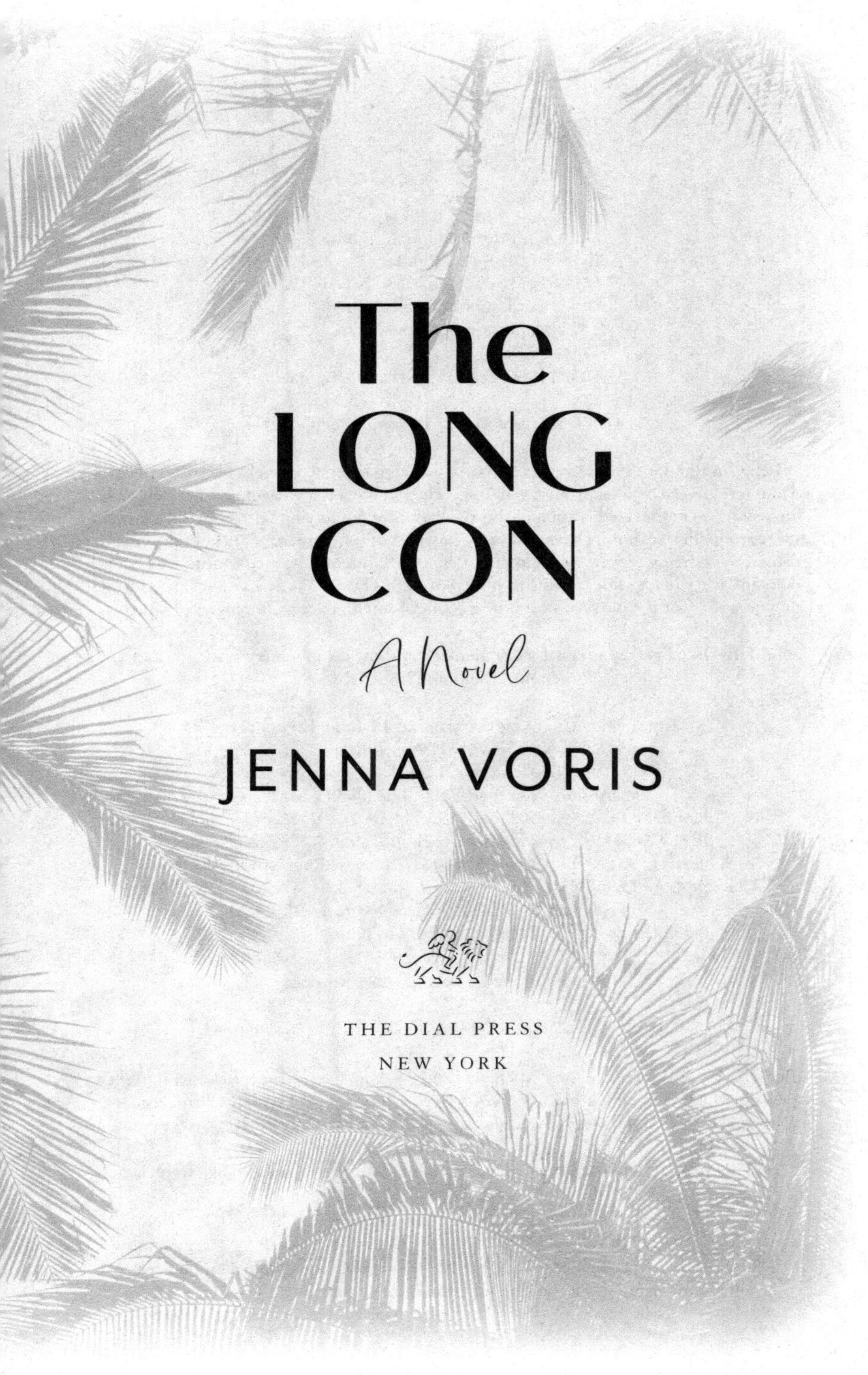

The LONG CON

A Novel

JENNA VORIS

THE DIAL PRESS
NEW YORK

The Dial Press
An imprint of Random House
A division of Penguin Random House LLC
1745 Broadway, New York, NY 10019
randomhousebooks.com
penguinrandomhouse.com

A Dial Press Trade Paperback Original

Library Of Congress Cataloging-In-Publication Data
Names: Voris, Jenna author
Title: The long con: a novel / Jenna Voris.
Description: New York, NY: The Dial Press, 2026.
Identifiers: LCCN 2025029781 (print) | LCCN 2025029782 (ebook) |
ISBN 9798217197286 trade paperback | ISBN 9780593977200 ebook
Subjects: LCGFT: Thrillers (Fiction) | Lesbian fiction | Novels | Fiction
Classification: LCC PS3622.O75 L66 2026 (print) | LCC PS3622.O75 (ebook)
LC record available at https://lccn.loc.gov/2025029781
LC ebook record available at https://lccn.loc.gov/2025029782

Printed in the United States of America

1st Printing

Book Team: Production editor: Michelle Daniel • Managing editor: Rebecca Berlant • Production manager: Katie Zilberman • Copy editor: Alicia Hyman • Proofreaders: Debbie Anderson, Judy Kiviat, Taylor McGowan, and Bridget Sweet

Title page art: AdobeStock/pla2na; chapter opener art: AdobeStock/siraphol

Book design by Diane Hobbing

The authorized representative in the EU for product safety and compliance is Penguin Random House Ireland, Morrison Chambers, 32 Nassau Street, Dublin D02 YH68, Ireland. https://eu-contact.penguin.ie

For Emily, for everything

The LONG CON

ONE

Chloe leans both elbows on the table, slicks on another layer of half-melted lipstick (L'Oréal Colour Riche Satin, shade: Worth It), and decides she's really not asking the universe for that much. Tonight, it comes down to three things—for the humidity to remain at a somewhat reasonable level, for the straps of her thrifted ball gown to stop coming apart around her neck, and for the aging millionaire at her table to stay awake long enough for her to take all his money.

Three perfectly reasonable requests, in her opinion.

Chloe eyes her reflection in the table's glittering centerpiece as she tucks the lipstick back down the front of her dress. Between the layers of wilted red tulle and the smooth wave of her normally unruly hair, she hardly recognizes herself in the decorative glass. The centerpiece does, however, give her a clear view of Logan standing against the ornate wallpaper behind her, a tray of overpriced hors d'oeuvres propped lazily in one hand. *Perfect.*

He's on time, she's ready to move, and her date for the evening is two glasses in to a wine-fueled monologue about software development. It's now or never.

"Ready?"

Priya's voice is barely audible over the chatter of the party and Chloe resists the urge to adjust the wireless earbud hidden behind her hair. She can't respond here, but there's a flicker of movement in the centerpiece as Logan steps away from the wall, tray passing effortlessly from hand to hand as he cuts his way through the dinner crowd.

"I was born ready, Priya, darling."

Chloe resists the urge to roll her eyes. Logan's always had a thing for dramatics, even in places like this. It's something she learned the day she found him building an illegal air-conditioning unit on the floor of their freshman dorm, insisting she should dump his lifeless, overheated body in front of the dean's office if he didn't finish by noon. Now, she blames his day job and the *Now You See Me* films for feeding his amateur magician's ego. Logan might have two different birthday parties booked tomorrow, but he's here tonight and their plan begins the way they all do—with Chloe sitting across from a mark too rich for his own good, who, despite everything, is still completely oblivious to the cunning tilt of her lips.

This one was almost too easy to corner. James Montgomery Webber, seventy-two. A tech billionaire who recently tore up half a mile of Miami beachfront to build a sprawling new office hub. He currently employs half the city and he's single-handedly funding half of Andrew Carlyle's senate campaign, which is how he scored an invitation to tonight's festivities. Right up front at an exclusive, donors-only dinner in one of the Carlyle hotels.

He wasn't necessarily the target Chloe would have chosen, but there's an art to these things she's learned not to push.

"Sandwich?"

Logan leans over their table, tray extended in Webber's direction. The warm scent of his cologne washes over them (Tom Ford, Ombré Leather), and Chloe risks a glance in his direction. Logan's mouth is turned down in an expression of bored disinterest, but there's a soft pink color painted across his already full lips. Because *of course* he found time to touch up. They both spent the last hour sweating outside, slipping their way through security checkpoints and locked doors, but god forbid Logan Amesfield show up to an event looking anything less than perfect.

Chloe grabs two tiny sandwiches off his tray and tries not to think about the frizzy curls currently sticking to the back of her neck. "Thanks."

Webber barely looks up. Light from the chandelier flashes off his diamond-encrusted watch as he waves Logan away, like the mere presence of a waiter at their table is an inconvenience. Again, Chloe barely refrains from rolling her eyes. If she were working tonight or wearing her usual catering uniform, Webber wouldn't spare her a glance either. He'd look right through her on his way to the bar, but tonight, she's off the clock. She's armed with four-inch heels and borrowed lipstick, and Logan's interruption gives her the opening she needs.

"What were you saying?" Chloe leans in, knee casually brushing Webber's under the table. "The app you're developing. What's it called?"

Webber blinks. The motion exaggerates the wrinkles around his eyes, but his forehead remains unnaturally still. "You mean Slique?"

"Yes! What a great name."

It's not. It's ridiculous, but everything about James Montgomery Webber is ridiculous. Chloe's not about to get picky now. She slides one finger up his arm, stopping just inside the crook of his elbow. "What does it do, again?"

She has him; Chloe feels it as Webber's gaze slides from her face to the neckline of her gown before finally dropping to her hand. He clears his throat. "It's a black car service. For luxury vehicles and on-call drivers."

"Oh!" Chloe blinks. "So it's like Uber?"

A hint of a smile touches the corner of Webber's mouth. "Not exactly. Imagine you land in a new city. Your regular driver is back home, and you don't know who to trust. What do you do?"

Chloe's pretty sure 99 percent of the population will never actually encounter that problem, but she tilts her head anyway, feigning confusion. "I don't know."

"Exactly." Webber grins, eyes still roaming unsubtly down the length of her body. "That's where we come in."

If there's one thing rich people love more than being rich, Chloe thinks, it's explaining in great, condescending detail exactly how rich they are. James Montgomery Webber has enough money to change the world yet here he is—drinking wine in the ballroom of a luxury hotel and breaking down the basics of capitalism to a girl fifty years his junior.

Some people don't deserve nice things.

Some people deserve to have their watches stolen.

It's only when Priya's voice comes through the earbud again that Chloe realizes she's instinctively tightening her grip, fingers curling into the fabric of Webber's jacket as she imagines him jumping into a solid-gold Slique car, filled to the brim with glittering Scrooge McDuck coins.

"Corner by the balcony. Four o'clock."

Priya is talking around a mouthful of food—probably the pad thai they all ordered for dinner—and Chloe's stomach growls at the thought.

"Really?" Logan asks. "That corner looks pretty exposed."

Chloe can practically hear Priya's eye roll through the line. "Have I ever been wrong, Logan?"

"Many times."

"About *this*?"

"Okay, no, but—"

"Then stop complaining. Let me know when you're ready."

Chloe releases her grip on Webber and shoots a quick glance toward the wall. The area Priya suggested *is* exposed, people wandering on and off the balcony on their way to the bar, but Priya has also never failed to find a security blind spot. Chloe pictures her in the back of her trusty orange Subaru, feet propped against the dashboard, romance novel in her lap as she tracks them through the party from several blocks away. If she says the corner is their best bet, Chloe will make it work. She gives herself three more seconds to plan a route and then, when Webber pauses for breath, she makes her move.

"Oh, I get it!" she exclaims, face lighting up. "Your app is like Charm."

"No, it's . . ." Webber breaks off, confusion threatening to crack the Botox-induced stillness of his forehead. "Wait, what's Charm?"

"That new rideshare app?" Chloe pulls out her phone. "The one with the armored cars? That's who you got the idea from, right?"

"I . . . no. We're revolutionizing the future of luxury transportation. I've never heard of *Charm.*"

"Sure you have! They're everywhere. I literally took a Charm car to dinner tonight. I'll show you."

Chloe opens her phone, screen deliberately shielded so Webber can't see she's tapping at nothing.

Priya snorts faintly in her ear. "I still can't believe that works."

"Right?" Logan mutters. "Dibs on gaslighting the next CEO. It's not fair Chloe gets to have fun while I'm stuck in a cummerbund."

"I think you look handsome."

"Please be serious, Priya, I look like a killer whale."

Chloe ignores them and stands, phone extended above her head like she's trying to catch a signal. "There's never any service at these things." She heaves a defeated sigh. "Come on, let's try by the window."

She starts toward the balcony without looking back and, because she's good at her job, because men like Webber truly believe the world is supposed to open for them, he follows.

Chloe weaves through tables of well-dressed donors and waitstaff, dodging photo ops and handshakes along the way. If Andrew Carlyle is really trying to fund a senate campaign, she thinks he can start by cutting his party budget. It's a Wednesday night in late June and this entire event is already several degrees of *too much.* This Carlyle hotel is nearly twice as big as the location Chloe works at across town—sleek and shiny with enormous floor-to-ceiling windows that face out over a private beach and the ocean beyond. It's all dripping chandeliers and ornate pillars and black-tie guests, a dazzling combination that might as well punch Chloe in the throat and call her an impostor for daring to con her way inside.

There's the governor sitting at a table near the front with his equally bored-looking wife. There's the weatherman from channel six, laughing animatedly as he downs another glass of champagne. There's Katherine Windey, who can apparently take a break from overseeing her own hotel empire as long as it doesn't require looking up from her phone. Rich people. Powerful people. People who seem completely unfazed by Andrew Carlyle's enormous, spray-tanned face beaming down at them from every angle. Chloe shivers and averts her eyes from the campaign posters as she walks. It's not like he's *actually* watching her. Carlyle's not even here yet, which is annoying considering this entire event is for him, but the image of his smooth, dark hair and too-white smile feels burned into her brain.

Chloe pauses next to the balcony with Webber at her side. She moves back and forth until Priya's hum of approval echoes in her ear, then stands on her tiptoes, pretending to wave her phone overhead. "I'm telling you," she says. "You have to see this app. I mean, what are the odds you both had the same—"

Something slams into them from behind. Chloe stumbles, heel snagging on the hem of her dress. She catches herself against the wall as wine sloshes over the rim of Webber's glass and when she whips around, she finds Logan staring back at them, face a portrait of nervous concern.

"Oh my god!" He reaches for her with one hand, the other still clutching a tray of what looks like snail carcasses. "I'm *so* sorry, are you two okay?"

Chloe's not, actually. She's pretty sure part of her dress ripped. There's a breeze tickling her ankle that definitely wasn't there before, but she forces herself to ignore it as Logan reaches for Webber next.

"I'm sorry," he repeats, dabbing at Webber's wine-stained tie. "Let me get you something for that, I'm—"

"Leave it." Webber slams his half-empty glass onto Logan's tray. "Just go. And get me another drink while you're at it."

Chloe can practically feel the annoyance rolling off him, frustration at the seemingly incompetent waitstaff mixed with the self-preserving instinct of not wanting to draw attention in a place like this. Logan seems to realize the same thing because he ducks his head, tray tucked against his chest like a makeshift shield, before turning and disappearing into the crowd.

Webber curses under his breath, wine still tracing scarlet trails over his rigidly pressed cuffs. "*Unbelievable,*" he mutters. "Tonight of all nights."

After another precarious second, Chloe finally succeeds in freeing her shoe from the folds of her skirt. She tosses her hair over one shoulder with as much disgust as she can manage. "I know. Are you all right?"

"I'm fine." Webber waves a hand, and this time, Chloe thinks the dismissal applies to her, too. "I should go find somewhere to clean up."

Chloe nods, doing her best to look disappointed as she focuses on his wine-splattered shoes. "Of course. Do you have a business card? Maybe we could stay in touch?"

One final trick. Something to fuel his ego when he leaves. Men like Webber, she's learned, don't have business cards. They walk through life with the expectation that everyone already knows exactly who they are and what they do, but the flattery works. Webber's expression softens ever so slightly as he shakes his head. "I'm afraid not. Enjoy the party, though. It was nice to meet you."

And then he's gone, another indistinguishable suit in a crowd of dazzling wealth.

Chloe watches his retreating back for another second before tucking her phone back down the front of her dress. *Easy,* she thinks. It's always easy with men like that. Even now, part of her almost wishes Webber would look down and notice that his watch is missing, the band of diamonds now stashed securely in Logan's pocket. Maybe then they'd have a real challenge.

"Got it," Logan mutters through the earpiece. "That was smooth."

Chloe rolls her eyes and plucks a half-empty glass of wine off a nearby table. "You pushed me into a wall, but okay."

"Technicalities. Who's next?"

Who's next? Because someone has to be. Because they didn't drive all the way across town and crash Carlyle's campaign dinner to stop here, not with an entire ballroom at their fingertips. Not with the rapidly growing mountain of unpaid bills on Chloe's desk.

"What about Carlyle?" Chloe asks, eyes flicking from table to table. "Is he here yet?"

Logan's snort is a gentle caress in her ear. "You want to go after your boss? I thought you liked your job."

Chloe resists the urge to tell him that no one actually likes their job. She puts up with her own long hours in the hotel kitchens for the healthcare. She does it for the discounted employee housing and the stability of a steady paycheck, because she has other people to worry about, not because she likes it. The thought of her shift tomorrow is barely a whisper in the back of her mind. Right now, the thrill of success makes her feel unbreakable. She wants something risky. She wants something fun. She wants to sink her teeth into this entire gold-plated room and call it justice.

Priya is typing; Chloe can hear the *click click click* of her acrylics through the earbud. "Doesn't look like Carlyle's here yet," she says. "Katherine Windey is at table seven, though, if you really want to rob a hotel CEO. Her properties are supposed to be better, anyway."

Chloe tilts her head. "Didn't she get arrested for embezzlement?"

"Everyone here has gotten arrested for embezzlement, Chloe. That's, like, their whole thing."

"Hold on." Logan's voice sharpens with interest. "Katherine's here? Is she alone? What's she wearing?"

"Oh my god, Logan," Chloe mutters. "You can't just ask what women are wearing."

"That's not . . . I'm asking about *The Brooch*."

Chloe grins into her drink. Logan's been after Katherine's jeweled bumblebee brooch since the ribbon-cutting ceremony of her new island resort last year. He thinks taking it would be good for his "street cred." Chloe thinks the idea of Logan having any sort of street cred is laughable. She normally wouldn't mind getting her hands on something that valuable, but this particular piece is usually pinned directly beneath Katherine's delicate, upturned nose. Even Logan and his sticky magician's fingers haven't found a way around that.

"No brooch," Chloe decides. "Not tonight."

Logan sighs mournfully. "It's a collector's item, you know."

"I know."

"I'd treat her right."

Chloe is about to respond when a flurry of movement at the ballroom entrance catches her eye. Another group of donors arriving late, bottlenecking in the doors as they take in the grandeur of the ballroom.

"On it," Priya says before Chloe can speak. "I'm pulling up a guest list."

Chloe downs the rest of her drink, keeping one eye on the door as she slides along the back wall. Maybe tonight could still be interesting after all. One of the new arrivals has an enormous, jeweled brooch pinned to her lapel—not quite as big as Katherine's but equally as obnoxious. Chloe is about to point it out when Logan sucks in a surprised breath. The sound is staticky in her ear, lighting some deeply buried survival instinct in the pit of her stomach.

Chloe's steps falter. "What?"

"Trouble," Logan says, voice already resigned to the worst. "Two o'clock. Blue dress."

Chloe cranes her neck, trying to catch a glimpse of who, exactly, Logan is talking about. *Trouble* could mean a lot of things—hotel security, a boss, a vengeful ex. Once, in Priya's case, it was all three. Chloe ducks behind another table, gaze flitting from one classically beautiful face to another. "Do you want to elaborate? I can't—"

There, to her left. A flash of blue silk. Ice tips down Chloe's spine and she stumbles to a halt in the center of the ballroom. "You've *got* to be fucking kidding me."

A few scandalized faces turn her way, but Chloe is long past caring. She's frozen to the marbled tile, glass still clutched in one hand, and it's all she can do not to crush the delicate stem between her fingers.

"What?" Priya's voice is frantic. "What's going on?"

Chloe opens her mouth, but nothing comes out. She's stuck, watching the woman in blue break away from the crowd and head toward the bar. Eventually, it's Logan who breaks the silence.

"Told you," he says, wry humor coloring every word. "Trouble."

TWO

The day Chloe realized she could have everything she wanted came five months after her twenty-sixth birthday, two weeks after someone stamped an eviction notice on her apartment door, and twelve days after her mother's funeral.

It was an unseasonably cool day in late June, the Miami sky thick with looming clouds, and she'd been parked outside her childhood home, waiting for her father to leave for work. She wasn't technically avoiding him. They'd just spoken on the phone yesterday, but the last thing Chloe wanted was to sit in that house with all their unspoken grief still darkening the space between them. She couldn't tell him she was getting kicked out of her apartment. She couldn't tell him she'd been fired for the second time in three months, and she absolutely couldn't tell him it was all her fault.

She'd still been slouched in the driver's seat with one foot propped against the dashboard when a shiny green Prius pulled into the driveway across the street. As Chloe watched, a girl hopped out of the car and into the back of a van that had been idling in the garage next door. As soon as the door swung shut behind her, the van reversed into the street, turned, and sped off around the corner, no doubt heading somewhere exciting and fun.

It was summer, after all, even if Chloe didn't think things like that mattered anymore.

She eyed the abandoned Prius, noting the way it gleamed in the driveway despite the lack of sun. How the girl had left both front windows down in her haste to leave. A Gulliver Prep school tote bag hung off the front seat, the corner of a laptop case just visible beneath the fabric. Chloe's fingers tightened around the steering wheel. Her own laptop had finally called it quits last week, the cherry on top of an absolutely terrible month, and here was this girl, leaving her own computer lying around like it was nothing. Like she didn't care.

Maybe she doesn't, Chloe thought distantly. *Maybe it should belong to someone who does.*

She was out of her car and across the street before she fully registered her intention, but when she slipped a hand through the car's open window and tucked the girl's laptop safely into her own bag, it almost felt like an awakening.

Chloe had pawned it for eight hundred dollars the next day—enough to hold off her landlord for another week, take her dad out for lunch, and buy an appropriately professional blouse to interview for a catering job at one of the Carlyle hotels. But the rush of taking that laptop didn't fade. She knew her father was still drowning in medical bills and funeral costs. She was suffocating under a pile of loans from a four-year communications degree that went exactly nowhere, so why couldn't she want more?

Why couldn't she take it?

Chloe never planned to come back to Miami after graduation. Most of her college friends had stayed in North Carolina. Even Logan moved to Orlando for a theme park job, but when her mother got sick, Chloe felt the last of her choices evaporate like cool morning mist. She never understood the pull of this city or why her mother had left the rolling Irish countryside to come *here* of all places, but that summer, Chloe carved out a place for herself, too.

She started working in the Carlyle kitchens. When Logan quit his theme park job, she helped him find an apartment downtown before asking, as casually as she could on one of their weekly phone calls, if he was still doing card tricks for fun. She learned where the summer tourists carried their money, how to slip valuables from hotel rooms without leaving a trace, and where to sell them for the best price. She learned how to style her hair and laugh harmlessly at people's jokes as she slid a hand into their back pockets.

By the time she met Harper Parisi a few weeks later, Chloe thought herself more or less invincible.

She and Logan had been crashing some corporate party in the back of a fancy steakhouse, posing as junior-level employees no one seemed particularly inclined to talk to. Logan had his eye on a blond woman to their right, but Chloe couldn't stop watching the CEO. He'd left his wallet in the pocket of the jacket that now hung off the back of his chair, gold money clip and all. If Chloe could just get his attention, if she could distract him long enough to turn his head, Logan would be able to grab it.

"I wouldn't do that if I were you."

Chloe narrowly avoided splashing a glass of eighty-dollar wine across the floor as she turned toward the voice. The blond woman Logan had been eyeing now stood at Chloe's shoulder, one hand propped casually on her hip. She couldn't be much older than them, but everything about her screamed wealth, from her bright, silky highlights to the tailored gingham fabric of her skirt.

"Do what?" Chloe asked innocently.

"Oh, please. You're not exactly subtle." Then, before Chloe could react, the woman lifted a hand. "Schwartz!" she called. "I didn't know you had a new assistant. Where did you find her?"

The CEO lifted his head, brow furrowing in confusion as if he was just now realizing that no, he *didn't* actually know why Chloe was at his party. He glanced toward the security guard in the corner and Chloe had just enough time to grab Logan before both men started in her direction. The last thing she saw as they ducked out of the restaurant was the cool tilt of the woman's smile as she slipped a hand into the pocket of Schwartz's unattended jacket.

The note came the next day, tucked in the back of Chloe's mailbox in a crisp, padded envelope.

Stay out of my way.
xoxo Harper

Chloe's stomach dipped when she found the gold money clip inside. It was one thing to admire the piece from afar. It was quite another to have it show up at her apartment, sent—undoubtedly—by a strange woman who shouldn't even know her name, much less where she lived. Chloe wrapped her fingers around the money clip one by one, squeezing until the cold edge bit into her palm, and that was how it started—with a woman in the back of a Miami steakhouse and the distinct feeling that the world had just shifted under her feet.

It became clear to Chloe very quickly that Harper was nothing like her or Logan. A quick scroll through her meticulously filtered social media feeds revealed she had more money than she knew what to do with and absolutely no qualms about showing it off. She was probably related to some hedge-fund manager or tech mogul, someone who didn't care that their daughter's only contribution to society was sitting on yachts and being hot. The point was that she had class and comfort—both the things that were supposed to make life worth living and yet there she was, pulling the same simple cons Chloe had spent the summer mastering. And she was doing them *better,* which was even more infuriating.

No matter where Chloe turned or what she did, Harper was always *there*—at galas and parties and city events, with her mouth painted a bold shade of crimson and her gaze locked on the same target Chloe had been pursuing all night. Sometimes Harper got there first. Other times, Chloe emerged victorious, pockets weighed down with things she hadn't even wanted just to prevent Harper from getting her hands on them.

There wasn't a point to their back-and-forth. Chloe didn't even like calling it a rivalry, but every time she and Harper inevitably crossed paths, it was immediately clear who had been invited and who had lied their way in wearing a thrifted gown.

So when Chloe watches Harper pause next to a glittering tower of champagne glasses across the Carlyle ballroom, she's not thinking about the watch in Logan's pocket or the hundreds of unattended purses in the coatroom. She's just thinking about how her night is about to get inevitably, exponentially worse.

"What the *hell* is she doing here?" Chloe mutters, turning her back on the party.

"I don't know," Priya says. "She's not on the guest list. Isn't she supposed to be in Italy?"

"Yeah, I was hoping she'd die in a tragic boating accident."

"God, can you imagine?" Logan says. "I feel like that would make her worse, somehow." He hesitates a second longer before asking, "What do you want to do?"

Excellent question. Right now, all Chloe wants is to march across the ballroom and wrap both hands around Harper's throat. She wants to throw her against the wall and demand to know why she's here, why she can't ever seem to leave them alone. Instead, she watches Harper pluck a champagne glass off the tower and pushes a frustrated sigh between her teeth. "I'll handle it."

"Chloe." Priya's voice sharpens. "Don't—"

Chloe reaches up and rips out her earbud before stalking across the ballroom.

When she learned Harper Parisi was spending the summer in some Italian chateau, Chloe spent an embarrassing amount of time hoping it was for some awful, life-ruining reason. Maybe her trust fund had dried up. Maybe she'd gotten fired from whatever boring, corporate job she'd been nepotism-ed into. Maybe she was pregnant and disappeared so no one would know if her outrageously dewy skin was finally dulled by the pain of childbirth. There would be some imperfection, she thought, some flaw to let her know that Harper wasn't as perfectly unshakable as she pretended to be.

But here she is, as dewy and stunning as ever with no sign of a secret baby in sight. She's standing in a quiet corner of the ballroom, champagne glass hanging lazily from one hand. Her nails are painted the same color she wore that day in the steakhouse (Chanel No. 895, shade: Sunlight) and Chloe thinks something about it feels purposeful. Like Harper applied it specifically for the possibility of this meeting. Her long blond hair is pulled into a high ponytail—some gravity-defying combination of sleek and voluminous that Chloe is definitely *not* envious of—and she's wearing a blue dress she lifted from a downtown boutique last winter.

Chloe inhales a sharp breath. Before she can lose her last thread of composure, she closes the distance between them and snaps, "Why are you here?"

The question comes out steady, but if Harper is surprised at the confrontation, it doesn't show. She turns, brows lifting as she slowly looks Chloe up and down, no doubt taking in her ripped dress and rapidly frizzing hair. "Chloe," she says at last. "You look . . . comfortable."

Chloe's grip tightens around the stem of her wineglass. She should have splurged on the taller shoes. Harper shouldn't get to look down on her now, like she has any moral ground to stand on. "*Why* are you here?" she repeats.

"Why do you think?" Harper waves a bored hand in the general direction of the ballroom. "I'm here to eat a very expensive dinner and support a worthy candidate."

"That's all?"

"Of course." Harper's eyes narrow ever so slightly. "Why are you here?"

Chloe bites the inside of her cheek, immediately wishing she could take the question back. Harper's always had this terrible knack for getting people to show their hand; Chloe hates that she still falls for it. "Nothing," she mutters. "Just stay out of my way."

She turns back toward the party, but Harper blocks her escape with one elegantly arched foot. "Oh, I see," she says, amusement flickering behind her green eyes. "Are you here for Collins? His wife just died and left him a yacht, you know. Or Teddy, maybe?" She gestures toward an ancient-looking man at table twelve. "He spent twenty thousand dollars on his granddaughter's wedding dress last month. Absurd, right? Or maybe you're here for Webber? Careful, he won't shut up about *revolutionizing the future of luxury transportation* or whatever bullshit app he's developing."

Harper's posture is relaxed, one hip resting carelessly against the table. Her hair spills over one shoulder as she glances around the ballroom, like she's making her own mental notes about who to seek out next. Chloe hates it. She grits her teeth and grinds out, "That's none of your business."

"Isn't it? I feel like I should know if you're about to ruin my night."

"I'm *not* about to—"

There's a soft touch at her elbow and Chloe whirls, ready to smash her wineglass into the face of the first person she sees. But it's just Logan, clutching a tray of appetizers and glaring pointedly at them both. "Do we maybe want to break this up?"

Chloe blinks and realizes that some of the dinner guests have started shooting curious glances in her direction. Because she and Harper are standing too close together, talking too intensely for an event like this. Because this happens *every time*—Harper's presence making her feel sharp and desperate, emotions too volatile to fit beneath her skin. She steps back and forces herself to breathe as Harper turns her attention to Logan instead.

"Look at you!" she says, trailing a hand down the arm of his borrowed uniform. "Nice cummerbund. Are these any good, by the way?"

She starts to pluck a shrimp cocktail off his tray, but Logan yanks himself from her grip. "Pleasure as always, Harper," he says before sliding Chloe another glare that clearly says *let's go*.

This time, Chloe listens. She slams her empty glass onto the champagne table and stalks back across the ballroom, Logan scurrying in her wake. Maybe Harper will choke on shrimp cocktail and save them both the trouble. "God," she mutters the second they're out of earshot. "I hate her."

"I know," Logan says. "Why is she here?"

The two of them aren't supposed to talk on the job. Chloe knows that. They aren't supposed to know each other at all, but this is probably one of those emergency situations where the rules go out the window. Chloe shrugs. "Who knows. She says she's here for dinner and to donate to Carlyle's campaign."

Logan pauses in front of his catering cart, pretending to refill his tray. "Is that it?"

"Of course not! She's a liar, Logan!"

Chloe's hands tighten into fists at her sides. For some unidentified reason, Harper is *here*. At Chloe's job, in her business yet again. There are plenty of terrible people to con in South Florida. Harper could talk her way onto any yacht in the marina, but no. She's in the Carlyle ballroom drinking champagne and shaking hands with conservative donors like she's the goddamn queen of England.

"Hey." When Logan touches her elbow again, his voice is soft. "Why don't we call it a night?"

Chloe immediately shakes her head. "No," she says. "We're not done."

"I don't like it either, but we still need a way out."

The corner of Logan's mouth turns down in a frustrated grimace and Chloe knows he doesn't want to leave either. He's probably thinking about his own dead-end job and Katherine Windey's unattainable brooch and all the different things he could buy with money like that. She's thinking about it too—the stack of bills on her kitchen counter, her dad all alone in his new apartment, the loans she doesn't know how to pay.

Of course they shouldn't leave, but Harper, as always, is a variable they can't predict.

Before Chloe can answer, a commotion breaks out on the other side of the ballroom. She turns as subtly as she can, apprehension stirring in her stomach at the new clamor of voices. The noise is coming from a table toward the front. From James Montgomery Webber, who's turning in frantic circles as he pats his suit jacket. Chloe can't hear him over the crowd, but the words on his lips are clear.

My watch. I can't find my watch.

The back of Logan's hand brushes hers, a silent warning, but Chloe refuses to look down. There's half a ballroom between her and Webber, even more space between them and the nearest exit, but the way forward is clogged with campaign signs and tables and the unmistakable feeling that something is about to go horribly wrong.

Across the room, Harper downs the rest of her champagne and turns toward the commotion. The only thing more embarrassing than Harper crashing her job, Chloe thinks, would be Harper watching her get hauled away in handcuffs. She's supposed to be better than this. She can usually do these kinds of jobs in her sleep, but it's an effort for Chloe to steady herself as she tugs Logan along the back wall.

They've almost reached the main entrance when the doors fly open and members of the Carlyle security team file inside, pulled by the flurry of raised voices. Chloe immediately turns in the opposite direction. She can feel her pulse now, pounding in her throat as she sorts through their options. Webber's watch is in Logan's pocket, tucked away and out of sight. Right now, no one is watching them. All they have to do is get out.

"Oh, that's terrible!" Harper's voice rises above the crowd, loud enough for Chloe to hear. "You lost something? Do you need help?"

She motions for the tables around her to stand so she can look under their seats and, as she leans over to lift a rogue napkin, Chloe swears Harper flashes her a wink. *She knows.* The realization is crystal clear. Somehow, Harper knows exactly what they did tonight and she wants to make sure everyone else knows it, too.

Logan ducks behind a lone catering cart as he fiddles with his earbud. Chloe remembers her own just in time, tucking it back into her ear as more guests turn to watch the search. "What do our exits look like, Pri?"

"Oh, you're back?" Priya lets out a distracted hum. "Sorry, I assumed something malfunctioned because there's no way you would actually *mute me during a job*!"

Logan sets his tray on the cart. "Must we do this now?"

"I don't know, why don't you ask Chloe?"

"Okay!" Chloe hisses. "I'm sorry. Next time I'll let you listen to every boring detail. What do our exits look like?"

For a second, the only sound is Priya's fingers against the keyboard. Then she sighs. "Honestly, not great. Why don't you give it a minute? They're not going to shut the whole place down for a Rolex. I bet that guy has, like, twelve more at home."

She's probably right, but Chloe doesn't think they have a minute. Harper is pulling up tablecloths and patting across empty seat cushions like she's starring in a one-woman show about the power of friendship and Chloe wants to win.

She wants to claim the victory here, snatch it from beneath Harper's nose.

She's about to suggest Logan take the watch and leave through the kitchens alone when Harper lets out a sharp gasp. The sound slides right through the growing pit in Chloe's stomach and when she tears her gaze away from the exit, Harper is standing in front of Webber's table with a diamond-encrusted band spilling between her fingers.

"Is this it?"

Chloe can't help it. Her mouth drops open, all subtlety forgotten as Logan's hands fly over his jacket, hastily checking and rechecking where the watch should be. When he looks up, his expression is incredulous, and Chloe knows.

Somehow, in the time it took Harper to run her fingers down Logan's arm earlier, she'd slipped their only prize of the night from his pocket without either of them noticing.

Across the room, Webber seizes the watch and refastens it around his wrist with shaky fingers. "Yes!" he says. "Oh, thank you! I was sitting here earlier. It must have fallen off."

But Chloe is hardly listening. She's still standing against the wall, fury prickling up the back of her neck, when Harper's gaze slides toward her again. It's a flash of a smile, so quick Chloe almost misses it, but the familiar lift of Harper's mouth might as well be burned into her skin. She'd know that expression anywhere, would recognize it across any room. Right now, it's victorious.

Right now, it says, *Your move, Chloe.*

THREE

There are three photos on the wall above Chloe's bed—a faded filmstrip of her and Logan from their first week at NC State, a Polaroid of her childhood dog, Beau, and a framed picture of her mother, standing on the beach with one hand lifted against the brilliant Miami sun.

Chloe still remembers the details of that specific evening—the nearly empty beach, the late November chill, her mother motioning her into the foamy water. *Come here,* she said, hand outstretched. *See that? All the way over there?*

It was a familiar game, one they hadn't played in years, but it always started like this—with her mother pointing toward the horizon and loudly proclaiming that if the two of them looked hard enough, they could see their family waving back at them from across the sea.

Chloe has never been to Ireland. She's never seen the Kilkee Cliffs or met most of the relatives her mother spoke of, but that day, she played along. She pretended, for once, like the recent diagnosis hanging over their heads didn't exist. Like she'd never heard the words *stage four ovarian cancer* in her life.

Of course, she said, shivering as the ocean lapped at the toes of her sneakers. *You kind of have to squint, though.*

Her mother laughed, the sound clear and lilting, and somewhere over their shoulders, Chloe heard the click of her father's camera.

Even now, part of her still thinks of that day on the beach as the Last Day. Her mother's descent had been quick after that, a sharp drop into tests and treatments and never-ending hospital hallways. Some people said they were lucky, that at least they'd had time to prepare a goodbye, but Chloe remembers those months only as a series of muted flashes and echoes. She hadn't been prepared for anything. All she knows is that one morning her mother had been standing on that beach with her arms outstretched, vibrant and alive like she wanted to swallow the world, and the next she was gone, leaving Chloe and her father to pick up the pieces.

Chloe stopped at one of those cheesy, beachside tourist shops a few weeks after the funeral and bought an obnoxiously iridescent frame with the money she'd gotten selling someone else's iPhone. The frame wasn't her style, but it was exactly the kind of bright, kitschy thing her mother would have loved.

Now, the framed photo from that day hangs above her bed in her dimly lit employee apartment behind the downtown Carlyle hotel. It catches the sunlight streaming through her ground-level window so when Chloe opens her eyes the next morning, the first thing she sees is the familiar flash of pastel glass patterned across her wall. It's almost peaceful.

Then the shrill blare of her alarm slices through the early morning haze and the feeling shatters.

Chloe groans, patting across the duvet until she finds her phone. It takes a solid thirty seconds of searching for the snooze button to realize the sound isn't her alarm at all. It's her ringtone. She jabs a finger at the cracked screen until the noise stops, then she shoves her head under the pillow and snaps, "What?" as Priya's expertly contoured face fills the screen.

"Good morning to you, too." Priya's voice is half muffled by the pillow, but Chloe can still hear coffee brewing in the background of her friend's immaculate, sun-soaked studio. "I had a feeling you'd forget to set an alarm last night, so this is a friendly reminder that you need to be at work in less than an hour."

Chloe lifts her head, double-checks the time, and bites back another groan. Of course she forgot to set an alarm. Of course she overslept. Her room is still a mess from the night before, ball gown hanging off the back of her chair, shoes kicked into separate corners. She was supposed to clean when she got back, to sort through her things while basking in the high of a job well done, but in reality, she'd barely had enough energy to tug off her clothes before collapsing face-first into bed. Judging from the makeup-stained dent in her pillow, this is the first time she's moved.

"Thanks, Pri," she mutters. "I appreciate you."

"That's better." Priya grins, leaning forward to swipe on another coat of mascara. She's perched on the padded seat of her vanity, one knee tucked against her chest. Her ring light casts a warm glow over her smooth brown skin and if the sharp cut of her eyeliner is any indication, she's already been up for hours.

Of all the wannabe influencers in southeast Florida, Chloe thinks Priya is most likely to make it, and not just because she has two years of an MIT degree helping her game social media algorithms. It's also because she unironically does things like wake up at dawn for hot yoga and once told Chloe she couldn't start her day until her "feelings have been adequately journaled." Like now, for example, she's swirling a reusable straw around a mason jar of green juice with one hand and winding a hot roller into her bangs with the other.

"We missed you last night," Priya says as Chloe finally hauls herself out of bed. "You didn't come back for dinner."

Chloe props her phone on her desk so they can continue talking as she riffles through her hamper. "I was a little preoccupied."

"Right. Getting conned by your bitter nemesis."

"She's not my nemesis."

Nemesis implies intention. It implies a goal. It implies that she willingly spends time thinking about Harper Parisi's inevitable downfall. She does, of course, but that's not because Harper is her *nemesis.* It's just because Chloe hates her.

Priya nods, but something about it feels placating, like even now, after almost a year of friendship, she doesn't quite believe it. "She *did* show up out of nowhere and ruin our job," she points out. "I hate to break it to you, but that's peak nemesis behavior."

Chloe doesn't answer. She finally unearths her work slacks from the floor of her closet and ducks out of frame to tug them on, ignoring the weird stain on the left knee.

The thing is, she's not sure Harper *did* show up out of nowhere. Sure, she's obnoxiously wealthy and impeccably connected. Her parents probably have one of those weird, seven-figure jobs only available to people okay with committing casual war crimes; so it wasn't unthinkable for her to attend one of Andrew Carlyle's donor events. Still, Chloe can't shake the feeling that something about last night feels premeditated.

"She just can't stand the idea that someone has something she doesn't." Chloe throws on the first black shirt she can find and starts searching for a pack of makeup wipes. "It's not like she needed that watch. It's not like she needs to do any of the things she does but that's never stopped her before."

Priya lets out a soft laugh. "Maybe she does. We don't actually know her."

But Chloe *does* know her. She knows Harper's type—beautiful, terrible people who've never lived in the real world, who think they're indestructible because no one has dared to tell them no. She scowls, resuming her search, but there are no makeup wipes on her dresser or floor. She's about to start opening drawers when she remembers the unopened packet still stashed in the pocket of last night's dress. She lunges across the room and starts tearing through the fabric.

"It's annoying," Chloe continues. "She could go anywhere in this city, anywhere in the world, probably, but she's always *here.* I mean, what's the point? Doesn't she have yachts to buy or taxes to evade or—"

Chloe stops mid-sentence, hand inside the pocket of her dress. She's found the makeup wipes, but there's something else here, too. It's smooth and slim, edges unnecessarily sharp, and when she tugs it into the open, Chloe finds a shiny black business card tucked inside her palm.

There's a single line of text stamped across the front—Nice lift. Better luck next time.

And on the back—Carlyle penthouse, Thursday, 09:00.

Something cold trickles down the back of her neck. Chloe runs a finger over the card's smooth face, remembering the envelope Harper slipped in her mailbox the day after they met. There have been more notes since, of course, all of them signed with a casual *xoxo Harper.* This is clearly another one of hers, but the card isn't what unnerves Chloe now.

It's the idea that Harper managed to slip it into her pocket unnoticed, that she apparently expects Chloe to drop everything and follow her instructions now.

Carlyle penthouse, Thursday, 09:00.

That's today, right before her regular shift is scheduled to start.

"Hello?"

Chloe jumps before remembering Priya still propped on her desk. She stuffs the card in her pocket and straightens, heart pounding unnaturally fast. "What?"

"What do you mean, '*What?*' You were the one talking."

"Oh. Right." Chloe shakes her head. "Never mind. I have to go, I'm running late."

Priya's eyes narrow, like she doesn't buy the excuse, but Chloe doesn't give her the chance to protest. She ends the call, shoves everything into her bag, and makes her way downstairs right as the hotel shuttle pulls up to the curb.

The Carlyle employee housing is technically only half a mile from the hotel, but the jagged maze of parking lots and back buildings makes walking almost impossible. That, combined with the damp Florida heat, means the shuttle is the only real way to get to and from work, regardless of how unreliable it is. Chloe collapses into one of the sticky plastic seats, anger heating her skin despite the bus's frigid air-conditioning. As the doors close behind her, she slips the card out of her pocket again. It's surprisingly solid in her palm, like it's made of plastic instead of paper. In the morning light, she can see the text is actually gold foil, because of course it is, words stamped into the matte background with razor-sharp precision.

Carlyle penthouse, Thursday, 09:00.

No sign-off, no signature. Just the expectation that Chloe will drop whatever she's doing to follow its cryptic instructions.

But even if she wanted to, she can't. She has a shift today. She needs to plan another job to make up for last night's failure. Harper might have taken Webber's watch out of spite, but Chloe still desperately needs the money. She rerouted most of her mother's medical bills to her apartment months ago, determined to pay off at least half while simultaneously digging through the interest of her own student loans, but she's not the only one living day to day.

Logan moved to Orlando because his company was one of the few in Florida that provided gender-affirming healthcare to trans people. He found a queer community in Miami too, but that didn't erase the fear of living in a state that's actively trying to stamp out his existence. He's wanted to leave for years, and these odd jobs are supposed to fund his way out. Priya only got through two years at MIT before her parents' hardware store went bankrupt. She boarded a one-way flight home and has been living two blocks from her family ever since, helping to care for her three younger siblings and working odd retail jobs while her parents struggle to make ends meet.

Most months, the three of them get lucky. Logan pawns items from the parties he books, Chloe slips into people's hotel rooms after hours, and Priya occasionally dips into their spreadsheet of saved credit cards. They make it work. They have a system.

But here they are, once again strapped for cash because Harper fucking Parisi wanted to parade around in a stolen gown and play hero for the night.

Chloe's knuckles whiten around the cracked edges of her phone as the shuttle pulls into the hotel parking lot. She's on her feet before the driver releases the doors, fueled by the lingering memory of Harper's taunting grin. Maybe this is all a trick. Maybe Harper has no real intention of meeting her in the penthouse today, but Chloe is done playing games.

The downtown Carlyle hotel is smaller than the one they infiltrated last night, but Chloe still curses its long, sweeping corridors as she half walks, half jogs toward the elevators. Her fingers ache, a year of pent-up anger bubbling to the surface. She managed to keep most of her frustration at bay while talking with Priya this morning. She was able to control it last night too, but this is different. It's one thing for Harper to ruin her jobs and steal her winnings, but it's quite another to show up and make demands here, at *her* hotel.

Chloe skids to a stop in front of the service elevator, steps inside, and taps her employee ID against the scanner three times before realizing she's not moving. Because *of course* she's not. She's never had access to the penthouse before and Harper can't change employee protocol because she feels like it. Chloe exhales a frustrated breath. She's about to give up and clock in like normal when she remembers the card in her pocket. Its smooth edges, the surprising weight. A jolt of disbelief slides up her spine.

"No way."

Chloe fishes the card out and, after a brief moment of hesitation, taps it against the scanner. Immediately, the penthouse button lights up and the elevator rumbles to life. *Unbelievable.* If she didn't hate Harper so much, she'd almost be impressed with the commitment. But when the elevator doors slide open into the penthouse foyer, Harper isn't waiting to greet her.

Instead, Chloe is alone in the nicest room she's ever seen, with absolutely no idea what to do next.

Only managers have penthouse access, and it takes exactly two seconds for her to realize why. This is where their celebrity guests stay, where athletes host viewing parties and VIP dinners, and where Andrew Carlyle launched his senate campaign last year. It takes up the entire top floor of the hotel, four fully furnished bedrooms dripping with chandeliers and shiny new appliances. There's a kitchen down the hall, a laundry room around the corner, and somewhere to their right a network of storage closets bigger than Chloe's apartment. Classical music plays from somewhere in the distance and she's about to follow the sound when the elevator lets out a sharp *ding* behind her.

"Jesus Christ!" Chloe jumps into one of the granite pillars as the doors slide open again.

"No, it's just me."

Chloe expected the Harper from last night, the cold, impeccably dressed con artist who lured her up here for a fight. She imagined gold jewelry and tailored clothes and a sharp crimson smile, but when Harper steps out of the elevator now, it looks like she's been yanked unwillingly from a poolside cabana. Her hair falls loose around her face, and a gauzy cover-up hangs casually from one shoulder. The black strap of a designer bikini peeks out from underneath and Chloe thinks she must have angered a very powerful god in a past life. There's no other explanation for why the universe would let her come to this weird showdown in stained pants and no-slip shoes when Harper looks like *this*.

"Funny," Chloe says as her pulse returns to normal. "This is *such* a funny joke, Harper. Is there a point or are you just here to waste my time?"

"What?" Harper steps into the foyer, platform sandals giving her a completely unnecessary extra few inches of height. "I'm sorry, why are you here?"

"I literally work here! You can't—" Chloe breaks off as Harper's mouth quirks in amusement. This is a mistake. She turns and jams a finger into the elevator call button. "Forget it. I don't know what your plan was, but you can leave me out of it. Oh!" She fumbles in her pocket until she finds the card. "And you can have this back."

She flings it across the room, half expecting Harper to roll her eyes and pout now that Chloe's ruined her weird little plan. Instead, she catches the card in one hand, brow furrowing as she reaches into her own pocket with the other.

"I don't know what to tell you, Chloe, but you're not that special."

Harper holds out her other hand and there, sitting in her palm, is a black card, nearly identical to the one Chloe tossed her way. The text on the front reads ALMOST. TRY AGAIN., but the back is the same—CARLYLE PENTHOUSE, THURSDAY, 09:00.

Chloe blinks, momentarily lost for words. "But you put that in my pocket."

"No, I didn't." Harper tosses Chloe's card back to her. "I'd never use that font. On a matte background? Please."

"Then why are you here?"

"Because I'm on *vacation,* Chloe. Not everything is about you."

It takes everything in Chloe's power not to strangle Harper right here, in the foyer of this very fancy penthouse. But she *does* look like she's on vacation, like this is merely an inconvenient stop in her otherwise perfect day.

And if Harper didn't set this up, if she didn't plan this . . .

Somewhere down the hall, the music stops. Static scrapes across the walls and then, right when Chloe's starting to worry that this is the start of a very weird indie horror film, there's a sound of rustling fabric, the soft scrape of a needle dropping, and the record starts over.

A crease forms between Harper's brows. "Is someone here?"

That, Chloe realizes, would have been an excellent question to ask five minutes ago. Slowly, she and Harper turn in the direction of the music. As they walk together down the sweeping corridor, there's a moment when Chloe wonders if they should fear the mysterious entity that called them up here alone. In reality, she's mostly annoyed. Dish duty after a brunch shift isn't fun but at least she knows what to expect. She wouldn't be standing shoulder to shoulder with Harper Parisi in the Carlyle penthouse, wondering if she's about to get stabbed or kidnapped or held for some exorbitant ransom no one in her life can afford to pay.

Eventually, the corridor opens into what looks like an office. The doors are propped open, giving Chloe a clear view of the polished black-and-white tile and the claw-foot desk sitting in the center of the room. A record spins on a turntable in the corner and it's not until Chloe takes a hesitant step forward that she realizes they're not alone.

A shadowy figure stands with one hand braced casually against the desk, haloed in light streaming through the enormous floor-to-ceiling windows. He looks, Chloe thinks, exactly like his campaign posters, a striking combination of broad shoulders, thick hair, and brilliant white teeth. It's the only thought that manages to form in her mind before Andrew Carlyle lifts a hand and beckons them forward.

"Ladies," he says, voice echoing in the empty space. "Why don't you take a seat. We have a lot to discuss."

FOUR

Even if Chloe hadn't spent the last year working in this hotel, even if she didn't spend last night purposefully avoiding his glossy campaign posters, she'd still know exactly how much power Andrew Carlyle holds from the casual way he beckons them forward now. She's seen the billboard ads, of course. She's seen the TV interviews and *Forbes* magazine covers and that one commercial that plays between episodes of *The Bachelor* where he's holding a baby crocodile and talking about tax cuts. Until today, she would have very confidently bet every penny in her paycheck that Andrew Carlyle had no idea who she was, but here they are. Standing in the middle of his hotel penthouse like it's the most natural thing in the world.

"Come in," Carlyle says, gesturing to the open chairs in front of the desk. "I see you got my invitation."

He's wearing salmon pink boat shorts, sandals, and a billowy linen shirt with too many open buttons. It looks like he's just stepped off a yacht, which, now that Chloe is thinking about it, is a very strong possibility. He also looks, more than anything, like he's expecting them.

The card in Chloe's pocket suddenly feels very heavy. In the instant it takes her to hesitate, Harper crosses the length of the office and casually drops into one of the empty chairs. She arches one manicured eyebrow in Chloe's direction and Chloe's face heats. She might not understand what's happening here but she's definitely not letting Harper take charge. She strides across the room and carefully perches on the edge of the other chair as Harper holds out the business card.

"How did this get in my pocket?" Harper asks. "I didn't even know that dress *had* pockets until I got home."

Carlyle shrugs. "A magician never reveals his secrets."

Chloe starts to point out that Logan once spent three hours telling her all the different ways to pull a quarter out of someone's ear, so *yes,* actually, magicians *do,* but Harper kicks her under the table.

"Ignore her," she says, flashing Chloe a pointed glare. "We're just a little surprised. It's not every day you get called to a Carlyle penthouse. This really is a gorgeous room, by the way."

Her voice is too sweet, dripping with false enthusiasm as Chloe leans down to rub her aching shin. *A little surprised* is an understatement. Somehow, Andrew Carlyle found a way through her defenses last night and slipped a card into her pocket. He knew she wasn't on the guest list. He might also know exactly what she was there to do and Chloe isn't going to sit here and pretend it's an honor to be invited to her own reckoning.

She scans the back half of the office, clocking the exits and windows as casually as she can. There's a row of shiny awards lining the file cabinets (a certified Five Star Luxury Hotel plaque; a national sustainability award; what looks like an Emmy, for some reason) and two framed diplomas on the wall to their left. The entire room is so stark and clean, glittering with new money, that she thinks it's a wonder it can sustain human life at all. The only hint of personalization is a photo on the edge of the desk—a young

Andrew Carlyle standing with a group of friends in front of what looks like a university library, holding a stack of books and beaming up through a rustic gold picture frame.

"That's from my last year at Cornell."

Chloe's gaze snaps up. Carlyle is watching her over the top of the desk, absentmindedly tracing a finger across the top of the frame. "Pretty, isn't it?" he asks. "It's not real gold, though, so I don't think you'd get much for it."

The words are so casual it takes Chloe a second to register the accusation. "I wasn't—" she starts, but Carlyle waves a hand.

"Of course you were. That's why you crashed my party last night, isn't it? It was quite impressive, really, but I'm going to have to ask you both to refrain from swindling my donors in the future. I have a campaign to fund."

Chloe's fingers lock around the leather armrests. *Is this a setup?* Did Harper lure her up here after all, just to push her off the gilded balcony? For a brief, wild second, she thinks of her father all alone in his new apartment, of her mother's family on some distant beach she'll never see, of Priya and Logan and all the people she's once again letting down.

Then Harper leans forward, one bare leg crossed purposefully over the other, and says, "Well, technically *I* didn't swindle anyone."

"Oh my *god.*" Chloe drags a hand down her face. She braces herself for the inevitable punishment, but to her surprise, Carlyle just watches them over his steepled fingers.

"Do you do that sort of thing a lot?" he asks. "You're very good at it. Very rehearsed."

Chloe is still struggling to form a coherent thought when Harper tilts her head to the side, blinking innocently up through her eyelashes. "Do *what,* exactly?"

"Come on. I'm not here to judge. I'm just curious."

"I'm afraid I don't know what you mean."

At least Harper is a good liar. There aren't many rules when it comes to conning hotel guests, but Chloe thinks not blatantly confessing her crimes to her boss is a big one. She doesn't think Carlyle has any real evidence that she tried to rob Webber last night. He might have glimpsed something in passing, but if he had anything substantial, Chloe doubts they'd be sitting around, talking this casually about her alleged offenses. No, Carlyle wants something and, for some reason, he thinks she and Harper can give it to him.

"I'm sorry," she says, leaning forward in her seat. "But I still have a shift this morning. Is there a reason we're here or—?"

"Do you know Katherine Windey?"

The question is aimed at her, so unexpected that the only thing Chloe can think to say is, "The brooch lady?"

"We went to school together, you know," Carlyle says, ignoring Chloe's outburst. "I always thought there was something serendipitous about the two of us ending up in the same city with our own chains of luxury hotels. I'm biased toward mine, obviously, but she's . . . very good at her job."

He says *good at her job* the way someone else might say *infested with flesh-eating bacteria.* Like it physically pains him to admit. Chloe waits for him to continue, but he doesn't look at her. Instead, his gaze slides purposefully toward Harper. "You've seen her new hotel, right? The Rivera?"

Harper nods stiffly. "I stayed there for a bit last month. It's nice. Apparently it's doing so well she's opening a new tower on the east side of the island."

"I know. It looks ridiculous."

"Wait." Chloe can't help it. She turns toward Harper. "You booked a hotel room in your own city?"

"It's called a staycation, Chloe."

"I *know* what it's called."

Carlyle lets out a humorless laugh. "Well, that's her thing, isn't it? The *staycation.* Modern-day luxury for tourists and locals alike. But I suppose when your hotel is on the country's most exclusive private island, you can say whatever you want."

There's an edge to his voice now, an irritated thread laced beneath every word. If it were anyone else, Chloe might point it out, but this is *Andrew Carlyle.* There's a power lurking beneath his dismissive tone and all of her retail job survival instincts are urging her not to push.

Harper, apparently, has no such qualms. "You don't sound bitter at all," she says, brows lifting ever so slightly toward her hairline.

"What?" Carlyle shakes his head. "No. Of course not. Did I technically own that property first? Yes. Should I have kept it after the hurricane? Definitely. But she bought it fair and square, and now she's getting profiled in *The New Yorker.* It's fine," he adds in a way that makes Chloe think it's very much not. "She got the island property, so I bought up her beachfront. She took one of my investors, so I poached her best clients. It's part of the game."

Everything is a game to rich people, Chloe thinks. She learned that a long time ago, but she doesn't particularly feel like playing this one. "I'm sorry," she says again. "I'm not trying to be rude, but I've never been inside a Windey hotel or taken a *staycation,* and right now I'm late for work, actually, so could this maybe wait until—?"

"I hosted a campaign event up here last week," Carlyle says, cutting through the rest of Chloe's sentence. "It wasn't anything elaborate, just a small gathering of local friends and donors, so of course I invited Katherine. I always invite her. I didn't think twice about it until everyone left, but . . ." He waves a dejected hand at the cluster of awards on his file cabinets. "I'm sure you've noticed by now."

If that's supposed to be an explanation, Chloe thinks it's severely lacking. She squints at the display of glittering awards over his shoulder, but nothing looks out of the ordinary. "Noticed what?" she asks.

"Nothing! Absolutely nothing! It's gone. She took my Florida Hospitality Award. Just snatched it off the shelf when no one was looking. She was always jealous I won that year. She always thought she deserved it, I know that, but *taking* it? From my own party? That's a new low, even for her, and—"

"Wait." Chloe holds up a hand as the words sink in. "That's it? I thought you had, like, a real problem."

"This *is* real."

"No, it's not." Chloe snatches her bag from the floor, earlier caution forgotten. For a single, blistering second, she doesn't care who Andrew Carlyle is or what he owns. "I'm supposed to be working right now," she says. "In *your* kitchen. I have a ten-hour shift on top of an event tonight and you called us up here to . . . what? Vent about your missing award?"

A piece of Carlyle's perfectly gelled hair comes loose, falling in front of his face as he looks imploringly up at them both. "No, Ms. Bly," he says. "I called you up here so you two can steal it back."

Chloe feels the shift in the air before Carlyle finishes speaking. It's the same prickling sensation from last night when she spotted Harper across the ballroom. Like she's holding a live wire between her teeth. She hesitates, swallowing over the sudden tightness in her throat. "And why would we do that?"

Carlyle scoffs and this time, Chloe thinks she catches a glimmer of frustration behind his smooth millionaire mask. "Stop pretending. You"—he points at her over the desk—"snuck into my dinner last night. You passed all my security checkpoints, tampered with my security footage, and almost walked out with another man's watch. Granted, James Webber isn't very hard to trick, but it's still an impressive feat to pull off alone."

Alone. The word echoes through the back of Chloe's mind. Despite all his influence and posturing, Carlyle doesn't seem to know about Priya or Logan. That's something, at least. A singular card to keep up her sleeve.

Chloe opens her mouth to speak, but Carlyle rounds on Harper next. "And you," he says. "You took that watch from under her nose last night. You weren't on the guest list either, but with your name and connections, no one would think twice if they saw you on a Windey property."

That gets Chloe's attention. "Connections?" she asks. "What connections?"

Harper doesn't answer. A muscle tenses in her jaw but other

than that, she might as well be carved from the same cold, thinly veined marble as the floor. The corner of Carlyle's mouth lifts in a mocking grin. "Oh," he says. "She doesn't know?"

Chloe's fingers tighten around the strap of her bag. "I don't know *what*?"

She doesn't like being kept in the dark. She doesn't like Harper knowing things she doesn't, but for once, Harper isn't gloating. Her eyes are fixed stubbornly on the wall behind Carlyle's desk and when she speaks again, it's with a strange sort of resignation.

"Katherine Windey is my mother."

Chloe's mouth drops open. She glances from Harper to Carlyle, waiting for one of them to crack, to tell her they're joking, but the longer they all sit in silence, the more she thinks the confession makes sense. She always knew Harper was wealthy. There's no way to fake her specific brand of glamorous ease. But *this*?

"Oh my god," she whispers, half to herself. "You're an *heiress*?"

Harper scowls, cheeks flushing a delicate shade of pink. "Can you not?"

"But you are!" Laughter bubbles in the back of Chloe's throat, completely at odds with the situation unfolding before them. "I . . . *how*? I've looked you up. Multiple times, actually, and I've never seen any connection to Katherine Windey. You don't even have the same last name."

"I know." Harper shifts uncomfortably in her seat. "My mother has always used her maiden name for business and we're both very good at making things disappear. I'm flattered you looked me up, though," she adds, some of her usual edge sliding back into her voice. "Can't say I've ever felt inclined to do the same."

But Chloe barely registers the insult. She's spent the last year searching for Harper's hidden weakness, a way to crack through her impenetrable façade, and here it is. Harper Parisi isn't some lonely, desperate outcast trying to make ends meet. She's the same kind of rich person the two of them have been conning all year and the only reason Carlyle wants her now is because she's Katherine Windey's daughter. Chloe couldn't have planned it better herself.

She bites back another grin as she turns to face Carlyle. "Okay, fine," she says. "Katherine took some award from your office. That's annoying, sure, but is it really that big of a deal? Can't you just ask for it back?"

"Ask for it back?" Carlyle looks mildly scandalized. "From *her*?"

Chloe nods. "Would that not be easier?"

"You tell me, Ms. Bly. If this was your prize, if you had finally won, would you give someone else the satisfaction of admitting they bested you?"

Chloe grimaces, resisting the urge to glance in Harper's direction. *No.* If it were her, if Harper stole the one thing she'd been chasing for years, Chloe wouldn't just ask for it back. She couldn't.

"Katherine's had a good year," Carlyle continues. "Don't get me wrong, but it's nothing compared to what I've accomplished. I know she's jealous. I'd probably feel the same if our positions were reversed. It's exactly what she wants and I refuse to stoop that low. She came into my penthouse on my invitation. If I let this one go, there's no telling what she'll come back for next."

Harper shifts forward in her seat and Chloe wonders if she's thinking the same thing—if she's trying to imagine herself looking Chloe in the eye and admitting defeat after a full year of slicing through each other's lives. "You can't give her the satisfaction," she murmurs. "She'd never let you live it down."

"Exactly," Carlyle says. "I want my award back. I want you to take it in a way she won't see coming and I want to win. I bet she has it sitting in the Rivera right now, waiting to rub it in my face the next time I stop by. That's where she's been living all summer, right?"

His last question is directed toward Harper. She shrugs, tension evident in every small movement. "I don't know," she says. "We're not really speaking at the moment."

"Well, find out. That's what I'm paying you for."

Chloe straightens, interest piqued by the last sentence. "You'd pay us? How much?"

The ghost of a smile flits across Carlyle's mouth. "Oh, I don't know." He tips his head back toward the vaulted ceiling, like he's just now considering. "Does five million dollars sound all right?"

"Five *million*—!" Chloe momentarily forgets how to breathe. She doesn't know how much she could've gotten for Webber's watch last night, but it's certainly not that. Even split between her, Priya, and Logan, five million dollars would be enough to pay off her debt and her mother's old medical bills. It would be enough for Logan to put a deposit down on a new apartment in a different state and for Priya to pad her family's finances for the foreseeable future.

It would be enough to buy Chloe a one-way ticket out of this city for good.

"Why would you . . . ?" She trails off, then starts again. "That's a *lot* of money."

Carlyle's answering smile is sympathetic enough for Chloe to realize that it's probably *not* a lot of money for him. "That award means a lot to me," he says. "It was my first national win, the culmination of decades of work. Katherine knows that. She knows it's personal and I want to see her face when she realizes it's gone. You can't put a price on that kind of win."

Yes, Chloe thinks, *you can.* You can put a price on anything, and five million dollars is well beyond any job she, Priya, and Logan have managed to pull. Harper's face is still carefully blank, but Chloe thinks she glimpses something flickering beneath the practiced stillness. Hunger. Ambition. For some reason, Harper hates her mother enough to genuinely consider this offer. Chloe sees it in the way her fingers flex at the sound of Katherine's name, nails digging into her thighs through the thin fabric of her cover-up. But there's also not a world where Harper doesn't walk away from this unscathed, pockets lined with millions of dollars. And even though Chloe is pretty sure Andrew Carlyle is nothing more than another unsuspecting mark too rich for his own good, that thought is enough to make her hesitate.

Because it *is* a lot of money. Too good to be true, in her experience. If Carlyle knew she crashed his party and tried to rob Webber, why wouldn't he threaten to turn her over to the authorities instead of striking a bargain? Why would he offer so high a reward if there was another easier, cheaper way to keep her in his pocket?

Chloe shoots to her feet and, before she can second-guess herself, blurts, "I have to think about it."

Carlyle's expression falters. "You have to *think* about it?"

Chloe nods, pulse quickening as Harper's eyes narrow in her direction. People like Andrew Carlyle, she's learned, are not low on options. If she refuses, Chloe has no doubt he'll find someone to replace her, someone willing to take the money and do his bidding without stopping to consider the consequences. But she's never had that luxury. Consequences are all she knows and if Carlyle wants to buy her loyalty now, Chloe wants to know how far he'll go to keep her.

"Yes," she says. "I told you, I'm late for work."

She bites her lip, bracing herself for Carlyle's reaction, but to her surprise, Harper stands, too.

"Chloe's right," she says, coming around the back of her chair so she and Chloe are facing the desk together. "We need to think about it. My mother owns dozens of hotels across the city. She could have stashed your award anywhere and we're not agreeing to something that wastes our time. We take our job offers seriously."

Chloe thinks the use of *we* is a little unnecessary. She's not doing this for Harper, but when she tries to step back, Harper wraps a hand around her wrist. Some of the color has returned to her face and she's using the same cool, disinterested voice from last night's dinner. Authoritative even here, in a penthouse that isn't hers to command.

Carlyle blinks, composure slipping back into place as he considers them. "I . . . okay. How long do you need? I'm here until four, but there's not a lot of—"

"That's fine," Harper says. "We'll have an answer for you then."

The two of them lock eyes across the desk, a mirror image of opposing wills. There's a similarity between them that Chloe doesn't quite understand, a grudging respect built from wealth and certainty and all the things she's never had access to. Harper's nails bite into her skin as they wait, but neither of them dares move until Carlyle finally nods.

"All right," he says. "Let's talk this afternoon."

Harper gives a dismissive snort and slings her pool bag over one shoulder. "We'll see. Chloe?"

Chloe doesn't have it in her to pretend, but as they turn toward the door, feet echoing against the polished tile, she swears she sees the corner of Carlyle's mouth lift. Like he already knows they're going to say yes. Like he's already won. For once, Chloe thinks she agrees.

Because who could possibly say no to five million dollars?

FIVE

Chloe makes it halfway down the hall before she realizes Harper is still clutching her wrist.

"Get *off* me," she snaps, yanking herself free and slapping the elevator call button.

"Oh, relax. I don't bite. That was a good strategy, by the way," Harper adds as the elevator light ticks toward the penthouse. "Telling him we need time to think about it gives us bargaining power."

"I'm not bargaining with anyone."

Already, there's a strategy weaving itself together in the back of Chloe's mind. She'll take Carlyle's offer, of course, but she'll take it alone. She'll divide the five million dollars between her, Priya, and Logan and nothing Harper says will change her mind.

"You're not?" Harper looks her up and down. "Do you not usually negotiate your offers?"

Chloe decides the fact that she isn't exactly getting regular job offers isn't relevant at the moment. The elevator slides open and she steps inside, pushing the button for the ground floor. Harper grabs the door before it can close. "Where are you going?"

"Back to work. Some of us aren't on a permanent *staycation*."

"I'm starting to think you don't know what that word means." Harper shoulders her way into the elevator. "Shouldn't we figure out a plan? Decide what we're telling Carlyle this afternoon?"

"There's no *we*. We're not working together."

"Oh my god, Chloe, get over yourself. He's offering us five *million* dollars. You wore a 2006 designer knockoff to a black-tie event last night. Don't act like you don't need the money."

"It's not about the money!" Chloe snaps, but her skin heats at the observation. It *is* about the money, obviously, but she's not about to let Harper know how much that part of the deal entices her. "Why do you care? It's not like you need it."

"Because my mother is a raging bitch who doesn't care about anything but her hotel empire. For once in my life I'd love for her to not get everything she wants."

The answer is too quick to be anything but true. Harper's arms are folded tightly over her chest, her chin set like she's daring someone to contradict her, and that, Chloe thinks, is her mistake. Because Harper might be good at slipping under people's skin. She might walk through life with the unearned confidence of a millionaire's daughter. But she's not invulnerable. Her feelings about her mother could not be clearer and Chloe knows exactly how to use them to her advantage now.

"Not my problem," she says. "I already have a team."

Harper scoffs, color flaring in her already flushed cheeks. "Please. Logan the wannabe magician and that girl from the hardware store? That's not a team, Chloe. That's just sad. You're telling me you don't even want to consider this?"

"Not with you."

"But *why*?"

"Because," Chloe says, the corner of her mouth lifting as the elevator finally comes to a stop. "I don't think you're as good as you think you are."

Harper's mouth drops open, but Chloe doesn't stay to hear

her response. She ducks into the hall and starts walking toward the kitchen, ignoring the frantic slap of Harper's sandals behind her.

"Are you kidding? I ruined your job last night. I walked away with that prize. I *won*."

"But that's not what Carlyle said." Chloe rounds on her so quickly that Harper stumbles into the wall. "He thinks *I'm* good, right? He picked *me* for my skill, because I snuck into his party without anyone noticing." She steps forward, directly into the rapidly dwindling space between them. "He picked you because of who your mother is. That's it. Nothing more."

Harper's eyes widen a fraction of an inch. She sucks in a breath and that's the only warning Chloe gets before she pulls back a hand and slaps her. Chloe's head snaps to the side, cheek stinging from the force of the hit. It's surprisingly strong for someone as delicate as Harper, wild for someone who usually keeps their emotions so carefully in check. Chloe can already feel the welt forming when she looks up, but she doesn't care.

Harper stands against the wall with one hand still raised, eyes bright, fingers trembling, and for the first time all year, Chloe thinks she looks afraid. Chloe grins, quick and vicious as she savors the almost imperceptible way Harper's back presses into the wall, away from her.

"You're *nothing,* Harper," she says, emphasizing every syllable of every word. "So I think you should leave me alone."

Then she turns and shoulders her way into the kitchen, tugging an apron off the hook as she passes and reveling in the bone-deep satisfaction of finally rendering Harper Parisi speechless.

"I NEED YOU both to know that this is the only acceptable reason to text me *Help! Level one emergency!* on a Thursday afternoon," Priya says, collapsing onto a lounge chair next to Chloe. "To review, an unacceptable reason would be something like, I don't know, telling me to leave work early because some Bravo star is cheating on their girlfriend in the Carlyle wave pool."

She glares pointedly in Logan's direction as he lifts both hands in the air. "That was one time!"

The three of them are sitting around one of the Carlyle's outdoor pools, Chloe still in her work clothes, Logan in a pair of swim trunks they lifted from the lost and found last week, and Priya in a breezy yellow sundress that makes her look like she's auditioning for a reboot of *La La Land.* There's a collection of mai tais sweating on the table between them, several palm trees swaying overhead, and just enough of a breeze to make the outdoors tolerable. Chloe isn't technically supposed to use the facilities during work hours, but as long as they stay tucked away in the corner, the rest of the staff usually leaves her alone.

Priya throws an arm over her face to block out the sun. "Not the point, Logan," she says. "I'm just saying that Chloe understands the urgency of the level one emergency. Bravo stars cheating on their partners are, like, level six at best, but a five-million-dollar job? I'd ditch my shift for that any day."

Chloe would be more flattered if Priya's current list of acceptable reasons to ditch her shift didn't also include "feeling tired" and "just not wanting to be there." She never needs an excuse to leave work, but when Chloe glances over the table, Priya and Logan are both watching her expectantly. She texted them an abbreviated summary of what had happened in the penthouse—deciding at the last minute to leave out Harper's slap—but now that she's sitting outside in broad daylight, nothing about the offer feels real.

"So you weren't kidding?" Logan prompts when Chloe stays silent. "You really met Andrew Carlyle?"

"No, she was *summoned* by Andrew Carlyle," Priya corrects. "Totally different vibe. Are his teeth really that white? I'm convinced they're CGI every time I see that crocodile commercial."

"Oh, same," Logan says. "Does he have terrible energy in person, too? I feel like he always looks like he's about to endorse fracking or something."

Priya snorts. "He looks like he tells people to go back where they came from."

"He looks like he'd deadname me for fun."

"He looks like if a men's rights podcast was a person."

"Okay, okay!" Chloe swats at them with her towel. "Yes to all of the above. It was weird, but he's rich. So . . ."

She trails off, letting the possibility of all that could mean unfurl between them. Five million dollars would be one hell of a prize to pass up, but she still can't shake the feeling Carlyle offered it too freely. That something about it feels too good to be true, even now.

Logan rubs a hand over his chin. "I mean, I have no ethical problem taking money from rich people, especially ones who run for office in the state of Florida. And if all we have to do is rob Katherine Windey, I think we should take the job."

Chloe shakes her head. "You just want to do a jewelry heist."

"Well, yes. I thought that was implied."

Priya leans back on her elbows, bottom lip caught between her teeth. "Jewelry heist aside, I still can't believe you didn't say yes already. What's there to think about?"

Chloe shrugs. "I just feel like we should consider the specifics."

"Like what?"

"Like . . . why anyone would pay that much money for an award that's genuinely useless. And how I don't trust Andrew Carlyle."

"No, you don't trust *Harper,*" Logan corrects. "Which is totally valid, but there is a difference."

"It's actually possible to distrust multiple people at a time, you know."

Priya picks the paper umbrella out of her glass, twirling it between two fingers as she thinks. "I don't like her either, but if we're doing this job, it sounds like we'll need her. She knows Katherine better than we ever will."

"I know," Logan says. "We should have guessed she had hotel money. I mean, look at her highlights. No one's going to the salon that often without generational wealth."

The three of them fall silent and Chloe tips her head toward the sky. The morning is mostly clear, but there's a dark cluster of clouds gathering on the horizon. She pictures the rain beating against the pool deck and lightning cracking overhead. She thinks of her mother, who loved storms despite the destruction left in their wake, and wonders if that same sort of damage is coming for her, too.

Priya releases a rough sigh. "It's not ideal," she says, "but Harper isn't bad at her job. If Carlyle is really set on hiring you both, I'd consider it." She hesitates, gaze turning distant. "That amount of money would be life-changing."

Chloe nods. "I know."

And she does, but that doesn't stop her from circling through option after option, desperately searching for one that doesn't include Harper Parisi. Priya must know that too, or she wouldn't have voiced the alternative. But that's how their friendship works. One of them has to be the voice of reason.

When Chloe walked into the City Center hardware store last year, she'd been looking for a can of paint to smooth over the cracks in her living room wall. The tall, tattooed girl mixing her paint had been so magnetically cool that Chloe spent a solid half hour trying to decide if she wanted to be her or be inside her before she finally broke down and called Logan for advice. He immediately told her that if Chloe didn't ask for her number, he would, which meant Chloe left the store that day with a jar of Sherwin-Williams (shade: Accessible Beige 7036) and a plan to meet Priya for brunch the next morning before their shifts. As the two of them sat across from each other in a cracked vinyl booth, it took Chloe exactly five minutes to realize the warmth she felt for Priya wasn't romantic at all. Instead, it was the same bone-deep familiarity she'd experienced the first day she met Logan. Like part of her soul had been tucked inside another person and she was only now realizing what it meant to be whole.

Now, Chloe can't imagine her life without Priya in it. There aren't many people who can recite strings of Python code and full episodes of *Jersey Shore* from memory. There aren't many people who would help her hack the Carlyle security system night after night, no questions asked, and there aren't many people, Chloe thinks, who would willingly back her on a job like this.

Logan reclines in his chair, pulling Chloe's attention back to him as another damp breeze whips over the pool. "If you don't want the job because you think it's bullshit or you don't trust Carlyle, fine," he says. "But you shouldn't say no because of Harper. She's already cost us enough and it might be worth talking to her."

Chloe grimaces. "That's pushing it."

"No, I mean it might be worth talking to her now. Because she's here."

Logan points across the pool deck and Chloe sits up so fast she almost sends the rest of their drinks flying into the bushes. Sure enough, Harper is striding toward them across the deck, casually dodging hotel guests and waitstaff as she goes. Chloe suppresses a groan. She wanted Harper to come back groveling, to fall on her knees and beg Chloe to take the job with her, but there's no trace of their earlier conversation on Harper's subtly tanned face. Instead, she's vibrant and glowing, like she really did spend her morning lounging by the pool while Chloe scrubbed ketchup from the dining room carpet.

"There you are." Harper drops onto the edge of Logan's chair, shoving his bag and towel to the ground in the process. "I've been looking for you all morning."

She's still wearing the same swimsuit and cover-up from before, but now her hair is pulled back in a loose braid. Priya raises a disbelieving eyebrow in her direction as Logan snatches his things off the ground and purposefully scoots to the opposite end of the chair.

"Looking for me?" Chloe asks. "Why on earth would you do that?"

Beg, she thinks as Harper pushes her sunglasses to the top of her head. *Admit how much you need this.*

Harper shrugs. "Just wondering if you've had time to . . . think about things?"

"Things like Andrew Carlyle offering us a disgusting amount of money to steal a hospitality award from your mom?"

"Shh!" Harper's shoulders stiffen and she whips around to glance nervously up and down the pool deck. "Are you trying to get caught?"

Now it's Chloe's turn to shrug as she tilts her face up toward the umbrella. "If Carlyle didn't want me to talk, he shouldn't have let me leave that office alive."

It's supposed to be a joke, but Harper doesn't relax. "It's because he thinks we'll say yes."

"And why the hell would he think that?"

"Maybe because it's five million dollars?" Priya mutters.

"Exactly." Harper waves a hand in Priya's direction. "I don't think anyone's ever told him no."

Chloe glares up at the umbrella, still purposefully avoiding eye contact. "I *didn't* say no."

"Right. You just said no to working with me."

"I don't know why that's such a shock. You're the one who's been making my life miserable all year."

Immediately, Chloe wishes she could take it back. The admission is too personal to put in Harper's hands after this morning. She shouldn't get to know how much those slights still affect Chloe or how often she still lies awake at night trying to figure out where she went wrong. Sure enough, Harper's eyebrows arch upward in clear amusement.

"Miserable? That's a little dramatic, don't you think?"

To Chloe's relief, Logan leans in, arms crossed as he surveys Harper across their shared lounge chair. "I don't," he says. "What about last night? We were clearly working that event and you still managed to make it about you."

Harper shakes her head. "That was a completely different situation. What if Webber hadn't found his watch? He owns, like, half the city. Carlyle wouldn't have just let everyone leave. Who do you think they would have searched first—the other guests or the waitstaff?" Her gaze lingers purposefully on Logan. "Honestly, the two of you should be thanking me for not blowing your cover. I don't do everything out of spite, you know. Is that so hard to believe?"

"Yes," Chloe says. She does most things out of spite. The idea that Harper wouldn't, that she's somehow *better* for it, is laughable. Harper opens her mouth again, cheeks flushed with indignation, and in that moment, Chloe thinks she looks almost human.

"I know you don't trust me," Harper says, "but this is a big job. If you don't believe me, believe that I wouldn't pass up five million dollars."

"Why?" Chloe asks. "You don't need it. Can't Katherine Windey just write you a check?"

There it is again, the subtle tightening of Harper's jaw at the mention of her mother. "Has it ever occurred to you," she says, "that there's a reason I haven't asked her to do that?"

We're not really speaking at the moment. That's what Harper said when Carlyle asked her about Katherine's summer plans. Chloe breezed over it at the time, still reeling from the shock of the reveal, but now she's wondering how deep that rift goes.

Chloe glances over to find the others still watching her. Priya gives an almost imperceptible shrug as if to say *why not?* and when she turns to Logan, he's wearing an identical expression of wary anticipation. They want to do it, Chloe realizes. Despite the risks and unanswered questions, both of them would accept Carlyle's job today, because five million dollars is too big a prize to give up. *Life-changing,* Priya called it.

And how can Chloe say no to that?

"Fine," she says, turning back to Harper. "Say we're interested. How are we supposed to work together when you haven't even apologized for last night?"

Harper's face falls. "That's what you want me to do? *Apologize?*"

It's like the word doesn't fit properly in her mouth, hissing between her teeth as she tries to force it out. Chloe nods, suddenly much more interested in where this is going. "Yeah, actually. That would be a great start."

For a second, she thinks Harper is going to hit her again. She certainly wants to because her hands curl into fists at her sides before she takes a deep breath and reaches across the table. "Chloe—"

"Don't touch me."

Harper's hand drops back into her lap. "Chloe," she says again, voice thick with exaggerated patience. "I'm sorry for interrupting your job last night. I'm sorry for everything that's happened this year and I'm sorry that you're obviously still letting it affect you."

Chloe rolls her eyes behind the safety of her sunglasses. *Of course.* Even now, in the middle of an apology that's supposed to be genuine, Harper still can't resist an obvious dig. But her jaw is clenched, expression almost pained as she waits for a response, and something about the raw disgust in her voice makes Chloe think this confession might be true. Even if it's not, she could put up with Harper for a few weeks, if she had to. They all could. And when this is over, she can take her cut of the prize money and go someplace far away, where she'll never have to think about Harper Parisi again.

"Just so we're clear," Chloe says, gaze fixed on the rippling umbrella, "I don't forgive you. For last night or that first time or for any of the things you've ruined since. I think you're opportunistic and selfish and the only reason you're speaking to us now is because someone offered you money." She hesitates, satisfaction unfurling in her chest as Harper leans in. She lets the silence hang a second longer, savoring the power, before continuing. "But I'm also not losing five million dollars because of you."

Harper blinks. "What are you saying?"

"I'm saying we should do it. We should take Carlyle's offer."

Chloe doesn't mention that she always intended to say yes, regardless of the risk. She doesn't mention that part of her likes seeing Harper this way—wide-eyed and wary, question still caught between her slightly parted lips. Chloe doesn't trust it, of course. She doesn't trust Andrew Carlyle either, but she's not doing this alone. She has Priya and Logan. They've spent the last year digging their way through the city's elite, unearthing their secrets and bleeding them dry. Why should this job be any different?

Harper's face tips cautiously in Chloe's direction. Her lashes shudder against her cheeks and, for a second, a languid heat drops into the pit of Chloe's stomach. Then, Harper stands, yanking Chloe unceremoniously to her feet as she goes.

"Well, it certainly took you long enough."

And just like that, the heiress is back, all traces of vulnerability gone. Chloe barely has time to gather her things before Harper is steering her across the pool deck and back into the cool embrace of the lobby.

The second trip up to the penthouse is quick, less intimidating now that there's a goal. The two of them march through the foyer and down the hall without bothering to check for additional security and when they round the corner, Carlyle is still sitting behind the desk, a slim silver laptop open before him.

"We'll take the job," Harper says by way of greeting. "But we have a few demands."

If Carlyle is surprised by their sudden entrance, he doesn't show it. "You do?"

"We do." Chloe raises her chin, trying her best to look like this confrontation is a joint effort. "And first of all, Andrew—can I call you Andrew?"

"No."

"First of all, Andrew," she continues. "We want six million."

Carlyle's eyebrows fly up. "Absolutely not."

"You said it yourself," Harper cuts in. "We're good at this. No one knows my mother like I do, but we also have lives. If you're expecting us to put ours on hold, we need something to make it worth it."

"In what world is five million dollars not worth it?"

Chloe folds her arms. "No one said it wasn't, but if that's all you're willing to pay, then you can't keep us on retainer forever."

"Two weeks," Harper says. "You only get us for two weeks."

"And you have to approve my time off," Chloe blurts, suddenly remembering the practical elements of this arrangement. "If I'm taking an unplanned vacation, my boss will have questions. You make sure everything goes through and that I still have a job when I get back."

Carlyle's face twists in a scowl. "I'm paying you five million dollars. I don't think you'll need a kitchen job after this."

"What can I say? I like the healthcare."

Chloe meets his eye across the desk. She forces herself to hold his gaze, to channel Harper's seemingly unwavering confidence as the seconds tick by. In the end, it's Carlyle who looks away first.

"Well," he mutters. "You really have thought of everything."

Harper flashes a winning smile. "That's our job, isn't it?"

"I suppose. When do you want to start?"

He extends a hand in Harper's direction, then Chloe's. His grip is firmer than Chloe anticipated, and she purposefully tightens her own. *Another job,* she thinks, lips pressed together to hide her grin. *Another mark too rich for his own good.*

"We were thinking Monday."

SIX

There are very few places, it turns out, to comfortably plan a Miami resort heist.

Logan's roommates banned Chloe from their building after she accidentally dropped a bowl of ramen on their freshly steamed carpets, but Chloe also refuses to let Harper anywhere near her own apartment. In the end, the four of them end up piling into Harper's room at the Carlyle, compiling notes on the smudged whiteboard Priya lugged across town.

They told Carlyle they'd start on Monday, which means they have only three days to figure out where Katherine Windey is keeping his stolen award and formulate a plan to both take it back and get out without raising suspicion. When she puts it like that, Chloe thinks it almost feels achievable. They've done this before, after all. Logan has yet to meet a lock he can't crack and Priya's never turned down an opportunity to hack a million-dollar corporation, but Chloe's confidence is somewhat marred by the knowledge that there are twenty-three separate Windey hotels scattered throughout South Florida. Some would be hypothetically easy to access, like the downtown property two blocks east. Others, like the Rivera, sit on a literal private island in the middle of Biscayne Bay.

"This is ridiculous," Logan mutters as he turns to pace another lap of Harper's suite. "That award could be anywhere. Katherine could have tucked it in the back of a closet or under a floorboard for all we know."

Chloe has been thinking the same thing, but Harper shakes her head. "Taking it wouldn't be enough," she says. "She'll want Carlyle to know she has it, too. She'll display it somewhere public—somewhere secure enough to prevent him from taking it back, but obvious enough to still rub in his face."

"That doesn't exactly narrow it down."

"It might, actually," Priya says. She leans forward and tugs her computer into her lap. "If she really wants Carlyle to know she has his award, we don't need to case every Windey hotel in the city. I'll just pull a list of the high-profile events Katherine's hosting this week and cross-reference the RSVPs to see if Carlyle is also invited."

Logan finally stops pacing. "You can do that?"

"Don't sound so surprised, Logan. It's insulting."

Harper grins, both elbows braced against the kitchen counter as she surveys them across the suite. "You're welcome."

"No." Logan points a finger in her direction. "You don't get a prize for basic group participation. That's the whole reason you're here."

It takes everything in Chloe's power not to laugh at how quickly Harper's face falls. *Good.* Maybe these next couple weeks will humble her, after all. Now that she knows Harper's secret, Chloe thinks it should be easier to pick her apart, but in reality, Harper remains just as much of an enigma as before—a glamorous ghost of a person who exists in curated photos and filtered social media posts. Her mother, unfortunately, is the same way.

Sure, there's the usual array of pictures from that very public embezzlement trial back in January, where Katherine Windey took the stand in a custom Armani blazer and answered every question so aggressively she made a prosecutorial intern cry. The charges were dropped, but not before *BuzzFeed* published an article titled "These Ten #Girlbosses Are Serving Courtroom Chic."

Katherine was number four. Chloe's still pretty sure she's guilty.

There's very little information about Katherine's personal life online beyond that. So far, Chloe's learned she was married to Harper's father—a software developer named Enzo Parisi—for almost twenty years before the two of them divorced during Harper's senior year of high school. She's learned that Enzo now lives in Ohio with a new wife and stepdaughter, and that Harper attended the University of Alabama on a softball scholarship. She's learned that the entire collection of Windey hotels is worth more than two billion dollars and, despite Harper living right here in the city, none of Katherine's press photos seem to indicate she has any family at all.

"Here." Priya straightens, flipping her computer around so the others can see her screen. "I got it. There are three black-tie events at different Windey locations across town next week, but Carlyle is only invited to two—the grand opening gala at the Rivera and a casino night downtown."

Chloe leans forward. "What's the third event?"

"Katherine's hosting some cocktail party on her yacht for the incumbent Democratic senator. Carlyle won't be there, obviously, so it's not relevant to us."

"And when's the gala?"

Priya's brow furrows as she scans the invitation. "Next Tuesday. Looks like it's the first time that new tower opens to the public."

Chloe nods. Harper mentioned the new tower in Carlyle's office yesterday. She hadn't thought anything of it at the time, but insights like this are probably why they're keeping Harper around. Chloe shoots a reluctant glance in her direction. "What do you think?" she asks. "If your mother's goal is to show off, which event would she choose?"

Harper's face is a mask of calm indifference, but Chloe catches the way her lashes flutter in surprise at the question, like she hadn't actually expected anyone to ask. "Probably the Rivera gala," she says. "I checked—she *is* living in the penthouse this summer."

"And Carlyle was super bitter about it," Chloe adds. "If she's expanding the hotel, that gala would be an opportunity to flaunt both victories." She glances toward Priya's computer, struggling to sort through the mess of tabs filling the screen. "Can you get into the Rivera cameras from here?"

Priya shakes her head. "Not by myself. I'd need an email for the head of security at least and it's not like any of us—" She stops midsentence, head swiveling toward where Harper still stands behind the counter, one hip casually braced against the granite. "You."

Harper looks up. "What?"

"How well do you know the Rivera's head of security?"

"Why?"

Priya's answering grin is deceptively angelic. "Because I'm about to phish the hell out of him."

It takes approximately twenty minutes for David Gabriel Armitage, head of security at the Rivera Windey hotel and noted Miami Heat superfan, to open an email claiming he's been gifted a pair of courtside tickets from a generous co-worker. It takes another two for Priya to slide her way into his computer and it takes less than thirty seconds for Chloe to decide she's never willingly trusting a hotel with her credit card information again. This is who's protecting her, after all—some guy with a six-figure salary and years of training who still managed to fall for a pretty lie and a flashy subject line.

Finding their way through the cameras, however, is a different story. It's an arduous process, so long Chloe finds herself half dozing against Harper's fancy pillows while Priya works, still absentmindedly scrolling through pictures of Katherine Windey on her computer. It's strange, she thinks, that she's never noticed the resemblance before. How Harper's eyes are the same pale green as her mother's, how their chins jut out in the same impetuous way. Chloe imagines herself tracing the line of it with a finger, slowly tilting Harper's face toward her for a better look. Just for an experiment, of course. For research.

"Shit."

Chloe startles at the sound of Priya's voice and hurriedly snaps her laptop closed. "What?"

"I'm stuck," Priya says. "I have access to the hotel, but I can't see the east tower. I don't know if they haven't installed cameras yet or if the feed isn't connected, but I can't see the ballroom or the lobby or anything remotely helpful." She pushes her computer aside and tugs a frustrated hand through her hair. "I have access to every fucking camera in that hotel except the ones that matter."

Chloe leans in, stomach sinking as she watches the grainy security footage flick across Priya's screen. Without access to the cameras in the newly constructed ballroom, they have no way to confirm if the award is actually there or not.

Logan resumes pacing, chewing nervously at his thumbnail. "Okay, so what do we do?"

"Hold on. I'm thinking."

Chloe clamps her mouth shut as Priya's eyes flutter closed. She's seen this before. Give Priya a few minutes of silence to work through a problem, and she'll have a solution in no time. Harper, however, lets out a frustrated groan from the other side of the suite.

"Do I really have to do everything around here?"

She shoulders Logan out of the way and snatches her purse from the counter. Priya shoots Chloe an incredulous look but before either of them can protest, Harper sweeps a hand toward the door. "You want to see that new tower?" she asks. "Fine. Let's take a little trip."

The Rivera resort sits just off the Miami coast, nestled between two gleaming white beaches on its own private island. Chloe grips the railing of the yacht as they plow through another cresting wave and pointedly ignores the queasy drop in her stomach. She doesn't love the ocean. Her mother's old bedtime stories always seemed to feature women luring people over cliffs to their deaths, or men waking up one day and feeling inexplicably compelled to walk into the sea. Chloe has lived through enough hurricane seasons to know exactly how destructive these waves can be, and she can't, for the life of her, figure out why rich people are always trying to sail.

When they finally dock at the Rivera pier, a crew of employees in dark green polos rushes over to help them disembark. As she watches them slide the gangway into place, it occurs to Chloe just how ridiculous it is for them to try to rob this place. They can't even get off this boat without help. They're in the middle of the bay with one way in and one way out, two miles of open water separating them from shore, and she expects to just walk out the front door?

"Thanks, Shay. I'll give you a call when we're ready to leave."

Harper's standing at the top of the ramp, tucking what looks suspiciously like a hundred-dollar bill into the captain's palm. Chloe's still unsure who this boat actually belongs to, but everyone greeted Harper by name when they arrived, offering her glasses of Dom Pérignon like it was water. Chloe stuffed the half-empty bottle into Priya's backpack when no one was looking and, as the three of them follow Harper onto the dock, the sound of clinking glass echoes in every step.

A woman waits for them at the end of the pier, wearing a lighter version of the green Rivera polo and clutching a tablet in one hand. Her short platinum hair is almost the same color as her pale skin, and it's not until she extends a hand in Harper's direction that she cracks the barest hint of a smile. "Welcome back, Ms. Parisi."

Harper plants a quick kiss on her cheek. "Hi, Lisa! Can I have a table for two on the terrace, please." She takes Logan's hand, ignoring his surprised grunt as she yanks him forward and tucks herself deliberately under his arm. "We'd *really* appreciate the privacy."

Logan seems to realize the implication at the same time Chloe does. His eyebrows fly toward his hairline and Chloe chokes back a disbelieving scoff. *That's* their cover story? That Harper and Logan are in desperate need of a private, romantic getaway at the Rivera? It might be more believable if Logan wasn't staring at their intertwined fingers like he fully expects Harper to sprout claws and rip out his bones.

"Sure." Lisa makes a note on her tablet before glancing pointedly in Priya's direction. "Just a table for two?"

"Oh!" Harper claps a hand to her mouth. "I'm sorry, Priya, I'm a terrible host." She pulls Logan aside and nudges Priya toward the front. "Lisa, this is *Priya Mishra.* The model," she adds when Lisa doesn't react. "You've definitely seen her around. She has, like, half a million followers. She's here to meet with Reed about our influencer program. Didn't he tell you?"

Priya offers Lisa a cool nod over the top of her knockoff sunglasses. If there's one thing she loves more than phishing hotel security officers, Chloe thinks, it's putting herself on company influencer lists. Priya might not have half a million followers or any sort of modeling experience, but Lisa doesn't look like she's about to fact-check Harper anytime soon.

Still, Lisa's brow furrows as she glances down at her tablet. "Reed isn't here today."

"Not here?" Harper's face falls in an enviably convincing display of dismay. She shoots another quick glance at Priya before angling herself toward Lisa and lowering her voice. "This could be a really important partnership, Lisa. Is there any way you can show her the new ballroom, at least? Let her see our event space?"

"I'm sorry, Ms. Parisi." Lisa shakes her head. "The east tower doesn't open until next week. We're still getting things prepped for the gala."

"She'll be quick!" Harper looks up at Lisa pleadingly. "Please," she adds when the other woman doesn't move. "For me?"

Her voice turns soft and imploring, and Chloe has no idea how anyone could say no to Harper when she's looking at them like that—all wide sea-glass eyes and slightly parted lips. Lisa hesitates, clearly weighing the consequences of interrupting her packed schedule with ignoring her boss's daughter. Eventually, she sighs and motions them to follow her up the beach toward a cluster of golf carts.

"Fine. But this is an exception, all right? If anyone asks, we already cleared it with Reed."

"Of course!" Harper nods eagerly. "Thanks, Lisa. I owe you one."

"You always do." Lisa shoots a narrowed glance in Chloe's direction as they walk. "I'm sorry, I didn't catch your name."

"Oh, don't worry about her," Harper says before Chloe can respond. "She's just Priya's assistant."

"That's what I thought. You two—come with me."

Chloe scowls as Lisa motions her and Priya into the back of a waiting golf cart. *That's what she thought?* Sure, Chloe's not dripping in designer clothes, but she doesn't think she looks like anyone's assistant. She turns to glare at Harper, but she and Logan are already gone, sliding into the back of a different cart. The sight of it sends alarm bells clanging through Chloe's mind and she hesitates, feet slowing over the sand.

"He'll be fine," Priya whispers, low enough for only the two of them to hear. "He can take care of himself."

She pats the leather seat beside her and, after another second, Chloe sits. She knows that. Of course she does, but it's not Logan she's worried about. Right now, she's mostly concerned about Harper and the hungry, purposeful way she's watching them leave.

The drive up to the Rivera is almost as harrowing as the trip across the bay. Chloe clutches the edge of her seat as the golf cart bounces over the sand, hair whipping across her face. When they finally stop in front of the sliding glass doors, she feels like she's stepping out of a car wash. Priya, however, still looks every inch the influencer, eyes glued to her phone like she couldn't care less where Lisa is leading them.

They really think we're famous, she texts Chloe as they step into a cool, air-conditioned hallway. *Do you think Harper could get me on the influencer list for real?*

Chloe thinks Harper would do almost anything to make other people believe she's important. Everything she's done today proves that—taking them to the Rivera, chartering a private yacht, keeping her plans close to her chest, then leaving them to do the hard part while she drinks cocktails on a beachside terrace.

She gives Priya's message a thumbs-down as Lisa slows outside a pair of towering double doors. Chloe knows they must be in the east tower, but the hallway they've been walking down is immaculately clean, free of the construction debris Lisa was so worried about. She doesn't know what the rest of the resort looks like, but Chloe has a feeling the only thing setting this tower apart is the lingering smell of wet paint.

Lisa levels a pointed glare in their direction, one hand resting on the doorknob. "Before we go inside," she says, "I want to reiterate that I'm only giving you this tour as a favor to Ms. Parisi. This tower isn't open until next week, so the fact you're here at all is an incredible privilege. Please stay with me, keep away from the center of the room, and don't touch the art. Understand? And no photos or videos while we're inside."

Priya makes a show of dropping her phone into her purse, but Chloe waits until Lisa's back is turned before opening her camera and hitting record. Then she slides her own phone into her pocket with the lens facing out. In the second before the doors swing open, Priya catches her eye over Lisa's shoulder and nods once.

Time to go.

The ballrooms in the Carlyle hotels are opulent and warm, dripping in shiny carved wood and centuries-old oil paintings. Chloe expects the new Rivera ballroom to feel equally stuffy, yet when Lisa motions them inside, she finds it's anything but. In fact, it's kind of like being inside of a very smooth, very expensive egg. Each wall is painted the same glossy shade of ivory, curving up toward a domed ceiling complete with an enormous crystalline chandelier. The far wall is made entirely of glass, a choice someone probably thought was *aesthetic* and *innovative*. In reality, Chloe thinks the unrestricted view of the ocean beyond is unnerving. That's how this whole place feels, really. *Unnerving*. It's too clean and too structured, numbered tables spaced too perfectly across the smooth marble tile. The rigidity makes Chloe want to break something, to put her fist through that weird glass wall just to see if she can.

Even the art lining the walls feels methodical—bright, abstract paintings and climbing sculptures of metal and glass set in every corner of the room. They glint out at her beneath layers of protective plastic, only half visible among the maintenance staff still milling around the perimeter. Chloe keeps her head down as she walks. She knew they wouldn't be alone today, but she didn't expect the ballroom to be this crowded, or this full of watchful eyes.

A few paces ahead of them, Lisa is still talking, explaining the ins and outs of the Rivera influencer program to a thoroughly engrossed Priya, but Chloe is no longer listening. Instead, she hangs back, glancing over both shoulders as she tries to catalogue the visible pieces of art. It does nothing to center her in the space. Between the swarm of employees and the remaining construction equipment, it's difficult to know where to look.

Chloe closes her eyes. She spent the better part of the afternoon pulling up image after image of the Florida Hospitality Association award, memorizing its shape from every angle. It's surprisingly simple—a smooth glass triangle sitting atop a sturdy wooden base with the association logo etched into one side and Carlyle's name carved on the other. Easy to pass over and easy to miss.

She'll want Carlyle to know she has it, too. She'll display it somewhere public—somewhere . . . obvious enough to still rub in his face.

That's what Harper said earlier. That's what their whole plan hinges on, and when Chloe opens her eyes again, she thinks she understands. She waits until Lisa launches into another part of her speech before sliding up behind Priya and lowering her voice to a whisper.

"Where is Carlyle sitting next week? For the gala?"

Priya hesitates. Chloe can practically see her thinking, cycling back through the stolen guest list as they round the far corner of the ballroom. Eventually, she nods and mouths, *twelve.*

Twelve. Chloe cranes her neck, scanning the rows of numbered tables until she finds the one she's looking for, right on the edge of the first row. If this truly is a game, if Katherine stole that award with the intention of displaying it here, she'd probably make sure Carlyle could see it from table twelve.

It's what Chloe would do, if it were Harper. She'd make sure it was visible from every seat.

Her gaze slides past the sculptures in the corner, bypassing framed Pollocks and Kandinskys until it lands on the gilded windowsill closest to the table. And a familiar-looking statue displayed right in the center.

It's kind of funny, Chloe thinks as she takes a slow, careful step to the right. Among the collection of priceless art, this award looks almost plain. If she hadn't burned the shape of it into her brain this morning, she wouldn't give it a second thought. But here's Carlyle's missing award, gleaming down at her from a windowsill in the Rivera ballroom. The glass triangle is duller than it looked in pictures, the wooden base less refined, but there's his name carved into the side.

There's five million dollars, just waiting for her to take it.

Chloe glances over her shoulder, instinctively clocking their exits. But even as she angles her hip forward and points her camera lens toward the windowsill, that same familiar, cautious refrain slides through the back of her mind.

Too good to be true.

For all Carlyle's talk of playing the game, for all their complicated plans and false identities, this reveal feels suspiciously easy.

Chloe falls back into step with Priya as Lisa circles the ballroom one last time. She's still talking, running through their outreach process and potential contracts, but Chloe is no longer listening. She's not thinking about influencer events at all.

In fact, when Lisa leads them back out the way they came, the only thing Chloe's thinking about is the familiar edge of Carlyle's missing award and how easily it would fit in the palm of her hand.

SEVEN

"Is this seriously the best you could do?"

Harper leans over the back of the couch, chin propped in both hands as she watches the video looping on Chloe's phone. They're all back in her hotel suite, heads pressed together in observation, and it takes every ounce of Chloe's self-control not to roll her eyes. Sure, the footage she captured in the Rivera ballroom is a bit shaky, but given the circumstances, she thinks she nailed it.

"No worries, Harper," she mutters, tucking her phone back into her pocket. "You can do it next time. How were drinks on the terrace, by the way?"

"Lovely, thanks for asking." Harper flashes Logan a conspiratorial grin. "Weren't they?"

Color blooms across the tops of Logan's cheeks. "It was fine."

Chloe scowls and pushes herself off the couch. *Traitor.* If she thinks about the two of them sitting alone on a sun-soaked balcony for too long, her vision goes red. She doesn't trust Harper, and her newfound interest in Logan feels like yet another example of her uniquely infuriating ability to worm her way under Chloe's skin.

"Does anyone else think that was a little too simple?" she asks.

Logan scoffs. "What part of renting a yacht, sailing to a private island, and sneaking into a closed ballroom feels simple to you?"

"First of all, *you* didn't sneak anywhere."

It comes out harsher than Chloe intends, her voice a pointed snap, and Logan sinks further into the cushions. Priya, however, tilts her head.

"It did feel easier than I thought," she admits. "The award was just kind of sitting there."

Harper rolls her eyes. "Of course it was. Contrary to popular belief, my mother isn't some wildly clever criminal mastermind."

"Didn't she get arrested for embezzlement, like, five months ago?"

"Exactly. If she was smart, she wouldn't have gotten caught."

Priya lets out an amused snort. "Fair enough. So, what's next? Should we send Logan back in tonight?"

"You really think he could pull this off alone?"

"Okay, wow." Logan shakes his head. "I thought we were friends, Harper. Nice necklace, by the way."

"Thanks, I got it—"

Harper stops, hand instinctively flying to her throat. Her eyes widen when she finds her necklace gone and Chloe bites back a grin. Sure enough, when she glances at Logan, there's a thin gold chain wrapped around his pointer finger.

He tosses it unceremoniously in Harper's direction. "You were saying?"

"Fine," Harper bites out. "That was impressive, but I don't think you understand what we're dealing with. The only reason we got onto the island today is because I took you. You can't just stroll up to the Rivera."

"You can't exactly stroll into the Carlyle either, but that hasn't been a problem for us," Priya points out.

"It's not the same. They don't even clear you to dock unless you have a room number."

Chloe folds her arms, one shoulder braced against the wall as she considers their options. "Why don't we book a room, then? If getting there is such an issue, we could just stay on the property."

Harper scoffs. "Do you have Rivera money?"

"No, but you do. Quite literally."

"I'm not booking *you* a hotel room."

"Then why are you here, Harper? If you can't at least *pretend* to be helpful, I don't see the point in having you around."

A strained silence falls across the suite, but Chloe doesn't back down. For a minute, she thinks Harper's going to fight back, to bare her teeth and snap like she did that day in the elevator, but when she speaks again, her voice is measured, almost practiced.

"Fine," she says. "If it's that important to you, I'll get us a room. But that still doesn't mean you can waltz into the new ballroom whenever you feel like it."

"Why not? I'd be a paying guest, right?"

"First of all, *I'd* be a paying guest," Harper says. "But no. That tower doesn't officially open until after the gala next week. I pulled a favor to get you in today, but that won't work again."

"Then we'll wait until the tower opens."

"And do what? You know how many priceless pieces of art my mother has in that room alone? There's a Rothko insured for ten million dollars. She'll have twenty-four-hour security, not to mention the cameras and sensors and regular hotel staff. It would be like trying to rob a museum."

Chloe's right in the middle of making a mental note to google *Rothko* when Logan straightens. "What if we had an invitation?"

The question is soft, hesitant, and for a second, Chloe wonders if she heard him correctly. "An invitation to what?" she asks.

"The gala. The one on Tuesday. There'll still be security, of course, but they'll be preoccupied with the guests. They won't care who's going in or out as long as they have an invitation." He glances in Harper's direction. "Would it be easier to take the award during an event like that?"

Harper opens her mouth, brow furrowed like she's about to protest, then stops. "You know," she says, "I actually think it might."

Logan grins and Chloe knows before he speaks again that they're both on the same page. "Gala heist?" he asks, one eyebrow raised in her direction.

Chloe settles back against the wall, smile tugging unbidden at the corner of her mouth. "Looks like we're doing a gala heist."

The next morning dawns thick and humid, mist coating the ground as the sun strains over the tops of the buildings. Chloe's sweating by the time the shuttle drops her off at the Carlyle's main entrance, but she manages to sneak up to Harper's room without any of her co-workers noticing. Saturdays are always busy in the kitchen. She doesn't have much time until she has to clock in herself, but Logan's already in the living room when she arrives, sitting cross-legged on Harper's couch with a tray of room service.

"Pastry?" he asks, extending a lightly glazed cinnamon roll in her direction.

Chloe shakes her head. She's thawed too many bulk orders of frozen dough to trust the Carlyle's breakfast menu. She yanks open the refrigerator instead, perusing Harper's collection of luxury yogurts as the bathroom door swings open.

"Good morning." Despite the early hour, Harper is already dressed, hair blown out and eyelashes curled in a way that suggests she's been up for hours. She sinks into an armchair by the window. "Aren't there usually three of you?"

"Priya has work." Chloe grabs a jar of blueberry cardamom yogurt from the top shelf. "Can I have this?"

"No."

Chloe takes it anyway. "I can't stay long either. What do we have so far?"

The plan, they decided yesterday, was simple. On Monday, the four of them will check into the Rivera hotel—Harper and Logan posing as a couple while Priya and Chloe reprise their roles of Niche Internet Celebrity and Devoted Assistant. Then they'll use the distraction of the gala to infiltrate the ballroom, swipe Carlyle's award from the windowsill, and smuggle it out under Logan's jacket.

When Chloe lays it out like that, she wonders why they haven't tried something like this before.

Harper reclines in her chair, coy smile tugging at the corner of her glossy mouth. "Well, I have two invitations to Tuesday's gala, for starters."

"You got them?" Chloe whips around, yogurt momentarily forgotten. "Already?"

"What were you saying about me *pretending* to help?"

"Don't start, you—" Chloe stops as the rest of Harper's sentence sinks in. "You only got two? There are four of us."

"I know. I figured Priya would be tucked away upstairs somewhere doing whatever the hell she does and you, unfortunately . . ." Harper's gaze lingers a second too long on the untucked hem of Chloe's shirt. ". . . didn't make the cut."

Chloe slams the refrigerator shut, skin heating under Harper's gaze. "So, what? I'm supposed to sit upstairs while you two do all the work?"

"That's the idea, yes."

"Hold on." Logan sets his tray aside, glancing from Chloe to Harper with open concern. "You want *me* to go with you?"

Harper nods. "Yes."

"To a public gala at your mother's hotel?"

"Why do you think I took you for drinks on the terrace?"

"I . . ." Logan's mouth opens and closes soundlessly. "Was that a *soft launch*?"

"It was a strategy. My mother probably knows I took a date to her hotel. If Lisa didn't tell her, she definitely saw the bill. What did you order—like, four vodka cranberries? If she's busy wondering who you are and how we met, she'll be less likely to notice anything else that might happen at her gala. It's a good cover."

"And your mother won't think it's suspicious that you suddenly want to attend her grand opening? I thought you weren't speaking."

"We aren't." Harper's jaw tenses even as her voice remains airy and bright. "But she knows I can't resist a good party."

Chloe stabs a spoon into her yogurt, caught between frustration and grudging respect. "You could have told us what you were planning yesterday," she mutters. "We're a team, you know."

"No," Harper says. "This week, *Logan* and I are a team. You're our backup."

There's a cutting retort already forming on Chloe's tongue when Logan steps between them. "I appreciate the vote of confidence, Harper," he says, "but charming people at parties is Chloe's thing. You should really ask her—"

"I'm not asking her. I'm asking you."

Chloe's knuckles whiten against the granite countertop. Sure, she'd rather throw herself off the balcony than spend a night as Harper Parisi's gala date, but hearing Harper dismiss the suggestion so easily makes the blood rush to her face. Because if there's one thing Chloe knows, it's that she's a damn good fake party guest.

"What's the problem?" she asks. "Worried you won't be able to take all the credit?"

Harper shrugs. "My mother isn't historically a fan of the women I date and neither are her donors. I don't know about you, but I'd like to avoid people looking at us while we're trying to commit a crime."

She says it casually, accompanied by a single wave of her manicured hand as if that statement doesn't blow apart Chloe's entire worldview. Everything about Harper, from her lavender Reformation crop top to the pearl studs gleaming in her ears, screams tragic heterosexual. If Harper has been out here bringing women to expensive black-tie galas, Chloe would have to rethink a lot of the insults she's been workshopping all year, especially since most of them revolve around Harper's existence feeling like a hate crime designed specifically for her.

"Is that something you do often?" she asks, face purposefully blank. "Date women to piss off your mom?"

Harper folds her arms. "No, Chloe, I'm not pretending to be

gay for attention. What are we? Twelve? If you want to kiss me in a ballroom full of Florida Republicans, be my guest, but I'd prefer to finish this job in one piece."

"So would I," Logan says. "If you want someone straight, you'll have to ask Priya."

"Exactly," Chloe says, trying very hard to pretend like the way Harper said *kiss me* isn't currently playing on a loop in her brain. "I'm not letting him go alone."

"We don't have a choice." There's an edge to Harper's voice now, an echo of the same frustration pulsing under Chloe's skin. "There are only two invitations."

"Then I'll find another way in. We crash Carlyle's parties all the time, Harper. I think I can figure it out."

"Because you work here. What—are you going to quit and start working for my mother instead?"

She intends it to be an insult. Chloe can tell by the way Harper's lip curls, but the words slip through her with a frigid clarity. *Are you going to quit and start working for my mother instead?*

"Yes," Chloe says, realization dawning even as she speaks. "That's exactly what I'm going to do. Think about it," she adds when Logan hesitates. "Being a guest is one thing, but if we also had someone on the inside? If I had a master key or knowledge of the back rooms like I do here . . ."

She trails off, already running through the list of possibilities. Why didn't she think of this before? She knows how easy it is to slip through a crowded ballroom in a catering uniform. She knows how little attention rich people pay their employees, and if Logan needs to be the one in thrifted formalwear, it only makes sense for Chloe to take his place on the other side.

She catches Logan's eye over the counter and knows he's thinking the same thing. Harper exhales, falling back into her chair once more. "You know, Chloe," she says. "That's actually a pretty good idea."

Chloe grins, unable to hide her satisfaction. "I know."

By the time she leaves for work, the three of them have sketched out the beginnings of a new plan. Harper will book them rooms at the Rivera, she and Logan will attend the gala as guests, and Chloe will go full method and apply to one of the open jobs on the Rivera careers website.

"I still think that's risky," Logan says later that afternoon when he, Chloe, and Priya are sprawled across their regular lounges during Chloe's lunch break. "What if they aren't hiring? Or what if they don't get back to you in time?"

The two of them have already filled Priya in on the new plan and, after a full minute of her gloating that *obviously* Harper was gay because "no one with money keeps their nails that short." Priya pulled out her laptop and fired up a program Chloe didn't recognize.

Now, her eyes gleam with a familiar wicked intensity. "Don't worry," she says. "I have it under control."

To Priya, *having it under control* apparently means hacking the Rivera careers website and deleting every application except for Chloe's. Regret twists in Chloe's stomach as she watches the files disappear one by one. Maybe this is too much. Maybe one of those applicants needs this job as badly as she needed hers a year ago. Maybe they also have a never-ending stack of bills and too many unread texts from their father piling up on their phone.

Chloe pushes the feeling away as Priya finally closes her laptop. Andrew Carlyle handed her a way out on a shiny golden platter. She'd be a fool not to take it, no matter the cost.

"There you go," Priya says as she tucks her laptop back in her bag. "One Rivera employee coming up."

"Don't tell Carlyle," Logan mutters. "It's probably in your contract that he can legally hunt you for sport if you start working for his competitor."

Chloe shudders. He's probably right; rich people are always trying to hunt things for sport. "I know. Did you two read my email?"

She spent most of her shift sneakily compiling every piece of information she could find on Andrew Carlyle into a single document. Newspaper articles, social media posts, magazine profiles. In photos, he's almost always accompanied by his wife—a willowy ex-model named Sonia who has the single most symmetrical face Chloe has ever seen—and, less frequently, by one of their two sons, both of whom seem to alternate between taking luxury international vacations on private jets and golfing with their Ivy League frat bros. The boys have the same square jaws and dark hair as their father, which is the only thing Chloe finds remotely interesting about them. She was working under the assumption that Carlyle wore some kind of toupee, but maybe that was wrong. Maybe all Carlyle children are born with absurdly good hair and the infuriating ability to look down their nose at the rest of the world.

But the thing Chloe really cares about is his history with Katherine Windey. According to her research, they really have known each other since college, and their antagonistic back-and-forth didn't start with a stolen hospitality award. The first time Katherine tried to buy a plot of beachfront land, Carlyle swooped in at the last minute with an offer no one could refuse. He built his first hotel on the acreage she sourced and the next year, Katherine opened a Windey property three blocks south, using the pull of the downtown social scene to attract his guests away from the water. That was how it went. When she expanded into Fort Lauderdale, Carlyle took Boca Raton. When he won the Florida Hospitality Award last year, Katherine got a full-page spread in the *Miami Herald* about her sustainable architecture techniques. It's like they're each other's shadow, a pair of toxic, capitalist soulmates, and Chloe wouldn't be surprised if Carlyle's senate campaign is another attempt to secure the upper hand.

Priya lets out a dismissive snort. "Oh, I read it. You know what's going on, don't you?"

Chloe leans back in her chair. "You have to be more specific."

"With Carlyle and Katherine," Priya says. "Come on, Chloe. They *totally* fucked. Or they're currently fucking. Trust me, it's one of the two."

"I don't know, Pri. He seems to really hate her."

"Exactly. Read a book. People who hate each other are always trying to fuck at least a little bit."

"Really? Is that the plot of . . ." Chloe cranes her neck to see the paperback peeking over the top of Priya's bag. "... *Hooked by Desire*?"

"Of course. In that one, the people who hate each other and also want to fuck are Captain Hook and Peter Pan. But don't worry," she adds, "Peter Pan's an adult."

That wasn't actually Chloe's first question but now that she's thinking about it, the logistics do feel a bit precarious. "I didn't know there was a market for that."

"There's an entire genre of books for people who want to fuck Peter Pan, Chloe."

Logan rolls over to face them. "Is there a genre of books for people trying to get their friend a job at the Rivera? Because that feels like the one we should be focusing on."

"Nice," Priya says, voice deadpan even as Chloe bites back a laugh. "That was *so* close to being genuinely rude. Your date with Harper changed you."

And just like that, Chloe's good mood is gone, replaced by the stubborn memory of Harper's hand on Logan's arm. The two of them will be together again next week, dressed to the nines, pretending to be in love, and Chloe can't put her finger on why that bothers her so much. She knows it's an act. It's the same vapid role she played at Carlyle's dinner, but something about Harper makes it feel personal. Like she'd gladly break Logan's heart if it meant watching Chloe suffer.

The thought hovers in the back of Chloe's mind for the rest of her shift. She manages to pull herself together long enough to hand in her time off request, but her manager barely looks up before tossing it onto his desk.

"Two weeks?" He shakes his head. "That's really inconvenient."

Chloe shrugs, eyes glued purposefully to the floor. "Yeah, well, my mom died. So it's kind of inconvenient for me, too."

It's not technically lying, she tells herself as her manager's face turns a brilliant shade of pink. Her mom *is* dead. It *was* really inconvenient for her. The fact that it happened last year is completely irrelevant to the current situation.

"My condolences." Her manager scribbles his signature across the bottom of the page. "Here. Just remember to pull your time sheets from the last six months before you go, okay? I need to give them to the finance guys."

He nods toward the door, where a man in an impeccably tailored navy suit lingers just inside the hall. Chloe nods. "Sure."

She has no intention of pulling her time sheets. If this job goes well, she might never have to set foot in a hotel kitchen again. She stuffs her signed paperwork into her bag and sets off down the hall, offering the looming finance guy a tight smile as she goes.

She's still thinking about the implications of next week's gala when her phone vibrates halfway through the dinner rush. There's a very frazzled-sounding Rivera hiring manager on the other line and Chloe ducks into the pantry, hoping they can't hear the obvious sounds of a working kitchen on the other side of the door. She forces herself to focus, to channel her nervous energy into charming her way through the basic interview questions, and it must work because after ten minutes, she's offered a job on the spot.

"I know it's unconventional," the hiring manager says, each word coated in a thick French accent. "But I'd be lying if I said we weren't desperate."

Chloe decides to pretend that's not a dig at her very obvious lack of housekeeping skills and says she'll be there Monday.

When she slides her phone into her pocket and steps back into the kitchen, it's like something settles in the pit of her stomach, too. Acceptance. Composure. This is just another job, another mark too rich for their own good, and she's walked too far down this road to turn back even if she wanted to.

Well, Chloe thinks as she ties her apron securely around her waist. *It's a good thing I don't.*

EIGHT

THERE'S A MOMENT IN EVERY JOB WHERE THE SCALE SEEMS TO HOVER between likely and impossible, where the slightest change could send it swinging in either direction. For Chloe, the tipping point for this one comes over the weekend, when she finishes her final shift at the Carlyle and the idea of next week hovers like a storm cloud on the very near horizon.

She throws herself into their plan, mapping out the next few days hour by hour, detailing how Logan will snag Carlyle's award from the gala, and how Priya will cause just enough of a distraction for them to get away with it. She prints blueprints of the Rivera stairwells, memorizes the curve of every hallway, and stares at the shape of the island until she can trace the outline with her eyes closed.

It's easy. Simple. As natural as lifting James Webber's watch from his wrist.

That night, the four of them sneak into Priya's hardware store after hours and use the 3D printer to make a copy of Carlyle's award from scratch. It's not an exact replica. It's not even particularly accurate, but it doesn't need to be. It just needs to be good enough for Katherine Windey not to notice the switch until the gala is over and the four of them are far, far away.

"Let me see." Logan plucks the replica from the machine. He weighs it in his palm, tossing it from hand to hand and then, in the time it takes Chloe to blink, it's gone.

Priya laughs as she unplugs the printer. "Think it'll be that easy?"

Logan grins and opens his jacket to reveal the award tucked in the inside pocket. "Probably."

He repeats the movement again and this time, Chloe sees how it works. Logan always says pickpocketing is like learning a new card trick—all about the misdirect. It's an art she's never quite mastered, but he makes it look effortless.

"I can still see it, you know."

Chloe looks up to find Harper watching them from the other side of the room, one shoulder braced in the doorway like she's afraid joining them inside will stain her otherwise flawless reputation. "The award," she clarifies, nodding toward Logan's jacket. "I can tell it's in your pocket. Even if no one sees you make the switch, it's obvious you're hiding something."

Chloe glances toward Logan's chest, where the printed award is, indeed, straining awkwardly against the dark folds of his jacket. As much as it pains her to admit, Harper is right. All the tricks in the world are useless if Logan can't walk back to his seat without raising suspicion.

"Maybe we could tailor it?" Priya suggests. "Deepen the pockets?"

Chloe shakes her head. "I don't know how much that would help. What if we—?"

"Oh my god." Harper pushes herself off the wall. "Move."

She strides across the room, shouldering Chloe out of the way as she goes. Logan takes a hesitant step back but before he can make a run for it, Harper grabs his arm and pulls him against her, purposefully angling her body across his left side.

"There." She flashes Chloe a sharp, satisfied smile. "Better?"

Chloe scowls, still rubbing an absent-minded hand over the spot where Harper's shoulder had knocked hers. It *is* better, actually. The outline of the award is perfectly hidden behind the curve of Harper's waist. The two of them look like a regular couple, pressed together for balance after one too many drinks at a fancy hotel gala, and despite herself, Chloe is once again treated to the memory of Harper's lips forming the words *kiss me*.

"Better than nothing, I suppose," she says, voice purposefully light.

Harper's grin widens a fraction of an inch. "Of course. God forbid anyone else have a good idea, right?" Her voice drops to a low, seductive whisper. "What's the matter? Worried you won't be able to take all the credit?"

It's the same question Chloe asked her yesterday. Her jaw tightens with fury, but Logan slips out of Harper's grasp before she can respond. "I think we're all just hoping this goes well," he says, gaze flicking briefly to the floor. "I like your shoes, by the way."

"My—?" Harper draws back, twisting to examine her sandals from every angle. "What did you do to my shoes?"

"Nothing. I just really like how they match your earrings."

Priya snorts and even Chloe has to bite back a grin as she watches Logan toss one of Harper's shiny pearl earrings into the air before pinning it deliberately to his own ear. Just like that, the tension shatters.

"Unbelievable," Harper mutters. "How the hell do you do that?"

And when Priya bursts out laughing, Chloe wonders, for the first time, if the four of them might actually be able to pull this off.

"I hate to bring this up," Logan says as they file back into the dimly lit alley outside, "but is there a chance someone at the Rivera would recognize Chloe? I mean, we were just there yesterday."

Chloe hesitates, trying to remember who they interacted with. The drivers probably shuttle too many people back and forth to remember faces and she has a feeling Lisa's job mostly consists of making sure Harper has everything she wants, not interacting with housekeeping staff. "I don't think so," she says.

"No, that's a good point," Harper says. "It wouldn't hurt to change your hair or something."

"I'm not changing my hair."

"Don't take it personally. We're just being cautious."

"No," Chloe snaps. "You want to give me a makeover."

There's a moment of strained silence as Priya locks the shop behind them and tucks her keys back into her pocket. "I mean this with so much love, Chloe," she says carefully. "But we all do."

And that's how Chloe ends up in Harper's hotel bathroom, glaring suspiciously at the array of hastily purchased hair products lining the counter.

"How long is this going to take?" Priya calls from the other room. She and Logan are sprawled across Harper's king-sized bed, flipping through late-night shows on the hotel TV. From where she's sitting, Chloe catches the occasional glimpse of them in the mirror—Logan watching as Priya pulls bottles of skincare serums from Harper's suitcase, sniffs them once, then sets them aside.

Harper chews on her bottom lip as she runs an appraising hand through Chloe's hair. "Not sure. I'll have to see how the color lifts. And stop touching my stuff," she adds as Priya dips a pinkie into a jar of moisturizer. "That's from Paris."

Priya's expression sours and she drops the bottles back into Harper's suitcase.

Harper turns Chloe's chair away from the mirror, then reaches behind her for a comb. "Ready?" she asks.

No, Chloe thinks. She's *not* ready to put the fate of her hair in the hands of someone who, until this week, would have gladly pushed her over the side of a luxury yacht. She doesn't even know what Harper's planning to do. She could end up looking like the model stamped across the box of drugstore bleach—overly spray-tanned and suspiciously cheerful with her freshly dyed blond hair chopped in a severe bob.

Chloe swallows hard. Her mother always had long hair. It's not something she thought she cared about until now.

"What was that?"

Harper's hands go still and Chloe realizes, with a humiliating jolt, that she must have said that last part out loud. "Nothing!" She shakes her head, face burning. "I'm not . . . I've just always had long hair. My mother did, too."

Enough. Chloe digs her nails into her palms, tiny pinpricks of pain to clear her head. Harper shouldn't get to know that. She shouldn't get to see this delicate, fragile piece of her, but Chloe doesn't know how to take it back. She braces herself for the inevitable taunts, for Harper's mouth to curl into that vicious, predictable grin, but it doesn't come. Instead she just nods. Like this, for some strange, inexplicable reason, is something she understands.

"That's fine," she says. "I don't have to cut it."

Chloe blinks. "You . . . don't?"

"No. I'll just shape it a bit in the front and give you a new color. Maybe some bangs? You can keep the length."

"Oh." Chloe grips the arms of her chair, embarrassed at the relief sweeping through her. "Thanks."

Harper doesn't answer. She just switches her comb to the opposite hand and goes back to work, methodically yanking through each tangle as Chloe tries not to let her discomfort show. It's a while before either of them speaks, but when Harper finally breaks the silence, her voice is low enough for only the two of them to hear.

"I've seen her play, you know. Your mother." Chloe sucks in a surprised breath, but Harper continues like she hasn't noticed. "My dad used to take me to the symphony every year around Christmas. I don't even like classical music. I think it's boring, but he used to study opera back in Bologna, which is wild, considering he ended up working at a tech firm in Miami. He always got us season tickets. I saw most of their concerts for a period of, like, ten years straight, but the holiday show was always my favorite."

Chloe digs her nails into the armrests. It's one thing to miss her mother in private, to remember her sitting onstage at the concert hall with her beloved cello resting between her knees. It's quite another, she thinks, to have someone else wrap their fist around those memories and yank them into the open against her will. She squeezes her eyes shut and tries, *really* tries, not to think about the way the spotlight used to catch in her mother's dark hair, how she'd bite her lip in the split second before the conductor lifted his hands, or how their home was always wild and bursting with music.

Of all the things she's had to adapt to this year, Chloe thinks the silence is the worst.

"That was my favorite, too," she says. Then, because she's genuinely curious, she adds, "You really remember her?"

Chloe can't see Harper from her seat in the chair, but she feels her working, still sectioning Chloe's hair with the end of her comb. Her hands are steady, but when Chloe turns to catch a glimpse of her face, Harper's jaw is set, like she's physically biting back a response.

Chloe swallows over the lump in her throat and tries again. "Harper, I'm—"

"Stop *moving*." Harper seizes Chloe's chin in one hand and yanks her head back to the front. "You're ruining my vision. And yes, I do," she adds when Chloe opens her mouth. "Sort of. I found her resume when I was looking you up and realized her name was in all my old programs."

"You said you've never looked me up."

Harper's nails dig into Chloe's cheek one by one. "I lied."

Then she grabs the box of dye from the counter, yanks on a cheap pair of plastic gloves, and starts mixing.

Chloe glares pointedly down at her lap as Harper works. It's easy to hate Harper from a distance, to let a year of icy resentment build between them and pretend not to care. It's different, however, to sit together in a damp, windowless bathroom, to feel the uneven thrum of her pulse in her veins and know they're on the same side.

Neither of them speaks until Harper finally steps back against the wall. She put her own hair up at some point during the process. Chloe's only ever seen her shiny and polished but the wispy tendrils curling around Harper's face now are almost soft.

"There." Harper waves a hand toward the mirror. "What do you think?"

Chloe glances warily over her shoulder, bracing herself for the transformation. She's fully prepared to hate it, to add this to the long list of Harper's indiscretions, but when she meets her own gaze in the mirror, she hardly recognizes the girl staring back. Her hair still falls past her shoulders, but the dark, unruly curls are gone, replaced by a pin-straight blowout. The color is lighter than Chloe expected too, a rich auburn that also feels strangely intentional. Not a fresh start, exactly, but closer than anything she's had in years.

"Oh." Chloe brushes her fingers through her new bangs before catching sight of Harper in the mirror, still standing over her shoulder. She lets her hand fall back to her lap. "I . . . it's not bad."

"You're allowed to say you like it, Chloe. It won't kill you."

But when Harper turns to gather the leftover supplies, Chloe catches the barest hint of a smile tucked under her constant derision. For the first time all week, she thinks it looks genuine.

The rest of the plan comes together quickly after that. A late-night meeting in Harper's suite, a list of notes sketched across Priya's whiteboard, a few ideas typed into Logan's phone. Strategies piling together until the momentum is too strong to look back. It's not until Sunday evening that Priya finally looks up from her computer and says, "I think we're ready."

They're in Priya's apartment today, sitting around the kitchen table as the setting sun paints the walls a brilliant shade of pink. The four of them could probably sit here all night, trying to plan everything down to the last detail, but Chloe has learned there's a balance with jobs like this. No matter how prepared she is, it always feels a little like walking into the unknown.

"Yeah," she says. "I think you're right. Is everyone packed?"

"Almost." Harper stretches her arms above her head as she stands. "Do you want me to bring a gun?"

"A—?" Chloe nearly spills a can of sparkling water across her lap. "I'm sorry, you have a gun?"

"You don't?"

"In what world would I have a gun?"

"It's not an unreasonable question, Chloe. You can literally buy one at the gas station across the street."

"I'm pretty sure that gas station also sells hard drugs to anyone who knows what to ask for," Priya says. "I don't exactly trust their judgment. We'll be fine," she adds when Harper opens her mouth. "What time are you checking in tomorrow?"

Harper dumps the rest of her things unceremoniously into her purse. "Probably around nine. The second room is under your name, so you can get there later."

"Right." Priya nods, typing a note into their shared file. "Logan and I will head over when I'm off work. Should be around noon."

"And I'll be there early for orientation," Chloe says. "So as long as Harper's ready, the two of us can start."

"Sounds good to me." Priya glances around the table as everyone starts to pack up. "Does anyone want a drink before you head out?"

Harper stands abruptly, purse in hand. "I don't think we need to keep pretending to like each other. Just text me if anything comes up. Otherwise, I'll see you tomorrow."

She strides out of the kitchen without a backward glance and Priya waits until the apartment door slams shut before pushing herself to her feet. "Thank god. Who wants wine?"

Chloe raises her hand. Between her regular work hours and this weekend's planning sessions, she's barely had a moment alone. Priya busies herself in the corner, but Logan remains at the table, eyeing Chloe warily over the top of his phone.

"You good?" he asks.

Chloe rubs an absent-minded hand over her forehead. "Just tired."

"Me, too. It's weird, right?"

"Which part?"

Logan nods toward the door. "Harper. Working with her. It's . . . not as bad as I thought it would be."

Chloe grits her teeth, ignoring the whisper of jealousy stirring in her stomach. She wouldn't go that far. Sure, Harper's presence isn't actively repulsive. She actually managed to be decently helpful this weekend, but that doesn't mean they're in the clear. "I don't trust it," she says.

Logan arches a brow. "The plan or Harper?"

"Harper." Chloe glances toward the kitchen, where Priya is still divvying up a cheap bottle of Moscato. "I think we should have a contingency plan. Some sort of backup in case this goes wrong."

Because Harper Parisi is a liability. She always has been. Her presence is a risk they have to take, but Chloe is still horribly aware of who would walk away unscathed if this job went wrong.

It certainly won't be her.

Priya returns to her seat before Logan can answer and slides two glasses across the table. "Here you go. My finest eight-dollar bottle."

"Thanks, Pri." Logan takes a glass, flashing Chloe a reluctant grin as he lifts it in a mock toast. "To five million dollars."

Priya laughs. "To millionaire CEOs and their weird hotel rivalries."

Chloe reaches across the table for the remaining glass. It's cool to the touch, surprisingly heavy. *Five million dollars.* She hoists it in the air.

"To grand larceny," she says, and drinks.

CHLOE DOESN'T GO home after leaving Priya's apartment. Instead, she digs around the bottom of her bag until she finds enough change and catches the next bus south.

Her father sold their house months ago, but Chloe has only visited his new place once. She blames her work schedule mostly, but she also can't stand the soulless, empty feeling of his new neighborhood. It's nothing like the vibrant area she grew up in and, even though she understands why he left, she thinks part of her will always resent him for selling her childhood home.

It's dark by the time she gets off the bus, palm trees catching in the orange glow of the streetlamps, and for a second, Chloe considers turning back. It's not like she can tell her father about Carlyle's offer. He doesn't know about that part of her life and she intends to keep it that way, but some small, distant part of her still longs for the comfort of telling *someone.* Of curling up between both her parents on the couch and blurting out her problems to people who wouldn't judge her. When she finally builds up the courage to knock, her father answers the door almost instantly.

"I know it's late," she begins. "I'm—"

Her father doesn't let her finish. Instead, his face splits into a wide grin and he pulls her into a hug, tugging her over the threshold and into the hallway. "Chloe," he cries. "What on earth did you do to your hair?"

Chloe laughs, the sound muffled against the soft fabric of his sweater-vest. "You don't like it?"

"No, it's cute! It's just . . . red."

"I know. I needed a change."

He motions her into the living room and Chloe tries very hard not to look at the boxes still stacked in the hall. She should have been here to help, to make the stress of moving a little more manageable. Instead, she's been breaking in to donor events and taking penthouse meetings with elusive CEOs.

"Sorry about the mess." Her father glances over his shoulder, light glinting off his wire-rimmed glasses. "It's still a work in progress."

Chloe crouches next to an unopened pile of boxes. "It's okay. Sorry I haven't been around."

"Busy at work?"

"You could say that."

She digs her fingers into the seams of a tightly sealed box until it pops open. There's a pile of dusty picture frames inside, and Chloe pulls them into her lap one at a time. There's her mother standing in front of the arts center downtown. There's her father's graduation, his cap and gown slightly askew as he sweats through the Florida humidity. There's her five-year-old self smooshed between the two of them at Disney World.

Simple memories. Happy memories. Memories she also tucked away for safekeeping.

"I love that one."

Chloe looks up to find her father pointing into the box. There's another photo at the bottom—her high school self sitting in front of her bedroom mirror as her mother winds hot rollers into her hair. Chloe doesn't remember the moment exactly. She could be getting ready for a dance or a piano recital or a school play, but she does remember the feeling. She remembers the heat on the back of her neck, the soft scrape of her mother's nails against her scalp, and her voice whispering, *you are radiant, inside and out.*

Sometimes, Chloe still finds herself surprised by the things her mother has missed. She met Logan and most of Chloe's college friends, she was there for graduation and the time Chloe brought her first girlfriend home, but she never got the chance to meet Priya. She never went with them to brunch or stayed at the Carlyle or saw Logan perform at the beach, cards spread between his fingers like glittering jewels. She never met Harper either and even though Chloe thinks that's for the best, she also knows with absolute certainty that she would not be here, on the brink of the strangest, riskiest job she's ever taken, if her mother were still alive.

"I'm not going to be around much next week," she says, keeping her tone light as she drops the picture back into the box. "I'm up for a promotion at work, so they're keeping me busy."

"Oh? What sort of promotion?"

Excitement flickers across her father's face and it takes everything in Chloe's power not to wince. He never judged her for taking the Carlyle job. He never implied she could do better or asked when she was planning to leave, and she hates lying to him now. "Just a new management position. Nothing huge, but if I make it through the week, there might be a bit more money coming my way."

For now, it's the only truth she can offer.

"That's great, Chloe. Congratulations!"

And this is why you're here, she thinks as her father pulls her into a tight, one-armed hug. This is why she told Carlyle yes and why she agreed to work with Harper. Because her father deserves security. He deserves to start over in a new house with a good, reliable daughter and he deserves to be happy without the threat of debt collectors banging down his door.

Outside, the sky is black, palm trees no more than shadows in the night. Chloe can still feel the lie lingering on her tongue, but as she turns back to the boxes and continues unpacking, there's something else there, too. A crackle. An itch.

In the instant before she swallows, Chloe thinks it tastes a bit like possibility.

NINE

"Can anyone tell me what our one rule is?"

Chloe quickens her pace as she follows her new manager across the sprawling Rivera lobby. She's been here less than an hour and she can already tell that Reed Maloney is going to be a problem. He's tall and wiry with sun-kissed white skin, a truly impressive mustache, and absolutely no regard for the group of employees trailing in his wake. He's also incredibly punctual, perceptive, and observant—three things Chloe learned after stepping onto the pier thirty-seven seconds past her designated arrival time to find Reed waving a literal pocket watch in her face.

Good qualities for a hotel manager, probably, but terrible in someone she's actively trying to trick.

Chloe dodges another luggage cart, almost tripping into her new co-workers in the process. There are three of them starting today—her, an older woman already wearing a name tag that says PANDORA, and a boy named Skip who can't be more than seventeen. They were all thrown into the lobby as soon as they arrived, Reed assuring them they'd fill out all the necessary paperwork at some point this week.

"We're just *so* understaffed right now," he said, dropping a freshly pressed Rivera housekeeping uniform into Chloe's arms. "Between the gala tomorrow and that server glitch over the weekend, we need you training ASAP."

If this were a real job, Chloe might have told him she didn't work for free, but she doesn't need the extra attention today, or for anyone to start looking into the "server glitch." Besides, the longer Reed delays onboarding, the longer her cover remains intact. Chloe glances down at her name tag as they walk. The name STASSI glints back at her, almost accusatory in the early morning sunlight. She makes a mental note to never again give Priya free rein over her fake identity and quickens her pace.

The other new hires are still a few feet ahead of her, Skip's brow furrowing as he half jogs across the lobby. It's not until he opens his mouth that Chloe realizes he's still genuinely trying to think of an answer to Reed's original question.

"There's only one rule?" he asks. "Didn't we get a whole handbook?"

Reed shakes his head. "Just the one."

"Is it 'the customer is always right'?"

"No." Reed finally comes to a halt at the concierge desk, turning to face them so quickly Chloe has to leap aside to avoid running into him. "The answer is '*Reed* is always right.' Do what I say, and you'll make it through today. Any questions?"

Chloe shakes her head, face purposefully blank as Reed looks them over. She's used to the first-day intimidation tactics. She got the same shakedown from the managing staff at the Carlyle, but Skip is clearly new to this. He thrusts a freckled hand into the air. "Yeah," he says. "When's lunch?"

Reed closes his eyes. "I think," he says carefully, "it's probably better for everyone if you don't speak."

He turns back to his computer, ignoring the way Skip's shoulders slump, and Chloe takes a moment to glance around the lobby. The last time she was inside the Rivera, Lisa led her and Priya through a side corridor in the east tower. They skipped the main lobby entirely but now that she's here, it's hard not to stare.

The Rivera doesn't have the classic, opulent glam of the Carlyle hotels, but something about the lobby feels sleeker. Less old money and more like they're standing in the middle of a very fancy spaceship. The perfection of it still grates on her, just like it did in the ballroom, but she's not surprised Carlyle is bitter about letting this island go. The hotel Katherine's created here is the epitome of everything he's not, every modern trend he's never been quick enough to capitalize on. Even the ocean sparkling outside the windows doesn't feel as unsettling as it did this morning on her trip across the bay. From the safety of the Rivera lobby, it's almost comforting. Maybe that's why rich people love it so much, Chloe thinks as she watches another yacht pull into the harbor. Nothing feels particularly threatening when you're sealed behind wealth like this.

She risks a glance down at Reed's watch behind the concierge desk. Just past nine. Priya and Logan won't be rolling in for another few hours, but Harper should be here any minute.

"Observe." Reed snaps his fingers in front of Chloe's face before sweeping an arm in the general direction of the lobby. "Hospitality is the cornerstone of everything we do, from catering to housekeeping to event planning. You're going to spend the rest of the morning up here learning how to interact with our guests and helping me welcome them into their home away from home. Once you learn the rules, you'll be able to apply them to your own separate positions."

"Rules?" Skip shoots Chloe a panicked glance out of the corner of his eye. "I thought there was only one rule?"

Chloe pointedly ignores him. She could smile at every Rivera guest and follow all of Reed's elaborate hospitality rules, but that wouldn't negate the fact that her resting expression usually screams "do not come near me ever." She's right in the middle of trying to school her face into some kind of welcoming neutrality when the front doors slide open and Harper strides into the lobby.

As usual, she looks pristinely put together in a matching linen lounge set the same creamy color as the tiles under her feet. Her hair tumbles down her back in loose waves, pushed off her face by a pair of designer sunglasses, and she's rolling a pink carry-on suitcase behind her. The sun also chooses that exact moment to break through the thin layer of clouds outside, filling the entire lobby with warm, golden light. Personally, Chloe thinks it's a bit much, but when Reed looks up from his computer, his grin is just as brilliant.

"Welcome back, Ms. Parisi. How was your trip across the bay?"

Without access to Harper's yacht, Chloe was forced to take the ferry to work this morning. She spent a full fifteen minutes trying to smooth her bangs into something presentable afterward, but Harper, of course, looks like she's just stepped out of a Drybar.

"Oh, it was fine," Harper says, already preoccupied with riffling through her purse. "Is the cabana bar open?"

"For you?" Reed flashes her a conspiratorial wink and Chloe resists the urge to roll her eyes. "Always."

"You're the best, Reed." Harper turns to go, then hesitates, gaze falling on Chloe. "I'm sorry, what's wrong with your face?"

Too late, Chloe realizes she's still trying to smooth her expression into something kind and approachable. Judging by Harper's raised eyebrows, it's not going well. She lets her face fall back into its usual scowl. "Nothing."

"Hmm." Harper considers her a second longer before unceremoniously dropping her purse into Chloe's arms. "Take my luggage upstairs, will you? I need a drink."

Chloe lets out a muffled groan, staggering under the sudden weight of the bags. It's barely nine in the morning. Anywhere else, Harper's excuse of needing a drink would be paper-thin. Someone would guess that she wasn't going to the bar at all, that she was actually heading upstairs with Chloe, but standing in the middle of a resort made from her family's money, it's almost believable. Reed seems to buy it, because he nods with the sage understanding that Chloe thinks only comes from someone who's also spent the last several years drinking before noon.

"I believe your mother is currently in a meeting," he says. "Should I let her know you're here?"

Harper shakes her head. "No, thank you. This trip is actually a surprise, so if you could keep this between us for now, I'd really appreciate it." She takes her key from Reed's outstretched hand, then jerks her chin in Chloe's direction. "Bags," she says. "Upstairs, now."

Chloe barely resists the urge to roll her eyes as Harper turns her back and sets off toward the elevator. Reed's smile drops.

He rips the lanyard from his neck. Chloe nearly gags at the overpowering rush of cologne (Dior, Sauvage) as he leans over to tag both bags with Harper's room number. "Here," he mutters. "Put everything in room 4002 and bring that key back when you're done. And use the employee elevator," he adds when Chloe starts in Harper's direction. "No one wants to see you working while they're on vacation."

Chloe's surprised Reed can't feel the heat of her glare through the pile of luggage between them. *Five million dollars,* she thinks as she staggers into the back. *You're doing this for five million dollars.*

She jams a finger into the elevator button, winding Reed's lanyard around her wrist as she waits. The card at the end is plain, battered from excessive use, but Chloe would recognize a master key anywhere. She smacks it against the sensor when the elevator arrives, foot tapping against the tile as the light climbs toward the fortieth floor. When she finally spills into the upstairs hallway, her arms are trembling under the weight of the bags.

God, what did Harper *put* in here?

Chloe tightens her grip and drags everything into the hall. The Rivera is built in a circle, each floor looking down into a sunny, plant-filled courtyard. If she turns right, she'll arrive at Harper's penthouse before the first curve and if she goes left, she'll pass Katherine's suite at the opposite end of the loop. She's supposed to meet Harper in the room right away but now that she's here, Chloe doesn't think it would hurt to take a lap. She's only seen this floor through blueprints and grainy security footage. It would be nice, actually, to get a sense of what they're dealing with. With one last glance over her shoulder, Chloe turns left, toward Katherine's suite and away from their original plan.

She makes it less than a dozen paces before Harper's voice crackles through the speaker in her ear. "What's going on? Why aren't you here yet?"

Chloe tilts her head, ensuring her hair still covers the earpiece. It's been easy enough to hide so far, but her hands are currently occupied with Harper's bags. She doesn't answer, quickening her pace around the far edge of the hall.

"I know you're there," Harper says. "What's happening?"

Chloe rolls her eyes. "Chill, Harper. I'm just looking around."

"Reed will wonder why you're taking so long."

Let him. Chloe will bat her eyelashes when she returns, blurt out a string of apologetic excuses about how this place is *just so hard to navigate* and how she's *never been anywhere this nice before*.

Reed might be good at his job, but she's better at hers.

She keeps walking, eyes fixed determinedly ahead until the hallway starts to curve. The only thing that sets Katherine's suite apart from the ones around it is the tiny mailbox nailed to the wall outside. *Amateurs.* Chloe bites back a grin and slows her pace ever so slightly. They might as well tape a sign to the door that says *someone important lives here and regularly receives mail!*

"Chloe," Harper starts. "What are you—?"

Whatever she's about to say is cut off by the sound of a door slamming shut. Chloe whips around to find a tall woman with bright auburn curls pulling a housekeeping cart out of a neighboring room. She jumps when she sees Chloe, one hand flying to her chest.

"Oh! You scared me."

Chloe takes a careful step back. "Sorry."

"No, it's fine." The woman waves a hand and Chloe catches a glint of something shiny between her fingers. Another master key, identical to the one hanging off Reed's lanyard. "Are you lost?"

"Yes, actually." Chloe glances helplessly down at the suitcase. "I'm looking for room 4020?"

"Room 4020?" The woman hesitates before craning her neck toward Katherine's suite. "Are you sure?"

"Pretty sure." Chloe shifts Harper's purse to her other arm, wincing as the weight of it bites into her skin. "I'm supposed to drop these off."

"*Stop it.*" Harper's voice is a sharp hiss of static in her ear. "Get out, Chloe. You look suspicious."

The other woman extends a hand, helping adjust the bag until it sits comfortably in the crook of Chloe's elbow. "I think you have the wrong room. That's Katherine Windey's suite."

Chloe's eyes widen, like this is completely new information. "Oh my god, really? I'm so sorry, I had no idea. Reed just told me to take these upstairs, but I'm not trying to disturb *Katherine Windey,* of all people."

Harper's frustration is evident through the earpiece. "Get out," she snaps. "Now."

But the other housekeeper just laughs. "It's okay, I promise. The layout can be a bit confusing, but you'll get used to it. And don't worry about disturbing Ms. Windey. We hardly ever see her."

"Really?" Chloe tilts her head. "Not even for housekeeping?"

"Nope. The managers always take care of her themselves. It's a little above our pay grade. Have you met Katie or Kristen yet?" Chloe shakes her head. "You will soon. One of them will probably rescue you from Reed at some point today. You said you were new?"

"Chloe."

There's an edge in Harper's voice Chloe can't quite identify. She ignores it and heaves a dejected sigh. "It's my first day, actually. Is it that obvious?"

The woman laughs again, then points toward the luggage tag on Harper's suitcase. "A little. But mostly because you're supposed to take those to 4002, not 4020."

"What?" Chloe scrambles to double-check the tag. "Oh my god, that's so embarrassing!"

"It happens." The woman gives her a quick pat on the shoulder before turning back to her cart. "I'm Megan, by the way. I need to get back downstairs but I'm sure we'll get to know each other after Reed takes you off hospitality duty."

"So he does this to everyone?"

"Unfortunately. It's kind of his thing."

"Tragic. I'm Stassi," Chloe says, remembering her fake name just in time. "Thanks for your help, Megan. I really appreciate it."

She makes it exactly two feet back down the hall before Harper explodes.

"What the hell? You know my room number!"

Chloe glances over her shoulder in time to watch Megan drag her cart into the waiting elevator. "Sorry, I forgot."

She can feel Harper seething on the other end of the line, but Chloe doesn't care. Instead, she's eyeing every inch of the hallway, memorizing the windows looking out over the bay, the art hanging outside each door, and the cameras drilled into the ceiling exactly four feet apart. She clocks the sleek, patterned wallpaper and counts the double-door entrance to each suite, memorizing the distance between Harper's room and her mother's. There's a mirror on the wall across from her, a sleek pane of glass reflecting every inch of the hall in stunning clarity. Chloe meets her own gaze exactly once as she passes, just long enough to slip a hand into the pocket of her uniform skirt and run a finger along the edge of Megan's master key.

Logan was right, of course. A good lift is all about the misdirect and it wasn't hard to pretend to struggle under the weight of Harper's bags. If they're lucky, Megan won't realize her key is missing until it's time to clock out. More than enough time for Priya to make a copy.

By the time Chloe reaches Harper's room, she's not thinking about Megan or Reed or the gala tomorrow. She's not even thinking about Harper, really. No, she's too busy basking in the satisfaction of a job well done, letting the warmth of it sink into her bones. It's not until the door flies open and Harper braces one hand against the gilded doorframe that she remembers why they're here.

"Delivery for room 4002," Chloe says, sweeping her arm in the direction of the luggage in a mock bow.

In the warm glow of the hallway, Harper looks carved from stone. For a second, neither of them moves. Then Harper seizes the front of Chloe's shirt in one swift motion. The bags fall to the floor with a dull *crunch* and Chloe has just enough time to picture all those vials of fancy Parisian skin cream spilling across Harper's designer wardrobe before the door slams shut behind them.

TEN

Chloe has spent the last year feeling constantly, viciously angry. The intensity comes and goes, of course, but most days, she's usually one wrong move away from spontaneous combustion. She's angry at the world for trying to drown her when people like Andrew Carlyle get to float. She's angry at her mother for leaving, at her father for accepting it, at herself for letting thoughts like that fester. It's a standard feeling now, almost comforting in its routine, because at the end of the day, the truth is this—the sun will rise, the world will turn, and Chloe will find something to be furious about.

It's part of what makes Harper's particular brand of nonchalance so irritating. Because no matter what happened between them, no matter what Chloe ruined or stole or cheated her out of, Harper never seemed to crack. Instead, it's been a year of delicately arched eyebrows and cutting smiles and notes scrawled with *xoxo Harper* slipped into her mailbox. It's been a year of wondering if Harper is just an excellent liar or if the world really lets some people get by with nothing to feel angry about. If maybe all Chloe needed was a designer wardrobe and a full bank account to make her problems disappear, too.

But when Harper's fingers knot in the front of Chloe's blouse, when she shoves her against the wall of her penthouse suite and slams the door behind them, Chloe thinks she sees it. Raw, unfiltered fury flickering behind her green eyes.

"What the hell?" Harper snaps. "What are you *doing*?"

Chloe shrugs as best she can. "I'm dropping off your luggage."

"That's not what I mean."

"Then please, enlighten me, Harper, because as far as I can tell, I'm doing my job."

"But this isn't just *your* job!"

"Oh my god." Chloe bats Harper's hand away, ducking under her outstretched arm and away from the wall. "Is that really your problem? You're still mad Carlyle hired us both?"

"I—no! We have a plan, Chloe. You're supposed to meet me here. I'm supposed to hand off Priya's flash drive for the computer downstairs. At no point did we discuss making detours to my mother's suite."

Chloe plucks the speaker from her ear, carelessly tossing it from hand to hand. "I thought it would be helpful to see what we're working with."

"You thought it would be *helpful* to introduce yourself by name and let everyone see you upstairs?"

"I literally work here, Harper. It's not weird for me to be on this floor."

"Oh my god." Harper lets out a frustrated groan. She starts pacing the living room, heels clicking sporadically over the tile. "You're going to ruin this."

Chloe's face heats with a familiar liquid fury. Had she drawn out her exchange with Megan to make Harper uncomfortable? Maybe. Is she still kind of reveling in it now? Sure, but she doesn't appreciate the insinuation that she's the problem here. "Excuse me?"

"I said you're going to *ruin this,*" Harper snaps. "My mother isn't some random Miami socialite. You can't just lie your way out of the Rivera and I don't think it's wise to broadcast the fact that we're here. If you don't understand the gravity of this situation, maybe *you're* not as good as you think you are."

She's breathing heavily now, cheeks tinged a delicate shade of pink, but Chloe is done listening. Harper wants to discredit her now? Harper, who practically begged her to take this job, who spent the last year leaving teasing, taunting notes in Chloe's things like they were friends, like they were *equals*. Harper, who stood behind her in the bathroom yesterday and talked about Chloe's mother with such kindness that Chloe almost believed it was real.

"You want to know why I took that detour?" Chloe asks, voice simmering with barely leashed anger. She rounds on Harper without waiting for a response. "Because we know *everything* about this hotel. We know your mother's schedule and where to find security blind spots and how to make it through the gala tomorrow. We know everything except who else might be up here. Housekeeping? Mail delivery? Room service? Do you have a list of people to watch out for? Because I do now."

Harper steps back, but the couch is in her way. She stumbles, hand scrabbling against the wall behind her as Chloe takes another step.

"I know it's hard to wrap your head around, Harper, but not everything is about you. I talked to that housekeeper because we should know who has access to your mother's suite and which managers to watch out for. I let her help me with your luggage so I could take her key, not because I have some weird obsession with ruining your life."

She does, of course. Chloe would like nothing more than to personally witness Harper's downfall, but that's not the point right now. She pulls the stolen key out of her pocket and flings it across the coffee table. For a minute, it's oddly reminiscent of that day in Carlyle's office, the two of them sketched against a background of dark wood with a single key card sitting between them.

Harper's gaze falls to the table. "You . . . you stole that? How?"

"How do you think?"

"I don't know, you've always been a pretty shit pickpocket, Chloe."

Chloe's teeth sink into her bottom lip, but it's not enough to entirely stifle her frustrated groan. This is going nowhere. Conversations with Harper never do. She knows exactly how this one will end and honestly, it's her fault for getting involved in the first place. For daring to think things between them could ever be different. She's about to head for the door when Harper's head tips back toward the ceiling. She drops onto the couch, shoulders hunched in something that looks startlingly like surrender, and the sight is so strange Chloe momentarily forgets her decision to leave. She's never seen Harper angry before, but she's also never seen her look like this—quiet and small and terribly human.

So, despite herself, Chloe takes a deep breath and tries again. "You don't know everything, Harper. I get that Katherine's your mom. I know this is your hotel, but we're in this together. We're a team and you have to trust me."

Harper's fingers dig into the cushion beneath her. "This isn't my hotel. My mother will leave the Windey properties to a lot of people, I'm sure, but I'm not one of them."

"That . . ." Chloe shakes her head. The fact that Harper might not end up a literal hotel heiress isn't doing much in terms of sympathy. "That's not the point."

Harper folds her arms defensively across her chest. "Okay, well, I've also never been on a team before."

"Wow, you don't say?"

"Can you *not* for, like, five seconds? I'm . . ." Harper breaks off, face twisting in clear discomfort. "My mother and I aren't close. We never have been, but the last month has been particularly . . . contentious."

"Why?"

"Not the point." Harper's gaze is fixed determinedly on the carpet, like she can only get the words out if she pretends Chloe doesn't exist. "The point is that I don't want her to know we're here. She can't know. Not just because it'll ruin the job, obviously, but because I don't know what she'd do to us if she did."

It's a convincing performance, Chloe will give her that. Her voice even wobbles at the end but unfortunately, Chloe has been psychologically conditioned to take everything Harper says with several enormous grains of salt. She has no problem believing Katherine Windey, *Forbes* list CEO and enviably fashionable millionaire, is just as petty and vindictive as her daughter. She stole Carlyle's award for the sole purpose of decorating her ballroom, but despite Harper's warning, Chloe can't wrap her head around the idea of her genuinely being dangerous.

"Honestly, Harper," she says, "your mother has the general bone structure of someone who started the Atkins Diet in third grade. I think I could take her."

A ghost of a smile flits across Harper's face. "That's what everyone thinks. They're usually wrong. You saw her trial back in January, right?"

Chloe hesitates, unsure how much snooping she's willing to reveal. She didn't pay much attention to the case when it was unfolding at the beginning of the year, but she also spent hours combing through Katherine's court documents last weekend, scouring the background of every video in a vain attempt to spot a glimpse of Harper. It really was a compelling case—a well-known local celebrity accused of embezzling investor funds and laundering money through her own hotels. Despite the array of evidence stacked against her, Katherine never once considered a plea deal. She took the case straight to trial and after three days of what the *Miami Herald* called "genuinely riveting questioning," the jury found her not guilty on all charges.

Even now, the general consensus still seems to be that she totally did it and—even more scandalous—she somehow got away with it.

"Yeah," Chloe says. "I heard about it."

Harper gives a halfhearted shrug. "Well, there you go."

It's not an answer, but something about her tone piques Chloe's interest. "You think she's guilty?"

"I think she's smart. I think there's a reason she's not in prison right now and I think she'll do anything to prove she still deserves to be here. Even if it means taking a random award from Carlyle's penthouse."

Chloe tips her head to the side, considering. Maybe Harper has a point. Katherine Windey spent the last several months hosting parties and attending city philanthropy events, throwing her money around in elaborate displays of wealth. It's like she's trying to rebuild her reputation, solidify herself back at the top of whatever corporate mountain she was scaling, and if the only thing standing in her way is Andrew Carlyle's rival hotel empire, Chloe can understand her desperation.

"So that's it?" Chloe asks. "You're afraid of her?"

Harper shakes her head. "We just . . . don't like each other."

"But *why*?"

"I don't know, Chloe. Why don't you like me?"

"Because you're a selfish, entitled bitch who's always in my way," Chloe says without hesitation.

Harper laughs, and some of the lingering tension dissolves. "Well, there you go," she says. "I don't think my mother ever wanted kids and she certainly didn't want me."

The vulnerability of the statement catches Chloe off guard. It reminds her of Harper's apology last week—so unexpected that it might actually be true. She mentally scrambles back through her Harper Rolodex, trying to remember the pieces she patched together last weekend. Her father's lucrative engineering career, her parents' seaside wedding in West Palm Beach, the years of Katherine deliberately showing up for events and parties alone, like the very idea of a family was beneath her.

"I don't get it," Chloe says. "If you don't want to see your mother, then why did you take this job? Why stay in the city at all? You could have moved to Ohio with your dad."

"Wow." Harper arches a brow. "You really did do your research. I'm flattered."

"That's not . . ." Chloe bites her lip, face heating at the implication. "I like to know who I'm working with."

"Of course."

But there's a small, satisfied smile tugging at the corner of

Harper's mouth. The sight of it leaves Chloe scrambling, sorting through the last several minutes in a futile attempt to figure out how she's once again managed to lose the upper hand.

"I already tried that, you know," Harper says. "I moved in with him the summer before college, but when I tried to come back the next year, he was already seeing someone. And then a few months later he was buying a house in the suburbs with a new wife and daughter. So it didn't really work out."

Maybe it's mean, but it takes every ounce of Chloe's rapidly waning self-control not to openly scoff. *That's it?* She knows what it's like to lose someone, to *really* lose them in a way that's impossible to reverse, and the idea that this marginally angsty backstory is some secret explanation for Harper's actions is laughable. Harper could pick up a phone and call both her parents right now, if she wanted to. She could buy a plane ticket and arrive on her father's doorstep by the end of the day but Chloe will always be fighting to remember the lilting cadence of her mother's laugh.

"No offense, Harper," she says, offense dripping from every syllable, "but I don't really care. If you can't handle being around your mom, you shouldn't have said yes to this job. You should have left it to me because I didn't come here to fuck around."

Harper's head snaps up, gaze cold and unyielding. "Neither did I."

"Then what are we doing?"

"You *don't—*" Harper shoots to her feet. "I'm trying to help you, Chloe. I'm telling you that my mother is unpredictable. You don't know her. *I* barely know her anymore and we can't risk her finding out why we're really here. If we're supposed to be a team, you need to trust me, too. That's it."

Trust. The word floats between them, half formed. Chloe doesn't trust Harper. She can't. The mere idea of it feels impossible but then again, the thought of them standing together and having this conversation would have felt impossible last week, too.

"I'm sorry," she says. "I don't. And I don't think we need to be friends for this to work."

Harper lets out a low laugh. "Don't flatter yourself. I don't want to be friends with you either. I'm just trying to finish this job."

"And you think you can finish it? Whatever it takes?"

Steel glints behind Harper's gaze, a quick flash of something solid and real. "Whatever it takes."

Outside, the sun burns hot and bright, outlining the carpet in liquid gold. The corner of Harper's mouth lifts a fraction of an inch and again, Chloe thinks it's strange for the two of them to be here together when the only thing she's wanted for the last year is to beat Harper at her own game. This conversation should have solidified her victory. She should have packed Harper's confessions and weaknesses away for safekeeping, but it's like they're linked somehow, bonded by something deeper than Carlyle's offer and Chloe can't figure out what it is.

She wants to, though. She wants to dig her fingers into the cracks of this hotel room and tear it apart, even if it's just to make Harper bleed.

"Okay." Chloe nods. "But if we're a team, that trust has to go both ways. We're all invested in this and we need to work together."

Harper shudders, like the mere thought of working with Chloe is enough to make her skin crawl, but she still extends a hand. "Fine. We're a team."

Chloe takes her hand, purposefully ignoring the cool brush of Harper's fingers against her own burning skin. "A team," she echoes, and shakes.

There's that flash again, the memory of standing on the other side of Carlyle's desk. She shook his hand just like this, pulled in by the same tantalizing promise of what could be waiting for her on the other side. The image vanishes as soon as Chloe lets go, but her own fingertips still prickle as she turns to leave.

Another deal, she thinks as she crosses the length of the suite and yanks open the door. *Another risk.*

She wonders how many more she'll take before the week is over.

ELEVEN

"Would it kill you to be a little less conspicuous?"

Chloe glowers into the shadowy hallway, suddenly glad no one can see her face over the mountain of tablecloths piled in her arms. "My bad," she mutters into her earpiece. "Next time you can come down here and do it yourself."

Priya heaves a dejected sigh. "I can't. I'm *famous,* remember?"

Another housekeeper rounds the corner before Chloe can remind Priya that her Instagram model alter ego doesn't actually exist. She snaps her mouth shut and presses her back against the wall, waiting for the other woman to maneuver her cart through the cramped corridor before releasing a sigh of relief. So far, no one's given her a second glance, but she doesn't know the other Rivera employees well enough to clock who might be a threat. She probably doesn't have long before someone in the laundry room notices a pile of freshly washed tablecloths is suddenly missing and she wants to be long gone before they do.

This morning, Chloe was fully prepared for Reed to lecture her about taking too long to deposit Harper's luggage, but when she finally made her way back to the lobby with Priya's flash drive curled in her fist, he barely seemed to notice. All it took was several minutes of apologizing where Chloe batted her eyelashes in her best impression of a lost baby deer who would never, under any circumstances, insert a Trojan horse into his concierge computer, before Reed lost interest and sent her downstairs to continue training.

After a year of working in the Carlyle kitchens, her first day in housekeeping was practically a vacation. Sure, there were rules and protocols she had absolutely no intention of learning, but at least there weren't any guests demanding her attention or requesting custom meal delivery. Her manager, a tired-looking woman named Kristen, spent approximately ninety seconds showing Chloe how to operate the rows of industrial-grade laundry machines in the basement before turning back to her own pile, oblivious to the way Chloe's gaze lingered on the ID and key cards clipped to her belt.

Apart from Reed, that seemed to be the general vibe—get in and get out. Mind your business and don't talk too much.

That was fine with Chloe. When it was time to clock out, she made a show of pretending to leave before ducking back into the laundry room, grabbing the stack of tablecloths, and slipping back into the employee stairwell.

Which is how she ended up here, letting Priya guide her toward the ballroom as she struggles to keep her grip on the pile. Very cool, normal behavior, in Chloe's opinion.

"Take that next left."

Priya's voice crackles through her earbud a second too late. Chloe skids to a halt and backtracks around the corner. "How much longer?" she mutters.

"Oh, it's not far," Priya says. "Three more turns."

"Three more turns" turns out to be four lefts and a right, quickly followed by the single steepest staircase Chloe has ever seen. She's sweating by the time she pushes her way into the corridor, arms aching around the tablecloths. "That," she gasps, "was *not* three turns."

"Sorry! Blueprints only show so much. You're fine."

That's easy for Priya to say. She's probably lounging in their hotel room right now, limbs sinking into a thick, fluffy duvet with her laptop propped on her stomach. Chloe grits her teeth and shakes her bangs out of her face. The sooner she's done here, the sooner she can join her.

The ballroom door is already cracked when she approaches, silver light streaming into the hallway. Chloe waits for someone inside to yank it the rest of the way open before calling, "Hold the door!" and shuffling forward as best she can. The employee on the other side steps back, just like she knew they would. They even help steady the tilting pile of tablecloths as she passes, too distracted by her uniform and her precarious grip to realize that every table is already draped with elegant folds of cream-colored cloth.

"Where am I going?" Chloe mutters as the door swings closed behind her.

"Table six. Over by the dolphin sculpture."

The table numbers from before are gone, replaced instead with tiny, intricately scripted name cards at each plate. Chloe turns in a circle, sparing a single glance toward the windowsill as she goes. Carlyle's award is still there, winking cheerily down at her. For a single, heart-pounding minute, she debates abandoning their whole plan and making a mad dash across the room. If it weren't for the employees still milling around, setting up for tomorrow's festivities as the security guards watch from the door, Chloe might try it. Instead, she tightens her grip and staggers toward the table Priya pointed out.

None of the other employees spare her a glance, too caught up in their own tasks to pay attention to Chloe's discomfort. *That's what looking confident and frazzled will do,* Chloe thinks as she approaches table six. *Act like you belong and people usually let you.* She lingers just long enough to find the hand-lettered name card she's looking for—Hunter Schroeder, the name on Logan's second-favorite fake ID. Then her toe catches on the edge of a chair and she falls to her knees.

Chloe's moving before she hits the ground. She rolls under the table and fumbles in her waistband for their printed replica of Carlyle's award. She took it from Harper's luggage this morning, purposefully ignoring the way the top was starting to lean ever so slightly to the left, and she can only hope Katherine will be too busy entertaining her guests to notice the tiny imperfections. Chloe digs two brand-new earpieces from one pocket and a roll of duct tape from the other. She tears off a strip with her teeth and clumsily secures everything to the underside of Logan's chair. *There.* All guests have to pass a three-step security clearance tomorrow night and even though Chloe's gotten into plenty of galas with her own trusty earpiece, it doesn't seem right to risk it now, especially with the printed award in tow. She adds another strip of tape for good measure before shoving the roll back into her pocket and dragging herself to her feet.

"Sorry," she says to no one in particular. "I didn't realize someone already brought the tablecloths. I'll take these back."

The few employees nearest to her nod, but hardly anyone looks up as Chloe gathers the fabric to her chest. As she straightens, her eye catches on Logan's name card again and this time, she can't help but notice the one next to it.

Harper Parisi.

It's fine, Chloe tells herself as she turns to go. It's all part of the plan. The sight of Logan's and Harper's names next to each other shouldn't give her anything to worry about and she's definitely not thinking about how it looks for all the world like they're a pair now. Like she's the odd one out.

And why wouldn't she be? Harper's whole thing is incredibly appealing. Her mother owns the literal island they're standing on and she conjures invitations to exclusive parties on demand. Chloe will never be able to replicate that kind of effortless success, no matter how hard she tries, and some small, bitter part of her wonders if her friends know that, too. If they're secretly glad Harper is here to do all the things Chloe can't.

"You good?" Priya asks.

The sound of her voice jolts Chloe back to reality. She swallows her resentment and turns to go. "Yeah," she mutters. "I'm just peachy."

The room Harper booked for Chloe, Priya, and Logan is only a few floors above the lobby. The others are already inside when Chloe arrives, digging through platters of room service charcuterie while Harper stands by the window, watching the scene unfold like she's allergic to fun. Compared to her room upstairs, this one is almost quaint—just a single king-sized bed, a desk, and a small couch facing a giant window that overlooks the sprawling pool and crystal-clear ocean below. It's not small by any means, but right now, every available surface is covered in fabric.

Jackets in alternating shades of black, navy, and maroon are slung across the desk, a pile of button-up shirts lies discarded on the floor, and there's a tangle of what look like bowties in the middle of the bed. Chloe takes a hesitant step forward, wondering if she missed some kind of memo. "What's this?"

Logan looks up at the sound of her voice. "Chloe!" he cries. "Look at this room. Look at this *cheese*! Can you believe people live like this?" He sighs into a handful of gouda. "I love you, sweet rich-person hotel. You're my everything."

Chloe grimaces as she steps around a pile of pleated slacks. "I'm actually more interested in the sample sale happening on your bed."

Logan shrugs helplessly. "Harper said if I wore the suit I brought to the gala, she would personally throw me into the sea."

Of course she did. They could have a dozen conversations about the importance of trust and teamwork and Harper would still find some way to tilt this week to her advantage.

"Sorry it's such a small selection," Harper says, one shoulder still braced casually against the wall. "It's all I could get delivered on such short notice."

"Right." Chloe tries not to think about how there are more

shirts in this room than in her closet back home. She glances at Logan. "You really didn't have other options?"

It's unheard of for Logan to show up unprepared when Chloe is pretty sure his roommates own the largest assortment of themed costumes outside of a Spirit Halloween. The amount of formal-wear stuffed in the closets of their tiny downtown apartment could probably put Harper's collection to shame, and Chloe regularly raids it for her own personal use. She once showed up to a black-tie event in a 1920s-inspired embroidered gown and not a single person knew it came from a costume set called "Great Depression Whore."

"I know," Logan says. "Weird, right? But apparently rich people don't wear clothes that come in resealable plastic bags. Look!" He grabs a handful of bowties from the mattress. "Real silk!"

Chloe is saved from answering by Priya poking her head out of the bathroom door, steamer in one hand and a half-empty cup of boba tea in the other. "Don't get him started on the silk, you'll be here all night." She leans a hip against the doorframe as she looks Chloe up and down. "Everything good downstairs?"

"Yup." Chloe nods, sinking onto the edge of the mattress. "Hunter Schroeder, Attorney at Law, is ready to go."

"You went with Schroeder?" Priya raises an eyebrow in Logan's direction. "I thought you hated being an attorney."

Logan shrugs. "He's not my favorite, but he always passes a background check. And I watched *Legally Blonde* last night, so I'm good to go."

Priya bites back a grin. "I'm good on my end, too. That concierge computer was perfect, Chloe. Did you have any trouble with the flash drive?"

Chloe shakes her head. "No. Why?"

"You were just a bit late. I wondered if your boss noticed you."

Chloe risks a glance at Harper. They both know why Chloe was late getting back downstairs. If she wanted the upper hand now, Chloe could tell the others all the secrets Harper spilled in her room. She could reveal just how much Harper's relationship with her mother affects her decisions, how there's probably no way for her to be completely objective with a job like this.

They could stop this constant back-and-forth and finally crown a winner.

"No." Chloe leans back on her elbows. "They had me running around so much I lost track of time. Won't happen again."

From the corner of her eye, she watches Harper's posture relax ever so slightly.

"Good," Logan says. "So we're all set for tomorrow?"

Priya's brow furrows as she picks up her computer. "I think so. You and Harper will arrive at the gala just before dinner. Your earpieces and the decoy award are under Logan's chair, so all you need to do is mingle until after dessert. It'll be too noticeable to have you both up and about during dinner, but there's a sweet spot right before the end of the night where everyone will be heading to the bar for one last drink before it closes."

"Before Katherine makes her speech," Logan says. "Got it."

"Exactly. She's supposed to talk about the tower expansion at the end of the night. It's the last thing on the schedule, so you have to make the switch while the bar is still open and people are walking around. You and Harper will make your way over to that corner, switch out the awards, and get the hell out of there before Katherine gets up to speak."

"And it won't be weird if we leave before the end of the night?"

Priya shakes her head. "Not if you're together. Just make it look like you're going off to bone."

Chloe grimaces at the thought. She knows the plan inside and out. She helped put it together but now that they're discussing it, she feels remarkably useless. Priya will be camped out in one of the beachside cabanas, guiding them through camera blind spots and navigating the party unseen. Harper and Logan will be enjoying a six-course dinner in a luxury ballroom and Chloe will be hovering pointlessly in the background as Harper slides into the role that usually belongs to her.

"Sounds good to me," Harper says. "It's been ages since I've attended a good party."

Priya's brow furrows as she turns back to her computer, like she's mentally running through a list of everything they still have to do. Chloe does the same, tucking her feet underneath her as she thinks. Their first day is coming to a close. They made it inside the Rivera and if they can make it through the next twenty-four hours, they'll be off this island for good. She can put up with Harper for another day, if she has to. She can grin and bear it through another pointless shift in the laundry room for five million dollars.

"Oh, one more thing, Harper." Priya glances over to where Harper still stands in the corner, watching the lights flicker on in the marina below. "Could you pull your mother for a conversation at some point after dinner? She'll probably be watching table twelve to see Carlyle's reaction and the last thing we need is for her to move the award or take it somewhere else before Logan can make the switch. If we can keep her occupied until her speech, we'll have a window."

Harper's expression doesn't change, but the line of her shoulders stiffens ever so slightly. "No."

"Seriously?" Priya looks up from her screen. "Why not?"

"Because I don't want to."

"Okay, my bad. I thought we were a team."

Chloe wonders if the others feel the temperature drop, too. The intensity of it drags over her skin, raising the hair on the back of her neck as Harper's smile turns frosty. "Is that your excuse for everything?" she asks. "I've done more for this job than all of you combined. I got us in here. I got us the invitations. You're standing in a hotel room I paid for and you still think I'm not contributing?"

"I didn't say that! I just don't get why it's such a big deal."

"You don't have to. It's none of your business."

The thing about grief, Chloe has learned, is that it's unpredictable. Sometimes, she'll go weeks without ever feeling its sting. Other days, the force of it knocks her to the ground. She still doesn't know how it works or why it's happening *here* of all places. But as she watches Priya and Harper glare at each other across the room, she's hit with the sudden, rib-crushing certainty that she'd do anything for the chance to talk with her own mother now.

Chloe closes her eyes as the familiar wave of nausea sweeps through her. This is how it's been hitting her recently, not the shortness of breath and panic attacks that had shadowed her last year, but in slow, churning ripples of unease. In the overwhelming urge to turn herself inside out. Vaguely, she's aware of Harper and Priya arguing, their voices bouncing off the ornate wallpaper. It's probably important, something to pay attention to, but Chloe doesn't care. She's drowning three stories above the shoreline and it's not until Logan slides a hand over her knee that Chloe remembers where she is. She blinks as the room comes back into focus and realizes she's shaking the bed, foot jumping up and down of its own accord against the carpet. She forces herself to still as Logan's grip tightens and she swallows over the slick coat of bile in her throat.

I'm fine, she thinks as she pats his hand in return. *It's just the usual.*

He'll understand. He's helped her through worse than this. Chloe clears her throat again and looks up in time to watch Priya throw back her head and groan, "That's not what I *meant.* You're being unreasonable."

"I know exactly what you meant." Harper pushes herself off the wall. "I'll be there tomorrow. We'll take the award and get the hell out of here, but I'm not having a conversation with my mother. That's not part of the plan."

Priya opens her mouth, but Harper doesn't wait to hear her response. Instead, she turns on her heel and storms out the door. Chloe winces as it slams into place behind her. The last thing they need is to draw attention to their room, and Harper's anger is starting to feel like a very strong, very destructive magnet for trouble.

"Nice." Logan releases Chloe's knee and turns back to his charcuterie. "That went well, I think."

Priya shoots him a frustrated glare. "Don't start. You know I had to ask."

Chloe exhales as the three of them fall into uneasy silence. The nausea from before is gone, replaced by a dull ache in the center of her chest. She tries to ignore it, running through the intricacies of their plan instead. This one is less complicated than half the jobs they've pulled in the last year. Everything should be fine, but Chloe knows with absolute certainty that if she has to lurk in the employee stairwells tomorrow while Harper and Logan parade around the ballroom, she's going to scream.

"I need to be there."

She doesn't realize she's spoken out loud until Priya looks up. "What?"

"I need to be at the gala," Chloe says. "Like, inside the ballroom. In case Logan needs backup."

Priya hesitates, nails tapping against the outside of her computer. "I wish you could be, but I don't see how. We can't get another invitation."

"Then I'll work catering," Chloe says. "That's the whole reason I took this fake job, right? So I could help? What's the point if I'm not even in the ballroom?"

"But you don't work catering," Logan points out. "You're in housekeeping and I don't think they'll let you staff Katherine Windey's gala on your second day. How are you supposed to get in?"

Chloe stands, making her way forward to peer out the window. Night is falling over the horizon, painting the sea a velvet shade of black. If she squints, she can just make out the corner of the hotel marina and the heavily guarded collection of yachts worth more than she'll ever make in her life. So much money just sitting there, waiting for someone to take it. So much wealth in the hands of people who've never cared about anyone but themselves. Chloe closes her eyes and imagines her fist wrapped around Carlyle's missing award. For a minute, the ache in her chest disappears, dulled by the promise of tomorrow's prize.

How are you supposed to get in?

Logan's question echoes between them as Chloe turns from the window. She meets his gaze across the room and nods once. "Why don't you leave that to me?"

TWELVE

By the time Chloe finishes her second shift at the Rivera, she's learned three things: to always trust the kitchen staff when they say something's worth tasting, to ignore the times Reed inexplicably locks himself in his office (it's clearly to do cocaine), and to never, under any circumstances, let anything happen to her uniform.

Even though they're in the basement for most of their shift, out of sight and folding laundry, the housekeeping staff are still required to wear the same uncomfortably stiff plaid skirt and pressed ivory blouse as the other employees. Chloe thinks the combination is more Britney Spears Music Video than luxury hotel employee, but god forbid it get wrinkled. Reed continually sends people back to the employee locker room for everything from scuff marks to pit stains and the rules for working one of Katherine Windey's galas are stricter still.

Chloe ducked into the kitchen this morning in time to catch the tail end of Reed's speech on the night's festivities. His list of designated gala employees appears to be random, but the Rivera is still so understaffed from Priya's cyberattack that Chloe suspects it's basically any kitchen staff they can spare. By the time she clocks out in the evening, most of the assigned employees have made their way to the locker room to get ready. Chloe follows, mentally running through the list as she goes.

Caroline, Mariah, Jaime, Asabea, Adeline, Olu.

Reed was very clear about how important it is for them to be punctual tonight but sure enough, Adeline is running late. Just like she was this morning.

Just like Chloe is counting on now.

The other employees are crowded in front of the single foggy mirror, too occupied with fixing their hair and steaming their uniforms to notice Chloe slip around the corner. Adeline's locker is in the second aisle, three spaces from the end. A glittery pink padlock holds it shut, and Chloe bites back a grin as she tugs a pin from her hair. *Nice try.*

The door swings open with a soft click. She glances over her shoulder to make sure no one's noticed the sound, then grabs Adeline's uniform from the bottom of the locker, relocks the door, and dumps everything down the laundry chute.

Good luck getting into the ballroom now.

Chloe has barely returned to her own locker when the door bursts open.

"Sorry," Adeline gasps. "I swear that ferry never leaves on time. Has Reed been down yet?"

She heaves a relieved sigh when the others shake their heads. Chloe holds her breath, listening to her fumble with the padlock, and right when she's beginning to wonder if she robbed the wrong locker, Adeline pokes her head around the corner.

"Has anyone seen my uniform?"

A few of the other employees glance up. Chloe purposefully busies herself with arranging and rearranging the single pair of shoes in her locker.

"Seriously?" Adeline asks when no one moves. "Did someone clean in here last night? My uniform's gone."

She starts storming up and down the aisles, crouching to search under the benches. As quietly as she can, Chloe slicks on a fresh coat of hairspray and reapplies her mascara. *There.* She's presentable. She's professional. She's ready to save tonight's gala from the brink of total disaster.

She's just zipped everything back into her bag when the locker room door flies open again. "Ready to go?" Reed asks, one hand braced against the doorframe. "We're needed upstairs in . . ." He trails off when he catches sight of Adeline still in her street clothes. "What are you *doing*? We're supposed to be there in five."

"I know!" Adeline turns in another hopeless circle. "My uniform is gone."

Reed's mustache twitches in clear frustration. "Well, it didn't just walk away."

"But I left it here last night! Don't we have extras somewhere?"

Reed glances toward the communal shelf, where earlier this morning crisply folded blouses and skirts sat in neat piles. Now, it's empty. He shakes his head. "Housekeeping must have taken them down to wash."

Yes, Chloe thinks, *housekeeping must have.*

Adeline throws a helpless glance at her co-workers but it's too late. Reed's frustration is evident as he rubs a hand across his slowly reddening forehead. "I don't have time for this. We're understaffed as it is and I need everyone who can work tonight in uniform. Can you do that, Adeline?"

She very obviously can't. From around the corner, Chloe watches her face fall. She gives herself one more second before slinging her bag over her shoulder and walking out into the open. "Oh!" She stops when she sees the others. "Sorry. I didn't mean to interrupt."

Reed gives her a quick once-over, beady eyes narrowing on her freshly pressed uniform. "What are you still doing here, Ms. Bly?"

"Just calling my dad." Chloe makes a show of sliding her phone back into her pocket. "Sorry, I know it's late. But I'm on my way out."

She steps around Adeline and makes it halfway to the door before Reed holds up a hand. "Have you worked parties before?"

Chloe hesitates for what she hopes is an appropriate amount of time. "My last job was in catering?"

"Thank god." Reed's fingers close over her shoulder. "You're working tonight."

"But—"

"All you need to do is hold a tray and look pretty. Please tell me you can do that, at least?"

Chloe clamps her mouth shut and nods as Reed motions everyone forward. Of course she can do that. That's the whole reason she's here. As they step into the bustling hallway, Chloe has just enough time to reach up and tap the speaker lodged in her ear before the door swings shut behind them.

DURING HER FIRST month at the Carlyle, Chloe worked an album release party for some reality show DJ. She didn't know his music. She hadn't even known his name, but whenever she glimpsed him in the hallway, one of her co-workers would dig her fingers into Chloe's arm and whisper *that's him!* with the kind of awestruck reverence usually reserved for church.

Chloe never really got the appeal. He was just another skinny, average-looking white guy with nice hair and too many shoes, but there had also been a *vibe.* A way he moved through the halls that suggested he was used to people watching him and that he welcomed the attention. She went home that night with the distinct impression that she was missing something, and that's exactly how she feels now, stepping into the Rivera ballroom to find the gala already in full swing. Like she should definitely know the people milling around her and they all definitely expect her to know them.

The protective tarps and lingering piles of construction dust are long gone. Now, the ballroom glows with silvery light from dozens of glittering chandeliers, illuminating the rows of tightly packed tables and well-dressed guests. Chloe recognizes a few influencers Priya follows milling around the open bar, a man in a sharply pressed navy suit who might be the mayor, and a group of fortysomething women who are way too beautiful to have normal jobs. She's just craning her neck for a glimpse of Logan or Harper when Reed ushers her into a dimly lit hallway lined with catering carts.

"Here." He shoves a tray of frothy pink cocktails in Chloe's direction. "Just stay in the back and don't speak to anyone. The last thing I need is people finding out it's your second day. And try to look like you want to be here, okay? It wouldn't kill you to smile."

Chloe takes the tray and forces her widest, most simpering grin as she imagines dumping the contents over Reed's head. "Better?"

He grimaces. "No, actually. That's worse. How is that worse?"

"What can I say?" Chloe mutters as she ducks under his outstretched arm. "It's a talent."

When she enters the ballroom a second time, it's not the guests or the décor or the stunning view of the sunset she notices. Instead, it's the familiar anticipation coiling in the pit of her stomach. Because she's been here before. She's done this exact thing dozens of times at dozens of parties and tonight is no different. The stakes might be higher, yes, but the end result, Chloe's learned, is usually the same. All she needs is an opening, a chance, and a handful of vapid, unsuspecting marks too rich to realize they're being played until she already has a hand in their pocket.

"How's everyone doing?"

Priya's voice is too loud in her ear. Chloe resists the urge to reach up and turn the volume of her speaker down. "Ready," she says.

"About time," Harper mutters from somewhere across the ballroom. "What took you so long?"

Chloe glowers into the crowd. "I was hooking up with Reed in the bathroom."

"Really?"

"No, Harper! I was scamming my way into an exclusive gala in the world's most poorly designed hotel; sorry it took me a minute."

"Ladies," Priya says, voice frustratingly calm. "Not to make this about me, but I didn't get to scam my way into anything. You're all attending a very fancy party without me and I'm pretty sure

Pitbull is at table four, so can we please respect my privacy during this trying time? You just need to cooperate for, like, three more hours."

Chloe resists the urge to roll her eyes. Priya had finally hacked her way into the new set of cameras when they came online this morning. It wasn't easy work by any means, but Chloe knows for a fact that she's currently sprawled across a plush linen lounge chair, monitoring their progress from the privacy of a cabana on the south beach. There's probably a collection of frosty, coconut-flavored drinks on the table next to her and a selection of Peter Pan erotica bookmarked at her side. She's not exactly suffering.

"Sorry, Pri. I'm ready."

"We are, too," Logan says. "Any updates?"

There's a moment of silence as Priya clicks through something on her computer. "Not much," she says eventually. "We're still on track for dinner to start in ten and it looks like Katherine is currently at table three."

"Brooch or no brooch?"

"No brooch, unfortunately."

"Damn." Logan exhales a long, dramatic sigh. "My white whale remains."

"What brooch?" Harper asks.

Chloe pictures the two of them sitting side by side at their table, heads pressed together so no one else notices their strange, one-sided conversation. She clenches her jaw and mutters, "That bumblebee piece she wore to the Rivera opening."

"One day, Chloe," Logan says, "I'm going to get you to do a jewelry heist."

Harper snorts. "That piece is hideous."

"Trust me, we know," Priya says. "Also, Carlyle just arrived a few minutes ago. He's at his table now and, in case you were wondering, that's definitely Pitbull at four."

Chloe cranes her neck over the sea of guests. She can't find Katherine Windey or Pitbull in the crowd, but she immediately spots Carlyle, sitting at the corner table with his wife at his side.

Judging by the relaxed, confident way he's lounging in his chair, Chloe doesn't think he's seen the stolen award sitting on the windowsill just over his shoulder.

"Let's avoid him if we can," she says. "I don't want to make this more complicated."

Right now, Carlyle still thinks she and Harper are working alone. He doesn't know about Priya or Logan, and Chloe wants to keep it that way.

"Agreed," Priya says. "Let's stick to the plan and get out of here. I'll check back in an hour. Try not to do anything stupid before then."

The static in Chloe's ear softens as Priya falls silent. *One more hour.* They just have to make it through dinner. Chloe imagines gathering at the cabana tonight, holding the award in her hands and knowing this could be the last job they ever pull, the last time she wonders how she's going to make it to her next paycheck.

There's a flash of movement to her left and Chloe turns in time to watch Logan rise from a table toward the front. She didn't notice him before and, as she tracks his path toward the bar, Chloe thinks she knows why. With his sharp black suit and crisp bowtie, he's indistinguishable from the other guests—distant and reserved and richer than anyone knows what to do with. The sight of it twists her stomach. She still can't see Harper through the crowd, but Chloe has a sneaking suspicion the two of them make a striking pair. They have to. Harper wouldn't have brought him to the Rivera terrace that day if she didn't think they'd be impressive, and she wouldn't have brought him here if people weren't talking about it now. It was part of her plan even then and Chloe can't shake the feeling that Harper Parisi has secretly been several steps ahead of them this entire time.

She turns away from the tables, pacing the perimeter of the ballroom in a vain attempt to clear her head. It's uncomfortably warm here and the longer Chloe walks, the more her muscles wind taut beneath her skin. She avoids the corner where Carlyle's award still glimmers from the windowsill, focusing instead on the strange collection of abstract art. A rising ocean wave, a blooming rose, something that looks like a young Leonardo DiCaprio, for some reason.

Chloe does a double take at that, certain she's seeing things, but when she glances over her shoulder, there it is—the abstract bust of swoopy-haired Leo staring down at her like a weird, surrealist corpse. She makes a mental note to ask Priya to find out who commissioned that particular piece.

"Are you just going to stand there or can I get a sangria?"

The voice is familiar, but Chloe's pulse still leaps at the sudden question. She risks a glance to her right and when she finds Harper standing a few feet away, the rattling thrum in her veins turns molten and sharp.

"Is that what this is?" she asks, glancing down at her tray with purposeful nonchalance. "I've been telling everyone it's very fancy juice. Reed will be livid."

To her surprise, Harper lets out a low laugh. She's swirling a cocktail pick around the edge of her empty glass, hair pulled back in a sleek bun that accentuates the sharp line of her jaw. Combined with her tailored silver dress and signature red lip, she looks more like the person Chloe's been resenting all year—wealthy, aloof, and completely out of her league. The look brings out the biting green of her eyes too, and Chloe remembers too late that they aren't supposed to know each other. She turns back to the party, ready to end this conversation, and finds that the crowd has shifted. From her position against the wall, she has a clear view of the ballroom for the first time all night. Straight over to table three, where Katherine Windey is grabbing another flute of champagne.

Chloe still can't believe she's never noticed the resemblance. How many times has she passed Katherine at parties just like this? How often has she watched Harper from across a room, committing every detail of her face to memory? Now that they're both here, the similarities are impossible to miss. They have the same blond hair, sharp chins, and full lips, but there's something else that extends beyond the physical. Chloe sees echoes of Harper in the way Katherine talks with her hands, how she leans into the conversation like she fully believes herself to be the center of everyone's world.

"You're staring."

Chloe tears her attention from Katherine's table as Harper leans a shoulder into the wall. "Sorry."

"It's fine. Most people stare when we're together."

"Probably because it doesn't happen often," Chloe says. "You're never in the same pictures."

"And exactly how many pictures of me have you seen?"

Harper's chin tilts in her direction and even though Chloe doesn't return her gaze, she still feels the pressure of it slide along the curve of her neck. She swallows, mouth uncomfortably dry. "Enough to know you wore that dress to your cousin's wedding last month."

Harper laughs again, a real, genuine laugh that shivers down Chloe's spine. It's the kind of sound she didn't think Harper could make, the kind that leaves her wondering if something about this is an act, too. Then, before Chloe can think of a response, Harper's smile drops completely.

"Do you have any champagne?"

"I . . ." Chloe blinks, taken aback by the sudden snap of her voice. "What?"

"*Champagne,* Chloe. Go get me champagne."

Harper shoots off the wall and slams her glass onto Chloe's tray with so much force the whole thing almost topples to the floor. Chloe stumbles, mouth dropping open, but Harper's no longer looking at her. Instead, she's glaring across the ballroom, to where Katherine is now staring directly back at them.

Shit. Chloe backs into the wall. Did Katherine see them talking? It would be one thing for her to wonder about Harper's last-minute invitation. Those kinds of questions would be expected, but it would be quite another for her to catch her daughter talking too closely with some random caterer.

"Go," Harper says and this time, there's an edge in her voice Chloe doesn't recognize. "Get out of here."

Static crackles in her ear as Priya draws in a breath. "What's going on?"

Chloe doesn't answer. She just reaches up and switches her earpiece off, fumbling with her tray as Katherine pushes herself to her feet. There's an instant where the crowd swells between them, where Chloe feels the press of an oncoming storm without the luxury of knowing when it will break. She turns away just in time, busying herself with a nearby catering cart as Katherine comes to a stop a few feet from where Chloe was standing seconds ago.

"What are you doing here?"

The question is clearly aimed at Harper. Chloe keeps her gaze fixed straight ahead, repeatedly loading and unloading her tray as Harper releases a long sigh.

"Hello, Mother."

"Don't do that." Katherine's voice is cool, a frosty echo of her daughter's. "You can't return my calls, but you can come to my party?"

"What can I say? There's something about a gala that really speaks to me."

If Chloe tilts her head, she can just make out Katherine's reflection in the glass wall to their left. She grabs Harper's wrist, yanking her around so they're both facing away from the crowd. "Why are you here?"

Harper shrugs, her face the picture of bored disinterest. "Why do you care?"

"*Because,* Harper. This is a very big night for me, and I don't have time to worry about you making bad choices in front of my guests."

"Oh my god." Harper barks out a laugh. "You have absolutely no right to lecture me about bad choices. I'm not here for you."

Katherine's grip tightens ever so slightly. "I know exactly what you're here for."

Chloe's body stiffens at the low accusation in her voice. *What does she think Harper's here for?* There's no way Katherine could know about their plan or suspect they're here on Carlyle's request, but something about the way her knuckles whiten around Harper's wrist makes Chloe think she's missing something. Harper's face tightens as her mother's nails dig into her skin. Her next inhale catches on a gasp of pain and Chloe moves without thinking, whirling to face them with her tray outstretched.

"Can I offer you a drink?"

The two of them pull apart, Katherine's hand immediately dropping back to her side. As soon as her mother releases her, Harper turns on her heel and stalks back into the crowd without so much as a glance in Chloe's direction, leaving her with nothing but a tray of very expensive sangria for protection. *So much for backup.*

Katherine, however, makes no move to follow. Her gaze sweeps from Chloe's face down to her freshly shined shoes. Her smile is still carved into place, but when she tilts her head and asks, "What's your name?," there's not an ounce of warmth in her voice.

Chloe takes a hesitant step back. She's pretty sure Katherine Windey can smell weakness. She's probably listening to the frantic beat of Chloe's heart right now and it's all she can do to remember the fake name pinned to the front of her uniform. "Stassi?" It comes out sounding like a question.

"Stassi," Katherine repeats. "And you're new here."

Chloe hesitates, trying to guess where this conversation is going. She's never doubted her ability to talk herself out of impossible situations, but her brain is currently short-circuiting, leaving her stuck somewhere between the wall at her back and Katherine's frosty glare.

"I . . . yes. It's my first week."

"Thought so." Katherine plucks a glass of sangria from her tray. "Word of advice, Stassi. If you want to succeed here, you can start by keeping your nose out of other people's business."

She's going to kill me, Chloe thinks. *She's going to toss my body in the ocean.*

Outwardly, she nods, trusty customer service smile still firmly in place even as her mind screams at her to run. "Of course."

"Good." Katherine drains the contents of her drink before setting it back on Chloe's tray. "Have a good night."

When she turns back to the party, it's like the air in the room vanishes with her. It takes everything in Chloe's power not to slump against the wall as she watches Katherine thread her way back through the crowd. *So much for getting in and out unnoticed.*

She's not afraid of Harper anymore. She's not even afraid of Andrew Carlyle, but as Chloe stares at the lipstick mark imprinted around the rim of the empty glass, she thinks she might be a little bit afraid of Katherine Windey.

THIRTEEN

If it weren't for the thought of five million dollars waiting for her tomorrow morning, Chloe might spend the rest of the night hiding in the kitchen, counting down the hours until she can leave this island for good. She's already facing the wrath of one millionaire. She doesn't want to provoke another. But when Reed snatches her tray of sangria and pushes her back into the ballroom with a heaping tower of entrées, it becomes clear she doesn't have a choice. Besides, Chloe reminds herself as she deposits plate after steaming plate onto the tables before her, she's come too far to give up now.

She circles the ballroom as dinner drags on, keeping one eye on table six, where Logan is doing an excellent job of pretending to know how to use the three different dinner forks, and the other on Katherine Windey.

Rationally, Chloe knows she's safe. She's standing in the middle of a very expensive ballroom surrounded by very rich, very important people. Sure, none of them are particularly invested in her wellbeing, but they *are* witnesses. It's not like Katherine could get away with murdering her in public.

She probably could, though, Chloe thinks as she collects another round of empty glasses from a nearby table. *She's gotten away with things before. She could throw you out of here right now and she'd probably like it.*

Chloe used to think rich people were predictable—simple, mindless marks too self-absorbed to think of themselves as targets—but every aspect of tonight unsettles her. Because sometimes rich people steal each other's hotel awards to prove a point. Sometimes, they're willing to pay five million dollars for someone else to get theirs back. Sometimes they build a glass hotel in the middle of the ocean just because they can. Every time she glimpses Katherine in the crowd, Chloe tries to imagine her swiping Carlyle's award from his office, tucking it in her purse, and carrying it all the way back to the Rivera to display at this specific party. It's so pointless, so incredibly irritating, and, Chloe thinks, it's exactly the kind of thing she'd do to Harper.

Logan's still at his table when Chloe circles back to collect the empty plates. He's deep in conversation with the woman to his left, one arm resting casually in his lap to hide the outline of the decoy award already tucked in his pocket. His shoulders are relaxed, voice natural as he laughs at something the woman says, but he scratches at his nose when Chloe passes. To anyone else, the movement would probably go unnoticed, but Chloe recognizes the signal immediately. *There's a problem.* When Chloe's gaze falls on the empty seat beside him, she immediately knows what it is.

Logan might be ready to go, waiting for Priya's signal to move toward the award, but Harper is nowhere to be seen.

Chloe dips her chin in response and lets her gaze drift around the ballroom. *Where the hell is she?* They don't have long until Katherine's speech. The kitchen staff is already prepping the ballroom for dessert, and if Priya's predictions are correct, their window to move through the crowd unnoticed is rapidly approaching. Logan might be the one making the actual switch, but Harper is his excuse to leave, the one who's supposed to drape herself over his arm and hide the outline of the stolen award from view.

Chloe's about to duck into the kitchen and ask Priya to track Harper down herself when a flash of silver catches her eye. She turns, squinting through the crowd, and—there! Harper is standing alone on the terrace, her back to the doors as she stares across the darkening sea. It's a striking image—the moonlight painting her in the same silver glow as her mother's collection of glass sculptures—but it's somewhat marred by the fact that Chloe knows Harper isn't supposed to be out there at all.

Of course she's not, Chloe thinks as she deposits her pile of dirty dishes onto a nearby catering cart. When is Harper ever where she's supposed to be? If Chloe wants something done, she obviously has to do it herself.

She glances over her shoulder, checking to make sure the other waitstaff are busy with their own tables before fading into the crowd. Reed is too preoccupied with his tablet to notice Chloe pass, but she doesn't breathe normally until she slips through the balcony doors and onto the terrace. The change in temperature is immediate. Chloe can practically feel her hair frizzing in the humidity, straining against the hairspray she applied earlier. She closes the door behind her, but Harper doesn't look up when it swings shut or when Chloe's footsteps crunch on the stone walkway. Instead, she remains at the balcony, one hand rubbing absentmindedly at her wrist where a ring of crescent-shaped marks is still imprinted against her skin.

Chloe opens her mouth, fully intending to ask what, exactly, Harper thinks she's doing out here. Instead, what comes out is, "Are you okay?"

Harper whirls at the sound of her voice, and Chloe thinks she catches a flash of genuine surprise before her expression hardens back into its usual haughty arrogance. She sinks back against the balcony, but when she speaks again, her words don't have their usual bite.

"Mind your own business, Chloe."

If they were anywhere else, Chloe might push. She might point out the strained, white-knuckled way Harper is currently gripping her wineglass or note the current of uncertainty in her voice, just to see if she'd break. She might revel in the power of it. Instead, she mirrors Harper's posture, leaning back until both elbows are braced against the balcony behind her.

"It's almost time. Don't you have a hot date to get back to?"

The corner of Harper's mouth lifts in the ghost of a smile. "Jealousy has never been a good look for you."

"I'm not *jealous*. I'm just making sure you're still in this."

Harper's teeth slide across her bottom lip. It's like she's physically biting back a response and for once, Chloe wishes she wouldn't. She wishes they would just throw everything into the open tonight instead of continuing to drift through this strange limbo. Sometimes allies. Almost equals. Harper closed off and guarded while Chloe tries not to cut herself on the idea of her.

She's still waiting for a response when she feels Harper stiffen. Her eyes narrow on something inside the ballroom and when Chloe follows her gaze, she finds Katherine weaving between the tables, hand outstretched as she greets her guests one by one. For a terrifying second, Chloe thinks this is it. Katherine's seen them again and this time, there's nothing to stop her from throwing them both into the ocean. But when she moves past the balcony doors, the humidity-fogged glass warping her image, Chloe almost believes her smile is genuine. Everyone else seems to think so, anyway.

The crowd practically parts around her and Chloe can't help but wonder if Katherine's making the rounds because she enjoys it or because she feels the need to prove that, despite everyone's best efforts, she's still here.

She only falters once, when Carlyle crosses her path on his way to the bar. If Chloe didn't know their strange, twisted history, she might have missed it. Carlyle's chin dips as he leans down to whisper something in Katherine's ear. She tries to wave him off, but he grabs her arm, pulling her back to him for a heartbeat too long to be casual. It's only a second, a quick, mirror-image flash of her own interaction with Harper and then it's gone. Katherine yanks herself free, Carlyle fades back into the crowd, and Chloe blinks as the swell of the party swallows them both once more.

Interesting. Chloe tucks the interaction away for later, another piece of this job to unpack when this is over.

Next to her, Harper drains the rest of her wine in a single, vicious gulp. She drags the back of her hand over her mouth and then, without warning, slams her empty glass back onto the railing and pushes herself up. She flings open the ballroom door, the motion sudden enough to make several heads turn in her direction, but Harper doesn't seem to care. She strides into the crowd, past the table where Logan still waits, and straight toward the exit.

Chloe swears under her breath, scrambling to follow as the balcony door starts to swing closed. She doesn't know where Harper's going or what set her off, but the anger billowing in her wake is impossible to miss. She's a beacon in a sea of careless wealth, a hurricane on an otherwise peaceful shore. She might as well stand up and announce their intentions to the entire ballroom. They can't have much longer before the bar closes and they lose their cover. Logan is counting on Harper to help him switch the awards and she's currently fleeing into the hallway of the Rivera.

Fucking hell, Chloe thinks as she slips through the doors after her. Tonight might go down in history as the day she finally snaps Harper Parisi's pretty little neck.

By the time she spills into the hallway, she's out of breath and Harper is already several yards ahead of her. "Hey!" she calls. "Where are you going?"

Harper doesn't answer. Instead, she quickens her pace, leaving Chloe stumbling in her wake as they round a sharp corner. How Harper manages to move this fast in heels is a mystery Chloe will never understand. She bites back a frustrated curse and tries again.

"I don't know if you've forgotten, Harper, but we have a job to do. You're supposed to be with Logan right now. And I need to be helping the others with dessert. If I'm not there, Reed will—"

"Oh my god." Harper lets out an exasperated groan. "Are you

seriously worried about Reed? He's probably doing a line in the freezer as we speak."

"I . . ." Chloe blinks. "Wait, how do you know he's doing cocaine?"

"First of all, no one says 'doing cocaine.' And secondly, everyone who works at this hotel is clearly high all the time."

"I'm not."

"Congratulations. Do you want a trophy?"

"No, I'm—"

"Enough, Chloe!" Harper rounds on her so abruptly Chloe almost trips into the wall. "Can I have, like, *one* minute where you're not hovering over my shoulder?"

Chloe really *is* going to kill her. Her hands curl into fists, nails biting into the damp skin of her palms. She has no idea why they're back here—throwing insults and jabs by whatever means necessary, dancing on the edge of a blade until one of them slips. It's like something flipped in Harper halfway through the evening, some invisible switch Chloe's never been able to locate, and she cannot believe they're having this conversation now, when their five-million-dollar prize is sitting just yards away.

"No," she snaps. "You can't. Not tonight."

A muscle feathers in Harper's jaw. "I'm not asking for the night off. Just give me a second."

"Can you not—I don't know"—Chloe pretends to check the time on her nonexistent watch—"wait *one* more hour until all this is over? You think the rest of us want to be here? You think we don't have shit to deal with? You're not special, Harper."

"Fuck you." Harper's face is flushed, color spilling down the long column of her throat. "You don't know anything about me."

She's always been taller, especially in formalwear, but against Chloe's flat, no-slip kitchen shoes, the difference is drastic. Chloe has to tip her head back to maintain eye contact as the two of them finally fall quiet. Harper's eyes are bright with a wild, almost feral gleam. It reminds Chloe of the time Harper slapped her, of the split-second crack in her otherwise impenetrable façade.

For a single heartbeat, Chloe wants nothing more than to shatter it completely, to dig her nails into the seams of Harper's armor and *pull.* "What is this?" she asks, lowering her voice even as the faint sounds of the party swell behind them. "What's going on?"

Harper shakes her head, lip curling in clear disdain. "Leave me alone, Chloe."

She turns to go, but her heel catches in the hem of her gown. She stumbles, hand flattening against the wall for balance, and the realization hits Chloe at once. "Are you . . . drunk?" she asks.

"What? No, of course not."

But it all makes sense now. Harper's recklessness, her mood swings, the careless way she dashed from the ballroom. Chloe grinds her teeth together, jaw aching from the sudden pressure. She can't believe she almost cared. She was actually concerned for Harper's wellbeing, momentarily worried enough to follow her into the hall, and *this* was the reason?

"Oh my god," she mutters. "You are."

Harper folds her arms, a defensive echo of her usual posture. She must decide there's no point arguing further because she gives a small halfhearted shrug. "Well, it *is* a party."

"Are you serious?" Chloe cannot believe they're having this conversation. "We're not here for the party! We're *working,* Harper. We're a team. We talked about this!"

Harper's head tips to the side, gaze sliding ever so slightly out of focus. "I suppose we did."

This time, Chloe does nothing to hide her growing frustration. She lets out a strangled curse, nails pricking into her palms as she imagines sinking them into Harper's exposed throat. "I knew it," she mutters. "I knew we couldn't work together."

"Please. You wouldn't have made it this far without me."

"Bullshit!" Chloe rounds on her, momentarily surprised by the ferocity in her own voice. "We would have figured it out! I know this doesn't matter to you, but the rest of us have people to take care of. We're not here for fun."

Harper's gaze hardens and for a second, she looks like herself. "Neither am I."

"Then fucking act like it! You don't get to lecture me about how dangerous your mom is and then do . . . *this.*" Chloe waves a hand vaguely behind her. "God, Harper, this is why everyone hates you!"

Harper's eyes widen, crimson lips parting as she sucks in a surprised little breath. It would be nice, Chloe thinks, if she could actually enjoy the satisfaction of this moment, if it wasn't ruined by the anger smoldering beneath her skin. She's just opened her mouth to unleash a year of pointed, pent-up insults when a familiar voice drifts around the corner.

"Just use the dinner trays I—no, it's fine. I'll be right back. Just make it work."

Whatever Chloe was about to say dies in her throat. That's Reed's voice coming toward them down the hall. The realization settles in the pit of her stomach, snuffing out the fury that was roiling there just seconds ago. She glances over her shoulder, already formulating an escape plan and realizes, with a jolt of horror, that there's nowhere to hide. This section of the hallway is remarkably bare and the next corner she could theoretically duck behind feels miles away. Too far to make a run for it. *Shit.*

Chloe whips around, panic lacing her veins with ice. She has no excuse for being out here in the middle of her shift. Stassi—her bumbling, earnest alter ego—isn't supposed to know Harper. The two of them don't have a plausible reason for being alone together and it'll take Reed half a second to realize that, too.

Harper must be thinking the same thing because she grabs Chloe's arm. "Don't run," she says. "That'll look worse."

Chloe's pulse hammers with every approaching footstep. "Do you have a better idea?"

She certainly doesn't. Her next plan involves throwing herself out the window and hoping for the best, but Harper's jaw is set in steely determination. Her eyes are too wide, the color of the glassy sea outside, and for a single, terrifying second, Chloe feels like she's drowning.

"Do you trust me?" Harper asks.

"What? No!"

"Oh my god, Chloe. Get over yourself."

Harper's fingers tighten around her shoulders. Her thumb skims over Chloe's collarbone and then, right as Chloe forgets how to breathe, Harper slides her other hand around the back of Chloe's neck and kisses her.

Rationally, Chloe knows there are a lot of things she could be thinking in the second before Harper's lips crash into hers, but when Harper tips her head to the side, mouth opening into the kiss, the only word running through Chloe's mind is *finally.*

Harper tastes like wine and salt and raw, unbridled desperation. Her hands are cold, a shock when every part of Chloe feels like it's burning alive, but when she tightens her grip and pushes Chloe against the wall, Chloe decides she doesn't care. She stopped being able to decipher pain from pleasure a long time ago. With Harper, it feels the same. There's a strange, molten pressure in the pit of her stomach and when Harper's hand slides over her hip, Chloe can't help the rough sigh that tears from her throat.

Here it is, she thinks. Here's something about them that finally makes sense.

"What the hell is this?"

Chloe jumps. There's a solid *thunk* as her skull connects with the wall and then Harper is shoving her away. Chloe stumbles at the sudden loss of balance. She bites back a wince of pain, and when she finally looks up, Reed's face is inches from hers.

"Reed!" Harper's eyes widen. She presses a trembling hand to her own flushed face, gaze darting from Chloe to Reed to the empty fork at the end of the hall. "Hi. We were just . . . this isn't . . . we didn't think . . ."

She trails off, but her appropriately flustered performance does nothing to soften the furious set of Reed's jaw. When he speaks again, Chloe gets the impression he's trying very hard not to lose what little composure he has left. "This is a restricted area, Ms. Parisi, even for you. I'm afraid I have to ask you to rejoin the party."

Harper inhales, lips parting as if to protest. Chloe knows she's staring. How can she not? She's spent the last year watching Harper from the opposite side of a ballroom, tracking her every movement and memorizing each angular line of her face. She thought she knew her. She thought there was nothing left to learn, but the revelation that Harper kisses like this—like Chloe is the key to her own self-destruction—leaves her unmoored.

She watches as Harper takes a step back, hands smoothing down the front of her dress. Then, without so much as a glance in Chloe's direction, she turns and slinks back down the hall. Reed waits for her footsteps to fade around the corner before rounding on Chloe.

"And *you,*" he snaps. "What the hell are you thinking? Abandoning your job? Kissing a guest? Do you have any idea what kind of position this puts me in?"

It's not that Chloe is having trouble thinking, exactly, but she's definitely finding it difficult to think about anything other than the hot press of Harper's hand on her waist and the sharp bite of nails against the back of her neck. "I . . . I'm sorry?"

"You're *sorry*?" Reed's face is quickly moving from red to purple. "You're kissing our boss's daughter at an event you're working and the only thing you can say is you're *sorry*?"

"Technically, she kissed me."

Reed closes his eyes and Chloe gets the impression he's seriously weighing the consequences of strangling her right here, in the hallway of the Rivera. "Go," he snaps. "Get out of my sight. Get back to work and stay away from her. We'll talk about this tomorrow."

He practically shoves her down the hall, but Chloe doesn't need to be told twice. She retraces her steps toward the ballroom, looking back only once to confirm Reed has disappeared around a corner, probably to complete whatever very important task she and Harper interrupted.

Harper.

Chloe shakes her head. Her pulse is still hammering in her throat, an incessant chorus of *finally, finally, finally,* but the thought of Harper reactivates her familiar shield of anger. Because what the fuck was that? How did Harper go from fighting her in the middle of the hallway to pushing Chloe against the wall to save her from Reed's prying questions?

To save your cover, Chloe reminds herself. *She did it to save the job, not you.*

Not that she knows what to do with that either. She could probably unwind every intricate detail of the last hour, go all the way back to the beginning of the year and still have no idea how she ended up here—in the middle of a luxury island hotel with the heat of Harper Parisi's mouth imprinted against her skin.

"Chloe?"

Chloe whirls at the sound of her name. For a wild, panicked minute, she thinks Reed is back, that he's somehow uncovered her true identity and is here to make her confess. Instead, she finds Logan striding toward her, one arm pressed awkwardly against his side in a vain attempt to hide the fake award still tucked in his pocket.

"Logan?" Dread pools in Chloe's stomach, amplified by the sounds of the party still drifting toward them down the hall. "What are you doing? You're supposed to be inside."

"So are you." Logan comes to a stop in front of her, jaw tight with something that looks remarkably like anger. "What's going on? Why aren't you answering?"

Shit. Chloe fumbles with her earpiece until she hears the familiar rush of static. In her haste to follow Harper from the ballroom, she'd completely forgotten to turn it back on. "Sorry," she says. "Sorry, I wasn't . . . what's up?"

"What's *up*?" Priya's voice is unusually cold. "Oh, nothing much, just trying to steal an award from a luxury island ballroom. What's up with you?"

Chloe winces. "Sorry."

"Stop saying that. Where have you been? Where's Harper?"

"Where's—" Chloe breaks off. "Isn't she back in the ballroom?"

Logan shakes his head. "We thought you went to get her."

"I did! We . . ."

Chloe squeezes her eyes shut as she hurriedly rewinds through the last several minutes. Harper pinning her against the wall. Harper pulling back as Reed approached. Harper setting off down the hall, in the exact direction of the ballroom. Chloe assumed she'd gone back inside. There's no reason for her to leave, but the truth of the situation is written all over Logan's face. For some inexplicable reason, Harper has vanished, and the voice Chloe's been purposefully stifling all week crashes through the back of her mind.

You can't trust Harper Parisi.

"Whatever you're doing, do it fast," Priya says. "It looks like they're getting ready to close the bar."

"What?" Chloe whirls in the direction of the ballroom. "We haven't even served dessert."

"They just did. You missed the final call."

Of course she did. Bold of her, Chloe thinks, to forget how precariously this plan came together. To believe, for even a second, that nothing would ever go wrong. She grabs Logan's arm and starts power walking them both back toward the ballroom.

"New plan. Logan will make the switch now while everyone's still walking around. Got it?"

Logan nods, but his mouth is tight with worry. "There's still the problem of getting out unseen."

"I don't care. You made it to me with that thing under your jacket. Just come out this side door when you're done and I'll sneak you out the back. You'll be fine."

What Chloe doesn't say is, *you don't have a choice.* She doesn't let herself linger on the danger of their new plan or acknowledge the risk out loud. They're so *close* and she's not going to let Harper, of all people, keep her from their five-million-dollar prize. She quickens her pace, dragging Logan behind her as they near the ballroom.

"Chloe . . ."

There's a warning note to Priya's voice that Chloe decides to ignore. "I know," she says. "We're coming."

"No, wait!"

Chloe starts to tug Logan around the corner, then yanks him back as Priya's voice rings in her ears. She flattens her back to the wall, hand flying up to muffle Logan's surprised grunt, and when she risks a glance into the hallway, she has to bite the inside of her cheek to avoid groaning out loud. Because Reed is standing directly in front of the ballroom door, gaze fixed on his tablet as he angrily keys something in.

How he managed to get back to the ballroom before them is a mystery Chloe can't even begin to unwind. Maybe he can teleport now. Maybe he cloned himself at some point during his managerial career and never reversed the process. Either way, when this is over, Chloe is going to send that man away on a very long, very remote vacation. Preferably somewhere far away from her.

"Sorry," Priya says. "I tried to warn you. Hold on—I'll find another way in."

Chloe closes her eyes. They don't have time for this. Priya just said so, but they also can't send Logan back through that door with Reed watching. No one's supposed to be in this hallway. Reed made that perfectly clear, and Chloe has a feeling he won't be as lenient with Logan as he was with Harper. He'd probably demand an invitation, and he'd definitely notice the strange way Logan's jacket puckers around their printed award.

He wouldn't notice you, though.

The thought drips down Chloe's spine like melted ice. Logan might not be able to walk through that door, but she certainly can. Reed already knows she's out here. He already lectured her for it, so what more does she have to lose, really? Before she can think better of it, she rounds on Logan and whispers, "Give me the fake."

Logan's eyes widen. "Now?"

"Yes! Reed won't let you in, but I'm supposed to be here. Give it to me. I'll make the switch."

Logan hesitates, apprehension clear on his face. Chloe doesn't blame him. She's achingly aware of her own inadequacy, of all the times Logan tried and failed to teach her sleight of hand. Just yesterday, Harper looked her in the eye and said, with a casual sort of finality, *you've always been a pretty shit pickpocket, Chloe.*

But Harper isn't here. They're backed into a corner and this sort of pressure, Chloe knows, is where she thrives.

She holds out a hand, motioning again for Logan to hand the award over. It takes him another second to comply, mouthing, *be careful,* as Chloe tucks it into the waistband of her skirt. She nods, shields the award as best she can with one arm, and steps purposefully into the hallway. Reed looks up when she rounds the corner and his face immediately falls from mild irritation to utter disdain.

"What are you doing?" he hisses. "I told you to get back in the ballroom."

"I know!" Chloe shrugs as helplessly as she can manage. "I'm sorry, I got lost."

"You are the bane of my existence, you know that?" Reed seizes her by the collar and practically shoves her through the door. "Get to work."

Chloe stumbles into the ballroom and immediately grabs a tray to hide the outline of the award pressing against her side. Some of the guests are already back in their seats, finishing up dessert as they talk animatedly with the people beside them, but others still mill around near the open bar. Her co-workers flit between the tables, collecting empty plates and refilling water glasses. Chloe pretends to join them. She slides the award from her waistband as carefully as she can and tucks it behind the tray. She has no idea when Katherine is planning to speak but judging by the crates of empty bottles behind the bar, she doesn't have long until it closes for good.

She moves toward the windowsill as casually as she can, careful not to let her gaze linger too long on any table. When she glances over her shoulder, Reed is still watching her from the doorway, expression hot with thinly veiled hatred.

"Can I get a distraction, Priya?" she whispers. "Reed won't stop watching me."

Priya exhales a rough snort. "Well, whose fault is that?"

Chloe resists the urge to snap back. Priya is right, of course. The only reason Reed knows her at all is because she let herself get caught up with Harper. It always comes back to Harper in the end.

She ducks behind another table, skin still prickling with the pressure of Reed's gaze. "I need something, Pri. I can't do anything if he's looking."

"I know. I'm working on it."

The windowsill is in sight now, award gleaming tauntingly down at her. Chloe tightens her grip on the tray, palms slipping against the plastic edge. The crowd is definitely thinning, people heading back to their seats with one last drink in hand, and when she risks a glance toward the front, she's just in time to watch Katherine stand up from her own table.

"Now," Chloe whispers. "Do it now, Priya."

She can't hear Priya's response over the roar of her own pulse. She has no idea what she's asking for, or what Priya is planning to do. All she knows is that they're out of time. Iron slides over Chloe's tongue—blood from biting at the inside of her cheek. She swallows it down, ducks around another strange, spiky sculpture, and then, just when she's about to ask again, a chandelier on the opposite side of the room flickers. There's a split second where a nearby table looks up, conversation faltering, before every light in the ballroom blinks out.

It's less than a second, barely long enough for anyone to draw breath, but it's all Chloe needs. She lunges forward and grabs the wooden base of Carlyle's award. She sets the fake one on the windowsill, whirls toward a nearby catering cart, and shoves the real thing into a bin of dirty dishes just as the lights pop back on.

Through her haze of adrenaline, she thinks she hears someone laugh. There's another voice, then another, and when Chloe looks up, the party is still in full swing, guests waving off the momentary intrusion as they settle back in their seats. Reed has left his post by the door, no doubt to hunt down whoever's in charge of facilities, but for once, he's not looking at Chloe. In fact, no one is.

"You okay?" Priya's voice is faint in her ear. "Did you get it?"

Chloe takes another steadying breath and forces herself to straighten. She's done this countless times, snatched larger, much more valuable items from under people's noses without batting an eye. This should be no different. "Yeah," she mutters. "I did."

She scans the ballroom one last time as she turns toward the kitchen. In the renewed glow of the chandeliers, Chloe can see every crystal, every gemstone, every stitch of expensive fabric around her in bitter, stunning clarity. She notices the way the tablecloths drape against the floor, the light bouncing off pairs of glasses, and she sees, with a spine-chilling jolt, who happens to be looking at her, too.

Chloe keeps moving even as her throat goes dry. She guides the cart toward the safety of the kitchen, pretending with every step that she doesn't see the tip of the award peeking out from behind a stack of dirty plates. And that she doesn't notice the hungry, purposeful way Andrew Carlyle watches her go.

FOURTEEN

In Florida summers, the heat is never the worst part. When the sun sets and the shadows stretch across the pavement, it's the humidity that lingers, pressing over the city like a physical, breathing thing. It's the first thing Chloe notices when she exits the Rivera after the gala with Carlyle's award stuffed in the bottom of her bag—the crushing pressure of the air around her and the familiar realization that people can still drown on dry land.

She dips a hand into her bag as she walks, fingers skimming over the sharp edge of the glass triangle. There it is, still buried unceremoniously in the same place it was thirty seconds ago. In the same place it has been since she dug it out from under a stack of greasy dinner plates and fled to the employee locker room. Reed will probably try to write her up for that, too. He's probably furious she left the party before he could deliver a proper punishment, but Chloe doesn't care. Let him try to fire her. By the time he looks for her tomorrow morning, she'll be long gone and several million dollars richer. Home at last.

Home.

Usually, Chloe thinks of Miami with a bland sort of derision. It's never been her favorite place, but as she makes her way toward the beach, there's a different sort of future unfurling in her mind. Regular dinners in her father's new condo, where she can tell him about her week without feeling ashamed. A new apartment with central AC and a window overlooking the park. Finally taking a real vacation and splurging on first-class plane tickets just because she can.

When was the last time she allowed herself to think like this, to imagine a life that didn't revolve around twelve-hour shifts and unpaid hospital bills?

Chloe quickens her pace, hands tightening instinctively over the strap of her bag each time someone passes her on the path. Despite the late hour, she's not alone out here. A line of hotel golf carts snakes through the sand beside her, drivers shuttling guests directly from the gala to the docks. Because god forbid Katherine Windey's millionaire friends walk the half mile to their waiting yachts. Chloe winces as another cart flies by, splattering her legs with sand. She moves off the path when she hears the next one approaching, already bracing herself for impact, but the cart just slows to a crawl. Then it stops.

"Need a ride?"

Andrew Carlyle sits in the back of the golf cart, jacket draped casually over one arm. In the yellow glow of the headlights, he looks surprisingly normal, shirt rumpled, cheeks tinged with the subtle flush of a man who spent the last several hours at an open bar.

Chloe shakes her head and turns back to the path. "I'm good, thanks."

"Are you sure?" This time, there's no mistaking the warning edge to his voice. "It's a long walk."

Carlyle pats the seat beside him, seemingly oblivious to the line of golf carts forming in his wake. Behind them, passengers crane their necks, searching for the source of the delay, and Chloe sighs. *Fine. This conversation will have to happen sooner or later, won't it? Maybe it's better to get it over with now.* Reluctantly, she climbs into the seat, perching on the very edge of the slippery leather as they start moving again.

"Thanks."

Carlyle ignores her. "Where is it?"

"Always so serious." Chloe glances toward their driver, voice purposefully light. When he doesn't react, she lets her gaze slide back to Carlyle. "Did you have a good night? Where's your wife, by the way? I was so looking forward to meeting her."

"Hand it over, Ms. Bly. I won't ask again."

His voice is low, but Chloe is pretty sure she detects a current of unease threaded beneath every word. She thinks of the awards displayed in his office, of his hand wrapped possessively around Katherine's arm, and swallows over the lump in her throat. She doesn't trust Andrew Carlyle. Part of her still thinks he's using them, forcing her across some invisible chessboard she'll never understand, but he clearly doesn't trust her either. This deal, however precarious, only works if they both hold up their ends of the bargain.

Slowly, Chloe reaches into her bag and pulls the award into the open. "Fine," she says. "And then we talk about payment."

"Sure." Carlyle waves an impatient hand. "That's fine, just hand it over."

He's too eager, Chloe thinks. The realization makes her want to hold tighter, to see what else he might be willing to trade, but Carlyle snatches the award before she can move. In the moonlight, his expression is almost hungry. Shadows darken beneath his eyes and when he whispers, "There you are," Chloe has the feeling he's forgotten about her entirely.

He holds the award up to the light, one hand gently caressing the wooden base. It looks like he's tracing the outline of his own name, ensuring that it really belongs to him, and there's a split second of satisfied silence before his expression turns distinctly stormy. He turns the award over in his hands, each movement sharp and agitated, and it's not until he flips it upside down that Chloe realizes why.

There, carved on the bottom, is a single line of text.

YOU'RE SO PREDICTABLE. XOXO —K

Panic, Chloe has learned, is usually hot. It feels like flushed skin and a relentless, racing heart, but dread is colder. It's paralyzing and bitter and when Carlyle tilts the award toward the light for a better look at the message carved into the base, Chloe feels the latter settle in the pit of her stomach. *Well,* she thinks bitterly, *at least you know where Harper gets it from.*

Then, Carlyle's knuckles whiten around the base of his award. "This isn't mine."

Chloe blinks. "I . . . what?"

"This isn't mine." His voice is rough, so low the wind nearly whips it away entirely, but the fury radiating from his side of the golf cart is impossible to ignore. "It's a fake."

His gaze pins her to the seat and Chloe realizes she was wrong before. Panic is usually hot, but the kind flooding her now, this bone-deep sense of slowly dawning horror, leaves her numb. *Isn't mine.* But it is. It has to be. Chloe pored over those images all week. They made an extra trip to the Rivera ballroom to confirm that this is the piece Katherine stole. The Florida Hospitality Award with Carlyle's name stamped on one side and their logo on the other.

"How . . ." Chloe has to start the question three separate times before it comes out. "How can you tell?"

"Doesn't matter. She knew I'd be here tonight. She knew I'd try to get it back."

Carlyle turns in his seat and, faster than Chloe can track, hurls the award out of the moving golf cart. *No!* Chloe lurches forward, protest catching in her throat as she watches it disappear into the night. She can't have finally bested Harper, only to be thwarted by her mother on the same night.

You're so predictable. That's what Katherine's note said. Like she'd known right from the beginning how irresistible this trap would be.

"But why?" Chloe whispers. "It's not valuable. You said she only took it out of spite, so why make a fake? Why bother with any of this?"

"Because she's *Katherine,*" Carlyle snaps. "Because this is *fun* for her. But you already knew that, didn't you? She got to you, too?"

"No!" Chloe slides backward across the seat. "She didn't . . . I barely spoke to her. I didn't know it was a fake."

"And why not? That's why I'm paying you, right? Because you're supposed to be *the best*?"

Last week, Chloe thought Carlyle's whole thing was mildly interesting—strange and intimidating, sure, but not explicitly dangerous. But here they are, sitting inches away from each other in the dark, and Chloe has the terrible feeling that she might have underestimated him. Gone is the talkative, eccentric man who marveled at her skill and offered her money. Chloe thought him an easy mark then, already wrapped around her finger.

Now, she wonders if the real mark has always been her.

Carlyle closes his eyes. He tugs at his bowtie until it hangs loose around his neck and when he looks up again, his composure is back. "This isn't working," he says. "I thought you and Ms. Parisi would get this job done, but that was clearly a mistake. Our deal is off."

"No!"

It's out before Chloe can think better of it and it takes every scrap of her remaining willpower not to clap a hand over her mouth. She thought Carlyle had sounded too eager before and here she is, showing her own hand. She might as well write *desperate* across her forehead. She takes a deep breath and tries again. "We still have time. We'll find the real award."

"I have absolutely no reason to believe that's true."

"We got this far, didn't we? You know anyone else who could pull that off?"

Silence stretches between them as the cart finally comes to a stop. In the waning moonlight, Carlyle's gaze feels bottomless, dark and empty as an oil slick. "Friday," he says. "I want that award on my desk by Friday or the deal's off."

"But . . ." Chloe shakes her head. "No. You gave us two weeks."

"And now I'm changing my mind."

The rest of Chloe's protests die in her throat. What is she supposed to say? That it's not fair? That he can't do this? Of course he can. Everyone on this island can do whatever they want. Katherine Windey can steal other people's awards and hold them hostage for fun. Andrew Carlyle can use whatever means necessary to get his back and no one will care.

The only person without a choice, as usual, is Chloe.

She clambers out of the golf cart, fists clenched at her sides. "Deal. We'll find it. You'll have it by Friday."

Carlyle's eyebrows lift as he looks her up and down. He probably finds her desperation amusing. He's probably playing her the same way she plays the rich guests at his parties, but Chloe doesn't care. She can't lose this job. She can't go back to scraping by when her vision of the perfect future is *right here,* and she certainly can't look her friends in the eye and tell them they failed. She lifts her chin, forcing herself to return Carlyle's gaze and eventually, he nods.

"All right," he says. "I'll see you on Friday. Now, if you'll please get out of my way, I have a boat to catch."

He steps around her without waiting for a response, heading across the dock without so much as a backward glance. *It's not like he needs one,* Chloe thinks bitterly as she watches him vanish into the dark. She just handed him all her bargaining power and the worst part is, she doesn't even care.

She glances over her shoulder at the distant, glittering outline of the Rivera. The others are probably together by now, waiting for her on the opposite side of the island. They're probably celebrating too, making lists of everything they want to buy when they get paid. That's what Chloe was doing earlier. It seems absurd now.

She sighs and turns back to where the golf cart dropped them off. "Don't suppose I can get a ride back, can I?"

But the driver is already gone, speeding away with nothing but a fresh pair of tire tracks in his wake.

Chloe groans and tips her head back toward the sky. *This,* she thinks as she hefts her bag onto her shoulder, *is going to be a very long night.*

FIFTEEN

Chloe finds the fake award half buried at the edge of the path, glass spiderwebbed with hairline fractures. Her legs ache from pushing through the sand, but she scoops it up anyway, ignoring the anticipatory dip in her stomach when she tucks it back into her bag. Ten minutes ago, it was her ticket out, the thing they risked everything for. Now, it feels like another example of her own inadequacy.

The Rivera glitters at her back as she walks and, for a second, all Chloe can think about is her mother, standing on the beach that day in November with her head tipped toward the sky. She thinks of her family standing on a different beach on the opposite side of the world and thinks, as she does most nights, about all the ways she's failing them.

She knows her mother's family through faded photographs and once-a-year phone calls. She knows them in the same distant way they know her, and it never used to bother her. Then her mother died, and the only link between Chloe and a world beyond Miami shattered. Even after the funeral, when two of her aunts invited her to visit, Chloe wasn't able to say yes. It's not that she doesn't want to go. She does. She *will.* But every time she tries to pick up the phone or send an email, something stops her.

What if her family doesn't like the person she's become? What if they all resent her for not visiting sooner, or for keeping her mother away from them all those years? What if they take one look at her and know every terrible, underhanded thing she's done since the funeral? That's not something Chloe can handle. Especially now, with the physical weight of another failure swinging against her hip with every step.

The south beach is technically closed at night, but Chloe fumbles in her pocket until she finds the key she swiped off that housekeeper yesterday and lets herself through the gate. If anyone happens to check the logs tomorrow, they'll see no record of her name in the system. They'll probably question Megan instead, sit her down in Reed's office and demand to know what she was doing out so late.

Maybe one day, Chloe will learn to care.

Most of the cabanas are empty, gauzy white curtains fluttering in the wind as she passes. The padded lounge chairs and carved wooden tables have all been wiped down in preparation for tomorrow's guests, but there's a light still flickering in the cabana closest to the water. When Chloe peeks her head around the corner, it takes a second for the others to realize she's there.

Priya's laughing at something Logan said, glasses pushed on top of her head as she pops open a bottle of wine. She only wears glasses when she needs to concentrate, insisting the bulky frames "ruin her aesthetic," but she doesn't seem to mind them now. Logan's shirt is halfway undone, his bowtie abandoned in the sand at his feet. His jacket is slung across the chaise and there, lounging against it like she didn't actively ruin their entire night, is Harper.

All the fury that was dampened by Carlyle's presence comes screaming back. Chloe throws back the curtain and snaps, "What the hell is she doing here?"

Priya looks up at the sound of her voice, nearly upending her wine in her haste to stand. "Chloe!" She ignores the question and yanks her into the cabana. "Come here, you gorgeous genius! You did it! We're rich!"

Logan swivels toward them in his seat, but Chloe doesn't hear what he says next. She's suddenly very interested in the side of his neck, where a bright red smear of lipstick stands out against his pale skin. *So Harper's kissing everyone, apparently.* The thought should be reassuring. At least her exchange with Chloe in the hallway was calculated instead of some passionate, spur-of-the-moment decision. That's for the best, actually; it means Chloe's allowed to be angry.

She yanks out of Priya's grip and rounds on Harper. Harper, who abandoned them in the ballroom. Harper, who almost ruined their plans, who's celebrating with them now like she belongs. "Where have you been?"

Harper barely looks up as Chloe approaches, one ankle crossed gracefully over the other. She dumped her heels in the corner, but she's still wearing her dress, which means Chloe is treated to a completely unwelcome memory of that same fabric bunching between her fingers.

"Where have I been?" Harper asks. "Here, of course. You're the one who's late." She gives Chloe a quick up and down, nose wrinkling at the sand caked into her uniform stockings. "Did you, like, crawl from the lobby or something?"

"Don't." Chloe leans forward, bracing both hands on the arms of Harper's chair. "Why didn't you go back to the ballroom? Why didn't you tell us where you were? You knew Logan was waiting for you to make the switch. That was the plan."

She's close enough to see the makeup smudged under Harper's eyes, the tiny, singular imperfection on her otherwise flawless face, but Harper's not wide-eyed and tense like she was in the hallway. In fact, when she uncrosses her legs and stands, forcing Chloe away from her chair, her expression is almost mocking.

"They closed the bar early," she says. "No one could have planned for that."

"Yes, we could have. You could have been in the ballroom like you were supposed to be and you could have done your job. Where else could you have *possibly* gone?"

Harper lifts a manicured brow. "What are you accusing me of?"

"I don't know. What are you hiding?"

Vaguely, Chloe is aware of Priya and Logan hovering on the other side of the cabana. She's aware of the sand in her shoes, of the way her feet ache from the long walk across the island, and of the fake award pressing through the fabric of her bag. Harper's head tips to one side, mouth curling in the hint of a smile, and for one searing second, Chloe thinks she's going to kiss her again. Then Harper pulls back and holds up her phone.

"If you must know, I stepped out to arrange our ride home. I thought we had time before the bar closed and I wanted to make sure Shay was ready with the boat."

Chloe blinks. "You . . . left to call a *boat*?"

"You're the one who wanted to leave as soon as possible."

Harper tosses her phone in Chloe's direction. Sure enough, there's a series of texts between her and the boat captain from last weekend, where they do appear to be coordinating a pickup. Chloe shakes her head. She expected excuses, of course, but something about this casual, harmless explanation prickles along the back of her neck. Harper didn't want to do anything when she stormed out of the ballroom. She was drunk and reckless, smashing through the party with hurricane-like abandon, and Chloe doesn't think she was struck with sudden generosity in their time apart.

Logan takes a hesitant step forward. "She *did* say she needed to call our ride when we sat down for dinner."

"Are you serious?" Chloe rounds on him. "You buy that? She abandoned you in the ballroom!"

"Not on purpose. We all thought we had more time to make the switch."

"Right. And did she tell you that before or after you kissed?"

The second it's out, Chloe wishes she could take it back. Logan's eyes widen first in surprise, then in annoyance. "I'm perfectly capable of drawing my own conclusions, thanks."

"That's not what I meant."

"What do you mean, then?" Priya asks.

Her smile is gone, replaced with a look of wary concern and it takes Chloe another second to realize it's because of her. Because she's the one getting in Harper's face and snapping at Logan after what the others still believe to be a successful night. She knows how it must look, but Priya didn't see Harper the way Chloe did tonight—reckless and volatile and flighty. They don't know how much of a problem she is, but Chloe's known it all year. She's just opened her mouth to explain when Harper lets out a breathy snort.

"Is that what this is about?" Her gaze rakes carelessly over Chloe's face. "You're mad I kissed someone else?"

Logan whips around so quickly he almost trips in the sand. "What? You two kissed?"

"Yeah, *what*?" Chloe echoes, face burning. "You can't . . . that has nothing to do with it."

Of all the things that happened tonight, kissing Harper might actually be the least relevant. It is, however, the most embarrassing, which is definitely why Harper's bringing it up now.

"It obviously does, Chloe," Harper says, voice thick with exaggerated patience. "What else could you possibly be upset about? That I had a glass of wine on the balcony?"

"Maybe the fact you got drunk and almost ruined our night? You ran out of the ballroom in front of everyone."

"So did you! All you've done this week is tell me that we're a team, that we're in this together, but you didn't trust me to be alone for a second. If you'd just let me go, none of this would have happened!"

Chloe's fists clench at her sides. That's not true. She knows it's not and Harper does too, but there's a defensive edge in her voice that makes Chloe think they're straying toward something real. *Here you are,* she thinks, pulse thrumming with barely contained fury. The woman who'd flinched away from her mother's touch and glanced at Chloe out of the corner of her eye with momentary vulnerability is gone. Here's the Harper from Carlyle's party last week, the cold, distant con artist waiting to strike. Maybe she's never been anything else.

"You can tell yourself whatever you want," Chloe says. "But I'm not the one who almost ruined our job. And I'm not the one lying about it now."

Harper rolls her eyes. "Please. Do I seem drunk to anyone else?"

Chloe watches Priya and Logan exchange a hesitant glance over Harper's shoulder. She's seen that look before. She knows exactly what it means. *Chloe's at it again. Chloe's so focused on beating Harper that she's making it our problem, too.* She wants to shake them, to grab them by the shoulders and force them to see that she's not the issue here.

But the longer she glares at Harper, the more Chloe's own memory fades. Because Harper *is* remarkably coherent for someone who was stumbling around the Rivera an hour ago, unable to control her own outbursts. Her gaze is focused, clear as the star-flecked sky, and when she speaks again, her voice is steady.

"You weren't in the ballroom either. You left because you cared more about watching me than following your own plan. I know you don't like me, but I'm a part of this, too. You're the only person who seems to have a problem with it."

"Because it was a mistake!"

Something flickers behind Harper's infallible gaze. If Chloe didn't know better, she'd think it was hurt. "What else do you want from me? We got the award."

"No, we didn't!"

Silence falls across the cabana, like everything within a mile radius suddenly inhaled the same collective breath. Even the wind seems to die, waves freezing on the shore as Chloe's outburst lingers between them, and for a minute, the stunned look on Harper's face is almost worth it. Her brow furrows, red lips parting in silent question, but it's Logan who speaks first.

"What do you mean?" he asks. "You have the award, right?"

His voice is rough, tentative, and suddenly, Chloe wishes she could take it back. This isn't how she wanted to tell them. Priya and Logan deserve better than a shouted confession in the middle of a fight, but she was too focused on clawing her way under Harper's skin to realize where it was heading. She digs the heels of her hands against her closed eyelids. Maybe she's cracking under the pressure. Maybe her hatred of Harper really is warping her perception. That's probably something she needs to unpack but right now, she just wants to go home.

She wants to stop imagining the phantom press of Harper's lips against her throat each time they make eye contact.

"No," she whispers, hands falling back to her sides. "We didn't get it. The award in the ballroom was a fake. Something Katherine set up on purpose. It was never real."

For a second, no one moves. Then Priya sinks onto the edge of the chaise. "No," she whispers, head dropping into her hands. "No, no, no."

It's the same refrain that's been echoing in Chloe's mind since Carlyle pulled her into his golf cart. She tugs the award from her bag and hands it to Logan. Now that she knows the truth, she can't stop wondering if she should have clocked this version's imperfections sooner. She remembers thinking that the glass should have been shinier the day she and Priya toured the ballroom, but she chalked it up to normal wear and tear.

"I don't understand," Logan says. "This is it. It looks exactly like the pictures."

Chloe gives a halfhearted shrug. "We managed to print a forgery, didn't we?"

"Not like this."

"Well, I'm sure Katherine Windey has a few more resources at her disposal."

Harper scoffs, arms folding in clear disdain as she glares across the cabana. Chloe watches her carefully, noting the way her nails dig into her biceps, leaving a trail of angry red marks to match the ones still lingering around her wrist. Harper's always been a good liar, but when she shakes her head and mutters, "Of course," Chloe thinks the contempt in her voice is real. Despite how easy it would be to believe, she doesn't think Harper knew about the switch, or the note her mother had carved into the bottom of the decoy statue.

"So what do we do?" Priya asks. She's twisting a lock of hair around her finger, her other hand tapping nervously against her thigh. "That was our only lead."

Chloe nods. She's been trying not to think about that. "I know."

"Are we just supposed to start over? Do we go back to searching every Windey hotel in the city? Do we guess and hope we get lucky? I'm not—"

"Hey." Logan sinks into the chaise and slides a reassuring arm around Priya's shoulders. "We figured it out once, we can do it again. We still have time."

Chloe winces. "We don't, actually. Carlyle wants it back by Friday. Three days from now."

"What?" Priya's head snaps up. "How do you know?"

"He found me after the gala. Gave us an ultimatum."

"But he can't do that."

"Of course he can. He can do whatever he wants."

"But *we* can't." Priya's voice is barely more than a whisper. "I'm sorry, Chloe. I know that's my job, but I can't conduct a search of that scale in a day. It's too big. We have nothing to work with."

"I know." Chloe wishes she could say anything else. She's already cycled through the same fears and come up with exactly zero solutions. She knows they're fucked and if she thinks about it for too long, she'll start to spiral, too.

"What about the other party?" Logan asks. "You said there were more last week."

Priya nods weakly. "There's a casino night at the downtown Windey."

"Why don't we start there? Narrow in on one location?"

He sounds hopelessly naïve. Chloe knows it's more complicated than that, and for Logan to suggest otherwise is nothing more than a temporary solution. She sags against the wall, watching the Rivera lights flicker on the other side of the curtains. "I still think it's here," she murmurs, half to herself.

Logan looks up. "What?"

"I still think the award is here."

Chloe doesn't know why she's so sure. She certainly doesn't have any proof, but there is a *feeling*. A faint buzz in the tips of her fingers. Because doesn't this all come back to the Rivera in the end? The hotel that Carlyle lost and the deal he's been furiously regretting for years?

Priya's expression sours. "Where? I've already combed through every inch of that hotel."

"Not everywhere," Chloe says. "We haven't tried Katherine's suite. It makes more sense for her to keep it there than at a random party downtown, especially since the award tonight was a fake."

She hears the desperation in her voice well before Priya's expression softens. She sounds just as naïve as Logan, but what choice do they have? She'll break into Katherine's suite herself if it means getting them out of here.

Chloe thinks of Carlyle standing on the dock, glaring over his shoulder at the Rivera. She thinks of his hands wrapped around the award, the way his knuckles whitened ever so slightly in the second before he realized it was a fake. What had given it away? What made him realize it had been switched in the first place? Maybe he'd sensed something off from the beginning, but Chloe keeps coming back to the second before Carlyle flipped the award over in his lap, to the way he fiddled with the base like he wanted to pull it apart.

Maybe he did.

The realization slides through the back of her mind, soft as a half-formed whisper. Maybe it wasn't just the statue Carlyle wanted back. Maybe there was something else hidden inside, tucked away in a spot where no one else would think to look.

Logan sighs and pushes himself to his feet. "Well, we can't do anything about it tonight. Let's get some sleep and regroup tomorrow."

Priya shakes her head, already reaching for her computer. "I'm fine."

"No, he's right," Chloe says. "You need to rest. You've been working nonstop since we got here."

"We still have the rooms tonight," Harper says. "I can extend our reservations through Friday if we need."

Chloe nods, the knot in her chest loosening ever so slightly. She likes action. She likes a plan and here's the first concrete step out of the dark. "Let's get some rest," she says, slinging an arm around Priya's shoulder. "This isn't over."

That's easier said than done. As they make their way back toward the hotel, Chloe sure feels like it's over and, more than anything, she's starting to feel like it's all her fault.

The four of them take the elevator in silence, sand spilling onto the marble floor as they ascend. The thought of sleep is intoxicating, tugging at Chloe's already heavy eyelids. All she wants is to collapse on the pull-out couch in their room, but when Priya and Logan step into the hallway, something makes her hesitate. Chloe turns, one hand braced on the elevator door, and finds Harper watching her from the corner.

"I told you," Harper says.

"Told me what?"

Harper shrugs. She pulls Priya's bottle of wine from her bag, uncorks the top, and lifts it directly to her lips. "Not to underestimate my mother."

SIXTEEN

That night, Chloe dreams of dark water, open sky, and a girl dressed in silver moonlight.

She's standing on an unfamiliar beach, bare feet sinking into the sand as a storm gathers on the horizon. Harper's there too, stoic and silent as she gazes out across the waves. She steps into the sea, current tugging at the hem of her gown, and when she glances over her shoulder, Chloe sees that she's holding a long silver dagger in one hand.

A trick, Chloe thinks, words half formed and hazy in her mind. *This isn't real.*

And still, she keeps walking, straight toward Harper until the ocean claims her, too.

There you are, Harper whispers. She turns the dagger over in her hands and for a second, Chloe feels the image shift. It's a pearl-encrusted cocktail pick. It's an ivory shotgun. It's her own fingers locked around Chloe's throat. It's a deadly, vicious weapon, and when Harper leans in, lips brushing over the shell of Chloe's ear, her voice feels like one, too.

What do you want?

The water rises around them, icy current tugging at their hips, but the arm Harper wraps around her waist is molten.

What do you want, Chloe?

Harper drags the edge of her blade over Chloe's bare skin, stopping only when the tip rests directly in the hollow of her throat. The touch is achingly gentle, a cruel, warped version of a lover's caress. Blood drips down her chest, but Chloe hardly feels the pain. She grins, fingers wrapping around Harper's, and when she answers, it's an exhale of every hidden desire locked inside her treacherous heart.

You. I want you.

Harper bares her teeth, lips hovering just above Chloe's as her grip tightens on the dagger. She leans in and Chloe inhales one final breath before the water closes over their heads, dragging them into a dark abyss.

Chloe shoots upright with a gasp, hands instinctively flying to her throat. They come away clean, of course, no sign of blood. Because she's not standing on some frosty, distant beach. She's safe and dry and . . .

And she's in her room at the Rivera, tangled in sheets on the pull-out couch.

She scrambles up as the events of last night come flooding back. The gala, the beach, the fake award sitting cracked and worthless in the sand. Chloe releases a tight breath and it's only then, when she's finally starting to sink back against the pillows, that she hears the knocking on their door.

At first, Chloe thinks it's the dream, an echo of last night's headache still pounding behind her skull. Then it happens again, too loud and insistent to be anything but real. She leans over and pats across the floor until she finds her phone.

Just past seven in the morning. Way too early for any sane person to expect visitors.

Muted sunlight falls through the crack in the curtains, tracing pale lines across the shiny tile. When Chloe pushes herself out of bed, she finds Priya already awake, sitting cross-legged with the blue-white glow of her laptop reflecting off her glasses. Her headphones are on, lip caught between her teeth, and she appears blissfully unaware of whoever's lurking outside. Logan, however, is still miraculously asleep, one hand dangling over the edge of the mattress as he snores contentedly. *Figures.* A hurricane could smash its way through the Rivera right now and he wouldn't budge.

When Chloe crosses the room and peers through the peephole, she wishes she could say the same. "Do you have any idea what time it is?" she asks, yanking the door open.

"Sorry. No one was answering their phones."

Harper breezes inside, dressed in a matching workout set and clutching a bright green smoothie. She looks like the star of a feel-good Nike commercial about finding your inner champion and—even worse—she looks like she's never heard the word *hangover* in her life. It's like last night never happened and Chloe has a single second to process that she herself is wearing an oversized t-shirt with the words I GOT RAILED IN BOCA RATON stamped over a cartoon drawing of a train before the door falls shut behind her.

"What are you doing up?" she asks, folding her arms over the train's inexplicably smiling face.

"Pilates."

"I . . . what?"

"It's very centering, Chloe. You should try it."

That wasn't actually why Chloe was asking, but Harper doesn't elaborate. Instead, she strides across the room and flings open the curtains before tossing a decorative pillow in Logan's direction. "Get up. We have work to do."

Logan lets out an unintelligible groan at the sudden burst of light and honestly, Chloe feels the same. It's too early for this. She's still trying to pull her thoughts into something semi-coherent, but she can't stop picturing Harper pulling a knife from the skintight fabric of her leggings and plunging it into the center of Chloe's chest.

When Chloe catches a glimpse of the ocean through the window, the only thing she can think about is the memory of Harper's lips, salty and frozen and pressed against her own.

Harper perches on the corner of the mattress, casually stirring her straw around what remains of her smoothie before glancing at Priya's computer. "So," she says. "What's the new plan, Pri?"

Chloe scowls at the casual way the nickname slides off Harper's tongue. The four of them aren't friends. She doesn't know what Harper is to her these days but she knows it's not simple.

Priya tugs off her headphones, glancing warily from Harper to Chloe. "When did you get here?" she asks.

Harper waves a hand. "Like, two minutes ago."

"Why are you dressed like someone who runs a pyramid scheme?" Logan calls from under his mountain of blankets.

"Because I went to Pilates this morning, okay? Can we focus?"

"Focus on what?" Chloe mutters. "Don't you have a brunch to attend?"

"Don't you have an award to find?"

It's objectively true, but the offhand way Harper says it lights Chloe's nerves. She knows she's not responsible for Katherine's fake or Carlyle's new deadline but in this moment, the accusation is clear.

They don't have anything to show for last night. And it's all Chloe's fault.

Priya groans and buries her face in her hands. "Can you two chill for, like, five seconds? I've been trying to phish the security director of the downtown Windey for the last two hours, so the *least* you can do is not claw each other's throats out while I'm working."

Chloe snaps her mouth shut. Harper's gaze drops to the floor and when she speaks again, she sounds almost sheepish. "Sorry, Priya."

"Thanks." Priya exhales, then glares pointedly at Chloe. It's not until her eyebrows lift that Chloe realizes she expects an apology from her, too.

"Right," she says. "Sorry. So that's the plan?" she asks, eager to change the subject. "You're phishing the security director again?"

Priya nods. "I think Katherine will display the award at another one of her parties and I think we need to be at the downtown Windey tonight."

"I like it," Harper says. "That's a good idea."

Chloe opens her mouth, rebuttal ready on the tip of her tongue. She *doesn't* think the award is downtown. She thinks it's at the Rivera, in Katherine's suite or somewhere similar, and she's dying to know what makes Harper so confident after the scene she caused last night. Chloe almost asks. She almost demands to know what Harper is thinking, but she tried to accuse Harper last night in the cabana, too. She tried to call her out and Harper twisted the conversation so thoroughly that even Priya and Logan believed her. She made Chloe the antagonist, the bitter rival who couldn't stand the idea of her own failure, so no, Chloe thinks, she won't bring it up here.

The next time she confronts Harper Parisi, she doesn't intend to lose.

"What if the award isn't there?" Chloe asks. "What if it's another fake?"

She keeps her voice measured, like she's merely curious and not bursting with furious accusations. Priya shrugs. "Then we regroup and try somewhere else."

"We don't have time. We need it by Friday."

"Yes, Chloe, I'm aware. But unless you have another idea, this is our best shot."

Priya glares at them over the top of her glasses and the rest of Chloe's theory dies in her throat. This isn't the bright-eyed, bubbly Priya she's used to. That girl is frustratingly perky, the textbook definition of a morning person, but somewhere between the gala and now, there's been a shift. Chloe sincerely doubts this version of Priya has posted her daily inspirational Instagram story or adequately journaled her feelings. In fact, when Priya leans down to snatch her computer off the couch, Chloe doesn't think she's slept at all.

"You do." Logan leans forward, pulling Chloe's attention back to the center of the room. "You have another idea, don't you?"

It's not really a question. Logan knows her too well for that, but Chloe hesitates. She doesn't want to fight. She doesn't want to discredit Priya's instincts or the plan she's clearly spent hours pulling together, but she can't shake the feeling they're heading in the wrong direction. Yes, Carlyle was invited to the casino party, too. It would be a perfect opportunity for Katherine to flaunt her victory, but he has no personal connection to that hotel. He wants the Rivera, the island that's just out of reach, and Chloe has a feeling Katherine knows it, too.

"I still think it's here," she says. "It's obvious Carlyle regrets selling this island. If Katherine's trying to win, she'll keep the award here. On her desk, on a shelf, on a windowsill in her office."

"There aren't cameras in Katherine's office," Priya points out. "There's no way for us to know what's inside."

"What if I got a key?"

"You . . ." Priya trails off, brow furrowing as she considers. "You want to go back to work? Didn't you walk out on your shift last night?"

Chloe waves a hand. "I'll come up with an excuse."

"That's an awfully big risk to take."

It takes every thread of Chloe's remaining self-control not to point out that everything they've done for the last year, every clever con, every quick-fingered robbery has been risky. Yes, it's entirely possible that Reed is planning to fire her the second she clocks in. It's possible he's already sent her face to every security guard onsite, but she didn't come this far to stop now.

"I'll be fine," she says when Priya opens her mouth to speak. "How long would I have?"

Priya hesitates, fingers tapping against the top of her computer. "Casino night starts at six. If we want to make it downtown in time to set up and get Harper inside, the latest we can do is the four o'clock ferry."

"I'll make that work."

Harper shakes her head, exasperation clear even on the other side of the mattress. "Just because you can, Chloe, doesn't mean you should. Priya's right. This could end very badly."

"This might be hard to believe," Chloe says, "but not everyone's as afraid of your mother as you are."

"Well, maybe you should be. You don't know what she's capable of, and breaking into her office is a huge risk to take without proof."

"You don't have proof the award is downtown either."

"Sure, but it makes sense. You're guessing based on . . . what? A *feeling*?"

Chloe twists her fingers in the hem of her shirt. If she hadn't been adamant about searching Katherine's office before, she is now, just to prove Harper wrong. Maybe she would concede if Priya or Logan pushed back. Maybe she'd let the whole thing go and accept their plan, but Harper's been lodged between her ribs for so long that Chloe doesn't think she'd recognize herself without this particular brand of pain. It's a part of her, a grudge scraped onto her very bones, and the longer she sits with it, the more she thinks she's right.

"Maybe it is a guess," Chloe says. She bends over to snatch her uniform off the floor and when she straightens, she lets her amicable mask slip, just a bit. "But the thing about my guesses, Harper, is that they're usually right."

Harper's eyes narrow, the only indication she understands the words for the threat they are, but Chloe doesn't stay to justify it. She grabs her shoes, storms into the bathroom, and locks the door firmly behind her.

One way or another, this ends today.

SEVENTEEN

Reed's pocket square is the wrong shade of green. It's not the biggest oversight in the world, but for someone so obsessed with detail, Chloe can only assume it means he stayed up all night planning her punishment, too focused on the details to notice he'd grabbed the wrong color on the way out the door. He's probably still thinking about it now as she walks toward him down the hall, stewing in his own personal Chloe-themed revenge scheme. She wonders if it includes scrubbing the ballroom with a toothbrush like some Victorian orphan or writing the words *I will not talk to my boss's daughter* until the urge to pin Harper against the nearest wall and physically claw the truth out of her vanishes.

But that might be good for her, actually, Chloe decides. It might help her think.

She plasters on her best customer service grin as she approaches. Physically, there's nothing for Reed to lecture her about. Her skirt is pressed, her bangs are pinned neatly back from her face, and even her shoes are polished and shiny, all traces of sand scrubbed away. She's the picture of innocence, the perfect employee, and that's exactly how she's going to stay.

"Good morning," she says, inclining her chin in Reed's direction. She tries to slip past him into the laundry room, but he thrusts out an arm, effectively blocking her path.

"You," he says.

Chloe raises an eyebrow. "Me."

"Where were you last night?"

"Last night?"

"Last night," Reed repeats. "After the gala? You left the rest of your team to clean up the ballroom without you."

Chloe tilts her head, blinking up at Reed with what she hopes is a convincingly harmless expression. "What do you mean? I left when the party ended."

The crease between Reed's eyebrows deepens as he glares from Chloe to the smudged screen of his tablet. "Your shift didn't end when the party ended. Your hours were on your schedule."

"But I didn't get a schedule. You just pulled me from the locker room and told me I was working."

They face off from opposite sides of the doorway, Chloe's face carefully blank, Reed's jaw clenched. After a moment of tense silence, he exhales a rough sigh and mutters, "I suppose you're right." Then, before Chloe can move, he leans in close enough for her to smell the peppermint on his breath and whispers, "I don't know what you're up to, Ms. Bly, but you're not fooling me. Don't let it happen again."

He's watching her carefully, waiting for her to break, but Chloe just smiles innocently up at him. Reed might be used to his employees stretching the truth to get out of a shift, but Chloe has been slipping into other people's skin for a long time.

"Can I clock in now?" she asks, glancing purposefully at the way Reed's arm is still blocking the door to the laundry room.

Reed ignores her. "Kristen was supposed to train you today, but she's out sick. Then I asked Megan, but she's at the dock setting up tomorrow's event."

"What event?" Chloe asks instinctively.

"Irrelevant." Reed's gaze flickers down to his tablet. "You know how to strip rooms, I'm assuming?"

Chloe doesn't, actually, but now doesn't feel like the time for honesty. "Of course."

"Good. There's a bin in the closet you can use to collect the sheets and dirty towels. Just dump it down the laundry chute when it's full and I'll send Allie upstairs to do the rest. Can you handle that?"

"I already said yes."

"And I don't have time for you to be wrong." Reed's mustache twitches with the force of his next exhale and Chloe has the feeling their lack of staff is the only reason she's still on the schedule. She's just surprised he hasn't brought up Harper yet. "Oh," Reed says, tucking his tablet under his arm. "And try not to kiss anybody while you're up there, okay? You're a lawsuit waiting to happen."

There it is. Chloe ignores the jab and reclines against the door-frame instead. "And you want me to strip *every* room?"

Reed rolls his eyes. "That's what I said, isn't it? There's a key waiting for you in the laundry room. Don't lose it," he adds, jabbing a finger in Chloe's chest. "Those things are a headache to replace."

His expression sours and Chloe wonders how much he lectured Megan for losing her key on Monday. She wonders if there were other consequences too, if she should add Megan's name to the long list of people who have every right to hate her.

"Got it," she says. "I'm going to start upstairs. The family in 4010 won't stop calling for more towels."

"I literally could not care less where you start as long as everything gets done. Go."

Chloe nods as Reed finally lowers his arm. He starts marching back toward the lobby, frustration evident in every step, and Chloe bites back a grin as she watches him go. *Perfect.* She wants him annoyed, actually. She wants him angry enough to keep her out of sight for the rest of the day and maybe, just maybe, she can pull this off.

There are two separate key card lanyards hanging behind the laundry room door—one hook labeled STASSI and the other labeled KRISTEN. Chloe loops the latter around her neck, then slides the remaining card onto Kristen's hook to disguise its absence. It's not like Kristen will notice. She's out sick today and Chloe thoroughly plans to exploit her managerial access in her absence.

Chloe drags the laundry bin from the closet, ignoring the way the front wheel sticks and rattles. She'll start upstairs, all right, but she has no intention of cleaning every room. Maybe the rest of the housekeeping staff know to leave Katherine Windey's suite alone, but this is Chloe's first week. She's just a new employee, someone struggling to learn the ropes, and she would never, under any circumstances disobey a direct order from her boss, who just explicitly told her to clean *all* the rooms.

When the elevator door slides open on the fortieth floor, Chloe is ready. She pulls her laundry bin into the hallway with a renewed sense of urgency, shivering as a strange flash of déjà vu prickles down her spine. She was just here on Monday, dragging Harper's luggage around the curve of the hall, stopping to pluck Megan's key from her hand, and reveling in the possibility of what could be waiting for her on the other side of every locked door. Now, the waiting corridor is empty, storm clouds gathering in a dark blur through the window. Usually, the rain would be a welcome relief but today, Chloe thinks it feels like a warning.

She turns from the window, tugging the laundry bin toward Katherine's suite instead. She's extremely aware of Harper's room on the other side of the curve, but when she rounds the corner and comes face-to-face with Katherine's door, her vision narrows to a single point.

The scanner attached to the doorknob and the red light blinking at the top.

Chloe pulls the key card from her pocket and holds it against the door. In the second before the light turns green, Chloe thinks she understands why people choose to walk away from things like this. A year ago, the anticipation squeezing her stomach would have been unbearable. She would have let it crush her, but now, it feels strangely familiar.

She's survived worse things. She'll survive this one, too.

The light on the door flickers green and Chloe shoulders her way inside. "Housekeeping?"

The question echoes around the sprawling room. She was pretty sure Katherine was gone, but her shoulders still relax when no one answers. She tugs the laundry bin over the threshold and lets the door fall shut behind her.

At first glance, Katherine's suite is almost identical to Harper's—the same glamorous overtones and cozy elegance dripping from every corner. The living room is painted a soft dusty pink, the patterned wallpaper the same color scheme as her housekeeping uniform. For a minute, Chloe is tempted to hold the fabric of her skirt against the wall to see if it's a perfect match. That feels like a detail Katherine Windey wouldn't miss. Across the room, a large mahogany desk sits against a looming floor-to-ceiling window. The smooth pane of glass is vaguely reminiscent of the ballroom downstairs, but the steep drop to the frothy waves is even more unsettling from forty stories up. Chloe averts her eyes as lightning pulses on the horizon. To her right a dishwasher runs in the corner of the kitchen and to her left, a partially cracked door leads into the bedroom. If she cranes her neck, she can just make out the corner of a neatly made king-sized bed topped with a truly disgusting number of decorative throw pillows. Chloe exhales a muted sigh of relief at the sight. Unless Katherine Windey is unnaturally tidy, another manager has already stopped in to clean, which means she's not in any immediate danger of being discovered by housekeeping.

She drags the laundry bin into the center of the room, then turns in a slow circle. If she stole someone's hospitality award as part of a long-standing, low-key erotic feud, where would she keep it? The desk, maybe? The file cabinet? Somewhere in the kitchen to catch the light? Unfortunately, the living room is frustratingly clean, nothing that screams "stolen property" or a conveniently placed neon sign pointing to Carlyle's award.

One thing at a time, then.

Chloe picks her way toward the desk, footsteps muffled by a thick cream-colored rug. At first glance, the desk is as empty as the surrounding room, nothing but a blank notepad, a wooden picture frame, and a single fountain pen sitting on top. When she yanks the top drawer open, Chloe finds the items inside equally disappointing. A stack of paperwork, a few concert ticket stubs, a loose collection of photographs.

Nothing that leads back to Carlyle. Nothing to suggest Katherine thinks about him at all.

Chloe slides the drawer shut, accidentally rattling a picture frame in the corner of the desk. She reaches out to steady it, but her fingers stop in midair when she sees the photo inside. A younger Katherine standing on a white sand beach with her back to the sea and a little girl pressed against her side. An icy jolt shoots down Chloe's spine at the familiar line of the girl's smile. It's Harper, no more than seven or eight, dressed in a billowy green sundress and smiling up at a man Chloe doesn't recognize.

He's broad-shouldered and tall, with olive-toned skin and a mess of dark curls. He smiles at the camera from behind a pair of narrow sunglasses and it takes Chloe another second to realize it must be Harper's father. Enzo Parisi, the software engineer who now lives in Ohio. His hand rests casually on Katherine's waist, but if it weren't for that small display of affection, he might as well be a stranger. Even here, Chloe can see the echoes of Katherine's features frozen in time on Harper's face, but there's no hint of her father's dark curls or easy smile.

Maybe that's why she hates her so much, Chloe thinks, noting the way Harper grips the hem of her father's shirt in the photo. It wouldn't matter how much Harper tried to distance herself from her mother. At the end of the day, she could never escape her own reflection.

Footsteps echo in the hall outside and Chloe freezes, one hand still holding the photograph. She listens until they fade around the corner, then shakes her head. She's not here for a Parisi family history lesson.

She hurriedly opens and closes the rest of the drawers before ducking into the kitchen and running a hand over the suspiciously bare counters. She tries the bedroom next, then the bathroom, pulling out every trick in her book as she goes. Knocking on walls, listening for a hollow shift under her feet. By the time she turns toward the bookcase on the far side of the living room, Chloe has to fight the urge to fling the contents across the floor.

Where is it? She was so certain she was right, so convinced she'd be able to rub Carlyle's award in Harper's annoyingly contoured face, that she didn't fully consider the possibility of failure. But that's what this would be, right? Another failure tacked to her ever-growing list?

Chloe gives up on the shelf and whirls, searching the living room one last time. As she does, the sun momentarily slides from behind the wall of stagnant clouds outside. It falls over the top of the desk, mahogany surface warming in the light, and something glints in the corner of her eye. On the other side of the room, half hidden behind an enormous fiddle-leaf fig, is a golden bar cart. It's easy to miss, tucked around the corner between the plant and a glass coffee table. The sun reflects off each gilded edge, and there, resting on the top shelf like it's the most casual thing in the world, is a collection of glittering statues.

Chloe is across the room in an instant. There could be more people in the hallway outside. Someone could be opening the door right now, reaching in to haul her away, and she wouldn't hear it over the blood rushing in her ears. The image of Carlyle's missing award is burned into her mind and as she fumbles through Katherine's own collection, the rush in her ears becomes a devastating roar.

This display is noticeably smaller than the one in Carlyle's office. It only takes up two of the bar cart's three shelves, a cluster of statues and plaques and weird, abstract shapes. Chloe sorts frantically through the display, wincing every time the glass clinks too loudly, but it's not until she ducks down to peer at the second level that her hand brushes something familiar.

A statue with a sturdy wooden base topped with a clear, distinctly uncracked triangle of glass.

Chloe's breath catches in the back of her throat. She snatches the award from the shelf, fingers trembling, but when she flips it around and reads the words carved into the base, every knot of anticipatory tension releases in a single hopeless groan.

FLORIDA HOSPITALITY AWARD: WINDEY HOTELS.

Because of course Katherine won this award a year after Carlyle. Of course it would be displayed here in her office and of course it would be too much for Chloe to expect her allotment of luck to hold.

Her nails dig into the wood, one by one. She was so *sure*. Carlyle's award was supposed to be here, contemptuously hidden in the very same hotel he'd lost. It made sense, she'd been certain of it. But the longer Chloe stands with the award in hand, the more that certainty wavers.

She'd missed something. They all had, somehow, and she can't shake the growing prickle of unease.

Chloe glares down at the statue in her hands. It glimmers up at her mockingly, the tip of the glass triangle so sharp she hardly dares to touch it. Then, partially out of curiosity and partially out of frustrated spite, Chloe grabs the base with one hand and pulls.

She doesn't know what she expects. She doesn't know what she wants, really, just that the thought of taking something like this and breaking it in her own two hands makes her feel powerful. At first, nothing happens. The statue remains stubbornly intact, but when Chloe tries again, nails digging into the groove where wood meets glass, she feels something loosen. The two pieces slide apart with a soft *pop* until she's left holding one in each hand, staring into the empty hollow left in the wooden base.

For a second, the only sound is the rattle of the air-conditioning and her own uneven pulse. The itch under her skin is back, the same spark she felt that first morning in Carlyle's office. Because this is what he was looking for last night. She's sure of it. This is how he knew the award from the gala was a fake—because it didn't open. It didn't have this strange, subtle design flaw that gave way to a perfect hiding spot.

And this, Chloe thinks, is why Carlyle wants his own statue

back so badly, why he's willing to pay an exorbitant amount of money for her and Harper to retrieve it. Not because he's sentimental or attached, but because there's something inside. Something valuable hidden in a place no one would think to look.

Chloe is still standing in front of the bar cart staring at the two halves of Katherine's broken statue when more footsteps echo down the hall. They pause outside the door, and that's the only warning she gets before the doorknob rattles. Chloe's head snaps up, pulse leaping into her throat. She has just enough time to tuck the award behind her back before the lock clicks and the door swings open.

EIGHTEEN

CHLOE REALIZES THREE VERY DIFFERENT THINGS AT THE SAME TIME. The first is that the navy blazer Katherine Windey is wearing was definitely featured in that *BuzzFeed* #girlboss article. The second is that she has Logan's favorite brooch pinned to her sharply pressed lapel, and the third is that the only reason Chloe's not being flung off the balcony for trespassing is because all of Katherine's attention is currently focused on the phone balanced between her shoulder and her ear.

"That's irrelevant," she snaps to whoever's on the other end of the line. "I want his campaign signs off my property tonight, otherwise it looks like an endorsement. Which, by the way, it's not." She kicks the door shut, back still facing Chloe as she shifts the stack of files she's carrying to her other arm. "I don't care. I went to school with a lot of people, that doesn't mean I think they should hold public office. Who said that?" A pause. "Okay, well, Marci from the *Herald* is a talentless hack who can barely string two words together; tell her to get off my dick. No, that's not an official quote, I—"

Whatever she's about to say next dies in her throat as she turns and finally locks eyes with Chloe. Katherine's mouth falls open, a line creasing between her perfectly manicured brows, but when she shifts her phone to her other ear, her voice is remarkably calm.

"Hi, Lisa? I'll have someone call you back." She hangs up, drops her phone onto her stack of files, and, without missing a beat, snaps, "What are you doing in my room?"

Chloe can usually stay calm in situations like this. Just last month she talked some guy in a black Dior suit into letting her tour his private jet, but something about Katherine scrambles her brain. Maybe it's the sharp, unyielding set of her jaw, or the memory of her fingers locked around Harper's wrist.

"I'm . . ." Chloe takes a shaky step away from the bar cart. "Housekeeping?"

Katherine scoffs. She brushes past Chloe on her way across the room and drops her files on the desk with a loud *smack*. "If you're going to lie, at least make it convincing."

"I'm not lying!"

"Really? Because this room isn't on the housekeeping rotation."

Chloe swallows over her rapidly tightening throat. *Pivot,* she thinks as Katherine folds her arms over her silky blouse. *New plan.* She bites her lip and stops trying to hide the tremor in her voice.

"I'm sorry," she says. "There must have been a mistake. We're understaffed and I haven't been trained yet and Kristen was supposed to help me but she called in sick, so Reed sent me up here to strip all the rooms and I had no idea this one was off-limits so—"

"Oh my god." Katherine pinches the bridge of her nose. "Please stop talking."

Chloe retreats another step. "I'm sorry."

"Stop saying that."

"I'm—" Chloe clamps her mouth shut to prevent another instinctive apology from slipping loose. The silence that follows is agonizing, but when she looks up again, Katherine's expression is marginally softer.

"Don't apologize when you have nothing to be sorry for," she says. "It makes you look incompetent. You said it was your first week, right?"

So Katherine does remember her from last night. Chloe nods, gaze darting instinctively toward the door. "Yes."

"Well, there you go. Everyone makes mistakes. But for future reference, you should never enter this suite without my explicit permission."

"Right." Chloe exhales a shaky breath. "Sorry. I mean . . . yes. Okay."

To her surprise, the corner of Katherine's mouth lifts in the barest hint of a smile. "Better."

It's strange, Chloe thinks, to see the expressions she's memorized on Harper fit so easily on someone else's face. Katherine opens one of her files and Chloe lets her gaze slide carefully back to the bar cart. Her arms are starting to ache from clutching the award behind her back. If she could just put it back together, she could drop it on the cart and leave before Katherine remembers she's supposed to be angry.

Chloe takes a tentative step to the side, hands fumbling to reassemble the pieces behind her back.

"Is there a reason you're still here?"

Katherine has one hand planted on her hip, sun glinting off the edge of her gilded brooch, and for a minute, the only thing Chloe can think about is Logan's voice saying, *one day, Chloe, I'm going to get you to do a jewelry heist.* Maybe that's her way out. If she snatched that piece off Katherine's lapel and ran, it would certainly distract from the broken award she'd inevitably leave behind.

"I . . . no." Chloe glances around the room, frantically searching for an excuse. Her eyes fall on the sweeping floor-to-ceiling window. "It's just . . . this view," she blurts. "I've never seen the island from this high up. It's beautiful."

If there's one thing rich people love more than being rich, it's explaining in great, condescending detail exactly how rich they are. The same principle that allowed Logan to pocket James Webber's watch last week, the one that's buoyed them all through countless cons and thefts. Chloe can only hope it holds true now.

For a second, Katherine's hand stills on the surface of her desk, head tilting as she looks over the collection of yachts docked safely in the Rivera harbor. Then she smiles. "It's nice, isn't it?"

"Totally." Chloe inches back as carefully as she can, taking advantage of Katherine's momentary distraction to finally slide the two parts of the award back together. "I think the marina's my favorite spot on the island."

Standing like this with her back to the office, the pale sunlight turning her hair gold, Katherine looks so much like her daughter that Chloe still can't believe she didn't notice the resemblance sooner. Unlike Harper's, however, Katherine's answering smile feels genuine.

"Do you sail?" she asks.

Chloe thinks of her dream last night, of the cold water closing over her head, and shivers. "No. I don't like the ocean. It's . . . intimidating."

"That's the point."

Katherine's expression turns inward and for a second, Chloe's not entirely convinced they're having the same conversation. Maybe that's all this hotel is in the end. An intimidation tactic. A strategic move. Another way to beat Carlyle at whatever game they're playing.

Chloe takes another step back. When her hip brushes the corner of the bar cart, all thoughts of open water vanish. She keeps her gaze locked straight ahead as she slowly lowers the award toward the surface. It's not easy to do from this angle. She's just bent her knees in an attempt to get closer when Katherine turns suddenly from the window. Chloe jumps, award slipping from her fingers, and the sound it makes when it hits the top of the cart feels loud enough to rattle the very pictures from the wall.

Several dozen excuses gather on the tip of her tongue, but Katherine doesn't seem to notice the disturbance. Instead, she braces one hand on the surface of her desk and says, "I want to apologize for how I spoke to you last night."

"I . . ." Chloe's mouth falls open, mission momentarily forgotten. "What?"

She's worked minimum wage retail jobs her entire life. She's had customers confront her about everything from the store's return policy to their opinion on her physical appearance, but never once has anyone tried to apologize. She doesn't think it's allowed.

"I want to apologize," Katherine repeats. "I was dealing with a number of . . . precarious situations last night. But I shouldn't have taken it out on you. That was rude."

"Oh." Chloe slides away from the bar cart as carefully as she can. "Sure. Thank you?"

She hesitates, waiting for the punch line, but it never comes. Something about Katherine feels different this morning. Softer. Like she's not actively out for blood. *Probably because Harper's not here,* Chloe thinks bitterly. She understands the feeling.

There's a beat of silence where the two of them watch each other from across the room, Katherine outlined in patchy sunlight, Chloe still standing suspiciously close to the bar cart. Then Katherine's phone vibrates across the surface of her desk. In the instant before she picks it up, Chloe catches the contact name flashing across the top of her screen. *Andrew Carlyle.*

And just like that, Katherine's expression shutters. "You should get back to work," she says. "I'm sure there are other rooms in need of assistance."

She's talking to Chloe, but she's looking at her phone, mouth tightening the longer it rings. Chloe nods and reaches for her laundry bin. She lingers just long enough to watch Katherine pick up the phone and snap, "I told you not to call me," before the door clicks shut and Chloe is once again alone.

She exhales, sagging against the wall. Her arms still ache from clutching the award and Chloe wonders if this is what runners feel like mid-marathon. Wrung out and tired and desperate for air. The corner of Katherine's mailbox presses against the small of her back as she strains to hear the rest of the conversation inside, but all she gets is the whisper of air-conditioning through the vent overhead. No hint of Katherine's voice or suggestion of what she and Carlyle might be discussing.

That's fine, though. Chloe straightens, readjusting her grip on the laundry bin. She might not understand the pieces falling into place around her, but she has a decent idea who might.

And, unfortunately, she knows exactly where to go next.

NINETEEN

Chloe walks into the Carlyle hotel forty minutes after the end of her shift at the Rivera, wearing a stolen pair of Harper's shoes and flipping the penthouse key card between her fingers.

She doesn't know if it's still active. She doesn't know if she'll make it past the security team downstairs, but she's been living on the edge for too long not to notice the ground starting to crumble under her feet. Chloe can handle Andrew Carlyle using her, but she's been around long enough to know there's something else here, too. Another layer to this job he isn't sharing. She doesn't expect honesty, or for him to suddenly start divulging all his secrets, but she does intend to get her friends out of this in one piece.

Two men in sharp navy suits block Chloe's view of the front desk as she enters. One of them holds a dark leather briefcase and the other glares down at his phone, pointedly ignoring the concierge before them. With a jolt, Chloe recognizes the first as the finance guy her manager met with last week. She doubts he'll recognize her, especially with her new hair and wardrobe, but she still ducks her head as she cuts through the lobby.

The waistband of her skirt is too tight, made for someone with infuriatingly narrow hips. Chloe has to tug it down three separate times as she walks before the hem finally stays in place. She pulled it from the bottom of Harper's suitcase before catching the ferry across the bay, taking advantage of the twenty minutes the others were out for lunch to sneak back into the suite. Not that Harper knows that, of course, but what's the point of having a master key if she's not going to use it?

Chloe joins the crowd filing into the elevators. She taps her penthouse card against the scanner, waiting as everyone filters onto their respective floors. By the time the final guest departs, she's sweating under her blouse and her skirt is once again riding up her thighs. She yanks it down as hard as she can, ignoring the sound of popping seams.

Harper probably has a tailor on retainer.

The penthouse foyer is as spotless as Chloe remembers, smooth tile glimmering in the hazy light from outside. She's half expecting some sort of security now that Carlyle hasn't actively invited her, some overly muscled hired help standing in the middle of the room and demanding to run a credit check. But the room is deserted, with nothing but the glow of the glittering chandelier to keep her company.

Music drifts down the hall, the same low, classical strains as before. Chloe's muscles wind tight beneath her skin as she follows it around the corner. It must hide the sound of her footsteps too, because when she stops in front of Carlyle's office, it takes a second for him to realize she's there.

"Ms. Bly." He does a double take, hands stilling on his keyboard, and Chloe feels a brief flash of satisfaction at the surprise etched across his face. The expression vanishes as quickly as it comes. "What are you doing here?"

It's more of a dismissal than a question, but Chloe forces herself to hold her ground. Harper would. She glared at Carlyle across the desk that first day like they were equals, and even though Chloe has no idea what it's like to walk through life with that kind of confidence, she *is* wearing a pair of eight-hundred-dollar shoes now. And girls with eight-hundred-dollar shoes probably don't let other people tell them what to do. She lifts her chin, forcing herself to channel a fraction of Harper's cool arrogance.

"I have a question for you."

Carlyle doesn't look up. "Do you have my award?"

"Not yet."

"I'm a very busy man, Ms. Bly, so if you haven't done your job, I don't see what there is to discuss."

Chloe ignores him. She crosses the remainder of the room, pulse hammering a hurried warning in her veins, and drops into one of the chairs on the other side of the desk. This kind of confrontation isn't new to her. In fact, it's almost familiar. This place is familiar, too. The same vaulted ceiling, the same vintage picture frame taunting her from the corner of the desk. The sepia vignette inside is the same too, a young Andrew Carlyle standing with his friends in front of the university library. Now that she's looking at it again, Chloe notices that the left side of the photo is jagged and torn, like part of it has been ripped off or tucked away. For some reason, the sight steadies her. Like no matter what Carlyle says, there will always be a few imperfections lurking beneath his surface, too.

She leans back in the chair, both elbows propped on the padded leather armrests. "That award must be very valuable to you."

A muscle tenses in Carlyle's jaw. "It is."

"Because it represents your win, right? It's a reminder of everything you've accomplished?"

"Exactly. I want it back and you—"

"Why did you hire us?"

Carlyle's hands rest on his keyboard. He's wearing another too-casual boat shirt, but when he looks up, Chloe senses the frustration rippling under every movement. *Good,* she thinks. She wants him on edge. She wants him on the defensive.

"I already told you. You and Ms. Parisi made a wonderful team at my dinner last week."

"But we aren't a team. And you didn't arrive until after I left, so how did you know what we were doing? How did you put this in my pocket?" Chloe wiggles the key card in the air, thumb rubbing absently over the raised text. "Why did you trust us to finish this job when we'd never even spoken?"

"You're trusting me to pay you for it. Funny how that works."

"I don't trust you. Just so we're clear."

Carlyle laces his fingers together with exaggerated patience. "Do you have a point, Ms. Bly?"

Chloe gives a casual shrug. "Just wondering why this particular award is so important. I mean, you're the one who started this feud with Katherine, right? You stole that first plot of land she wanted."

Something flickers behind Carlyle's eyes. "Is that what she told you?"

"She didn't have to. The records aren't hard to find."

If Chloe's being generous, she probably has one, maybe two minutes before Carlyle tosses her out of the penthouse for good. But if she can keep him talking, if she can slide under his skin long enough to loosen his tongue, she might get the answers she needs. To her surprise, Carlyle takes the bait.

"Interesting." He shakes his head, as if to clear a particularly irritating memory. "And what do those records say, exactly?"

"That she sourced the land," Chloe says. "That she'd been working with developers for months, collecting permits and arranging inspections and then you swooped in last minute with a deal no one could refuse."

"Exactly. I had the better offer. I can't control how she feels."

Chloe purses her lips, head tipped to one side like she's genuinely considering. "I mean, I'd be annoyed if I spent all that time working on a project only for someone else to take all the credit. You can't be mad that she's stealing your awards when you're the one who started this in the first place."

A shadow of that made-for-TV smile tugs at the corner of Carlyle's mouth. "Do you know how I knew she wanted that land? Do you know how I knew exactly what she was doing with those developers or how badly she needed it to work out? Because she *told me.* Over and over again, for months after we both moved to

Miami. All she could talk about was how excited she was for that first hotel. She didn't think twice about who she was telling. Do you want to know the real reason she's sneaking around and stealing awards from me now?"

Chloe's fingers curl into the armrests. There's a wild, almost gleeful gleam in Carlyle's eye as he waits for her answer, like he wants nothing more than to tell her how powerful he really is. "I don't know," she says. "Because you were a bad friend, apparently?"

"No, because she *lost.* Everything she's done since she opened the doors of that first hotel has been to prove me wrong. I'm the only reason she exists."

Chloe doesn't think that's particularly fair. She's not Katherine Windey's biggest fan, but she doesn't like Carlyle's thinly veiled attempt to take credit for someone else's accomplishments. She shrugs, the gesture infinitely more relaxed than she feels. "I don't know. I heard she has a Rothko insured for ten million dollars. Seems like she's doing fine."

"Of course she'd pick a Rothko. Art that derivative always makes people feel important." Carlyle's face is still infuriatingly smooth, but when his hands flatten against the desk, there's tension lined in every finger. "You have to know who your enemy is before you can best them. That's your strategy with Ms. Parisi, isn't it? Do you know what she wants?"

Chloe shrugs, ignoring the uncomfortable prickle at the back of her neck. "Five million dollars, I'm assuming."

"Oh, you can do better than that. Didn't you see her that first time I brought you together? All she wants, really, is for someone to *notice her.* To tell her she's important and pretend to care. Try that next time you talk to her and see where it gets you."

He's enjoying this, Chloe can tell, and the worst part is, she thinks he's right. She thinks that *is* what Harper wants, deep down, but the casual way Carlyle says it, like he's handing Chloe a loaded weapon, makes her bristle on Harper's behalf.

"Know your enemy. Got it." Chloe lets the phrase settle in the air between them before straightening ever so slightly. "So what's up with the finance guys downstairs? Are you getting audited?"

Carlyle's brow lifts ever so slightly, the only hint of surprise on his otherwise imperturbable face. "I have no idea what you're talking about."

"Oh, I'm sorry. Is it a secret? The managers were having everyone pull their time sheets before I left, so I figured it was something like that."

Chloe's never been particularly good at cards. She can't, for the life of her, seem to develop a consistent strategy, but she is very good at bluffing. Sometimes, that's all it takes to sway a game in her favor. She doesn't know if her accusation is true and doesn't particularly care if it is. Honesty isn't the point. She's more interested in Carlyle's reaction, and what he might let slip in the process.

Carlyle's eyes narrow on her across the desk. His gaze is dark, unreadable as the sea clawing at the Rivera's coast.

"What do you want?"

Chloe's answer is immediate. "The truth. What did you send us in there to steal?"

"My hospitality award."

"That's all?"

"If you have something to say, Ms. Bly, just say it."

Tension coils in the line of Carlyle's shoulders. It feels like last night in the golf cart when he snatched the award and threatened her job, but this time, Chloe thinks she might have the upper hand.

"I get that you and Katherine have this . . . thing," she says, eyes never leaving his face, "but why is this single award so important to you? Didn't Katherine win one the next year? Wouldn't she have a statue just like yours sitting somewhere in one of her hotels? I get that you don't want to ask for yours back, but I don't understand why you'd offer two people you've never met five million dollars when that award is objectively worthless."

Say it, Chloe thinks, edging forward in her chair. *Tell me what I'm really looking for.* This is the answer she wants, an explanation for why the idea of this job has always sat like hot coals in her stomach, but the longer she watches, the more Carlyle's discomfort seems to fade. He leans back in his chair, fingers steepled before him, and when the corner of his mouth lifts into a smile, Chloe has the feeling she's made a fatal, devastating mistake.

"Oh, Ms. Bly," he says, tone noticeably lighter. "You're certainly not as smart as you think you are. That's an excellent point, though. Why is there money on the table when you're going to do exactly what I say, regardless of what I offer?"

"Hold on," Chloe starts. "That's not—"

"Do you think this is a negotiation? Do you honestly think you have any power here? I know exactly what you've been up to all year—robbing my hotels, my guests, my donors. I know all about your little friends, too. What are their names?"

Cold slices down Chloe's spine as Carlyle holds up one finger. "There's Logan Amesfield. Graduated from NC State with a theater degree, a truly unfortunate choice, and now works as a boardwalk magician and part-time clown for children's birthday parties. He's originally from Orlando but you convinced him to move down here last year and now he lives on Northwest Sixth? Near the stadium, right?"

He doesn't give Chloe the chance to respond, holding up another finger instead. "Then there's Priya Mishra. She went to MIT for two years before moving home to support her family. Now she spends half her time taking Instagram pictures and the other half working at the hardware store in City Center. And you." Carlyle's gaze rakes over Chloe's face with alarming ferocity. "You also graduated from NC State with a communications degree. You're from Miami, but you only moved home when your mother fell tragically ill. What was it? Ovarian cancer?"

Chloe's nails slice into her palms. "Don't—" she starts, but Carlyle ignores her.

"I'm sorry for your loss, by the way," he says, that same savage glee still dancing in his eye. "And when you're still so young? That must have been difficult."

He leans forward and it takes everything in Chloe's power not to draw back. "So you're right," he says. "I really *don't* need to pay you, because if that award is not back on my desk by Friday evening, I will turn every scrap of information I have on you three—every damning piece of criminal evidence—straight over to the authorities. I will bury you and your friends so deep you'll wish you never heard my name. You think every precinct in this city doesn't already work for me? You think it wouldn't be enough to put you all away for a long, *long* time?"

There's the ground, cracking again under her feet. Chloe always thought it was possible that Carlyle knew more than he was letting on, but when he didn't bring it up that first day, she assumed the threat had passed. If he knew about Logan and Priya, if he even suspected, Chloe was certain he would have used her friends as leverage the day he brought her and Harper into his office. But it seems she misjudged the entire situation. He's always been saving it for a moment like this.

I told you. For a minute, the voice in the back of Chloe's mind sounds suspiciously like Katherine's. *Always so predictable.*

"You . . ." Chloe swallows over her rapidly closing throat. "You made a deal with me. My friends have nothing to do with this."

"Oh, I know." Carlyle settles back in his chair. The tension that lined his face earlier is gone, replaced with cruel satisfaction. "And I'm not unreasonable. If you hold up your end of the bargain, there's no need for it to come to that. We can forget this entire conversation ever happened. I might even put the money back on the table, as a gesture of goodwill. I'm merely trying to make sure you understand what's at stake if you fail. Is that clear?"

Chloe's fingers ache around the edge of her chair. She saw a flash of this person last night, but here's the real Andrew Carlyle, sitting across from her with his mask off at last.

You have to know who your enemy is before you can best them.

Carlyle must have known her from the second Chloe asked how much he was willing to pay. He's been tightening the noose ever since, so gradually she didn't notice the trap until it was too late.

"Is that clear?" Carlyle repeats. He's still watching her across the desk, mouth curled in obvious amusement. "Can you finish the job?"

Chloe grits her teeth. Of course she can. She doesn't have a choice. "Yes."

"Then get to work."

Carlyle turns back to his computer like she's nothing more than a speck of dust on his impeccably shiny shoe, and Chloe knows it's because he won. Because he thinks he's better than her. As she pushes herself to her feet, she thinks he may be right.

"Oh, and Chloe?" Lit by the glow of his computer screen, Carlyle's grin is positively lethal. "If you're going to throw around accusations in my office, you'd better bring proof. Otherwise, you just look desperate."

Chloe's shaking by the time she spills out onto the sun-warmed sidewalk. She starts walking back toward the bay, not slowing until she rounds the corner and leaves the gleaming façade of the hotel behind. Only then does she exhale and slowly open her fist.

There, sitting in the center of her palm, is a receiver, nearly identical to the one she just pressed to the underside of Andrew Carlyle's desk. She flicks it on and holds it against her ear, straining to hear over the crowded street.

". . . and a large black coffee, please. As soon as you can."

The words are followed by a muffled click, like someone setting a phone receiver down, before the sound of typing resumes. Carlyle back to work, oblivious to the bug lurking inches below his computer and the hole she just smashed in his defenses.

Funny, Chloe thinks as she starts walking again. *Maybe he's not as smart as he thinks he is either.*

TWENTY

By the time Chloe makes it back to the Rivera, her hair is impossibly tangled from the trip across the bay and there are no fewer than four blisters forming on the bottom of her feet. She knows she can't avoid the others entirely, but she still braces herself when she opens the door to Harper's suite, excuses for her absence already formed.

Music is playing from somewhere in the kitchen and by the look of the immaculately clean entryway, Harper's getting ready to leave. The same pale pink suitcase Chloe carried upstairs now sits packed and waiting against the wall.

"Hi," she says, letting the door fall shut behind her. "What's going on?"

Logan ducks out of the bathroom at the sound of her voice. "There you are," he says, rubbing a towel through the ends of his damp hair. "Where have you been?"

"And what are you wearing?" Priya looks up from the couch lowering her headphones so they hang around her neck. "You look like a Hallmark movie villain."

Chloe trails a hand down the front of Harper's blouse, suddenly self-conscious. It's one thing to steal designer clothes, but it's quite another to have her friends see how hard she was trying to be someone else. "This isn't mine," she mutters.

"Oh, we know." Harper appears in the doorway to her bedroom, gaze raking down the length of Chloe's body. "It's clearly mine. You shouldn't wear that color, it washes you out." She glances at Priya. "Do you really think I dress like a Hallmark villain?"

"It's not your fault," Logan says hastily. "It's hard to pull off that much suede."

"Exactly," Priya says. "It's very 'I'm going to tear down your beloved community center, then tell the male lead his small-town girlfriend doesn't understand him.'"

Harper's brow furrows. "Thank you?"

Chloe scowls and kicks her shoes into the corner. "What's with the bags?" she asks. "Are you going somewhere?"

"Um, yeah?" Priya glances from Harper's packed suitcase to her own. "We talked about it this morning, remember. We're catching the four o'clock ferry downtown for casino night?"

"Right," Chloe says quickly. "Of course. You found it, then? The award actually is downtown?"

Logan hesitates. "Not exactly. Here." He pulls a frosty bottle of water from Harper's refrigerator and slides it across the counter. "You look parched."

It's only when her hand makes contact with the cold glass that Chloe realizes she hasn't eaten all day. Her last sip of water was at the beginning of her shift hours ago and now that the adrenaline of the afternoon is wearing off, the ache in her stomach is impossible to ignore. She drains half the bottle in a single gulp, dragging the back of her hand across her mouth to avoid spilling on Harper's blouse. It's probably dry-clean only. The silk probably dissolves in water like cotton candy. When she looks up again, the others are watching her with identical expressions of wary concern. It takes another second for Chloe to realize how she must look—rumpled and windswept, standing barefoot in the kitchen wearing Harper's clothes.

"So?" she prompts when no one speaks. "What's going on?"

"That feels like a question for you, actually." Priya stands up from the couch, laptop cradled in the crook of her arm. Her hair is still tied back in a messy bun, but she looks better than she did this morning. Like she actually managed to get a few hours of sleep in Chloe's absence. "Did you get into Katherine's suite?"

"Oh, yeah." Chloe waves a hand. "I stopped by this morning. The award wasn't there."

"You . . ." Priya trails off, gaze sliding pointedly in Logan's direction. "Okay. That would have been nice to know, Chloe."

"Why?" Chloe asks, unable to keep the bitter edge from her voice. "It's not like I found anything useful."

Logan shifts against the counter. "Are you sure? You searched the whole suite?"

"Pretty sure. Katherine came back before I could, like, rip up the floorboards or anything, but—"

"She came back? She found you in her office?"

"No!" Chloe shakes her head. "I mean *yes,* but it's not like she caught me doing anything wrong. I just told her I was new and didn't understand how housekeeping worked."

Chloe decides to omit the part about temporarily vandalizing Katherine's own award collection. That would require admitting that she *did* almost get caught, and judging from the way the vein in Priya's forehead is starting to pulse, she doesn't think that piece of information is particularly relevant.

Harper lets out a derisive snort. "You think she believed you?" she asks. "*You,* Chloe? Of all people? You can't keep underestimating her or someone's going to get hurt."

Chloe rolls her eyes. "I don't know how many times I have to tell you, Harper. I can handle your mother. I saw an opening and I took it. It's exactly what anyone here would have done."

"Except she saw you! She saw us together last night too, and I promise, that's not nothing to her."

"I don't know, she was perfectly nice to me today, so maybe the problem in that relationship is you."

Harper gives a dismissive scoff, but as she turns away, something about her expression feels fragile. It's the same way she looked out across the sea last night, like her entire façade is one pointed comment away from shattering.

"Okay, okay." Logan steps between them. "This is fine. It's good, actually. If the award wasn't in Katherine's office, then it's definitely downtown. Problem solved."

No, Chloe thinks, *it's not.* But when Harper folds her arms, exhaling through her nose in a way that clearly says *whatever,* Chloe knows how it will look if she refuses to move on, too.

"Fine," she mutters. "I'm in. What's the plan?"

Logan sags against the counter, muttering something that sounds suspiciously like *oh, thank god* under his breath, but Priya remains rooted to the carpet.

"Are you really?" she asks. "I know this is . . . a lot, but we're supposed to be a team, Chloe. We need to communicate with each other. With *everyone,*" she adds, glaring pointedly in Harper's direction. "You can't disappear all afternoon. You can't do things like that without telling us. How are we supposed to work with that?"

The same thing she'd lectured Harper about on their first day at the Rivera, at the gala, in that beachside cabana. *We're supposed to be a team.* Chloe folds her arms, heat flaring defensively in her chest.

"I didn't *disappear.* I was just trying to find that award, same as you. And I was going to put everything in the group chat after my shift, but I got distracted."

"Distracted by what?" Logan asks.

Chloe hesitates. Dropping her unapproved visit to the Carlyle penthouse doesn't feel like a particularly welcome addition to the conversation. "Nothing. It's not important."

"Yeah, right." Harper gives her another pointed up-and-down look. "You're not dressed for nothing."

"I went for a walk."

"In my clothes?"

"Maybe," Chloe snaps. "It's not my fault they look better on me."

"Okay, first of all, they absolutely don't."

"Stop it." There's an edge to Logan's voice now, a tension Chloe rarely sees. "This is what we're talking about. We can't finish this job if you're always at each other's throats."

That's true of course, but old habits die hard. Chloe's fingers curl at her sides as she remembers the heat of Harper's hands on her last night in the hallway. She *could* work with that Harper, if she had to. She'd almost welcome it. But the Harper standing before her now is slippery and vague and so completely unknowable.

"Fine," Chloe bites out. "If you *must* know, I went to see Carlyle."

Harper's eyes widen. She falls back a step, face draining of color, and Chloe barely gets a second to revel in her surprise before Priya slaps a hand against the top of the speaker, cutting off the music in the room.

"You did *what*?"

Chloe swallows nervously. "It's nothing. We . . . just talked about the job."

"And you don't think that's something we should've discussed beforehand?"

"It's not a big deal, Pri. I just want to know why he cares so much about that specific award and why he's willing to pay five million dollars to get it back."

Harper tucks a strand of loose hair behind her ear, face still unnaturally pale.

"Why does that matter?" she asks. "It's his money. He can do whatever he wants with it."

"There's more to it than that," Chloe says. "I know there is."

"With all due respect, Chloe, who cares?" Priya's voice is firm, completely devoid of its usual humor. "That's not our problem. We're here to find his award. That's all."

"That's literally what I'm trying to do!" Chloe looks from her to Logan, searching for a singular thread of their usual comradery. "Why can't you trust me?"

Harper lets out a short, sharp-edged laugh. "Oh, I don't know, Chloe, maybe because you're endangering everyone in this room."

Chloe rounds on her right as Logan's hand comes up to grip her shoulder. "I think what Harper means," he says, voice deliberately calm, "is that we're in a very delicate situation. Of course we trust you, but there's a lot on the line. This isn't the time to be impulsive."

"I'm not being impulsive! Carlyle is lying to us. You have to know that."

"No shit, Chloe!" Priya snaps. "He's literally running for senator! You think he got this far by being a lovely person? He's a liar. *We're* liars! Why is that suddenly an issue for you?"

"Because we deserve to know what we're risking! If we make the wrong move because he's withholding information, he's not going to get us out. He doesn't care. He knows about everything, Priya. He knows about you and Logan. He knows where you live and what you do for work and if we don't find that award by Friday . . ."

Chloe trails off, unable to complete the threat. Silence falls over the room, broken only by the wild thunder of her pulse. Then Logan's hand falls back to his side. "What do you mean?" he asks, voice hoarse. "You said . . . I thought we were safe."

Chloe did, too. It was easy to brush off last week's donor event. They'd left empty-handed, and Carlyle had no definitive proof they ever intended to take anything more. But the other jobs—the year of lifted jewelry and stolen credit cards and valuables plucked from one hotel room after the other—couldn't be explained away.

"No way." Priya shakes her head. "He's bluffing. He might know about me and Logan, but he doesn't have proof that we've ever stolen from him."

Logan starts pacing, hands raking nervously through his hair with every step. When his gaze lands on Chloe, it's completely devoid of its familiar warmth. "Really?" he asks. "You couldn't have left him alone for two more days? You didn't think, for one *second,* that it might be a bad idea to piss off a CEO with more money than god?"

Chloe flinches at the sudden ferocity in his voice. "You think this is my fault?"

"Well, it's certainly not mine."

"It's not like I paid him a visit for my own personal enjoyment." Chloe digs the speaker out of her pocket and flings it in Logan's direction. "I went to plant this. That's all."

She waits for the collective exhale, for everyone to realize she really did have a plan, but Priya just laughs. "So what? We can listen to his meetings now? That doesn't change the fact that your little visit endangered everyone in this room."

"That's not fair," Chloe snaps. "He'd still have that footage whether I went or not. Our conversation today didn't change the fact he was always going to turn us in."

"He doesn't have anything," Priya insists. "I'm telling you—he's bluffing."

"We don't know that."

"I do. I wipe those cameras myself. It's impossible."

"Or maybe you messed up, Priya!" Chloe cries. "You're not perfect."

It's too much. Chloe knows the instant the words leave her mouth. They're too pointed, too sharp, and Priya's expression creases with hurt.

"Fuck you, Chloe. I've been up here all day. I'm the one phishing security directors and getting camera access and risking detection every time I switch angles. I'm the one combing every square inch of this hotel while you're off making conversation with a man who doesn't care if we live or die. But sure. What do I know?"

Chloe reaches for her arm. "That's not what I—"

"I know what you meant," Priya says. "Do you need me to remind you how much I need this job? How many people are counting on me to make ends meet?"

"Of course not. I know what we're risking."

"Well, you're doing a pretty shit job of showing it." Priya slings her backpack over her shoulder and turns toward the door. "I'm going to wait in the lobby. See you when the boat leaves."

She leaves without another word, letting the door slam behind her with a heavy *thud*. Chloe recoils at the sound. Guilt churns in her stomach, burning up the back of her throat, but when she glances at Logan, he just shakes his head.

"Sorry," he says. "But she's right. You can't do things like this without telling us. We're all on the line here. She's worried about her family—"

"We all have families."

"And we all need this job." Logan straightens and reaches for his suitcase. "We're going downtown tonight. We're getting into that party and we're going to find Carlyle's award. You're more than welcome to take the four o'clock ferry with us, but if you're not going to help, I think it's probably best if you stay here."

Chloe bites back a rueful laugh. "So that's it, then? You know best? Five million dollars on the table and suddenly that's all you care about?"

"No, Chloe." Logan's voice has a quiet sort of finality she's never heard before. "I care about you. You're just too selfish to see it."

Then he's gone too, and Chloe shivers as the lock clicks into place behind him. Silence falls across the living room, broken only by the echo of Logan's voice in the back of her mind.

You're just too selfish to see it.

Maybe he's right. Maybe part of her always suspected she'd be the reason this job failed, too.

For a single heartbeat, the room is so quiet, Chloe can hear the rush of waves against the shoreline outside. Then Harper reaches across the counter for a bottle of wine. "Well," she says, an infuriating little half smile once again tugging at the corner of her mouth. "That was very dramatic."

It takes everything in Chloe's power not to lean over and smack the bottle from her grip. "Shut up."

"I mean, you're only hurting yourself." Harper continues like Chloe hasn't spoken, prying open the bottle with a loud *pop.* "I don't understand why you can't let things go."

Chloe bares her teeth. "Yeah. I wonder why."

She starts toward the door, but Harper extends a leg to the side, blocking her path. "You can't keep blaming me for everything, you know. We have a plan. We'll find that award tonight, we'll get paid, and then we never have to see each other again. You're the only one causing problems here."

"Because I'm right! I'm right about Carlyle and I'm right about you. *You* are the one who ruined our job last night and you're the one still keeping secrets now."

Harper shakes her head, still infuriatingly calm as Chloe practically vibrates with fury. "Incredible," she says. "You really are obsessed with me."

"Oh my *god.*"

Chloe tries to move around her, but Harper shifts to the side, still blocking the only escape route. "Let's say you're right. Say Carlyle isn't being honest and you figured out his deep, dark secret. It's still none of our business. That's how this game works."

"Then maybe I don't want to play."

"Or maybe you're tired of losing." Chloe can't tell if it's the heat or the proximity, but Harper's cheeks flush. Her next words come out silky and low, almost imperceptible in the shrinking space between them. "Face it, Chloe. The only liability here is you."

Chloe shoves her away. At least, she tries to. Her fingers curl in the smooth fabric of Harper's shirt but instead of pushing her aside, she lets out a low, frustrated groan and yanks Harper against her.

She was surprised last night in the hallway, her body short-circuiting the instant Harper's lips met hers, but Chloe is awake now. She's here and she's *mad,* every cell in her body screaming with the same insatiable need. Harper's mouth parts under hers, more surprised than anything, but Chloe doesn't care. She slides a hand possessively around Harper's neck, and then Harper's kissing her back, wild and ferocious and desperate.

It shouldn't make sense. Chloe shouldn't be able to guess where Harper wants her based on the way her breathing shifts. Harper shouldn't know about the sensitive spot right under Chloe's jaw and she definitely shouldn't be able to find it so quickly, teeth nipping at the delicate skin until Chloe's head lolls against the wall.

"This is *mine,*" Harper hisses. Her hands tear at the buttons on Chloe's shirt. "Give it back."

Chloe lets out a ragged breath as air slides across her chest, cooling her skin. She captures Harper's bottom lip between her teeth and bites until a small gasp of pain tears itself from Harper's throat. "No. I hate you."

Harper's answering grin is vicious. Chloe feels it pressed against her lips like a warning. "You don't."

She does. Of course she does. But what was the last year if not the teasing, infuriatingly long buildup to *this*? Chloe threads her fingers through Harper's hair, yanking until her head tips back and she can plant hot, biting kisses down the column of her throat. Harper's pulse hammers against her mouth. Chloe is certain hers is just as wild and still, she tightens her grip.

"I do," she gasps. "I hate you."

She yanks at Harper's shirt until the material wrinkles in her hands, until Harper breaks their kiss long enough to pull it over her head and toss it aside. For a paralyzing second, Chloe can't decide what to touch first. The sharp line of Harper's collarbones, the freckled plane of her stomach, the curve of her breasts still hidden behind the pale pink lace of her bra. She's never seen this much of Harper before. Before today, she would have claimed she never wanted to, but the truth is more complicated.

The truth is, if they'd done this that first day, if Chloe had slammed Harper against the wall of that corporate restaurant the way she'd always thought about, she doesn't think they would've ever been able to stop.

Harper lets out a choked laugh. "You're a bad liar, Chloe. You always have been."

The wall at Chloe's back is working overtime to keep her upright. She presses her lips together, swallowing the moan building in the back of her throat as Harper claims her mouth in another hot, hungry kiss.

"I'm not lying. I hate you. You're ruining my life."

It doesn't sound remotely convincing, but when Harper pulls back, eyes bright, lips swollen, Chloe thinks she looks equally undone. She has just enough time to revel in the simple, senseless victory of it before Harper drops to her knees.

"Then say it again," she whispers. "Tell me you hate me, and I'll leave you alone."

Chloe opens her mouth. She wants to say it. She should, but before she can form the words, Harper's mouth sinks against the inside of Chloe's knee and every thought in her head blinks blissfully white. Chloe bites back another embarrassingly desperate moan and winds her trembling fingers into Harper's hair.

"Say it." Harper's voice vibrates along the inside of her thigh. "Say that you hate me."

"I . . ."

It's like Harper's reached inside her chest and smashed a fist through every wall Chloe spent the last year building. Harper tightens her grip, fingers sinking into the creases of Chloe's hips as her mouth slides up her thigh and Chloe doesn't want her to stop. She doesn't want to think about anything other than Harper's mouth on her but she also knows that if this happens now, if she gives in before finishing what she came here to do, it'll ruin everything.

Chloe closes her eyes, hand falling back to her side. "*I hate you.*"

It comes out in a low, breathless gasp. Harper's hands go still around her thighs. Slowly, she sits back on her heels and when she lifts her chin to meet Chloe's gaze, her expression is surprisingly blank.

Chloe swallows over the lump in her throat. "I hate you," she repeats. "I want you to leave me alone."

This time, her voice is steady. Harper's hands fall back to her sides. Chloe pulls away as best she can, suddenly aware of her unbuttoned shirt and the way her skirt sits hiked up around her hips. She yanks it back down. Somehow, the thought of Harper seeing her like this, furiously trying to pull herself together, is worse than the thought of Harper seeing her undone. She keeps her gaze locked on the floor as Harper grabs her shirt and slowly pushes herself to her feet.

There's a moment where Chloe feels Harper look at her—

really look, like she's trying to memorize the shape of this exact moment. She doesn't look up. She can't. If she does, there's a very real chance Chloe will kiss her again. Then Harper turns. Without another word, she walks into the bedroom and shuts the door firmly behind her.

The lock slides into place with a soft *click* and it's like the sound breaks whatever spell has been keeping Chloe upright. She slides down the wall, landing in a crumpled heap on the carpet. *What the hell are you doing?* The thought clangs through her mind like a warning. The one that follows, however, is exponentially worse.

Why don't you want to stop?

TWENTY-ONE

LATER THAT AFTERNOON AS THE SKY FADES INTO A STORMY GRAY, Chloe sits in an empty chair at the edge of the beach and thinks about fate.

She should be happy. She won. She finally knows why Harper has never been able to leave her alone, why she's always gone out of her way to insert herself into Chloe's life. Because Harper *wants* her. Maybe she's wanted her all year and everything she's done this week, every feint, every lie, every hot and cold mood swing can be explained by the practiced, purposeful way she grabbed Chloe's waist upstairs.

It's the kind of power Chloe's always wanted. She was the one to say no, to push Harper away, but as she listens to the waves crash against the shore now, she doesn't feel like the victor. Because here she is—alone on the beach next to a marina filled with million-dollar yachts and the only thing she can think about is Harper Parisi. The soft wave of her hair, the insistent press of her mouth, the way she exhaled Chloe's name like she was biting back a curse.

If she were here now, on her knees in the sand with her mouth pressed against the inside of Chloe's thigh, Chloe doesn't think she'd turn her away.

She slides down in her chair, face heating even as a cool breeze whips off the ocean. She's lost track of the cons she's pulled this year, but Harper has always been a constant. A challenge, something to look forward to. When Chloe thinks of the future, there's never a version where she isn't sneaking into luxury hotels and stealing other people's money. It's a guarantee, something she can control, but the thought of infiltrating another party tonight, of possibly waking up tomorrow and doing it all over again, is debilitating.

Maybe this isn't worth it. Maybe this, like so many things in her life, is nothing more than a coping mechanism that went too far.

Another gust of wind cuts through the thin fabric of Chloe's shirt, whipping the waves into foamy, cresting peaks. She knows there's a storm coming. It turns the ocean a dark, oily gray and sends the yachts swaying side to side against the pier. Chloe watches the bows dip dangerously toward the water and thinks of Katherine Windey, who's somehow rich enough to believe she can conquer something as unknowable as the sea. She thinks of Carlyle, memorizing people's weaknesses like he needs them to breathe. That's what power does, after all. It protects the cruelest, most twisted versions of people and that's why Chloe's spent so long chasing it. That's why she's still planning to swallow her pride tonight and finish the job she started.

And that's why now, when so much of what she wants feels just out of reach, Chloe does the one thing she always wants to do when things feel heavy. She pulls out her phone and calls her dad.

He answers after the first ring, voice so cheery it nearly breaks her heart. "Chloe! How are you?"

"Fine." The lie is easy now; Chloe feels it roll off her tongue. "How's your week been?"

"Can't complain. Tomorrow's the last day of summer school, so I'll actually get a real break before the semester starts." He pauses before asking, "How's that promotion coming?"

It takes Chloe a minute to realize what he's talking about. She's told so many lies this week that it's impossible to remember who knows what. "Oh. That. I don't think I'll get it."

"Don't count yourself out yet, Chlo. What do I always say?"

"To keep your receipts for tax season?"

Her dad laughs. "And?"

"And," Chloe says, "that the most successful people in the world usually only get that far by being really fucking annoying."

"That's my girl."

Chloe grins, relaxing into the soft embrace of the chair, and for the first time all week, the knot under her ribs starts to loosen. Most days, it feels like she and her father are still fumbling through the dark, trying to learn how to move forward as a pair instead of a trio. Chloe doesn't know if they'll ever figure it out but sometimes, when the familiar rasp of his voice washes over her, she thinks there might be a future for her outside the relentless cycle of jobs. A way to feel comfortable and secure without throwing herself at the mercy of people like Andrew Carlyle.

Chloe swallows over the rising lump in her throat and forces the thought away. "Hey, Dad?"

"Hm?"

She hesitates, momentarily unsure what to say. Eventually she settles on, "Did you always know you wanted to be a professor?"

The line falls silent as her father considers. "I don't know. I knew I wanted to teach. I was good at it and after my first semester, it felt like a good fit."

Right, Chloe thinks. *Because that's how things usually work.* A normal life. A step-by-step plan. Logical, rational moves up some hypothetical corporate ladder. "Do you ever think about leaving or trying something new?"

"Honestly? No." There's a rustle of fabric and Chloe pictures her dad sinking deeper into his favorite leather armchair. "Where is this coming from?"

"I don't know." Chloe stares across the water, watching the waves break apart over and over again. It's almost four. The ferry will be leaving soon to transport them back to the mainland. "I don't know," she says again and then, so quiet she's not sure she means to say it out loud, "I don't think I want to do this anymore."

As soon as the words are out of her mouth, Chloe doesn't know if she's referring to her dead-end job in the Carlyle kitchens or the one looming over her shoulder tonight. Both feel equally exhausting. Both weigh on her in ways she doesn't quite understand, but when her dad speaks again, she has the strangest feeling he knows exactly what she's trying to put into words.

"You don't have to do anything forever," he says. "That's the thing about life, Chloe. You can change your mind whenever you want."

Chloe grins, drawing her knees against her chest. "You sound like Mom."

"Well, she was always the smart one."

"I know. I really miss her."

"Me, too."

They don't always talk like this, like her mother is really, truly gone. Chloe spends most of her time actively avoiding that topic but today, with no one around to see her cry, it's comforting to know she's not alone. "I want . . ." She has to start the sentence three separate times before she gets the words out. "I just want her to be proud of me."

"Oh, Chloe." Her dad exhales, voice thick with unshed tears. "She would be. She was. I promise."

Chloe doesn't think that's true. Her mother would probably have a lot to say about her current situation. None of it would be particularly flattering. She swipes the back of her hand across her face before the tears can fall. The air smells like rain, like any second the sky will open and soak her to the bone.

The beach around her has emptied, guests seeking shelter indoors as a group of Rivera employees folds up the chairs left behind. They'll tell her to leave eventually. She'll join the others on the ferry and finally finish what they set out to do. She'll never have to set foot on this island again if she doesn't want to and her father will finally be right.

Her mother *would* be proud of her.

At the marina to her left, another group of employees walks back and forth across the pier. At first, Chloe thinks they're also working to shield the yachts from the rain, but when she turns her head, she realizes they're all loading boxes of what looks suspiciously like top-shelf tequila onto the deck of someone's boat. It's not until another wave sends it rolling that she can finally read the name stenciled across the back.

The Windey.

Chloe wrinkles her nose. She remembers Reed telling her the other housekeepers were at the marina, setting up for a party tomorrow. Of course it's one of Katherine's. Of course they're still prepping for it now, loading carts and boxes belowdecks even as a storm threatens to break overhead. Because Katherine's too focused on making Andrew Carlyle suffer to think about something as trivial as the weather.

Chloe sighs and drops her feet into the sand. "I should go," she says into the phone. "I still have a shift tonight."

"Sure." Her dad clears his throat. "Thanks for calling, Chloe. I love you."

"Love you, too."

Chloe ends the call, phone resting in her hand as she listens to the patter of footsteps up and down the pier. She wonders if it's possible to combust from the weight of the secrets she's keeping, if one day her father will look up to find her splattered across the walls of a luxury hotel room.

After another second, Chloe opens her group chat with Priya and Logan and types, *What's happening with Katherine's boat?*

To her surprise, Logan responds a few seconds later.

I'm pretty sure it's a cocktail party for that Democratic senator. Why?

Right. Chloe remembers now—Priya hunched over her computer in Harper's suite, laughing at the thought of Katherine hosting Carlyle's opponent after she'd just attended his dinner. She watches two figures in green polos heave a heavy-looking box onto the deck and closes the thread without responding.

Her fingers move instinctively across the screen, ignoring the low-battery warning as she swipes through her social media accounts one by one. A mindless habit, something to occupy her hands while her mind frantically sorts through every frayed, incomprehensible thread of information.

Andrew Carlyle with his $5 million reward for an objectively useless trophy. Katherine Windey planting decoys at her own gala, just to elicit a reaction. Harper on the Rivera balcony, etched against a moonlit sea. Harper with her teeth bared, Harper pressing a silver dagger to Chloe's throat, Harper gazing up at her with wide, molten eyes and kiss-swollen lips. Harper, Harper—

It was as if the mere thought called her into existence. Harper's latest post slides across her screen—a golden hour snapshot on a white sand beach—and Chloe pauses, thumb hovering a breath above Harper's artfully filtered face.

The picture isn't from today. The blue waves and crystal-clear sky make that very obvious. It's annoying enough that she's posting old content for likes, but Chloe is even more irritated by the fact that she can pinpoint the exact month this photo was taken by the color of Harper's hair. It must have been back in February or March, when she momentarily tried to go brunette. The result was more of an ashy blond, but Chloe remembers it with alarming clarity because it was also the month Harper showed up to the country club where Chloe had been sweet-talking a table of wealthy donors, spilled a glass of merlot down Chloe's back, and slid into her spot at the table the instant she fled.

It's one of those maddening, toe-curling memories that still make Chloe want to rip off her own skin. She'd been dripping onto the floor of the country club bathroom with her thrifted dress plastered to her body when Harper entered a few minutes later. She took an infuriatingly long time reapplying her lipstick before dragging her gaze down the length of Chloe's body and murmuring, "What a mess."

Then she flashed a wink so quick Chloe still wonders if she imagined it and walked out like nothing happened. The next morning, Chloe found a note tucked in the purse she'd brought that night, a half-folded sheet of paper that just said, *red isn't your color, you know.*

That's who Harper is. That's what Chloe needs to remember now. It doesn't matter how good she felt pressed against her in the hall, or how deliberately she kissed Chloe in the privacy of her room, because none of that is real. Harper only exists to play games and Chloe can't believe she's falling for it again.

She glares at Harper's username in her recent searches, willing it to disappear. To be fair, the only reason it's at the top is because she can't stop looking at her account, and Chloe doesn't care enough about anyone else to keep tabs on their thirst traps. The only other people she's looked up since arriving at the Rivera are Reed, who has absolutely no social media presence, and Skip, the boy who was with her on the first day of training.

She taps on his account instead, desperate for a distraction. Skip's page consists of a grainy picture of what Chloe assumes is his family dog, and a photo of the Rivera lobby with the caption *new digs.* Yesterday, his stories were nothing but glamour shots of other people's yachts and today is no different. She taps through photo after photo of him on the deck of some boat before realizing, with a jolt, that it's the same yacht floating in the marina across from her now. Skip was one of the people setting up for Katherine's party and the photo evidence is everywhere. A picture of him leaning against the railing, another from the back with his arms spread in the classic *Titanic* pose, a selfie taken belowdecks, grinning up at the camera with another employee Chloe doesn't recognize. She's about to close out of the app when something in the corner of the picture catches her eye.

Skip's standing in what looks to be Katherine's personal cabin. Boxes of supplies for tomorrow's event are stacked against the wall, overflowing into the hallway, and there's a desk similar to the one in her office just visible over his shoulder. A slim silver laptop sits in the center and there, in the corner just to the right of Skip's smiling face, is a familiar-looking statue.

A wooden base topped with a smooth glass triangle.

Chloe shoots out of her chair. She clicks back into Skip's story and screenshots the image, zooming in as much as she can, but there's no mistaking what she's looking at. Carlyle's missing award gleaming from the corner of Katherine's desk.

Because there's a cocktail party tomorrow. Because Katherine's hosting Carlyle's political rival on her own personal yacht. Because she's going to smile and shake hands with the very people trying to keep him out of office, offer those pictures to whichever paper will write her the best story, and sit back as they plaster themselves across the city. She'll probably mail him a copy herself, content in the knowledge that his stolen award is clearly visible in the background of every shot.

"Oh my god," Chloe breathes. Another gust of wind whips across the marina. Foamy water slides across the pier and as she watches Katherine's yacht sway from side to side, she knows exactly what needs to happen next. "It's on the fucking boat."

TWENTY-TWO

For the first time in her life, Chloe wishes she was wearing her trusty pair of hideous, company-issued no-slip shoes.

Her sandals slide across the sand so badly that she eventually rips them off, clutching them in one hand as she sprints back up the beach. The stormy haze momentarily obscures her view across the bay, but when Chloe glances back over her shoulder, there's no sign of the approaching ferry. *Good.* That means she still has time.

She bursts through the door and back into the lobby, ignoring the scandalized looks of the guests still perched at the cabana bar. Her bare feet skid across the slick tile as she rounds the corner, but Chloe doesn't stop. She just steadies herself against the wall, ducks under someone's outstretched arm, and keeps running toward the elevators. She's pretty sure someone's telling her to slow down. It might be Reed, eyes widening on the other side of the concierge desk, but Chloe doesn't care. She has a job to finish and there's only one phrase clanging through her head now.

It's on the boat. She's keeping it on the boat.

Because of course she is. Why didn't Chloe think of it before? Katherine laughed when Carlyle showed up at her gala. She called him predictable and left him stewing outside in the sand, but this? Neither of them put the clues together in time.

Chloe skids to a stop in front of the elevators. There's already a crowd waiting to board, but she shoves her way inside, typing text after frantic text to Priya and Logan as they ascend. By the time she reaches the penthouse, she's trembling with barely contained anticipation. She sprints down the hall and slides to a breathless stop outside Harper's suite.

"Harper?" Chloe pounds a fist against the door. When no one answers, she fumbles in her pocket for the master key and pushes her way inside. "Hello?"

The lights are still on, golden patches spreading across the carpet, but the living room is empty except for her own hastily packed bag. Even Harper's suitcase is gone, vanished from its spot by the door. Chloe swears under her breath and yanks her phone from her pocket. 3:45. Fifteen minutes before they're all supposed to board the ferry. Maybe Harper already left. Maybe Chloe missed her in her mad dash through the lobby. She starts for the door, hurriedly typing out another message in her thread with Priya and Logan. She's barely pressed send when the bedroom door opens.

"Chloe?"

Harper pauses in the doorway, brows lifted in clear surprise. At some point in the last hour, she'd changed into a white pinstriped pantsuit and slicked her hair into a low ponytail. She looks like an heiress, like this entire place really is hers to command, and for a brief, heart-pounding second, Chloe's mouth goes unspeakably dry.

"Chloe?" Harper snaps a finger in her direction. "What are you doing?"

Right. Chloe gives her head a deliberate shake. "Where are they?" she asks.

"Who?"

"Priya and Logan. We need to talk."

Harper lifts a delicate brow. "They took the earlier ferry."

"They . . . ?" Chloe stops. "What? No."

She crosses the room, peering out the window across the bay. With the gloom, it's hard to tell which lights belong to which boat, but she flattens a hand against the glass anyway. "No," she says again. "We're leaving at four. We're supposed to go together."

"Yes, but Priya needs her car for the gala. I said I'd wait for you if they went over early." A crease slides between Harper's manicured brows. "She put it in the group chat. You didn't see?"

"My phone died." Chloe turns her back on the window. "You need to call them, then. Tell them to come back."

"I don't take orders from you."

"It's not a suggestion, Harper!"

Something must have changed in Chloe's expression because to her surprise, Harper actually listens. She puts her phone on speaker, and they both wait in uneasy silence as it rings through to Logan's voicemail.

"Again," Chloe says when he doesn't pick up. "Try Priya."

But Priya doesn't answer either. Harper tries them both again, the tinny ring the only sound in the otherwise empty suite, before finally giving up.

Chloe swears under her breath. "They're looking in the wrong place."

"Is that it?" Harper folds her arms over her chest. "I know you're upset you didn't find the award yourself, but the party—"

"It's not at the party! It's on your mother's yacht!"

Harper's eyes widen. Her lips part in a perfect crimson *oh* and when she takes a step back, the orange glow from the lamps momentarily softens her features. *There you are,* Chloe thinks. Here's the version of Harper she wants, the one who blurted secret confessions in this very room and kissed her like she didn't know how to do anything else.

Harper's throat bobs. "Are you sure?"

Chloe nods. She tells Harper about the yacht party, about the employees on the dock and Skip's accidental picture. When she's done, she half expects Harper to scoff, to push aside her theory like she has so many times already but instead, she just laughs.

"It's on the boat," she says, gaze unfocused and glassy. "Of course it's on the boat."

She laughs again, louder this time, and Chloe takes a hesitant step back as the sound bounces off the walls.

"Sorry," Harper gasps, waving a hand in Chloe's direction. "It's just so fucking predictable. My dad wanted us to get a boat for years, you know. He grew up sailing and always wanted me to learn. All their friends had boats, but my mother refused. Said it was too much work and she didn't want us coming home smelling like a fishing barge. Then he left and three months later she bought that yacht. Do you know why?"

Chloe shakes her head. She knows alarmingly little about why rich people buy yachts and kind of wants to keep it that way.

Harper bares her teeth. "Because of *him,*" she snaps. "Because Carlyle got one for parties and she couldn't stand the idea of being left behind. Hers is bigger, too. By eight feet. I'm sure that's important for some reason, but she's never let me onboard to see."

There's something uneasy about the way Harper paces the suite, a wild animal prowling its cage. Chloe folds her arms, bracing herself against the unease trickling down her spine. "So that's why you took this job?" she asks. "Because your mother doesn't want you on her boat?"

"Because she doesn't want me to do *anything*. Every party she threw, every event she hosted, every hotel she opened—those were hers. She didn't want me there. She didn't want me at all, but this job? It's *mine*. It's my work, my reward, my life, and she can't—"

Harper breaks off and Chloe gets the feeling that they're straying dangerously close to something real. Selfishly, she wants to know what it is. She wants to dig it up, to hold whatever confession Harper's been keeping up to the light, to see if it's the missing piece she needs.

"What?" Chloe asks. "What is it? Because from my perspective, all we need to do is get that award and get out."

Harper lets out a growl of frustration. It's ragged and low, not unlike the sound she pulled from Chloe's throat earlier this afternoon, but now, with the space rapidly shrinking between them, it feels like a threat. "I told you. My mother and I don't get along. She's not a good person."

Chloe shrugs. "Neither are we."

"It's different with her."

"Why? Because it's personal?"

"I don't expect you to understand, Chloe, but I don't need a lecture from someone who has a perfectly nice family waiting for them back in the suburbs."

The words twist in Chloe's gut. Before she can think better of it, she snaps, "My mom's dead, in case you forgot, so forgive me if I think you're being a little dramatic."

Harper flinches, drawing back like Chloe has physically struck her. "That's not what I meant."

"What did you mean, then?"

The seconds stretch between them in silent protest, every cell in Chloe's body winding tighter the longer they wait. She'll snap sooner or later. Maybe she'll take Harper down with her, but right now, this conversation is nothing more than a waste of time. Their prize is sitting forty stories below their feet, unguarded and alone on a luxury yacht, and all she wants is an answer.

"So that's it?" she asks when Harper doesn't move. "This is all part of some family drama?"

Tell me, she thinks. *Let me decide if you're worth it.* The unease is back, the same thing Chloe felt walking into Carlyle's office earlier this afternoon. Like something is about to go terribly, irreversibly wrong. Like she's going to turn around to find the moonlit dagger from her dream lodged between her shoulder blades.

Harper exhales a rough sigh. Her ponytail falls over her shoulder, just enough to obscure her face from view, and when she speaks again, her voice is so quiet Chloe almost misses it. "You learn a lot of things when your parents split up, you know. Like sometimes you find out your dad had a debilitating gambling problem and sometimes you learn your mother dealt with it by having an affair. You know. Casual things."

Chloe doesn't know what she was expecting, but it certainly wasn't that. She blinks, cycling through several different reactions before landing on, "Oh."

Harper lets out a low laugh. "Exactly. I knew about the gambling in high school. It was kind of hard to miss, but I didn't know about . . . the rest until recently."

It's one thing, Chloe thinks, to know the truth or suspect someone of lying. It must be quite another to live in blissful ignorance, only to have your entire worldview shattered by an inconveniently placed piece of information. She thinks about Harper's actions this week, all the specific, pointed hatred toward her mother. It felt purposeful, more than a simple desire to get under Katherine's skin, and it was. Harper wanted to hurt her mother in the same way she was hurt and Carlyle's job gave her the perfect outlet.

"Is that why she didn't want you at the gala?" Chloe asks. "Does she think you're going to talk?"

Harper nods, a wry smile playing at the corner of her mouth. "She's afraid I'm going to tell everyone her deep, dark secret."

"Are you?"

"Maybe." Harper's teeth slide viciously over her bottom lip. "You know why she hated being on trial? It had nothing to do with the arrest. It's because people look at her differently now. She can't hold her flawless, perfect life over my head anymore, especially after something so public. I just wanted to remind her that she's not invincible. I didn't want her to get away with this, too."

The conviction in her voice is electric. It burrows under Chloe's skin and ignites her own lingering frustration. Because why is Harper talking like the job is already over? They could finish it tonight. Despite herself, Chloe almost laughs. Of course it's going to end like this—her and Harper left alone to finish the job they started.

With the slowly darkening sky to their left and the lamps throwing amber shadows across her face from behind, Harper looks as hazy and ethereal as the woman from Chloe's dream. Her expression is tense, guarded, and when her gaze flicks to Chloe's mouth, Chloe wonders if this is the whole story. If there's not something else lurking in the shadows, waiting for her to let her guard down before reaching out to strike.

She shakes the thought away and looks up. They've already wasted too much time. If Harper's still lying to her now, it's a risk Chloe's willing to take. "Then let's go," she says. "Let's get it now, just the two of us."

Harper's eyebrows arch delicately toward her hairline. It's a ludicrous idea. Chloe knows it, but interest sparks behind Harper's gaze as she considers. She still wants it. She's still unwilling to give up her victory if there's a chance to best her mother, and that's what Chloe is counting on now.

"You want to go without them?" she asks.

Chloe nods. "I do. I think we should go now."

The first day they met, Chloe remembers feeling like the world tilted under her feet, shifting to orbit around a new kind of sun. She feels it again now when Harper's jaw sets in steely determination, when she nods and lifts her chin like it's the most obvious thing in the world.

"Okay," she says. "Let's do it."

TWENTY-THREE

"Is he still not picking up?"

Chloe leans over Harper's shoulder, watching as she dials Logan's number again. It rings half a dozen times before Harper gives up. "No," she mutters. "Neither of them are."

Maybe that's a sign. Maybe that's an indication that what they're about to do is a very bad idea, because Chloe thinks Priya and Logan should definitely be back on the mainland by now. They're probably sitting in front of the downtown Windey, tracking the guests streaming into the party from the back of Priya's Subaru. They're probably waiting for Harper to check in and they're probably not thinking about Chloe at all.

But right now, she and Harper are crouched in the sand outside the marina, using the beach's natural slope to shield them from view. The staff who were working on Katherine's yacht are nowhere to be seen. The boxes they were hauling down the pier are gone too, no doubt secured on board in anticipation of the coming storm. Chloe shivers as another gust of wind cuts through the palms overhead. "What are you thinking?" she asks.

Harper's eyes narrow on the dock overhead. "I'm thinking it's their loss. We need to move."

Unfortunately, Chloe agrees. She swipes her bangs out of her face before readjusting the strap of her backpack across her shoulders. She changed into her uniform on the way out, complete with her trusty pair of chunky, despicably ugly no-slip shoes. Her socks are already sagging around her ankles, but at least she blends in. No one would question her presence on the pier tonight, especially with Harper. All they have to do is board Katherine's yacht, grab the award from the corner of her desk, and tuck it in Chloe's backpack without attracting attention. Easy. Simple.

After the week they've had, Chloe really doesn't think she's asking for much.

She stands and grabs the cardboard box she stole from the mailroom on their way outside. "All right," she says. "Let's go."

Harper casts one last glance over her shoulder before heading up the beach. Her footsteps are steady on the damp sand, no sign remaining of the uncertainty that rattled her upstairs. Now, every movement feels calculated, from the swing of her arms to the soft bounce of her ponytail, and Chloe does her best to replicate it as she pretends to struggle under the weight of the empty box. The wooden planks creak under their feet when they step onto the pier, white paint just starting to peel where the wood meets the sea. They pass a few lone guests along the way, but no one stops them until Harper turns toward her mother's yacht.

"Hold on." A security guard in a dark green polo straightens from where he's been leaning against a post. "This is a private dock."

Harper keeps walking, flashing him a brilliant grin as she goes. "Yes, I'm aware."

She reaches for the railing, but the guard blocks her path, both hands braced firmly on his belt. "Private means no one allowed."

"I know what it means." Harper's voice is so sickly sweet it makes Chloe's skin tingle. She extends a hand in the guard's direction. "I'm Harper Parisi. That's my mother's boat. I'm sure you saw the staff loading up for her event tomorrow. We just have a few more things to drop off."

One day, Chloe thinks, she might get used to Harper's uncanny ability to chameleon herself into every situation. In the ballroom last night, she was elegant and unshakable, designed to protect herself from her mother's judgments. With Priya and Logan, she was carelessly assertive, but now, standing in front of her mother's boat with her family hotel glittering at her back, everything about her feels effortless.

The guard hesitates, glancing over his shoulder at the line of waiting boats. "I didn't know there'd be another delivery tonight."

"Of course you didn't. My mother's a very busy woman. Do you expect a personal phone call every time she needs to stop by her own pier?"

"No, but I—"

"But *what*? Do you need me to call her? Tell her you turned me away?"

Harper pulls out her phone, thumb hovering over the screen, and that's all it takes for the guard to decide he doesn't get paid enough for this. He inclines his head and motions them onto the pier.

"Apologies, Ms. Parisi. Please, take your time."

The shift in Harper's demeanor is immediate. She gives the guard a rough pat on the back before slipping past him. "We won't take long, promise!"

Chloe follows her onto the ramp, box braced uncomfortably against her hip. "Nice," she mutters as the guard resumes his pacing. "I think you traumatized him."

"Please." Harper rolls her eyes. "He works for my mother. He's already traumatized."

She climbs the rest of the way with ease, leaving Chloe to struggle her way up the ramp alone. The railing is cold under her palm, slick with saltwater, but Chloe doesn't let go until she's standing with two feet solidly on the deck. Even in the harbor, she can feel the ocean under her, rising and falling like some long-slumbering beast. Now that she's here, it's easy to understand why so many of her mother's stories began this way—with a girl standing alone at the edge of the sea, foolish enough to think it could grant her every desire.

Chloe shivers and turns toward the back of the ship, where a dimly lit staircase leads belowdecks. "Let's get this over with."

Easier said than done. Despite the smooth, shiny exterior of the boat, the staircase looks like a death trap—six narrow, incredibly creaky steps disappearing into the shadows below. Chloe hesitates at the top, but Harper doesn't seem to mind. She takes the stairs two at a time, landing on the deck below with a solid *thunk*.

"What?" she asks when Chloe lingers on the deck. "Afraid of the dark?"

It's impossible to see through the gloom, but Chloe can picture Harper's expression—eyes wide, brows lifted, the mocking tilt of her lips the only sign that the question isn't entirely innocent. There's a second of strained silence before a switch flips and light floods the narrow hallway. Chloe blinks, squinting into the cramped space below.

To the left of the staircase is a narrow kitchenette, pots and pans hanging from the wall in neat rows. The single shelf above the makeshift counter is lined with jars of clearly labeled spices and cooking oils, probably loaded in by the staff in anticipation of tomorrow's event. Because nothing says *cocktail party for your mortal enemy's political rival* quite like a dash of paprika.

Beyond the kitchen, a hallway stretches toward the back of the boat, lined with tightly closed doors. One of them, Chloe realizes, must lead to Katherine's cabin. One of them holds their prize.

She has to duck to avoid smacking her forehead on the low ceiling as she inches down the stairs. When she straightens, Harper's already yanking open the first door. It's just a bathroom, complete with a pink tile sink and matching hand towels, but the door makes an obnoxious slamming sound when Harper drops it back into place.

"Careful," Chloe says. "We don't have to rush."

Harper grabs the next doorknob, pulling it back with the same forceful enthusiasm. "I'm not rushing. I just want to be done."

"No, you want to find the award first," Chloe mutters. She peers inside the second door, shaking her head when it's nothing more than a storage closet. When Harper tries the third one, however, it doesn't budge.

Locked.

Chloe starts to sling her backpack off her shoulder, but Harper holds up a hand. "Let me."

She reaches into her pocket and pulls out a small leather pouch. The drawstrings look worn, like she's opened and closed them countless times, and her initials are embroidered into the side with pink, flowery script.

"Oh my god." Chloe bites back a grin. "Is that a *custom* set of lockpicks?"

Harper tucks the pouch back into her pocket. "Maybe."

"Where do you even get something like that? I mean, it's *monogrammed.*"

"Monograms aren't weird, Chloe. It's actually a very convenient way to keep track of your things."

Chloe snorts. "Sure. By the way, how's your MLM going? Recruited enough entrepreneurial boss babes to reach the next level of your exciting new business opportunity?"

Harper's gaze slides toward her as she slips the end of her first pick into the lock. "Not everyone who owns monogrammed things runs a pyramid scheme."

"I'm pretty sure the Venn diagram of those two personality traits is a circle, actually." Chloe hesitates, watching Harper twist the second pick with her free hand. "Where did you learn how to do that, anyway? I didn't think they taught lock picking in prep school."

"I didn't go to prep school," Harper says. Then, quietly, "I went to a finishing academy. There's a difference."

Chloe laughs, surprised at the way the sound makes Harper's own mouth curl into a hesitant grin. She twists her pick again, changing the angle so it comes in higher, and Chloe pretends not to notice the way her hands flex at the subtle movement. She's spent a majority of the last few hours thinking about Harper's hands. Hazard of the job, apparently. Now that she knows what it feels like to have them tangled in her hair and pressed beneath the fabric of her shirt, it's difficult to think about anything else.

"There!"

Something clicks in the lock and Harper pulls back. Chloe shakes her head to clear the annoyingly persistent image of Harper's fingers curled around the outside of her thigh. She's just reaching for the doorknob when the deck overhead lets out an ominous creak.

The two of them freeze, heads snapping toward the ceiling. Another wave swells beneath them, sending the yacht tipping subtly from side to side, but Chloe keeps her feet rooted to the deck even as her heart pounds. Silence falls down the hall. She and Harper wait for one minute, two, and then, just when Chloe's pulse is beginning to slow, the sound comes again.

The distinct click of footsteps making their way up the gangway.

Harper dives for the light switch and the entire level plunges into shadowy darkness. Chloe shrinks against the wall, hand fumbling behind her for the doorknob. *This is not happening.* She didn't come this far to be caught lurking in the bottom of someone else's ship with Harper Parisi, three feet short of their goal. She sucks in an involuntary breath as the footsteps continue across the deck, heels clicking directly overhead.

"Shh!" Harper clamps a hand over Chloe's mouth, pressing them both against the far wall. "It's her."

Chloe's first instinct is to push Harper away. She can smell the lingering musk of last night's perfume (Hermès, Eau des Merveilles), feel the sting of Harper's nails against her cheek, but those two words stop her cold. *It's her.* Katherine Windey, pacing the deck mere inches above their heads. Too late, Chloe remembers the empty box she left sitting upstairs.

Harper tenses as the sound grows louder, hand still pressed firmly over Chloe's mouth. It's another minute before Chloe realizes the footsteps are moving away from them, heading upstairs toward the captain's chair instead of down to the lower deck. Slowly, Harper lowers her hand. Chloe uncurls her own fingers from the sleeve of Harper's blazer.

"Sorry," she whispers, but Harper doesn't seem to notice. Her eyes are trained on the ceiling, like she still expects her mother to fly down the stairs and wrap a hand around her throat. A muscle feathers in her jaw, completely at odds with her smooth, impassive expression, but before either of them can speak, something shifts in the depths of the ship.

There's a click, a rough scrape, and then the engine roars to life.

Chloe staggers back. She grips the door for balance as the deck sways beneath her and it's not until they start moving backward against the waves that she realizes, with slowly dawning horror, what's happening. Katherine Windey isn't here for an evening checkup or a random visit. She's not wandering the deck for fun. She has a party to attend, a casino night hosted at her own downtown hotel, and she's not taking the ferry across the bay when she has a perfectly good yacht to show off.

Harper's eyes widen, as if realizing the implications at the same time as Chloe. "What do we do?" she asks, voice barely audible over the sound of the engines.

Personally, Chloe thinks the only thing they can do is accept the fact that they're about to die in the middle of the bay. That feels like the most logical explanation. She sways in time with the sea, doorknob pressing against her hip. *The doorknob,* she thinks hazily. *The cabin. The award.*

Five million dollars.

Chloe forces the very detailed image of Katherine Windey dumping her body into international waters from her mind. "We keep going," she says, voice significantly stronger than she feels. "We got this far, right? Let's finish it while she's distracted."

Chloe yanks the door open and together, they stumble into the cabin. Harper fumbles for a light, but it does little to illuminate the cramped space before them. A green floral rug takes up most of the floor, stretching from a small bookshelf in the far corner all the way to an armchair near the door. There's a single porthole drilled into the back wall and Chloe has to avert her eyes as a wave of saltwater splashes against the glass. Besides that, the only other piece of furniture is a dark mahogany desk.

But it's not like that time in Katherine's office. It's not like their mad dash through the ballroom either. This time, Chloe doesn't have to search. A small collection of statues sits in the corner of Katherine's desk, clearly arranged in a purposeful display. They catch in the light, bright reflections bouncing around the room despite the dreary weather outside, and there, right in the middle, is the one currently haunting Chloe's dreams.

"*Oh.*" Harper spots it at the same time she does. Her voice is breathy, stunned, and she crosses the floor as if in a trance. "It's here."

Chloe hesitates, one hand still pressed against the wall to keep from tipping over. Could it really be that easy? They've hit too many roadblocks, run up against one too many false promises for her to be completely certain of anything, but she still pulls her sleeve over her hand and plucks the award from the desk. She means to hold it up to the light, to examine it the way she did the one in Katherine's office, but Chloe knows before she even turns it over that this one is real. It's heavy in her palm, glass edge pricking her skin, and when she tilts the base, there's Carlyle's name etched into the wood.

"Let me see." Harper reaches out a hand, but Chloe hesitates.

"Careful," she mutters. "Fingerprints."

"We're literally about to steal it, Chloe. I don't think that matters."

Harper lifts it from Chloe's grasp, and it's only when she has it clutched in both hands, fingers curled possessively around the glass, that some of the tension finally melts from her shoulders. She flips it over, examining every inch as Chloe casts another uneasy glance toward the door.

"Here." She slings her backpack off her shoulder. "Put it inside. We should hide upstairs until she docks."

Chloe reaches for the award, but Harper doesn't move. Something shifts behind her neutral expression as she peers down at the statue. It's a subtle change, one Chloe might have missed if she hadn't spent an infuriating amount of time memorizing Harper's face.

"We're safer here than we are upstairs," Harper says. "Might as well lock the door and wait until she docks."

Chloe can't stand a lot of things about Harper Parisi. Her personality, for one. Her condescending little smirk when she thinks she's right or the way her hands fit perfectly in the curve of Chloe's waist, like they're made for each other. But most of all, Chloe hates how good Harper is at her job.

How even now, with everything they have to lose, she still desperately wants to trust her.

"Fine," she says, motioning toward her backpack a second time. "Can we at least put it away? That's five million dollars right there."

"I know." Harper's expression is dark, almost hungry, and Chloe has a sudden memory of Carlyle in the golf cart outside the gala. That's how he looked at her, shadows carving deep hollows in his face, and that's how Harper is looking at the award now. "I just need to check."

She steps back, award still clutched in her hands, and alarm bells clang in Chloe's mind as she watches Harper grip the base with one hand. She grabs the glass triangle with the other and pulls.

Chloe lurches forward. "What are you doing?"

But Harper doesn't answer. She doesn't even look up. She just tightens her grip and tries again. This time, the pieces slide apart. Just like they did in Katherine's office. There's a quick flash of motion as something tumbles from the base, landing in the middle of the desk with a soft clatter.

A flash drive, nearly identical to the one Priya used to infiltrate the Windey security system earlier this week. It's nothing fancy, just a slim gray plastic case covering the USB underneath. If Chloe didn't know any better, if she didn't see the way Harper goes still across the desk, she might think it was completely ordinary.

Here it is, she thinks as she takes a tentative step forward. Here's why Carlyle wanted this award back so badly. Here's why he was willing to pay an exorbitant amount of money for them to retrieve it. It was never about the sentimental value. It was always about the thing hidden inside.

And if he told Harper and not you . . .

If Carlyle told Harper what he really wanted while lying to Chloe every step of the way, then all those itchy, paranoid feelings plaguing her this week have been correct. Harper isn't her friend. She's not her equal. She and Carlyle have been in this together and Chloe has no idea why.

"So," Chloe says, doing her best to act like this is the most normal thing in the world. "What's that?"

"What?" Harper looks up, that same little smile still playing across her lips. "Oh, nothing."

"Doesn't look like nothing."

It comes out more forcefully than Chloe means. They're barely a foot apart with nothing but the desk between them. She's close enough to grab the flash drive herself if she wants, and Harper must be thinking the same thing because her gaze flickers to Chloe's face.

"It's nothing," she says again.

"Don't lie to me."

Whatever warmth Chloe felt between them earlier is gone, replaced by cold, calculating indifference. She half expects Harper to give another exasperated smile, or make some pointed comment about how she's unstable and paranoid, and maybe she is. Maybe there's a perfectly reasonable explanation for all of this. Then Harper laughs and the last of Chloe's reservations melts away.

"Funny," she says, plucking the flash drive from the desk. "This isn't a negotiation."

The deck tilts ominously under their feet and before Chloe can reach out to stop her, the door to the cabin bursts open. They both jump, flash drive clattering to the desk as Harper whirls. *It's Katherine,* Chloe thinks, head whipping toward the noise. *It's the security guard from the pier or one of Carlyle's friends come to finish the job.*

Instead, she finds Logan standing in the doorway with one shoulder casually braced against the wall.

"Hey," he says, looking from her to Harper. "What did I miss?"

TWENTY-FOUR

For Logan to appear here, on a yacht in the middle of the bay, is so absurd, so completely *him* that Chloe can't help the sharp laugh that escapes her. He might as well have emerged in a puff of smoke carrying a rabbit and a top hat.

"Logan." Harper blinks, surprise finally cracking her mask of calm. "You're supposed to be on the mainland."

"I know." Logan shrugs, letting the door close behind him as he crosses the threshold into the cabin. "But you were so insistent we take the earlier ferry that Pri and I figured we should probably stick around to see if Chloe needed help." He flashes her a wink. "Glad we did."

Harper's smile turns brittle. "How sweet."

"It's not, actually," Chloe says. "It's called being a team. That's what we are, remember? If Carlyle wants that flash drive, we'll hand it over together."

Logan nods, coming around the desk to stand at her shoulder, but Harper just sighs, like this conversation is the most inconvenient thing in the world. "Oh, Chloe. That's an admirable thought, but you were never in charge here."

Her hand slips into her waistband and in the second before it reappears, Chloe wonders, vaguely, if she's going back for the lockpicks, if maybe she'll emerge with another monogrammed accessory. By the time she realizes she's wrong, Harper has one manicured finger resting on the trigger of a silver revolver.

"Get back," she says, weapon trained in their direction. "Both of you."

Once in college, Chloe got incredibly wine drunk on Greek row, made out with two different lesbians dressed as Robin from *Stranger Things,* and woke up the next morning with a horrible case of the flu. She sat in bed for the rest of the week, sipping chicken noodle soup from a coffee mug and marathoning three seasons of *Bones.*

It wasn't an intentional choice. She'd just happened to scroll past a picture of Emily Deschanel wearing a Wonder Woman costume while under the influence of too much DayQuil and everything sort of spiraled from there. The irony of pirating a show about crime-busting FBI agents was not lost on her. Logan made sure to point it out each time he stopped by her dorm with supplies, but Chloe didn't care. She fell asleep every night with visions of decomposing corpses and SWAT team raids peppering her dreams.

But even though she spent an embarrassing amount of time watching Seeley Booth read people their rights, even though she's lived in Miami her entire life, Chloe has never actually been this close to a gun before. Maybe that's why this entire situation feels like a throwaway plotline from the tenth season of some cable network crime procedural. Maybe that's why it feels like she's watching herself from somewhere outside her body as the world narrows to a singular point, like she's still stuck inside that dream where Harper puts a knife through her heart.

"Interesting." Chloe glances from Harper to the weapon and back again. "Was your monogram guy not up for customizing this one, or . . . ?"

Harper jerks her chin to the side. "Against the wall."

Despite herself, Chloe obeys. Harper's finger is unnaturally steady on the trigger. Maybe she practiced for this. Maybe she saw Chloe on the other side of every bullet. It's a devastating contrast to the woman who softened under her touch just hours ago, who kissed Chloe like she wanted to sink into her bones.

Logan slowly raises his hands, breath shallow as he presses his back into the wall of the cabin. "Is now a bad time to remind you that I *did* ask if we should get a gun last year?" he whispers.

Chloe rolls her eyes. "Yes."

"And you said asking that question made me seem like a Republican?"

"I said *yes,* Logan!"

"Enough!"

Harper's still standing in front of the desk, the two pieces of Carlyle's award strewn across the surface. As Chloe watches, she picks up the flash drive again, sliding back the cap to reveal the small USB plug beneath. It looks completely normal—no fancy monograms, no labels, nothing to indicate it's worth anything at all—but Harper visibly exhales at the sight.

If Chloe was hesitant before, there's no doubt in her mind now. Harper came here for that flash drive and that flash drive alone. Returning the award was nothing more than a convenient excuse to disguise Carlyle's true motives.

"What is it?" she asks. "If you tell me, we can—"

"Shut up, Chloe." Harper rounds on them, her movements less careful now that she has the flash drive in hand. Her hip knocks against the desk, causing one of the other awards to fall to the floor with a loud *thunk*. Chloe flinches at the sound.

"What is it?" she repeats. "What are you doing?"

"I said, *enough*."

Harper's hand tenses as she shifts the gun from Chloe to Logan. Next to her, Logan lets out a frightened squeak, but Chloe doesn't back down. Slowly, as carefully as she can manage with the waves still tossing beneath her feet, she takes a step forward.

"What's on the flash drive?"

"I told you. It's nothing."

"It's clearly not, Harper. I thought we were a team."

Harper laughs, the sound bouncing off the walls in a cruel echo. "God, Chloe, you're so gullible. We were never a team."

Chloe figured that part out herself, actually. She suspected it the morning she pulled a key to the Carlyle penthouse from the pocket of her thrifted ball gown. He never actually admitted to putting it there. Harper was the only one close enough to slip it to her that night and everything she has done since, every story, every lie, every false apology only solidified the theory in Chloe's mind. It's infuriating, she thinks, to be surrounded with indisputable evidence that she's been *right this whole time* and not be able to properly gloat.

"So that's it?" she asks. "You're going to take that back to Carlyle and sell us out for . . . what? More money?"

There's a wild gleam in Harper's eyes now, almost frantic as she looks down at the flash drive. Like she doesn't have to worry about being careful because she's already decided to burn this place down when she's done. "It was never about the money, Chloe."

"It's always about money!" Chloe cries. "What's he offering you?"

"It's none of your business. Don't push."

"Or *what*? You'll shoot me? Seems like an awfully big mess to clean up."

"Maybe we shouldn't push her on that one," Logan whispers, but Chloe ignores him and takes another step away from the wall.

"Tell me," she says. "What did Carlyle offer you?"

Harper's gaze flicks over her shoulder to where Logan still stands against the wall. "What about him?"

"Who cares about him?"

"You do," Harper says. "Very clearly."

"Do you think I took this job so the four of us could hold hands on the beach?" Chloe takes another step, hands still lifted as she inches closer. "If Carlyle just wants the flash drive, that's fine. You don't have to tell me what's on it, but we can still bring it to him together. This is our job, isn't it? Let's finish it."

Chloe can feel Logan watching her, open-mouthed from his

place against the wall. She ignores him, keeping her gaze locked on Harper as an almost imperceptible tremor rattles her expression.

"This was never your job to finish, Chloe."

For the first time since entering the cabin, Chloe thinks Harper sounds uncertain. Goosebumps rise on the backs of her arms. It's cold in here, but Chloe can't tell if it's due to the storm or the bone-chilling realization that Harper, of all people, might actually be in over her head.

"Why?" she asks. "Did you make another deal? What does he have on you?"

Harper shakes her head, finger flexing across the trigger. "That's none of your business."

"You made it my business when you started waving a gun in my face, actually! Do you even know how to use that thing?"

A muscle tenses in Harper's jaw. She looks like she's fighting something, chewing back words. They're only a few feet apart now, nothing but a desk between them as Chloe takes a hesitant step. The deck lurches to one side. Another award tumbles to the floor behind them and Chloe winces at the sound. Gun or no gun, they aren't being subtle. They need to get out of here before Katherine hears the commotion and comes down to investigate.

"Fine." Chloe lifts her chin, forcing Harper to meet her gaze. "You made a deal without me. You don't have to tell me anything, Harper, but let me *help* you."

Harper laughs, but this time, something about it feels forced. "And why would you do that? You hate me, remember?"

How could she forget? That's the entire reason they're here, after all, because Chloe couldn't stand the thought of Harper Parisi claiming another prize for herself. She would have plunged that moonlit dagger through her own chest, just for the satisfaction of knowing Harper couldn't.

"I know," she says. "I do. I hate how good you are at your job. I hate how you're the only one who can keep up with me and I absolutely despise the way you make me feel."

Harper goes rigid. "And how, exactly, do I make you feel?"

There it is, Chloe thinks as she closes the remaining space between them. That's what she's counting on. That somewhere under the threats and anger is the same girl who sat in Carlyle's office and wanted him to tell her she was special. She cups a hand around the back of Harper's neck, thumb trailing a slow line down her throat. Her vision narrows to the pulse pounding under her finger and for a second, Chloe forgets about the flash drive.

You have to know who your enemy is before you can best them.

A low sound breaks in Harper's throat, vibration humming under Chloe's touch. She lowers her weapon another inch, eyes fluttering closed as she whispers again, "How do I make you feel?"

The frustrated groan that catches behind Chloe's teeth isn't entirely fake. Maybe Harper has been preparing for this inevitable betrayal all week. Maybe that's why every kiss tasted like frantic desperation, but when Chloe leans in and presses her lips to Harper's, she doesn't think it's over. She kisses her deeply, taking her time, and when Harper's lips part on a half gasp, half sigh, she knows she's close.

She trails a hand down Harper's arm, reaching as subtly as she can for the hand still holding the flash drive. "It's us, Harper," she whispers. "It's always been us. We can finish this together."

Harper shakes her head. "We can't."

"We *can*. Let me help you."

"No, you . . ." Harper closes her eyes and tries again, weapon falling back to her side. "You don't get it. You need to get out of here. As soon as we dock, you need to leave the flash drive and run."

"Not without you."

A soft, frustrated sound slides out of her. "This isn't a game, Chloe. You were never meant to get away with this."

"I . . ." Chloe's fingers tighten on Harper's wrist, inches above the flash drive, but she can't make herself move. "What?"

Harper drags the back of her hand across her face, gun still hanging loosely from her fingers. "You're the scapegoat. Carlyle hired me to get this back. That was always the plan. I'd get the payout and if anything went wrong or my mother started to suspect us, every piece of evidence would lead directly to you. The housekeeper with the master key who worked at the Carlyle before coming to the Rivera."

Chloe pulls back as the words crash around her. No, that's not possible. She's too smart for that. She would have noticed if it was a setup. *But* . . .

But didn't Harper encourage her to take this job in the first place? Didn't she goad Chloe into applying for that housekeeping job too, while explicitly allowing her to think it was her idea? Wasn't she the one steering Chloe into every situation, masking her sinister intentions behind a year of their own hostility? Of course Chloe didn't recognize it. She was too busy figuring out how to play Harper to realize the plan unfolding behind her back.

"Are you serious? You're going to let me take the blame? For a fucking *flash drive*?"

She shoves Harper away right as another wave catches under their feet. Harper stumbles, eyes wide, and she probably would have caught herself on the desk if Logan didn't slip away from the wall, taking advantage of her distraction to come around her other side and extend a foot into her path.

"Careful," he says as Harper trips over his shoe. She lands in a disgruntled heap on the floor, hands instinctively opening to break her fall, and the flash drive flies from her grip. "We'll take that back, actually."

Chloe grabs it right before it slides under the desk. "Go!"

She turns toward the door, but the two of them barely make it a foot before Harper lets out a frustrated growl. She rises up on her knees and snatches one of the fallen awards off the floor. *University of Alabama,* Chloe thinks vaguely as Harper winds up to throw. *Softball scholarship.*

"Logan! Duck!"

The warning comes too late. The statue whizzes through the air, so close Chloe swears she feels the wind ruffle her hair, and slams into the back of Logan's head. He goes down hard, taking Chloe with him. They sprawl across the deck and Chloe instinctively tightens her fist around the flash drive.

"Shit," Logan groans. "Is it bad? It feels bad, Chloe."

"Um . . ." Chloe scrambles to her knees, disentangling herself from Logan's body as she goes. She presses a hand to the back of his head and winces when her fingers come away wet with blood. "Um, no. It's fine."

Behind them, Harper staggers to her feet. Gone are her tears and momentary insecurity. When she turns on them, gun raised in their direction once more, she looks like a killer ready to finish the job. "Give it back."

Chloe stands to face her, purposefully putting herself between Harper and Logan. "Tell me what's on it."

"It's none of your business."

Stall her. Chloe glances wildly around the cabin wishing, for the hundredth time, that rich people weren't so frustratingly boring with their modern minimalist aesthetic. There's barely anything for her to hide behind.

"So you don't know," she blurts. "Carlyle hired you to steal it, but he didn't tell you why. Doesn't seem like he trusts you very much."

Harper's lip curls. "There's a reason he hired me and not you."

"Oh, I know." Chloe narrowly avoids tripping over a side table as she backs toward the door. "He told me all about you that day I went to his office. So many interesting things. Do you want to know what he said?"

"Enough!"

Harper shoves the table out of her way. It falls to the ground with a loud crash and Chloe jumps back as pieces of broken glass fly across the deck. The movement temporarily dislodges the flash drive from her grip. It falls soundlessly to the floor. Harper's gaze follows, narrowing on the ground, and Chloe reads her intentions in the instant before she moves.

They both dive at once, the contents of Chloe's backpack scattering across the rug as her fingers curl around the flash drive. Maybe she should let it go. Maybe she shouldn't fight like this, but Harper and Carlyle were both willing to destroy her for this information. Some bitter, twisted part of Chloe won't rest until she knows what it is. She pushes herself to her feet right as Harper's hand locks around her ankle.

"Give it back!"

There's a flash of cold metal against her calf and Chloe realizes it's Harper's gun, caught between their bodies as they grapple on the floor. She grits her teeth and tries to kick it away, narrowly avoiding Harper's face in the process.

"Stop it!" Harper's nails dig into her ankle. "Let it go."

"Put the gun down!"

"No!"

Chloe is not a particularly athletic person. She knows this because every four months, Priya decides to start marathon training "for real this time" and inevitably ends up dragging Chloe along to some new, aesthetically pleasing workout class. Her resolve lasts approximately two weeks, Chloe's lasts less than twelve minutes, and they usually decide to never speak of it again. Now, Chloe wonders if she's been vastly underestimating the health benefits of Pilates because when Harper hooks an arm around her neck and pulls, she momentarily sees her life flash before her eyes.

This is not how you die, Chloe thinks, writhing in Harper's grip as her air supply narrows. If it is, she's going to become the bitchiest, most vengeful ghost of all time. She's going to haunt Katherine Windey's yacht for the rest of her life. Vaguely, she's aware of Logan struggling to rise a few feet away, of the flash drive cutting into her palm as her vision goes black at the edges. Chloe swipes a hand behind her, aiming for Harper's face but ends up connecting with the barrel of the gun instead. It flies across the rug and Harper's grip momentarily loosens.

It's enough for Chloe to throw her weight to the side and dislodge herself. She staggers to her feet, coughing as air fills her lungs again.

"Chloe!" Logan's on his knees, still clutching his head with one hand. The other is pointing over her shoulder, to where Harper's gun now sits abandoned in the middle of the room. Chloe immediately understands what he means. She lunges for the weapon, but Harper's there before she can get a good grip.

"That's mine!"

She's on top of Chloe now, one knee pressed painfully into her spine. She reaches down and starts prying Chloe's fingers open one by one until she's able to snatch the flash drive from her palm.

"Mine," she repeats breathlessly. "I got it. He'll know I got it."

She tucks the flash drive in her pocket and Chloe groans, one hand still wrapped around the barrel of the gun. "What *is* it?"

"Let go, Chloe. I don't want to hurt you."

"I'm finding that very hard to believe right now!"

Chloe digs her fingers into the fabric of Harper's blazer. Her heartbeat hammers rapid-fire in her throat, hands aching as she strains toward the flash drive. Harper is still behind her, fumbling to regain control of her gun, but Chloe isn't going down that easily. She drives her elbow back and up, directly into the soft curve of Harper's stomach. Harper's breath releases in a single choked gasp and Chloe throws the rest of her weight back, twisting in an attempt to trap Harper's body beneath hers. But Harper is too fast. She rolls out of the way, still struggling to draw breath as Chloe lunges for her again, and in the instant before Chloe's hand locks around her throat, there's a soft warning click.

Then a shot fires next to Chloe's ear and all coherent thought cracks apart.

Chloe sees the flash, feels something whiz past her face and for a second, she thinks this is it. She really is going to die on a yacht in the middle of the Atlantic. She clamps her hands over her ears as Harper collapses in the opposite direction. For a minute, everything is still.

Quiet.

Then Harper lurches to her knees. She presses a frantic hand to her chest, but her pinstriped jacket remains strangely spotless. No sign of blood. Chloe's pulse pounds in her ears. She fumbles toward Logan's crumpled form, but aside from his head wound, he appears unhurt. Miraculously, Chloe thinks she is, too.

Then someone gasps.

Chloe whirls toward the sound and finds Katherine Windey standing in the doorway, one hand still gripping the wall. She's wearing a pantsuit not unlike the one Harper has on now, black-and-white stripes perfect for a casino night party. If it weren't for the blood slowly soaking through her shirt, she'd look for all the world like a completely normal person on her completely normal—albeit very expensive—boat.

But the hand pressed against her side does nothing to hide the blood dripping through her fingers. It's shockingly bright against the fabric of her pantsuit, so out of place in the crisp, curated office that Chloe momentarily wonders if she's imagining things. She squeezes her eyes shut but when she opens them again, Katherine is still watching them, open-mouthed.

Then, before anyone can move, her eyes flutter closed and she collapses to the floor.

TWENTY-FIVE

It takes an unexpectedly long time, Chloe learns, for someone to pass out. Or maybe that's just her own panic, stretching every second into something inescapable. Across the room, Katherine's chest rises and falls in short, shallow breaths. Blood pools across her pristine deck and as Chloe watches it stain the edges of the rug, she has the brief, wild thought that someone will probably have to call housekeeping when they get back. Reed is going to be pissed.

She slumps forward, hysterical laughter bubbling in the back of her throat. She's suddenly very aware of the engine idling under her hands and wonders, through the haze of panic, when the yacht stopped moving. At some point, Katherine must have left her position at the wheel to investigate the commotion downstairs, but Chloe can't, for the life of her, remember if she noticed the change. Now, the only movement comes from the waves sweeping them further from shore, Logan struggling to rise on the ground next to her, and Harper's trembling hands wrapped around a literal smoking gun.

"Oh my god." Harper rocks back on her heels. "Oh my god, I didn't . . ."

She's too pale, pupils blown wide as she stares down at her trembling hands, and Chloe thinks that no matter what Carlyle promised her, no matter what she thought she'd receive, Harper would never purposefully end it like this. She staggers to her feet, gun clattering to the floor. Despite herself, despite everything, Chloe still reaches for her.

"Harper . . ."

The sound of her name seems to crack through the numb veneer of shock. Harper blinks, hand slowly dipping into her pocket. Chloe pictures those manicured fingers curling around the flash drive. She thinks of their multi-million-dollar payout tucked right there against the curve of Harper's hip, and hauls herself to her feet.

"Harper, don't—"

But it's too late. Harper knocks her aside and bolts for the door.

Chloe stumbles, a pained hiss slipping between her teeth. She turns in time to watch Logan throw himself in Harper's direction, a truly valiant attempt considering his still-bleeding head wound, but it's no use. Harper sends him crashing back to the deck as she leaps over her mother's crumpled form and disappears into the hall.

Chloe swears under her breath. "Don't," she snaps when Logan tries to follow. "Stay here."

She sprints into the hallway, footsteps pounding up the stairs as she chases Harper onto the main deck. Most of the remaining daylight faded behind the clouds in the time they were belowdecks. Now, it's dark, sea and sky blending together as cold drops of rain start to fall. Chloe blinks water from her eyes and turns in a frantic circle. *There.* A flash of Harper's golden hair at the back of the ship. Chloe follows, ducking as the rain falls harder, faster, but by the time she reaches the stern, Harper is gone.

"Harper?"

Chloe braces her hands on her knees, struggling to catch her breath. *Where did she go?* They're on a fucking yacht. It's not like Harper decided to swim ashore. She yanks a hand through her hair, pushing her wet bangs off her forehead. One of her ears is still ringing, a tinny, high-pitched whistle that drowns out most coherent thought, and maybe that's why she doesn't hear it sooner. The slow, monotonous clink of chains unwinding.

Chloe surges forward, gripping the railing as the realization hits her. "Harper! Wait!"

But it's too late. An engine revs to life somewhere below and when Chloe leans over the railing, there's Harper, crouched in one of the bright orange lifeboats. Her hair is dripping down her back, blazer clinging to her shoulders as she squints into the rain. For the first time since leaving shore, Chloe takes a good look at their surroundings. She thought they were heading across the bay, but the waves must have pushed them back when Katherine left the wheel. She can barely make out the smudges of light in the distance, the beckoning glow of what she assumes is the Rivera, and for a second, Chloe's anger gives way to deep, terrifying dread.

"Wait!" she calls. "You don't have to do this!"

But Harper just glares up at her through the rain, face nothing more than a pale smear against the encroaching waves. "This can't have been for nothing, Chloe."

The lifeboat lurches forward, disappearing over the crest of the next wave, and the rest of Chloe's frustration comes out in a single vicious scream. "I don't know how to drive a boat!"

She wants to break something. She wants to throw herself overboard and chase that lifeboat down herself. She wants to shake Harper for doing something so recklessly dangerous, but no. She's stuck on a yacht with an incapacitated captain, a magician with a head wound, and no way to reach shore.

Chloe sprints back the way she came, taking the stairs down to the cabin two at a time. Saltwater drips off her skirt, pooling on the deck beneath her as she drops to her knees beside Katherine, who's still sprawled in the doorway.

"You should feel for a pulse," Logan says weakly. He's still on the ground, back braced against the wall, but when he brings a tentative hand to the back of his head, the bleeding looks like it's stopped. "That's what they do on *Grey's Anatomy.*"

Chloe shoots him a glare. "Not helpful."

"I know a lot about medicine, Chloe."

"Enough to know you're severely concussed right now?"

"What?" Logan blinks. "No, I'm good. Your face is just a little swirly and I think I threw up in the corner."

Chloe ignores him, fumbling with Katherine's wrist instead. She can only deal with one crisis at a time and when she finds a pulse, faint but steady under her clammy fingers, her body involuntarily sags against the doorframe. *Alive.* For now, at least, they're all alive.

"Hello? Can anyone hear me?"

Chloe jumps at the sound of the voice, palm involuntarily landing in the pool of blood slowly spreading across the deck. She wipes it on her skirt as the sound comes again.

"Chloe? Logan? Anyone there?"

This time, Chloe recognizes it. She reaches a trembling hand up and twists the earbud that's still miraculously lodged in her ear. "Priya? Is that you?"

"I mean this in the nicest possible way, Chloe, but who the fuck else would it be?"

And even though she knows Priya's been here the whole time, even though Chloe felt her every step of the way as this new plan unfurled, the sound of her voice steadies her now.

Logan lets out a soft laugh, head tipping back against the wall. "Hey, Pri," he says.

"Oh, thank god," Priya mutters. "What happened? I heard a gunshot."

Chloe releases a shaky breath. "Harper." It's the only explanation she can manage. "She shot Katherine."

"Holy shit. Is she . . . ?"

"No." Chloe still has one hand pressed against Katherine's side, monitoring her breathing as she tries to stop the flow of blood. It's not working. She can still feel it streaming through her fingers. "She's unconscious, but alive."

Priya swears again. "And you two? You're okay?"

Chloe's not quite sure how to answer that. Harper is gone. She and Logan are stranded in the middle of the ocean with an incriminating weapon sitting on the rug behind them. If Katherine Windey dies on this boat, there'd be no question about who's to blame.

"We're okay," Logan says.

Chloe nods. She wants to confirm, to say something more, but her throat closes and her next exhale comes out wobbly and weak.

"Oh my god," Priya says. "Are you *crying*?"

"What? No." Chloe swipes the back of her hand across her face. "Sorry. I just wish you were here. Can we never do this again?"

"Sure. Next time we build an elaborate trap for Harper Parisi, we won't be as mean to each other. I'm sure it'll be just as convincing." Priya hesitates before adding, "Did you at least get the flash drive?"

Chloe's head snaps up, gaze locking on Logan. His face is still twisted with pain but as she watches, a slow, lazy smile stretches across his face. "Don't ask me things like that, Priya," he says. "It's insulting."

He opens his fist and there, in the center of his palm, is the flash drive from Carlyle's award. Snatched from Harper's pocket in the instant she tried to push him out of the way. A subtle flick of the wrist. A well-timed distraction. That's all Logan's ever needed to do his job.

Priya exhales a long sigh of relief. "I love you guys, you know that, right?"

"Thanks." Chloe's fingers dig into the deck as the yacht crests dangerously over another wave. "I would tell you to save it for when we get back, but I think we're quite literally about to die at sea."

Logan winces as he struggles to his feet. "You don't happen to know how to drive a boat, do you, Pri?"

"Um . . ." Priya's nails tap against her keyboard with alarming speed. "Well, I'm currently looking at a wikiHow article titled 'How to Solo Drive a 100 Foot Power Yacht.' Does that sound helpful?"

"Not particularly."

"Okay, well, I also called the coast guard. They should be on their way. Can you get to a radio? Or somewhere to relay your coordinates?"

Chloe's not even sure she knows what coordinates are, but this, at least, feels doable. "Yes. I think all the equipment is upstairs."

"Good. You just need . . . in the back."

Priya's voice cuts out and Chloe presses a finger to her ear, willing her closer. "Priya?"

". . . if you . . . north . . . Chloe?"

There's a beep and then the line goes dead.

"Huh," Logan says, plucking his own earbud out and turning it from side to side. "That's not good."

Chloe bites back another frustrated scream. If she dies here, she's going to *kill* Harper. She's going to kill Katherine Windey and whoever sold her a yacht in the first place. As she stares down at the slowly growing pool of blood in the door, the terror she's managed to keep at bay claws back to the surface, hovering just behind her breastbone. She can get them out of this, surely. She's weaseled her way out of worse situations. She's having a hard time thinking of examples at the moment, but they definitely exist.

Chloe exhales through her teeth and removes her hand from Katherine's side. She's about to lift the hem of her shirt to check the bleeding when Katherine's eyes fly open. She sucks in a breath, fingers locking around Chloe's wrist and this time, Chloe actually does scream.

"Holy shit!"

"You!" Katherine's grip is incredibly tight for someone who's currently bleeding out on the deck of her own ship. "What . . . where are we?"

Logan leaps back, eyes wide, and Chloe's response catches in her throat. She's still half convinced this is Katherine's ghost, come back to haunt them for everything they've done this week, but when Chloe lifts the hem of her shirt, she finally sees the wound for what it is. The bullet didn't strike Katherine directly, grazing the length of her side instead. When Chloe looks over her shoulder, she finds the bullet embedded in the cabin wall, less than an inch from where Katherine was standing.

"Oh my god." Chloe doubles over, relieved tears stinging the backs of her eyes. "I thought you were dead!"

Katherine's brow furrows. "Why would I be dead? I'm—" Then she sucks in a breath. "Oh. She *shot* me."

"Yeah." Chloe wipes her bloody hands on her skirt. "And then you passed out, so. That was a little dramatic."

Katherine's face pales, gaze turning purposefully toward the ceiling. "I don't like blood."

That, Chloe thinks, is actually the most normal thing she's heard about Katherine Windey all week. She pushes herself to her feet as thunder rumbles overhead. They're still swaying dangerously from side to side and when Katherine tries to follow, face twisting in obvious pain, Chloe knows they can't wait this out.

She helps her stand, one arm looped around her waist for balance. "Please tell me you can drive us out of here."

"What . . . ?" Katherine blinks as she finally takes in her ruined cabin. "What the hell did you do?"

"I'm going to be so real with you, that's the least of our problems. Can you get us home or not?"

"Ignore her." Logan still has one hand pressed to his injured head, but he extends the other in Katherine's direction. "I'm Logan, by the way. Big fan. Love your work. Just want to let you know that I wasn't really involved in . . . any of this."

"Seriously?" Chloe smacks his hand away. "*Now*?"

"I can drive," Katherine says. The words come out in a strangled, painful groan and for a minute, she looks so much like Harper that Chloe's pulse stutters.

"Keep pressure on that," she says, nodding toward the wound in Katherine's side. "If you bleed out, I swear to god I'm going to kill you."

Slowly, the three of them make their way down the hall, staggering up the stairs one at a time. Logan's feet seem to slide out from under him the second they hit the main deck. He falls to his knees, wincing as he gingerly brushes the back of his head.

"Stay here," Chloe says. "Hold on to something. I'll take her upstairs."

Logan shakes his head. "No, I'm fine."

"Did you or did you not just say you threw up in the cabin?"

Katherine's eyes narrow in Logan's direction. "You did *what*?"

"Nothing!" Logan sags against the railing, one hand looping around the slick metal bar as Chloe turns to go. "Go on, be safe."

The rain is falling harder now, blurring Chloe's vision. It's an effort to keep them moving up the next flight of stairs toward the bridge. "I need a radio," she calls over the wind. "Something we can use to get help."

"There." Katherine points as best she can. "Right above the wheel."

Chloe feels her way across the controls as the ship lists from side to side. Katherine must have a death wish. There's no other reason anyone would take a boat out in this weather.

She doesn't realize she's said it out loud until Katherine lets out a pained sigh. "It wasn't raining when I left."

"We literally live in Florida! Check a forecast next time."

Somewhere in the back of her mind, Chloe's single remaining thread of self-preservation reminds her this is *Katherine Windey*. She probably shouldn't be talking to her like this. She should probably be more polite, but when Chloe flips on the radio to find nothing but static, she actually thinks she's letting her off easy. She growls in frustration and turns the dial off.

"Okay, plan B. Can you get us to shore?"

Katherine nods. Her jaw sets in steely determination, but when she tries to step forward, she sags against the controls, unable to support her own weight. Great. Chloe's going to take that as a no. On to plan C, apparently.

"Can you walk me through it?" she asks.

Katherine looks up, rain running down the side of her face. "What are you going to do?"

"Drive the boat," Chloe snaps. "What the fuck do you think?"

A sharp gust of wind whips through her blouse as she takes the wheel, plastering the wet fabric to her chest. Briefly, she thinks of Harper, alone in the storm. It would be fitting for her consequences to catch up with her out here, where not even her family name or Carlyle's money could save her. Chloe grips the wheel and shakes the thought away.

If there's one thing Harper Parisi does, it's deliver. She was always going to make it out of this, even if she had to drown Chloe to do it.

"That's the throttle," Katherine says, pointing to a lever on the dashboard. Chloe ignores the water pooling under her palm and grabs for it. "It's in neutral, so you'll have to ease it forward. Just go slowly and point us toward those lights."

Chloe inhales, trying to center herself at the controls. That makes sense. It's intuitive, like driving a car, but when she squints into the distance, the lights of the Rivera seem impossibly far. Another continent. Another universe. Katherine sinks to the deck, back braced against the controls as she presses one hand to her side. Deep wound or not, she's still in bad shape and Chloe doesn't actually want to follow through on her promise to kill her if she bleeds out.

She glances over the wheel to where Logan still sits on the deck below. She can't tell if he's watching them through the storm, but his presence steadies her. She squeezes the throttle in her right hand, slowly pulling it toward her as she spins the wheel to the left. The boat rumbles to life beneath them, then starts moving forward.

"I feel the need to tell you," Chloe says through gritted teeth, "that I really, *really* hate the ocean."

Katherine's head tips back, pain evident in every labored breath. "Funny," she says. "I hate being shot."

Chloe groans. She wants to respond, but all her energy is currently focused on keeping them steady over the churning waves.

"Who are you?"

It takes Chloe a second to realize Katherine's still talking to her. She tightens her grip on the wheel, palms slipping as she struggles to keep the yacht straight. "I work here."

"Don't lie to me."

"I do! Ask Reed. He loves me."

Katherine lets out a dry laugh. "I don't trust Reed Maloney's opinion on anything."

For some reason, that makes Chloe laugh, too. This whole situation is so ridiculous and she's so *mad* that it's all she can do. Mad at Katherine for taking the boat out in weather like this. Mad at Harper for betraying them. Mad at herself for not seeing the signs sooner. "You stole Andrew Carlyle's Florida Hospitality Award," she calls over the wind.

It's not a question, but she still feels Katherine stiffen beside her. "I don't know what you're talking about."

"Don't lie to me," Chloe says, parroting her mocking tone. "I don't care that you took it. I don't like him either, but that's why I'm here. He hired me to steal it back."

"Of course he did." Katherine's face twists in pain as they hit another wave. "He's so *dramatic.*"

That's one way to put it. Chloe spits out a mouthful of rainwater and asks, "Did you know about the flash drive?"

She doesn't know what it is about driving through a storm that's making her so talkative. She doesn't like Katherine. She's actually pretty terrified of her, but the thought of capsizing the boat this far from shore is worse. She needs something to fill the space between them as her sweaty palms slip across the wheel.

"What flash drive?"

Chloe risks a glance in Katherine's direction. Despite everything, Chloe doesn't think she's lying. She doesn't look like she has the strength for it. "He hired us to steal that award," she says. "Or at least that's what he told me, but there was a flash drive hidden inside. That's what he really wanted. Did you know it was there?"

"No." Katherine shakes her head. "I just knew that award was important. I knew he'd notice if I took it, and I knew it would annoy him if he couldn't get it back right away."

Talk about dramatic. Chloe flips her bangs off her forehead, ignoring the halo of water droplets that shakes loose at the movement. "So you really don't have any idea what could be on it?"

"No."

Chloe remembers the way Harper advanced on her downstairs, the almost zealous gleam in her eye when she snatched the flash drive from Chloe's grip. Whatever it was, Carlyle was determined to get it back. He made a separate, backdoor deal with Harper to do it, and Chloe has only ever seen him that determined about one, frustratingly specific thing.

"I think . . ." Chloe trails off, then tries again. "I think it has something to do with you."

"With me?" Katherine's head falls back against the controls. "*Why?*"

Chloe pulls the throttle toward her ever so slightly, urging them faster across the waves. "I don't know. Don't shoot the messenger."

"Why not? My daughter shot me."

"Well, that's not exactly my fault, is it?"

For a minute, Katherine looks like she wants to argue. It occurs to Chloe then that even if they do make it out of this, Katherine could very well turn them in anyway. Why would she implicate her own daughter when Chloe and Logan are right here, the perfect scapegoats for Harper's crimes? She tenses, but when Katherine speaks again, her voice is noticeably softer.

"They were working together?" she asks. "Harper and Carlyle?"

"Yeah," Chloe says. "They were working together the whole time, I think."

Another wave slams into the side of the boat. Water slides across the deck and Chloe flinches as it soaks through her shoes. There's saltwater in her mouth and pooling in the small of her back. Katherine falls silent and it's not until Chloe looks down that she realizes her eyes are fluttering closed.

"Hey." She nudges her with a foot. "Katherine?"

When she doesn't answer, Chloe releases the throttle and drops to her knees on the deck. She grips Katherine's shoulders, hands sliding over her wet skin as she feels for a pulse.

"Stop it." Katherine makes a halfhearted attempt to shove Chloe off. "I'm fine."

But she's not. Her lips are too pale and she's shivering from something Chloe doesn't think is the cold. "Don't do that," Chloe snaps. "Just . . . we're almost there, okay?"

She drags herself to her feet and squints toward shore. The lights are still there, but they're distant and blurry and . . . *and how is that possible?* They look further away than when they started sailing. Chloe chokes back a frustrated sob and grabs the throttle again.

Beside her, Katherine's hand curls in the hem of Chloe's skirt. "Harper?" she asks, voice hoarse. "Where is she? Is she all right?"

"Um." Chloe decides it's probably not the best time to tell the woman currently bleeding out beside her that her daughter has disappeared into the storm. "She's fine. She's . . . somewhere."

If Katherine notices the strange hitch in Chloe's voice, she doesn't comment. Her grip tightens in the damp fabric. "What did she tell you?"

Chloe shakes her head, focused on steering the yacht toward the line of multicolored lights blinking at them across the waves. "You're going to have to be more specific."

"Does he know? Did she tell him?"

"Tell him *what*?"

But Chloe has the distinct impression Katherine's not actually talking to her at all. Her eyes are glassy, breath coming in short, shallow bursts, and the only thing Chloe can think about is keeping them moving, tracking the lights as they grow steadily larger. It's not until she squints across the waves that she realizes it's not the yacht that's moving. It's the lights, and they're coming straight toward her.

The flashing red and green of two approaching coast guard boats.

Chloe sags against the controls, relief coursing through her as one of them pulls alongside the yacht. She has the brief thought that this too is something that belongs in a network crime procedural, before Katherine's hand slips from her skirt.

"Help!" Chloe cries. "Over here."

There's a sharp clang of metal as one of the officers tosses a line between the decks. He pounds up the stairs toward her. Another shadowed figure heads toward Logan, and Chloe staggers away from the controls. Her knees give out and as she crumples to the deck, she feels Katherine's hand close over hers. Her fingers are icy and in that instant, everything Chloe's done this week comes flooding back. The gun downstairs, peppered with her fingerprints. Her false employment at the Rivera, the stolen key cards, all the times she snuck into places she didn't belong. Katherine has every reason to turn her in now, to end this, but instead, her grip tightens ever so slightly.

"Thank you," she whispers, and then her eyes flutter closed.

"I . . . wait." Chloe crawls toward her in the rain. "Katherine?"

But there's a hand on her arm, tugging her gently away as someone else takes the wheel. Chloe's fingers dig into the wood beneath her. Without the adrenaline to keep her upright, she can barely lift her head as the yacht starts moving toward shore with renewed urgency. She can see the island now, the Rivera shoreline peppered with blue and red flashing lights. Are they for her? For Katherine? Did Harper call them here as a final checkmate?

Chloe pictures the Miami police department speeding across the bay in an army of little cop boats, sirens blaring and lights flashing, and chokes on a delirious laugh.

The hand on her arm tightens. Someone else is bending over Katherine, checking her pulse, asking her questions. Or maybe those questions are for her. Chloe can't tell.

"Ma'am." The officer leaning over her is tall, his voice warm even as his face slides in and out of focus. "Can you tell me your name?"

Chloe nods before realizing it's not really a yes or no question. "Chloe," she says.

"Chloe. Are you hurt?"

She shakes her head. "Did you see a lifeboat? A woman in a lifeboat?"

The two officers exchange a look and Chloe wonders if she's

making any sense. Her teeth are chattering and suddenly, she can't get warm. "A lifeboat," she repeats. "Her name is Harper."

"Chloe." The officer holding her arm tries again, voice gentle. "Are you hurt?"

The shoreline is visible now. Chloe can see the outline of the Rivera glittering through the storm and thinks, again, how utterly ridiculous it was to build a hotel on an island.

"Unresponsive." The officer standing over her whips out a walkie-talkie. "She's probably in shock."

Yes, Chloe thinks. *Probably.*

It's the last thing she remembers before the dark claims her.

TWENTY-SIX

Every single one of Chloe's worst memories takes place in a hospital. A side effect, it turns out, of watching her mother slowly fade against the colorless walls of an ICU. Chloe's never been a patient herself, but apparently sailing through a low-grade tropical storm and running what one paramedic referred to as "a pretty concerning fever" requires a certain level of care.

She doesn't remember the rest of the trip across the bay. She doesn't even remember getting to the hospital. All she knows is that one second she was drifting in some strange, half-delirious sleep, haunted by the image of Harper disappearing into a bottomless sea, and the next, she's opening her eyes. There's a monitor in the corner by her bed, a needle taped under the skin of her hand, and her father dozes peacefully in the chair next to her.

"Dad?" The word slips out before Chloe can stop it.

Her father jumps, glasses sliding to the end of his nose. "Chloe!" He visibly relaxes. "You're awake."

Debatable. She can still feel the swell of the waves beneath her, pushing the walls back and forth as she blinks into the bright, sterile light. "Where am I?"

"County Hospital?"

"*What?*" That shocks her out of her daze. "No!"

"Don't worry! They gave you some fluids to bring your temperature down, but you should be free to go in a few hours. You're okay."

Her father runs a hand through her hair, calm and reassuring, but it's not her health Chloe's worried about. She's sore and achy, sure. She can still taste the saltwater on her lips, but hospitals aren't cheap. She knows this from years of working through her mother's bills and here she is, racking up more debt of her own. She buries her face in her hands. "I'm sorry." Then another thought hits her. "Wait, where's Logan?"

"I'm here!"

Logan's voice comes from somewhere to her left. Chloe turns in time to see him draw back the curtain that separates her bed from the others. He grins down at her, fresh gauze wrapped around his head. Chloe has a strong suspicion he's been told to lie down too, but when he leans over and takes her hand, she decides not to care.

"Hi," she says.

"Hi." Logan looks her up and down. "You look terrible."

Chloe rolls her eyes, unable to stop the grin spreading across her face. "Where's Priya?"

"She went to get snacks. She'll be back any minute."

Her father pushes himself out of his chair. "Well, I'm going to stretch my legs for a bit. Let you three talk." He pauses long enough to pat Logan's shoulder on the way out before giving Chloe a pointed look. "And when I get back, you're going to tell me everything, okay?"

Chloe nods, gaze dropping to her lap as a hot rush of shame overtakes her. Logan waits until her father closes the curtain behind him before speaking again.

"It'll be fine," he whispers. "He's cool."

That might be objectively true, but Chloe doesn't think anyone's cool enough for this. "Did you tell him . . . anything?"

"Not really. I said we made a day trip to the Rivera after work, someone tried to rob Katherine Windey's yacht, and you saved the day by steering it back to shore."

"Right," Chloe mutters. "The totally believable story that starts with us hanging out at a luxury hotel."

Logan laughs, but before he can respond, the curtain yanks open again, flooding Chloe's bed with a new burst of cold, artificial light.

"Oh my god!" Priya's eyes widen and the hand that's not currently clutching half a dozen brightly wrapped candy bars flies to her mouth. "Chloe, you look terrible!"

Chloe scowls. "Okay, it cannot possibly be that bad."

Priya slides onto the foot of the bed, dumps her snack collection between them, then throws her arms around Chloe as best she can. "It is," she murmurs into her hair. "I missed you."

"Is that all they had?" Logan asks, pointing down at Priya's haul.

Priya pulls back, eyeing him reproachfully. "Sorry, the five-star charcuterie platter was sold out."

For a minute, Logan looks genuinely nostalgic, and Chloe bites back a grin as she leans against Priya's shoulder. Their fights might have been manufactured—blown out of proportion to lull Harper into a false sense of security—but she still hated watching her friends walk away. It felt wrong, like yanking out one of her ribs, and she's not ready to let either of them out of her sight. She reaches for Logan's hand, then winces at the painful twinge in her wrist.

Now that she's not fighting for her life at sea, Chloe can't help but notice her strange collection of bruises and aches. Her knees from where they'd slammed into the deck. Her shoulders from hauling Katherine up two flights of stairs. Her neck where Harper grabbed her. She rubs a careful hand over her throat and asks, tentatively, "Has anyone seen Harper?"

Priya shakes her head. "They found the lifeboat washed up on the mainland, but no sign of her."

"She definitely made it," Logan says. "She's too stubborn to die at sea."

"Sure." Priya grimaces. "But only because it would reveal her true form as an evil witch who steals people's voices and destroys their kingdoms."

Chloe sighs and rubs a hand down her face. She doesn't know what to think. She doesn't even know what she wants, but she knows Harper too well to think she'd go down easy. "How far do you think she got before she noticed it was gone?" she asks.

Logan shrugs. "Who knows. She was escaping in a lifeboat through a storm. She must have had better things to do than check her pockets."

Priya shudders, her grip tightening around Chloe's arm. "God," she mutters. "I can't believe she *left* you there."

"I know." Logan's expression sours as he brushes a finger along the ridge of his bandage. "I can't believe she was working with Carlyle."

"I can. If he wanted to hurt Katherine, her daughter would be the best ally. Makes it personal."

But that's the part Chloe can't quite figure out. She can still see Harper's wild, terrified face if she closes her eyes, the steely determination in the set of her jaw. *There's a reason he hired me and not you.* Whatever Carlyle has on Harper feels deeper than blackmail, but Chloe doubts they'll be able to unwind it now.

She shakes her head, ignoring the dull ache still throbbing behind her eyes. "Did you figure out what's on the flash drive, Pri?"

Priya's eyes light up. She reaches into her backpack and when she pulls out her laptop, her grin turns sharp, humming with barely contained anticipation. Chloe knows this look. It's the *Priya has hot gossip* smile, the one that means she's either about to announce something Chloe has absolutely no interest in—like the time she saw one of the guys from *Love Is Blind* doing a body shot off a cocktail waitress who was not his fiancée—or about to change the world.

There's usually no in-between.

"Do you remember Katherine's embezzlement trial back in January?" Priya asks.

Chloe nods. How could she forget? "They found her not guilty. The evidence was inconclusive."

"Right." Priya boots up her laptop. "But do you know *why* it was inconclusive?"

"Because she hired a hit man to pay people off?" Logan asks.

"No. Because she didn't do it. None of that evidence was real."

She flips her laptop around, scrolling through pages and pages of what look like bank statements. They must have come from the flash drive, and Chloe can't tell if it's the lingering effects of her time at sea or if she really doesn't understand what she's looking at.

"What do you mean?"

"I mean it wasn't her." Priya highlights a line of text toward the top of one document. "Someone was embezzling money, of course. All those charges had to come from somewhere, but they weren't from Katherine's accounts. They were from Carlyle's."

Chloe straightens, pulse quickening. She drags the laptop toward her, scrolling through the document as Logan leans over her shoulder. "You're saying he framed her?"

"Exactly." Priya nods. "It's a really good forgery. It fooled the police, anyway, and most of the prosecution. He covered his tracks too, but the reason there wasn't enough evidence to convict her is because there *literally* wasn't enough evidence."

Logan rubs a hand over his forehead, brow furrowing in concentration. "But this is his flash drive, right? His award? Why would he keep something like that?"

"He'd need a record of it somewhere, even if it was just for personal use," Priya says. "And if it's on a separate drive like this, he wouldn't have to risk it sitting on his personal computer."

"And he could hide it somewhere safe. In a place no one else would think to look."

"Oh my god." Chloe lets out a low, stunned laugh as the pieces that have been eluding her all week finally snap into place. "I thought he was being audited, or something. I thought that was why he got so defensive when I brought it up, but he knew I suspected there was something else inside that award. When I saw him after the gala, he assumed I'd been talking to Katherine. He thought I knew about the fake."

Priya nods. "That must be why he changed the deadline on us," she says. "He didn't want to risk you switching sides because if Katherine ever found it . . ."

She trails off and the three of them fall silent, staring down at Priya's laptop. Chloe can understand, to an extent, the breadth of Carlyle's feud with Katherine. There's a maddening frustration that comes with always having someone one step ahead. She knows what it's like to stand in someone else's shadow, trying desperately to claw her way free. She understands the desire to snap that bond altogether, but she also thinks there's a difference between petty theft and framing someone for white-collar crimes.

That's what Harper had planned for her, though. If everything went according to that plan, Chloe would be the one in custody now, fighting off charges for crimes she didn't commit.

Maybe Harper and Carlyle are more alike than Chloe realized.

Logan shifts uncomfortably against the wall. "Not to be the voice of reason in this incredibly exciting discovery, but we *did* find it. We have it now, and I don't think Carlyle's going to let that go."

Chloe nods. She's considered that too, of course. She knows she can't go back to her catering job. They might not be able to stay in the city, but without the payout they were promised, the three of them are right back where they started. Stuck. Scrambling. Desperate for a way out.

"Can we figure that out tomorrow?" Chloe asks. "I . . . I just really need to talk to my dad."

Logan's expression softens. "Of course. Whatever you need."

He plants a kiss on the top of her head before returning to his own bed. Priya squeezes her arm on the way out and Chloe closes her eyes. When she opens them again, her father's back, settling down in his chair. Instinctively, she reaches out a hand. He takes it, thumb moving over her knuckles in smooth, calming circles. There are so many things she could do in this moment, Chloe thinks. She could lie. Run away. Push him aside like she's been doing for the past year. But Chloe doesn't think she wants that anymore.

Instead, she takes a deep breath, opens her eyes, and tries something new. She tells her father the truth.

The only reason Chloe walks into the Carlyle hotel the next morning is to drop off her keys and hand in her official resignation.

They let her out of the hospital late last night. Chloe let her father take her home and she slept curled on his couch in the deepest sleep she'd had in weeks. When she woke up, she didn't even remember her dreams. Priya and Logan will come by tomorrow to help clean out her employee apartment, but until then, the only thing tying Chloe to this place is a single slip of paper and a year of complicated memories. She drops the resignation letter in her manager's mailbox and wonders if somewhere, in a different hotel across the bay, Reed is wondering what happened to Stassi the housekeeper. It's fitting, Chloe thinks, that in the end, neither place gets to keep her.

She says goodbye to her favorite co-workers on her way out, stops to grab one last panini from the kitchen, and is halfway across the lobby before her gaze catches on the elevator. Despite the warnings clanging in the back of her mind, she still has that penthouse key tucked in her pocket.

She knows for a fact that Carlyle is in Tampa. His face was plastered across the third page of their local paper this morning, bright-eyed and grinning like a very important possession of his isn't currently missing in action. This time, he won't be upstairs waiting for her, but Chloe can't help wondering if Harper might be, instead.

It's a foolish, utterly unsubstantiated idea. There's no way Harper stuck around after failing to deliver the one thing Carlyle wanted. She probably fled as soon as she realized the flash drive was gone. She's probably running from her mother too, from all the things she did on that boat, but . . .

But what if?

Chloe still can't figure out how Harper fits into all this. When she, Priya, and Logan sat down the night before entering the Rivera to make a contingency plan, they hadn't really known the role Harper would play. All they knew was that it felt too perfect, too forced. Harper showing up at Carlyle's party the night they both received penthouse key cards. She'll probably never face a single consequence for the part she's played, but that doesn't mean Chloe's ready to let it go.

How can she, when the memory of Harper's pale, panicked face still plays behind her eyelids each time she blinks? How can she when she truly believed, for a minute, that there was something real under Harper's desperate, frantic kisses?

Maybe she'll never know. Maybe they're always going to haunt each other.

Chloe takes a deep breath, nails digging into her palms. No matter the outcome, she needs to be sure. So she pulls the penthouse key card out of her pocket and takes the elevator up to the top floor for the last time.

It's just as empty as she remembers, lights off, furniture draped in long white sheets for cleaning. The door to the office is closed, but when Chloe grips the handle, she finds it unlocked. The room looks the same as she left it, bare and cold and professional. The only thing missing is Carlyle's laptop and, when she runs a hand underneath the desk, she finds her bug is gone, too. Harper would have told him about it, of course. That's why Chloe brought it up in the suite that day. It was always meant to be a distraction, something to make him think he'd bested her yet again. She leans down and plucks a second one from underneath the chair, biting back a satisfied grin as she tucks it in her pocket. They'll have to see if Priya can pull anything interesting from it this afternoon.

Chloe walks around the desk in a slow circle, opening a few

drawers as she goes. They're still full of office supplies and notepads, but there's no sign of anything personal. No sign of Harper. She's surprised at the way her chest aches at the thought, but the pain doesn't immobilize her anymore. She got her closure. Harper had underestimated her one too many times and finally paid the price.

She closes the last drawer and the force of it accidentally jostles the picture frame at the edge of Carlyle's desk. It falls to the floor before Chloe can catch it, shattering over the cold tile. Chloe drops to her knees, hurriedly scooping up the broken glass as best she can. The frame is cracked too, and as she sets the pieces back on the desk, she thinks it's a shame she's no longer in the business of crime.

It really does look like real gold. She could probably sell it for a decent price.

She picks up the photo last. A young Carlyle standing with a group of friends in front of the university library. Just like Chloe suspected, the left half of the image has been tucked back, hidden inside the frame, but it unfolds in her hands now. Her pulse quickens as she recognizes Katherine standing on Carlyle's other side, grinning widely with both arms around his neck.

Because they were friends, once, Carlyle said. Chloe almost believed him.

She can feel the tattered edges of something slipping through the back of her mind the longer she stands there. She grabs for it, wanting a conclusion, but it falls through her fingers. The Katherine in the photo looks so much like her daughter, especially here when she's several decades younger and smiling at the camera. Chloe remembers thinking the same thing about that family photo in Katherine's office, how strange it was that she couldn't find any hint of Harper's father in her face.

But there's something familiar in the slant of Carlyle's grin here, the angle of his single raised eyebrow. Chloe's fingers tighten around the photo's creased edge. She remembers all the times Harper's expression twisted at the mention of her parents, all the times Chloe thought Harper and Carlyle felt too similar. At the time, she'd chalked it up to coincidence. A side effect of running in the same wealthy circles. *Sometimes you learn your mother dealt with it by having an affair* Harper said, bitterness coating every word. Because she loved her father. She loved Enzo Parisi, the software engineer with the kind smile and love of fishing, who moved to Ohio to start a new family. Because Harper wasn't speaking to her mother currently, because whatever they'd discussed last had slashed some heavy, uncrossable rift between them.

Chloe swallows hard, remembering the way Katherine gripped the hem of her skirt on the yacht. *Does he know?* she asked. *Did she tell him?*

She did, Chloe realizes, and the thought drips down her spine like ice. Harper told Carlyle everything and that's why he hired her. That's why he wanted them both, not just because of Harper's connection to Katherine, but because she was willing to do whatever she could to make her mother hurt.

All she wants, really, is for someone to notice her.

Carlyle told Chloe as much in his office that day, looked her in the eyes and smiled like he wasn't actively manipulating the one person who'd been so very desperate for his approval.

"Holy shit," Chloe whispers. She can't bring herself to say the next part out loud, but as the photo slips through her fingers, the words seem to echo across the walls.

Carlyle is Harper's father.

TWENTY-SEVEN

"You know," Priya says, glancing around the table with barely disguised glee. "I think we should all take a minute to acknowledge the fact that I was right."

They're all sitting in Chloe's dad's condo, working their way through plates of home-cooked lasagna. The living room is still cluttered, still piled with moving boxes, but this time they're full of Chloe's things instead of her father's. She moved in less than a week ago and already, this place feels more like home than her Carlyle apartment ever did. Like now, for instance, she can have her friends over for dinner without worrying about where everyone is going to sit.

"Please, Priya." Logan waves a fork in front of his face. "Can we not? I'm eating."

Priya shakes her head. "No. I want you to say it with me. Say 'Priya, you were right, I'm sorry for doubting you. Carlyle and Katherine totally fucked.'"

Chloe grimaces into her plate. "To be fair, you also said that everyone who hates each other wants 'to fuck at least a little bit.'"

"Okay, and? You're going to tell me I'm wrong?"

Chloe is saved from answering by her father sweeping out of the kitchen with another basket of freshly baked bread. "Here," he says. "There's more in the oven if you need."

Logan immediately grabs for it, inhaling the thick aroma wafting up from the basket. "Mr. Bly," he says, with all the reverence of someone about to break out in prayer, "I think I love you."

Her father laughs and as he heads back into the kitchen, Chloe thinks it wouldn't be a surprise if he asked Logan to move in, too. He loves company. He loves hosting, and she hasn't seen him this happy in a long time.

When she got home from her visit to the Carlyle last week, Chloe dropped her bag on the couch and said, "I quit," loud enough for her father to hear from his room down the hall.

"Oh?" he said, poking his head around the corner. "Any idea what you want to do next?"

Chloe shook her head. Honestly, she's not even sure how she's going to pay off this new set of hospital bills. She's not sure how to build a resume either, but she knows she's going to do it right. No more infiltrating black-tie galas, no more late-night cons, no more secret, under-the-table deals.

The doorbell rings somewhere down the hall and Chloe's father hurries to answer it. Priya watches him go before eyeing Chloe across the table. "So, how's the unemployment treating you?"

Chloe stabs her fork into her lasagna. "Fine. I've been jobless for less than a week, though, so ask me again in a few days. I might have a different answer."

"God, I wish that were me." Priya sighs. "What have you been doing with all your free time? Any big summer plans?"

Chloe shrugs. In a perfect world, she'd buy a one-way ticket out of Miami International. She'd show up on her aunt's doorstep and wander the hills of her mother's childhood village for the rest of the summer, before returning home and giving her next steps some real, serious thought. "I don't know. I'd love to visit Ireland, but flights are expensive. Especially in the summer."

"Tell me about it." Logan tears into another piece of bread. "My sister just got a job in San Francisco. She wants me to visit and I don't know how to explain to her that I have, like, twelve dollars in my bank account."

"Amateur," Priya says. "You've survived worse than that."

"But I have standards now, Priya. I slept on a five-star mattress last week. I know what a thread count is."

Chloe pushes her fork around her plate as guilt claws its way up the back of her throat. She knows Carlyle's deception isn't her fault. According to Harper, he never intended to pay them anyway, but she can't help feeling responsible for their collective lack of funds.

"Chloe?" Her father is back in the dining room, brow furrowed in clear confusion. "You have a visitor."

Chloe looks up and nearly drops her fork.

Because there, standing in the entryway of her father's condo, like it's the most normal thing in the world, is Katherine Windey. She looks surprisingly chipper for someone who almost bled out on a luxury yacht last week. Her hair is pulled back in a low bun, wispy strands curling around her face in the heat. She's wearing a light blue blazer over a white t-shirt and jeans and, even though the look is distinctly casual, Chloe has a feeling the blazer alone cost more than her entire wardrobe. Then Logan lurches forward in his seat and Chloe notices the gold bumblebee brooch pinned to Katherine's lapel.

She shoots to her feet before Logan can make a grab for it, then immediately regrets it. It's not like Katherine's the president. Chloe's the only one standing, fork still clutched in one hand as the others wait in silence. She shakes her head, dozens of questions hanging on the tip of her tongue. In the end, the only thing that comes out is, "Why?"

Katherine glances around the condo, gaze unreadable as she takes in everything from the overly crowded kitchen table to the newly hung photos on the wall. "We didn't get a chance to finish our conversation. Is now a good time?"

Chloe doesn't think there's ever a good time to have a conversation with someone like Katherine, but something about her tone makes her think this isn't a request. She steals a glance toward her father, who's still lingering in the doorway. He might know most of the details of last week, but that doesn't mean she wants him involved now.

He steps forward as she opens her mouth, clearly sensing the rising tension. "Why don't you talk out on the patio?" he suggests. "I can clean up in here."

Chloe nods gratefully, voice still stuck somewhere in the center of her chest. She drops her fork back onto her plate and motions for the others to follow.

Of all the things that have happened to her in the last few weeks, Chloe thinks that leading Katherine Windey through her father's home is one of the strangest. Katherine probably finds the whole thing terribly boring, the beige walls and scuffed furniture a far cry from her galas and ballrooms and million-dollar yachts. By the time Chloe opens the back door and lets the others file onto the patio, every cell in her body feels coiled tight. Logan grabs her arm as he passes.

"Chloe," he whispers. "*The Brooch.*"

Chloe shakes her head. "Don't even think about it."

"But it's literally right there."

"Sorry, bud." Priya pats him on the shoulder as the door slides shut behind them. "Some things just aren't meant to be."

There are only a few pieces of flimsy plastic furniture on the patio. Katherine swipes a pile of dead leaves off her chair before perching gingerly on the edge, hands braced on the armrests like she's afraid the whole thing might snap. Honestly, it might. Everything out here is at least two decades old.

"So," Chloe says, breaking the uncomfortable silence at last. "How are you doing?"

Katherine shrugs. "I've been better."

"Right. And . . . how did you find me?"

"I have my ways. Just like you have yours." Katherine's gaze skims over Priya and Logan. "Interesting crew you have here. Nice to see you again, Logan."

Priya offers her a hesitant wave, but Logan ignores the greeting, staring so intently at the brooch Chloe thinks there's a decent chance he'll snatch it off her blazer and run. She swallows over the anxious lump in her throat and turns back to Katherine. She should have known this was coming. The world has been quiet for too long, letting her relax for a few days too many, and now Katherine is here to turn it back on.

"If you're going to arrest us, can you wait until my dad leaves?" Chloe asks. "He wasn't involved in any of this."

"Arrest you?" Katherine's brow furrows. "Do I look like a cop?"

"I . . . no. I just . . . we were on the boat when everything happened, so—"

"So what? You didn't shoot me."

Logan's heel connects with her shin under the table and Chloe stops, drawing in a sharp gasp of pain. Right. Of course she didn't, so why is she confessing her crimes like this is some sort of trial? She clears her throat and tries again.

"What's your story, then? What did you say happened?"

Katherine gives a noncommittal shrug. "We were on our way across the bay to a party at my downtown hotel when I realized someone stowed away on the boat. They tried to rob me, failed, and then escaped in the lifeboat. Thankfully, a few of my employees were on board to help fight them off."

"Really?" Priya lifts an eyebrow. "And people actually believed that?"

"Of course." Katherine's expression turns steely. "That's what happened, isn't it? What else would I be saying?"

Chloe opens her mouth, then closes it again. For whatever reason, Katherine has very purposefully crafted her and Logan a way out. She's letting them go when she could easily implicate them for working with Carlyle in the first place, and Chloe supposes she should feel grateful. But she's negotiated with millionaires before. There's always a catch, always something they want in return.

"And you don't want us to say it was Harper," she says. "You don't want to admit your own daughter shot you."

Katherine's jaw tightens. "That would be . . . less than ideal, yes." She hesitates before adding, "I haven't heard from her since that night."

"I don't know where she is, if that's why you're here."

It comes out harsher than Chloe intends, but it's the truth. She hasn't seen Harper since she pulled the trigger and left them stranded on that ship. It probably wouldn't be hard to find her now, if they tried. Katherine could trace her credit cards or track her phone, but Chloe has a feeling she likes not knowing.

Easier for her to pretend nothing's wrong if Harper's not around to remind her.

Silence falls across the patio, broken only by the creak of Logan leaning back in his chair. "Carlyle's still in Tampa," he offers. "Maybe she's there, too."

Chloe shakes her head. Regardless of the circumstances, she knows Harper is no longer working with Carlyle. She wouldn't be surprised if he drove her out of town himself for failing to bring him the flash drive. That was all he wanted from her, after all. Harper lied and cheated and sacrificed everything for him and he still cast her aside like she was nothing. Wordlessly, Chloe pulls a photograph from her pocket. It's the one she took from the penthouse, a young Carlyle and Katherine standing with their friends in front of the campus library. She smooths it out on her leg, then slides it across the table.

Katherine's face remains remarkably still. "That's not mine."

"I know."

Chloe lets the words hang between them, refusing to lower her gaze. She wants Katherine to admit it, to confirm the truth Chloe's been turning over in her head since yesterday. That Carlyle is Harper's father. That Katherine lied about it for years, hid the truth from her own daughter, and let Harper believe their own little family was perfect. Maybe Katherine isn't directly responsible for everything that happened last week, but Chloe still thinks if she cared about Harper half as much as Harper cares about her, none of them would be here.

"We . . ." Katherine folds her arms, gaze lifted stubbornly toward the line of trees behind them. "We were friends, once."

Chloe lifts an eyebrow. "That's all?"

For a minute, she thinks that's it. Then Katherine's jaw tenses, and when she speaks again, her voice is barely audible over the wind in the trees. "No one knows," she whispers. "No one has ever known. Not my family, not my husband, especially not Andrew."

"But you told Harper."

"Because she deserved the truth. Because she was so *angry* with me all the time and I wanted to give her something real. I didn't think she could hate me any more than she already did."

Rookie mistake. If there's one thing Chloe knows, it's that Harper Parisi has an incredible amount of space for hate in her heart. It's one of the things she admires about her.

"That's why she did this, you know," she says. "Because she wanted someone to notice her. She wanted someone to care and she knew it wasn't going to be you."

Katherine flinches, gaze finally dropping down to her lap, but Chloe doesn't back down. Maybe it's not fair to put this on her. Maybe Chloe has no right to lecture her like this, but Harper's gone. Chloe might never see her again and there's a part of her that still feels horribly responsible.

Priya breaks the silence, leaning across the table to give Katherine's hand a reassuring pat. "It's okay," she says. "I have my ex blocked on literally everything, but he messaged me on Pinterest yesterday asking if I could please not get a restraining order against him. He didn't frame me for embezzlement or anything, but I know how you feel."

Katherine yanks her hand out of Priya's grip. "That's—" She stops, lips parted. "I'm sorry, *what*?"

"He messaged me on Pinterest. Can you believe that? I didn't even know you *could* message people on Pinterest."

"No, I . . ." Katherine stands, brushing the dirt from her jeans. "Who is framing people for embezzlement?"

Priya flashes Chloe and Logan a sly grin and together, the three of them stand. They're always going to be good at this, Chloe thinks. If this is the last job they ever pull, at least they'll go out together.

"I think you know," Chloe says. "And if I had to guess, there's probably pages and pages of very explicit evidence hidden on the flash drive we recovered from Carlyle's award. The one Harper was so insistent she take back. And we might have, allegedly, stolen that flash drive from her on the boat."

Logan nods. "Exactly. It might also be in your pocket right now. Allegedly, of course."

Katherine blinks. Her hand flies to the front pocket of her jeans and when she pulls out the small silver flash drive, her mouth falls open. "Who the hell are you?"

Chloe ignores the question. "It's all there," she says. "You can do whatever you want with it."

"And let me guess. You three want something in return?"

Priya shrugs. "I think it's only fair. Carlyle was willing to pay a lot of money to get that back."

"Of course he was." Katherine rolls her eyes, but as she slides the flash drive back into her pocket, Chloe thinks the corner of her mouth lifts in the faintest touch of admiration. "Fine. You did save my life, after all."

Chloe shakes her head. "I didn't have a choice."

"You could have left me on that boat. You could have waited for the storm to pass or someone to happen upon us, but you didn't. Thank you." Katherine plants both hands on her hips. "So, what was he paying you?"

"Five million dollars."

"Five *million*—" Katherine rubs a hand over her forehead. "Fine. But if I can ask for one thing in return, could you please use . . . discretion in the future when it comes to my family? The things you know could hurt a lot of people."

Chloe pretends to consider, head tipping to one side as she taps a finger against her chin. "Of course," she says. "That's your business. But in case we need a reminder . . ." She nods toward the brooch pinned to Katherine's blazer. "That's a nice piece."

Next to her, Logan lets out a choked gasp. Priya steps pointedly in front of him, but not before Katherine notices the commotion.

"This?" She unpins it from her lapel. "I got this at a flea market in Orlando. It's worthless."

"Not to me."

The four of them stare at one another across the table. Katherine shakes her head and for a minute, Chloe wonders if she's gone too far. Then Katherine laughs.

"Fine," she says. "If that's what it takes to earn your discretion, you can have it."

There are a lot of things to be discreet about, Chloe realizes. How easy it was to hack the Rivera security system. That Harper Parisi shot her own mother. The extent of Katherine's relationship with Andrew Carlyle. Complicated things. Messy things. She could probably ask for more. Chloe has a feeling Katherine would give them whatever they wanted right now, but this feels like more than enough. She waits until Katherine drops the brooch in her waiting palm, then grins.

"Of course," she says. "It's a deal."

Katherine looks at the three of them, standing shoulder to shoulder on the grimy patio. For a minute, it seems like she wants to say something else. Chloe watches the uncertainty dance behind her eyes for a split second before she shakes her head and disappears back into the house.

"Oh my god!" Priya sags against the railing as the patio door slides shut. "We got hush money-ed!"

Chloe laughs and hands the brooch off to Logan, who mutters something that sounds vaguely like *come to papa* as he holds it up to the light. Getting "hush money-ed" sounds so dramatic. It's not like she ever plans to spill Harper's secrets. The part of her that hustled and scraped and dreamt of revenge is gone, pulled apart by their sudden, explosive end.

"Is that thing really worthless?" she asks, glancing at Logan across the patio. "This whole time you just wanted to, like, steal it for the vibes?"

"Who cares if it's worthless?" Logan flings one arm around Chloe and the other around Priya. "At least I was right."

Chloe laughs as he pulls the both of them into a crushing embrace. "About what?"

"About you," Logan says. "I knew I could get you to do a jewelry heist."

TWENTY-EIGHT

On a cool night toward the end of September, Chloe sits in a pub overlooking a slowly darkening beach and lifts a frosty glass of cider to her lips.

Ireland is beautiful year-round. She knows this because most of her cousins' favorite songs talk about Irish summers like they're currency, something to be scooped up and kept in pockets. Even so, Chloe thinks there's something special about now, when the air turns cool and soft. Miami doesn't have seasons like this. The best way to mark the shift is by tracking the hurricanes, but tonight, there's a breeze wafting through the open window behind the bar and Chloe is very pleasantly drunk.

She always thought visiting Ireland would hurt. In the weeks before her flight left, she tried to prepare herself for it. She closed her eyes and forced herself to imagine the bone-deep ache of walking the streets of her mother's childhood home, to feel the pain of seeing her face in every rolling hill and blade of grass. But, surprisingly, it's not grief she feels now. It's more of a *remembering*.

She scattered her mother's ashes in the sea during her first week in Kilkee, surrounded by her grandparents and aunts and half a dozen cousins she'd never met. They all have her mother's nose and her own soft, crooked smile. They share her love of folk songs and homemade desserts and, as the days have turned to weeks, Chloe has started to find pieces of herself in this city, too.

She was supposed to stay for a week. She'd booked herself a hotel up the road, but the minute her aunt Erin realized she was staying with strangers, she helped Chloe pack her things and practically dragged her into the spare room above her kitchen. It's been three weeks now, but Chloe doesn't mind. Her aunt's guest room is smaller than the one she used at her dad's condo, but it's the first place in a while that feels like home. When Chloe throws back her curtains and opens the windows, she can see all the way down to the beach and the water glittering beyond.

That's the best way to view the ocean, she thinks. *With both feet planted firmly on the ground.*

Now, she's learning to love this strange little seaside town the same way her mother learned to love Miami—one day at a time. It isn't hard to do. Chloe loves watching the tourists drag their surfboards to the beach every morning, despite the chill. She loves playing cards with her uncles around the same table her mother used growing up. She loves the flower boxes in town and Gillian's pub and, most of all, she loves Meg the bartender and the uncanny way she always seems to know exactly what Chloe needs.

"Here you go."

Chloe looks up as Meg slides two glasses toward her across the bar. Another cider, white ring of bubbles frothing cheerily around the rim, and a plain glass of water. Meg nods pointedly at the latter.

"You have to finish that before you start another," she says. "That's the rule when you're drinking alone."

Chloe grins, resisting the urge to tell Meg she's been far drunker on less. "Thanks. Can I get some—"

Meg slides a glass of ice across the bar before Chloe can finish. She moves on to the next customer, attention seemingly fixed on their order, but Chloe catches the brief, conspiratorial wink Meg throws her way.

Last week, her cousin Finn threw his arm around Chloe's shoulders after a particularly raucous night at Gillian's and yelled, *she likes you, you know,* directly into her ear.

Chloe had tried to push him away, but Finn was insistent. *I'm serious,* he said. *If you ask her out, she'll definitely say yes.*

Chloe's been back to Gillian's several times since then. She's watched Meg scrub the bar, tattooed biceps flexing with each long, deliberate stroke, and tried to imagine those same arms wrapping around her instead. For some reason, the image draws a blank.

Sorry, Chloe told Finn that night. *She's just not my type.*

It's the only thing that feels close enough to the truth.

Now, she pours her water into her waiting glass of ice, purposefully ignoring the other patrons crowding in at her back. The bar is decently packed for a Wednesday night. There's a football game playing behind the bar—Spain versus England. If there's one thing Chloe's learned in her three weeks abroad, it's that the Irish don't need their own team in the game to celebrate. They're going to cheer for whoever's playing England and revel just as hard if they lose. She should get out of here before the game gets too exciting and the bar fills up in earnest.

Outside, the sun slips over the horizon inch by inch. The time difference was jarring at first. It took Chloe almost two weeks to get used to the fact that night for her was still the middle of the afternoon back in Florida, but now, she almost prefers it. The thought makes her feel weightless, like no matter how fast her shadows run, they'll never be able to fully catch her. Still, she should call her father on her walk home. They haven't spoken in a few days and now that the semester is in full swing, he's sure to have a few good stories tucked up his sleeve.

Before she left, Chloe used Katherine's money to pay off most of his condo and almost all of their debt. It's not gone, of course. It's never that easy, but for the first time in years, Chloe doesn't feel like she's one disaster away from combusting.

She thinks her father feels the same way. He's been sending her letters recently, stuffed with entire albums' worth of photos from home—the garden he's starting out back, a particularly brilliant sunset on their favorite beach, and picture after picture of his new puppy. For some reason, he seems to have forgotten that he can text her pictures and Chloe doesn't care to remind him. She likes sticking photos from home in the cracks of her mirror. Sometimes, she'll pass them around the village and tell all her cousins' friends about the twelve-thousand-square-foot World Erotic Art Museum in Miami Beach or the luxury hotel that sits on its own private island in the middle of the bay, just to see their reaction.

Her friends send her postcards, too. Logan's latest was addressed from his new Brooklyn apartment. He used his share of the money for a down payment on a tiny little brownstone and put the rest toward new headshots and dance lessons. He's always going to be a performer. Just yesterday he told her and Priya over FaceTime that he had to physically restrain himself from snatching someone's wallet from their very exposed, very tempting back pocket, but Chloe has a feeling the days of card tricks and coin tosses are finally behind him.

Priya's letters always arrive on a custom set of rose-scented stationery. Even though they talk constantly, she still insists on sending long, diary-like letters every few weeks "like they do in *Pride and Prejudice*" and Chloe doesn't mind. Even with Katherine's money, Priya wasn't able to make it back to school this fall, but Boston, Duke, and NYU all let her defer until the winter.

"I just need to make sure my family is okay," she told Chloe last week. "I'm going to do everything I can to set them up, but trust me: When I leave, I'm not coming back."

Chloe grinned and promised to visit as soon as she was settled. It's something she's still getting used to—the idea that she actually has time to pursue the things she wants. She really could make a visit to wherever Priya ends up next year. She could visit Logan right now, if she wanted, just hop on a plane and fly straight through to JFK. She's spent so long weighed down by grief and debt and dead-end jobs that the thought of something more has always been just that—a thought. A hazy, half-formed idea never quite solid enough to grasp. Now, however, it's like the world is slowly unfurling itself at her feet. It's beckoning, waiting for her to decide what she wants to do with it, and Chloe thinks it's never been this easy to breathe.

She taps a fingernail against her glass, tracing droplets of condensation down the side. She's just started in on her fresh cider when someone slides into the seat beside her. It's not a strange occurrence with the pub filling up like this, but Chloe feels the displacement in the air before they speak, like a stone falling through dark water.

"I'm surprised to see you in a place like this. I never took you for a sports fan."

It's funny, Chloe thinks, how the sound of that voice still lifts the hair on the back of her neck. Some primordial combination of anticipation and dread. She gives a slow, rueful shake of her head, gaze fixed purposefully on the screen over the bar. "I'm surprised it took you this long to find me."

"Please. I've known where you were for weeks."

"Is that so?"

Chloe turns just enough to catch the speaker's profile in the corner of her eye. Harper sits on the barstool next to her, one leg crossed over the other as she drums her fingers against the bar. She's dressed the same—belted suede miniskirt and a formfitting black top—but her nails are painted a soft shade of green. It's such a departure from her usual color that for a minute, Chloe can't help but stare. Harper's hair is shorter too, chopped to just above her narrow shoulders. Despite herself, Chloe thinks it suits her.

"You cut your hair," she says.

Harper shrugs, still not quite meeting her eye. "I needed a change." She pauses before adding, "You look well."

"I mean, the last time you saw me, I was stranded in the middle of the ocean. I hope I look better than that."

The bar behind them erupts as someone onscreen makes a particularly daring penalty kick. The bartenders start pouring a new round of drinks and Chloe looks up in time to catch Meg's eye, pretending not to notice the color rising in Harper's cheeks at the reminder of their last conversation. She keeps waiting for the familiar thread of satisfaction, for the delight that usually comes with leaving Harper unmoored, but nothing happens. For the first time since they've known each other, Chloe isn't scrabbling for the upper hand. She has the advantage here and when Meg comes to a stop in front of them, she feels remarkably steady.

"What can I get you?" Meg asks.

Harper purses her lips. "Do you have Veuve?"

Meg's eyebrows fly toward her hairline in a way that clearly says, *does it look like we have fucking Veuve Clicquot?* before Chloe intervenes.

"She'll have a gin and tonic, Meg. Put it on my tab."

Meg lets out a dismissive snort before turning to help her next customer. Harper watches her go, lips curled in amusement. "She's very pretty."

Chloe ignores her. She's not doing this now. It's been over a month since she watched Harper's lifeboat disappear into the storm. It's not like she expected a postcard, but she still tenses each time she opens her mailbox. Like one day, she'll find a note tucked somewhere in the back, sealed with a kiss and signed off with a mocking *xoxo Harper.*

Chloe takes another long sip of her drink, fingers tightening around the glass. "What are you doing here?"

"Oh, you know." Harper waves a hand. "Taking a vacation, seeing the sights. This really is a lovely town. I see why you like it."

Her voice is purposefully light, but something catches in her throat on the last word. The slightest hitch in her breath. If Chloe didn't know her so well, she might have missed it. She waits, swirling the contents of her drink around the half-empty glass. After another minute of stubborn silence, Harper's shoulders sag.

"I don't really have anywhere else to go," she mutters.

"That's not true."

"Really?" Harper scoffs, and it's only then that Chloe realizes the hair and nails aren't the only changes. Harper's signature red lip is gone, replaced by a pale shade of pink. The rest of her face is noticeably clear of makeup and if the dark circles under her eyes are any indication, she hasn't been sleeping. It's so unlike the Harper she's used to. She looks terrible, breakable. More human than Chloe has ever seen her. "You want me to go home and pretend one of the most powerful people in the city doesn't, like, actively want me dead?"

Chloe shrugs. "He's probably more worried about an impending embezzlement case. If I had to guess, he's not thinking about you at all."

Harper flinches, but she doesn't take the bait. "Do you still have the flash drive?"

"No." Chloe shakes her head. "I left it with your mother. I want nothing to do with it."

Meg chooses that moment to arrive with Harper's gin and tonic. She slides it across the table with more force than necessary, sets a handful of napkins between them, and disappears back into the fray. Harper picks it up, takes a tentative sip, and immediately sets the glass down.

"That's revolting."

Chloe laughs. "You're the one who ordered a gin and tonic."

"Actually, *you're* the one who ordered a gin and tonic."

"Right, because you walked into this place and said, 'why don't I see if they have Veuve?'"

Harper rolls her eyes. She twirls the straw around her drink in silence, knocking the shriveled chunk of lime against the rim of the glass. When she speaks again, her voice is barely audible over the crowd.

"I didn't know what was on that flash drive."

In the weeks since Chloe left town, she's spent an infuriating amount of time replaying every conversation she ever had with Harper. She's sorted through them again and again, run them forward and backward in a halfhearted attempt to figure out where she went wrong. Was Harper ever honest with her? Was she really plotting Chloe's demise while simultaneously kissing her breathless?

Chloe isn't sure. She doesn't think she'll ever get answers but looking at Harper now, set against the backdrop of a crowded seaside pub, a small, delicate part of her still wants to believe this is real.

"Did you know about the frame job?" she asks.

To her surprise, Harper shakes her head. "I didn't know about any of it. He just told me he wanted it back. He said it would annoy her if I was the one who took it, that he didn't trust anyone else to do the job, and that he was so *glad* I came to him. That she had no right to keep us apart all these years."

Each word is bitter, forced out through clenched teeth. Harper's hand curls around her glass. Her knuckles press against her skin, as if desperate to escape, and for a minute, Chloe thinks the whole thing might shatter.

"I'm sorry," she says.

Harper bares her teeth. "I don't want your pity, Chloe."

"What do you want, then? Why are you here?"

She braces herself for another cutting retort, but it doesn't come. Instead, Harper seems to sink into the contours of the barstool. "I don't know."

Chloe drains the rest of her cider. She sets the glass down on the bar, pats her mouth with one of the napkins, and decides it's time to go. She's never been good at turning her back on things. She used to view the trait as an asset, but a few weeks ago, her new therapist asked, very bluntly, what exactly Chloe thought would happen if she left a conversation without having the final say. Chloe considered for a while before finally admitting, *I suppose it feels like losing.*

Her therapist had nodded, like that was exactly the answer she'd expected. *Sure,* she'd said. *But has it ever occurred to you that you might be the only one playing the game?*

Chloe slides a few crumpled euro across the bar for Meg and stands. Harper makes no move to follow. She's still staring at the bar, brow furrowed, and it's not until Chloe grabs her purse that she speaks again.

"She hasn't done anything with that flash drive, you know. No one knows what's on it."

Despite herself, Chloe laughs. "Of course not. She's probably waiting for the right moment. She probably wants to make it hurt."

Harper looks up. "How do you know?"

"Because it's what you would do."

Chloe doesn't mean it to be insulting. It's just a fact, but Harper flinches, drawing back like she can physically escape the words. "I don't want to be like her," she says. "I don't want to be like . . . them."

Has it ever occurred to you that you might be the only one playing the game?

Maybe part of Harper sees that version of their future, too. Maybe she still pictures the two of them decades from now, locked in this same twisted rivalry with no regard for the people around them. Chloe slings the strap of her bag over one shoulder. "Go home, Harper. You shouldn't be here."

"I can't."

"Yes, you can. Book a one-way to Miami. Put that platinum card to good use."

"No, I—" Harper runs a frustrated hand through her hair. "She won't want to see me. I left her, Chloe. I left all of you, but she could have—"

She breaks off, lips pressed together as if to prevent the last word from escaping. Chloe hesitates. If there's one thing she's learned this summer, it's that she is incredibly ill-equipped to deal with Parisi family drama. It's bizarre and treacherous and *messy,* and still, she can't help but remember Katherine curled on the deck of her ship, begging Chloe to tell her if Harper was all right even as she bled out in a storm. She thinks of Katherine sitting across from her on the patio, making secret backdoor deals to protect Harper even after she fled, and thinks, despite everything, that those aren't the actions of someone who doesn't care.

"I don't know," Chloe says. "I think you'd be surprised." Then, before she can stop herself, she leans down and rips the remaining napkin in half. "I don't know how long you're in town, but if you're still here on Thursday, my aunt likes to cook dinner for everyone. It's a lot of fun and you don't have to worry about intruding. Seriously, most of them didn't know me before I landed, and I promise we didn't stay strangers for long. Here's the address. Come by if you're free."

She slides the top half of the napkin in Harper's direction. Harper's fingers close around it, one by one. Her lips part in a soft, wordless circle, and Chloe turns to go. She doesn't need to see Harper's reaction. She doesn't particularly care what it is. She pushes her stool against the bar, offers Meg a friendly wave, and walks right out the door, content with the knowledge that she can still leave Harper Parisi speechless.

The air outside is cool, a pointed reminder of the oncoming fall. Chloe sucks in a lungful as she heads away from the center of town. It's later than she thought, the moon just starting to sink below the horizon, and most of the businesses lining the street are closed. Shadows gather on the sidewalk despite the orange glow of the streetlamps. Somewhere to her left, the ocean unfurls into the beach again and again, waves turning silver, then gray, then black. Chloe stops just before the curve of the road and steals one final glance over her shoulder.

Gillian's is still visible on the corner, light pouring merrily through its open windows. More and more people are streaming inside but as Chloe watches, one figure emerges alone. She can't see her face through the gloom, but she doesn't need to. Even here, in a city she's never been to, surrounded by people who don't know her name, Harper walks like she expects everyone to sink to their knees when she passes. She turns, face momentarily tilted in Chloe's direction, and for a breathtaking minute, Chloe thinks Harper is looking for her, too.

Behind them, the waves beat against the sand in a relentless, unyielding rhythm. Strange, Chloe thinks, for Harper to disappear on one side of the Atlantic and resurface here, as if spat out by the sea. She thinks of the game she used to play with her mother, waving across the ocean in hopes of reaching their relatives on some hazy, distant shore. Maybe there's a past version of herself on a Miami beach now, frozen in time and still squinting toward the horizon. Maybe somewhere, there's a past version of Harper, too.

Chloe inclines her chin ever so slightly in Harper's direction. Then she doesn't look back again.

Somewhere behind her, Harper is walking back to whatever luxury B&B she booked for herself. Maybe when she gets there, she'll find the other half of Chloe's napkin tucked in the bottom of her purse, right where Chloe left it. For a minute, Chloe lets herself picture Harper pulling it out, nose wrinkling at the lingering smell of gin, and holding it up to the light to read the three hastily scribbled lines.

> You're nothing like them. Trust me, I'd know. xoxo
> —Chloe
> P.S. It was nice to see you.

ACKNOWLEDGMENTS

When I was in college, I had a journalism professor tell me to my face that I "lacked the work ethic for a writing career." It's a classic piece of my lore and whenever I tell that story today, people tend to react one of two ways—either by telling me that guy sucks (true) or by wondering why I'm still thinking about something that happened nearly a decade ago. Why haven't I let it go? The answer is because I've never actually let go of anything in my life and because I learned there's nothing more powerful than spite and the desire to prove a sixty-year-old Midwest professor wrong.

This book in particular exists mostly out of spite. It exists because after a full year of only hearing the word *no,* I was determined to write something that made everyone say *yes.* And now if that professor ever picks up this book on a whim, he'll have to read an entire acknowledgment section celebrating the people who made this book a reality.

Personally, I think our collective work ethic is pretty great.

As usual, this book would not exist without my rock-star agent,

Claire Friedman. I'm continually awed by your ability to see potential in my roughest of rough drafts, especially when I can't. Thank you for encouraging me to try something new, for telling me to make this one "more chaotically Florida," and for heeding all of my unhinged astrology-based requests. The stars truly did align for this one!

To my incredible editor, Katy Nishimoto. It's rare to meet someone who not only gets exactly what I want my work to say but who also treats it—and me—with such enthusiasm and kindness. But here you are! I truly couldn't ask for a better partner for my adult debut and I'm so grateful you saw something in this story. Thank you for loving it as much as I do. And thank you for making an offer the week I happened to be in New Orleans so I could celebrate with copious amounts of beignets!

To the entire team at Dial: Whitney Frick, Avideh Bashirrad, Raaga Rajagopala, Debbie Aroff, Madison Dettlinger, Hope Hathcock. It's no coincidence that you publish some of my very favorite books and that is truly a testament to the people who work here. Extra special shout-out to JP Woodham for all the support and for answering my endless questions.

Thank you to Molly von Borstel, Faceout Studio, and Donna Cheng for creating the sultry, mysterious, "Hot Girl Reading at a Pool" cover of my dreams!

It's funny that writing is such a solitary activity because stories don't exist in a vacuum. So many people helped bring this one to life. To my family, for the lifetime of support and for moving to Florida at exactly the right time. To Serena Kaylor, Sasha Peyton Smith, and Emma Benshoff for escaping with me into the West Virginia wilderness and forcing me to write via peer pressure. The Seeley Booth cameo in this book is for you. To Sophia DeRise, for always being my first reader and for telling me all about the time you worked housekeeping at a hotel filled with celebrities. To this day, I think you're the only person in the world who's been kicked out of the (real-life) Carlyle hotel for wearing an Alice Cullen graphic t-shirt. To Chelsea Yedinak for answering all my legal questions and for explaining the difference between fraud and embezzlement no less than fifteen times. To Maria Rapisarda for living with me while I drafted this book. If you look closely, you can find the name of almost every *Vanderpump Rules* cast member hidden in the pages, as a treat. To Alexis, Caysi, Carissa, and Sarina, for everything.

To the booksellers and librarians who have been such vocal advocates of my work over the years. You're a huge part of why I continue to write books at all and I'm so grateful for all the support. And of course, shout-out to my favorite local indies One More Page Books, Old Town Books, and East City Bookshop.

And, of course, to Emily. I was working on this book when we met and a little part of me thought I might manifest a hot hotel heiress or a charming, plucky con woman in my near future. Instead, by some incredibly lucky twist of fate, I managed to manifest you—brilliant and kind, steadfast and joyful. Chloe and Harper could literally never! The Rothko shout-out in this book is for you, but the love is, too. All of it.

© VANIA STOYANOVA

JENNA VORIS is the author of multiple young adult books, including *Every Time You Hear That Song, Say a Little Prayer,* and *Made of Stars.* Originally from Indiana, she now lives in Washington, D.C., where she spends most of her time perfecting her road trip playlists and desperately trying to keep her houseplants alive. *The Long Con* is her adult fiction debut.

jennamvoris.com

Instagram: @jennavoris